WHAT PEOPLE ARE SAYING ABOUT *WINDSHIFT*:

In telling the story of the Women Air Service Pilots (WASP) during WW2, *Windshift* entertains and enlightens simultaneously. Ms. Faulkner writes about their sacrifice, their commitment, and what they endured to fulfill their collective sense of duty and patriotism. The sad truth is our lady warriors were treated as second-class contributors to the American victory by both the government and the public. Their strength, their sense of humor, and honor made them unique. Joyce Faulkner has written a story that is a must read on many levels.

~ Michael "Moon" Mullins, award-winning author of *Out of the Mist: Memories of War*, *Vietnam in Verse: Poetry for Beer Drinkers*, and co-author of *Kings of the Green Jelly Moon*.

Don't start this book if you don't have time to finish it! WINDSHIFT will grip you and charm you and hold on to your heart. The characters are developed to perfection and at least one of them will feel all too familiar. Are you ahead of your time or know someone who is? Then you'll "get" this intimate look into the lives of women who paved the way for the rest of us who don't live within the confines of convention either. Thank you, Joyce Faulkner, for telling our story.

~ Carmen Stenholm, award-winning author of *Crack Between the Worlds*.

This book challenges all women to think about how they got to where they are today. These four women pilots were true pioneers and passionate. Their determination, hurt, tears, strength, and fighting-back attitude make you wonder …. would I have that kind of courage?

~ Marlyce Stockinger, Branson.com

Joyce Faulkner's extensive research for *Windshift* springs to life through her fresh voice and effortless style — a combination that captivates the reader. The characters of this story, which illustrates blatant sexism during World War II and the shame of our government's lack of pay, benefits, and support for the WASP, linger long beyond the final page.

~ Bonnie Bartel Latino, former columnist for Stars and Stripes newspaper in Europe, and co-author of *Your Gift to Me*, a military romance novel.

Shirley, Emmy, Dolores, and Mags leap off the page into our imaginations, thanks to Faulkner's skill as a storyteller. Her descriptions allow readers to confront the characters as living people. Gradually we learn their back-stories and come to understand and forgive their flaws. We worry about them, applaud their successes, share their tears, and mourn their losses. We come to know them as friends because Faulkner never steps between her characters and her readers. She doesn't add her own commentary or interject her own ideology. She just narrates their stories, letting us get to know each of these women as we might get to know a neighbor or colleague through their own words and actions.

~ Carolyn Poling Schriber, award-winning author of *Beyond All Price*

Windshift takes the reader on a journey with four women who are caught up in change greater than themselves. We gain and lose along with our heroines and in the end we are rooting for all of them to achieve the ultimate triumph.

~ Paul R. Bruno, The History Czar®

Triumph in the face of adversity, grace under pressure, and the "civilian" valor of our Women Air Service Pilots (WASP) come together in a compelling and inspiring read that is a tribute to the brave, pioneering spirit of our female pilots.

~ Sandra Beck/ Military Mom Talk Radio

Sweeping. Riveting. One of the best novels I've read in years. Come let Shirley, Emmie, Delores, and Mags wing their way to your heart. Joyce Faulkner is one of those rare storytellers who spins words into gold. *Windshift* is so well written that you'll forget you're reading a story. Even before the propellers are turning, you'll be strapping on a pair of goggles and a leather helmet — and climbing into a cockpit to make history.

~ Kathleen M. Rodgers - author of the award-winning novel *The Final Salute* and soon to be released *Johnnie Come Lately*.

I read the first few chapters on the fly, got to the fifth at 11PM one evening and read until dawn to finish. Have not done that in a very long time. Joyce Faulkner's portrayal of the pioneering WASP, makes one wonder at glass ceilings and female stereotypes still enforced on us today. Quick read, thought provoking, inspiring and entertaining!

~ Joanne Quinn-Smith, 2009 National SBA Journalist of the Year
Publisher, PositivelyPittsburghLiveMagazine.com
2010 Stevie Award Finalist for Best Media Website or Blog

WINDSHIFT

by

Joyce Faulkner

COPYRIGHT: 2012 JOYCE FAULKNER

Library of Congress Cataloging-in-Publication Data

Faulkner, Joyce, 1948-
  Windshift / by Joyce Faulkner.
     p. cm.
  ISBN 978-1-937958-05-3 (hardcover) -- ISBN 978-1-937958-06-0 (pbk.) --
ISBN 978-1-937958-07-7 (e-book)
  1. Women air pilots--United States. 2. World War, 1939-1945--Participation, American. 3. World War, 1939-1945--Fiction. I. Title.
  TL539.F38 2012
  629.13092--dc23
                              2012013159

Cover Design: Joyce Faulkner

This novel is inspired by the Women Air Service Pilot (WASP) program during World War II. The characters, events, and locations are fictional.

Thanks to the members of the Sharon Rogers Band and to Herman Bailes Cox, the leader of Buddy's Big Band.

Red Engine Press

Printed in the United States

ii

Women Air Force Service Pilots (WASP)

During World War II, the people of the United States pulled together in an unprecedented effort to defeat the enemy. The country put aside societal rules for the duration allowing women to serve in the military as nurses and administrators. At home, young girls, housewives, and older men went to work in the factories. Most extraordinary of all, given the attitudes of the time, more than a thousand women signed up to participate in the war effort as pilots.

The Women Air Force Service Pilot Program (WASP) began as two separate organizations led by two famous aviatrixes. The WAFS (Women's Air Ferry Service) was Nancy Love's idea for recruiting experienced women pilots to ferry military aircraft around the US. With Jackie Cochran at the helm, the Women's Flying Training Detachment (WFTD) was established in 1942 to prepare women pilots for military flying. In 1943, Jackie Cochran combined the two groups and they became known as WASP.

The standards for women were higher than for men and the training was exacting. They 'checked out' in an assortment of military aircraft and performed such duties as delivering newly built or repaired aircraft to military bases in the states, towing targets, test flight, dogfight training, and transporting military brass.

Pilot status was highly sought after by American men of the era. Men viewed female pilots with suspicion and hostility. WASP flew military planes and obeyed military protocol. However, the military considered them civilians and denied them military pay and benefits. In 1944, the Army petitioned Congress to militarize the group. The WASP Militarization Bill failed because of the public perception that women were taking jobs that should belong to men. Women's Air Service Pilots were disbanded in December 1944. Nine hundred and sixteen women were on active duty at that point. Thirty-eight died in the performance of their duties.

To those who know it's hard...
and do it anyway...
and love doing it...

CHAPTER 1 — THE WINDSHIFT INN

"The country is at War — not just our young men — all of us."
~ George Maxwell, CEO American View Communications
September, 1943

I'm a pilot. It's an unusual occupation for a woman, but I didn't have a choice. I had some trouble in college and wanted to quit. As you can imagine, Father objected. Then he did a story on Amelia and realized I might be useful. He bought a small plane and paid for my lessons. For five years after that, I flew him from place to place. It was handy for the editor of a magazine and he could keep an eye on me — the perfect daughter gone wrong.

I'd still be his personal pilot if it weren't for the war. He heard through his connections that Jackie Cochran was recruiting women pilots for a special assignment. He thought if I was part of the program, I could send him newsy little nuggets from time to time. I think he also felt bad he didn't have a son to send off to fight Tojo or Hitler. He arranged for my interview before I ever heard about the Women's Air Force Service Pilots. What could I do but supply the man his paternal bragging rights? After all, it got me out from under his thumb. Almost.

I am a cautious, mediocre pilot but I was accepted into the program anyway. Father must have put in the fix. Training began in May of 1943 at Avenger Field in Sweetwater, Texas. There were twenty girls in my class. Every one of them was much more qualified than me. We lived in long barracks that we called bays and it was one long pajama party. I kept to myself. I didn't want to disappoint Father again so I worked hard to keep up. Fourteen of us graduated in August. Our initial mission was to ferry aircraft around the country for the Army. My first assignment was in Cold Creek, Ohio — two hours south of Cleveland by train. We tested new planes as they came off the *Wiley Aircraft* assembly line and then delivered them to Camp Morgan in California.

1

Jackie Cochran arranged for us to stay in a boarding house just outside Cold Creek with the unlikely name of *The Windshift Inn*. The owner was a widow in her late forties by the name of Myrtle Jones. She worked as a welder during the day and cooked for her guests in the evening. One thing I can say about Myrtle, she kept a nice neat place. I always felt better when I was at the inn.

I was assigned to the third floor, which was divided into two big rooms. The south dormitory was the largest, filled with six workers from the aircraft factory. The WASP took the north suite, which had room for four girls. Each of us had a bed, a dresser, a nightstand, and a small writing table. I was disappointed that there wasn't a wardrobe. You need to hang things up for them to look nice. Other than that, the space was adequate. I was the first one to check in so I got my pick of beds. I chose the one without a window.

I was unpacking when a plain young woman came in and threw her bags on the bed nearest the door. "How ya doing, Hoss?"

"I beg your pardon?"

"I'm Emmie Hopkins." She shook my hand.

I thought she should do something about all those freckles — stay out of the sun or bleach them or cover them — and her bangs were too long for someone her age. "My name's Shirley Maxwell," I told her and went back to hanging my clothes on the freestanding rack Myrtle found for me.

Emmie pulled open the top drawer of her dresser and dumped the contents of her suitcase into it. I pretended not to notice. "I think one of your dresses is out of order there, Shirley," she said and then laughed when I hurried to check it. "Gotcha!"

I never liked being teased — it was seldom funny and it always hurt. "Who else is staying here, do you know?" I tucked a lavender sachet into the pocket of my robe before I hung it on the rack facing right, just before my blouse section.

She kicked her shoes off and lay down on her bed, wrinkling the bedspread. I could only hope she intended to straighten it before we went to dinner. "Delores Lieberman? She's that gorgeous girl from Pittsburgh. Always has a bunch of guys mooning over her? Was in my bay at Sweetwater? Helluva pilot."

"Is she the one with that big blue stone?"

"She comes from a family of jewelers — collects sapphires, the lucky dish."

I arranged my toilet items on my nightstand. First my hairbrush, then my soap, hand crème, tooth powder, and toothbrush — they go in a small half circle. I wasn't comfortable with how Myrtle made the bed so I remade it and felt better. "Will Delores be here today?"

"I imagine she might. I haven't talked with her since Sweetwater when we dumped her in the fountain after she checked out in the AT-6."

No one ever dumped me in any fountain. Tradition or not, I felt it was unfriendly, disrespectful, and undignified. Of course, I needn't have worried. No one tried.

Myrtle stood in the doorway to the suite. "Are you ladies ready for a little tour? It's five-thirty. After about six, I'm busy with dinner so maybe you can tell your friend when she gets here." I was glad to see she wore a hairnet. It's nice to know the cook cares about things like that.

Emmie sat up. "Sure, Miz Jones. I'd love to take a tour." Her voice had a tinkly quality — like a child's music box. I hate wandering around someone else's house so they can show off their stuff, but I didn't want to be left behind so I nodded.

"Well, come on then." Myrtle was a big woman — broad shouldered and thick waisted, but her most striking feature was behind her. When she turned to lead us out the door, Emmie covered a giggle with her hand.

3

I've always been of the opinion that overalls do not flatter the female form and they did nothing for Myrtle. However, all of the girls working at the factory seemed to favor them. There were at least a half-dozen pair hanging on the clothesline out behind the inn every day.

Emmie and I followed Myrtle down the hallway to the bathroom. "There will be ten of you sharing this facility. That means baths should be taken the night before because you'll only have ten minutes apiece in the mornings. The housekeeper will have clean towels hanging on your rack by 1 pm every day."

The tub smelled like bleach. I ran my finger along the edge of the sink. It was spotless. I checked for hair in the drains, but didn't see any. As I straightened up, I felt Emmie and Myrtle's eyes on me.

"I love a nice clean bathroom," Emmie turned to Myrtle and smiled. "Don't you, Shirley?"

"Uh, yes. Very nice."

"You won't have to worry about a thing, Shirley." Myrtle put her hand on my shoulder. "I run a tight ship here at *The Windshift Inn*."

I nodded, trying not to pull away from her hand. They were being nice, I think.

We trudged down the back stairs. At the landing of the second floor, Myrtle paused. "There are eight private rooms on this floor. As you can imagine, folks pay more for them — and they like quiet. This is an old house with wooden floors. After 9 pm, I'd appreciate it if you would remove your shoes and keep your voices down so as not to disturb our other guests."

"Who lives here, Miz Jones?" Emmie asked.

"You can call me Myrtle, everyone does." A beam of light came in through a round colored-glass window above the landing. I noticed Myrtle had a bit of a moustache around the corners of her mouth. It was nothing a pair of tweezers couldn't help, but it was there

4

nevertheless. I touched my own upper lip. It seemed smooth but I made a mental note to check in a mirror when the tour was over.

"Thanks, Miz Myrtle. Who lives on this floor?" Emmie peered down the dark hallway. On second thought, Emmie was what men call cute rather than plain. She looked like she was smiling whether she was or not.

"Right now, we have a couple of rooms reserved for muckety-mucks at the factory. Of course, old Mr. McKensey has lived in 2D for the last 16 years. He was the first one I took in after his son was killed. The other rooms are filled once in a while."

"What if we wanted private rooms?" Maybe I imagined it, but Emmie seemed offended.

"My contract with Jackie Cochran states you will share the north dormitory, but if you want to pay the extra, I don't see why you couldn't have a private room." Myrtle glanced at Emmie and then back at me.

I preferred living alone, especially after having to share a bay with three other girls during training. However, I didn't want Emmie and Myrtle to think I was rude. "That's okay. I was just asking."

"It would be a place to put visiting relatives, isn't that right, roomie?" Emmie grabbed my arm and squeezed it, like we were partners or something.

We continued on down the stairs behind Myrtle. You could tell the kitchen at *The Windshift Inn* was Myrtle's pride and joy. It was the largest room in the house with two stoves, an icebox, a refrigerator, and extra cabinets.

I sniffed but there wasn't a trace of mildew.

"There's always sandwich fixings in the icebox," Myrtle said. "I make bread every day and we have peanut butter and a variety of jellies in the cabinets. I keep milk and homemade apple juice as well. If you want soda pop, you'll need to bring it in yourself. I have a Victory Garden out back. I use your ration coupons for coffee, meat, and cheese but I can't always get enough meat for everyone. I either stretch it or make meatless meals. Just so you know."

"So it's okay to come down in the middle of the night for a glass of milk?" Emmie asked.

"Long as you wash the glass afterwards and put it away." Myrtle's fingers were thick and calloused. I decided to cream my hands after the tour was over.

"I'm happy to help out in the kitchen if you want," Emmie said.

I never thought of offering to help. Father's cook would have been insulted if I messed around in her business.

"Be down here around 6 o'clock." Myrtle seemed pleased.

"I'll come too," I said not wanting to be left out.

When Myrtle chuckled, her football-sized breasts shook. "Well, I never thought I'd have a crew. Glad to have you though. There's always something to do."

She led us into the dining room. It was large but a long mahogany table and sixteen chairs filled most of it. A matching sideboard sat under a tall window with lace curtains. It was clean but I spotted a new spider's web above the curtain rod. I made a note to come back in here with a broom before dinner.

"A piano!" Emmie squealed as Myrtle took us into the parlor. "Is it a player type?"

"No, sorry. This was my grandmother's. You have to play it the old fashioned way."

Emmie wrinkled her nose. "Do you play, Shirley?"

I held up my index fingers. "Chopsticks."

"Let's hold out hope for Delores." Emmie ran a knuckle over the keys.

"Not to worry, I plink out a few tunes in a pinch," Myrtle said. "If we get desperate, there's the radio. We spend most nights here in the parlor playing games."

"I think we're going to have tons of fun, don't you?" Emmie squeezed my arm again. She acted like we were best friends.

"If you have clothes you want us to wash, please have them in a bag on your bed by 9 am. If you want us to do your laundry, that'll be an additional two bits a week. If you want us to iron anything, that will be another dime. If you want to do your own, there's a tub in the basement, which is available in the evenings. There are a couple of irons and ironing boards down there as well." Myrtle opened the basement door and pointed. Emmie and I nodded. I had no intention of letting anyone do my laundry. I hoped it wasn't musty down there, but I was too polite to ask.

"And then, in nice weather, there's the veranda." Myrtle stepped out onto the painted planks of the covered porch. It stretched across the front of the inn and along the left side. Two large oak trees added even more shade. Rocking chairs, lounges, and wooden gliders provided plenty of outdoor seating.

Emmie parked herself on a bench swing hung from the ceiling of the porch with chains. "Come on, Shirley." She pointed to the seat beside her. I sat down and we drifted back and forth. A breeze lifted Emmie's bangs and I noticed an ugly scar over her right eye. So that's why she wore them so long.

Myrtle sank into a high-backed rocker and stared off into the distance where an orange plane buzzed an airport. We could see the runway from the porch.

"Is that where we will be flying the planes from the factory?" It seemed small to me.

"Oh no. *Wiley Aircraft* has its own airstrip. That's *Jerry's Flying Service* — a small school for pilots run by a friend of mine, Jerry Kline. He's got a contract to teach the workers if they want it. That was Mr. Wiley's idea. He says people who know how to fly build better planes."

"That's smart," Emmie said.

"Jerry rents planes too — but the majority of his income is from *Wiley*." Myrtle's chair squeaked under her weight. A blue bus appeared on the dusty road leading up to the inn. "Here come the girls from the factory. Grant is running a little early tonight."

"They have their own bus?" Emmie asked.

"Mr. Wiley wants to make sure everyone has a way to get to and from work."

"That's nice of him," I said as the bus pulled into the turn around.

"Look at that!" Emmie said under her breath.

A beautiful young man was driving the bus. I couldn't take my eyes off of him. Neither could Emmie, apparently.

"Who is that?" she asked.

Myrtle waved to the driver as several young women climbed out. "That's my boss, Grant Logan."

"How come you don't ride the bus, Miz Myrtle?" Emmie curled her legs up under her as the swing floated back and forth.

The driver caught me looking at him. Blood rushed to my cheeks and I pretended I was reading the *Wiley Aircraft* sign on the bus door.

"Oh, Sugar. I do in the mornings, but in the afternoons, by the time everyone gets into the bus and Grant makes the route, it's forty-five minutes to an hour before he gets here. I got too much to do so I catch a ride with Jerry Kline most days. He usually leaves off a student about the time I want to go home."

Grant pulled out of the turn around and headed back towards town, gears grinding, smoke curling out of the exhaust.

"How come he's not in the service?" I shaded my eyes and stared after him. It was unusual to see an interesting man without a uniform.

"You couldn't see it from here, but Grant wears hearing aids. Even so, you need to turn toward him so he can read your lips. It's a shame, really." Myrtle nodded as each of the workers filed into the inn, chattering with each other and laughing.

"What happened to him, Miz Myrtle?" Emmie asked.

"He got the measles when he was about four. Fever went through the roof and they thought they were going to lose him. It was a few years before they realized just how bad his hearing got after that. People just thought he was a slow learner. He's a dear though. The whole Logan family is good people. They own a general store in downtown Cold Creek. Don't know what folks around here would have done without the Logans during the Depression. It had to be hard on them, but they kept a lot of us going by extending credit. They have two younger sons in the Marines. Nice boys!"

"It must be frustrating for him when all the other men are gone," I said.

Myrtle stood up. "The boy makes up for it in other ways. He makes us crazy with all the gas mask drills at the factory. For a while there, he made us jump through hoops a couple times a week. On top of that, he is the air raid warden. It's just as well he cranks the siren himself otherwise he wouldn't be able to hear it. Well, ladies. It's been nice chatting with you, but I need to see to dinner."

"We're coming, Miz Myrtle." Emmie jumped up and I followed.

"Come on in, I got some green beans that need snapping," Myrtle held the screen door and beckoned us in. "And one of you can set the table."

"I'll set the table," I volunteered, thinking of that spider web in the dining room.

9

"Okey, dokey." Myrtle followed us into the kitchen. "The dishes are in the sideboard. There will be twelve of us tonight."

"Guess that means I've got bean duty." Emmie picked up a brown bag sitting on the back porch and sat down with a big bowl Myrtle handed her.

It didn't take long to dispose of the spider and set the dining room table. When I came back into the kitchen, Emmie held up a bean that refused to break. Stems were scattered on the floor around her, but the bowl wasn't even half-full. "I don't think we're gonna be done with these in time for supper, Miz Myrtle," she said.

Myrtle was mixing cream into the butter to stretch it, biscuits were baking in one oven, and a peanut casserole sat cooling on the counter. "How much longer do you think it's going to take you?" She peered into the almost empty bowl. "They need to cook at least a half hour."

"Three days?" Emmie's mournful tone made us laugh.

"I'll help you." I'd never touched a bean before, but it wasn't that hard. We finished in ten minutes, however, that night the beans were a bit crunchy, much to Emmie's dismay.

"Oh, Myrtle," I said. "The beans are delicious. This is the way they serve them in Paris. I fell in love with them when I was in France with Father, but haven't been able to get them prepared this way since we came home."

Emmie beamed. The rest of the guests chewed away with curious looks on their faces. Old Mr. McKensey scowled and gummed a mouth full for several minutes. He left the rest on his plate. Apparently, he wasn't all that impressed with the French version of green beans.

Everyone helped clear the table and by 8:30, we congregated in the parlor. The factory girls paired up to play checkers. Mr. McKensey grumbled about the noise as he went up to his room. I looked at

Myrtle anxiously, but she shook her head and touched her index finger to her lips as if to shush me.

Emmie and I sat on the piano bench and I demonstrated a rousing chorus of Chopsticks. Myrtle joined us and played a passable version of *Don't Sit under the Apple Tree*. Emmie sang off-key and at full volume. The others stopped their games to stare and then giggle. I would have died of embarrassment. Not Emmie, she kept on singing until the final chords. When it was over, the room was quiet.

"Wow, Emmie. That's some singing," Myrtle acknowledged.

"You think? My husband used to tease me when I sang for him."

"Well, you know how men are." Myrtle winked at me while Emmie searched through the sheet music for another song.

The door burst open at that very moment and we were spared. Delores Lieberman had already captured two beaux at the train station, I guessed. An Army sergeant held her suitcases and a Marine corporal balanced her trunk on his back.

"Mrs. Jones?" Her eyes searched the room.

"Here I am." Myrtle stood up from the piano. "You must be Delores. We've been expecting you."

"The train from Pittsburgh was delayed. I spent a few hours sitting on some pretty hard benches at Pennsylvania Station." Delores' blue-flowered silk dress and open-toed pumps were a bit much for travel, if you ask me. She probably wore her hair on top of her head, pushed back and up from her temples to keep her curls in check, but she looked like she was going to a party. The extraordinary sapphire I had remembered dangled between her breasts. It was obvious the men were gaga over her.

"Delores!" Emmie embraced her.

Delores kissed Emmie's cheek, leaving a round red smudge. "When did you get in? I was hoping to be here this afternoon so we could

11

catch up. Did you know they sent Susan Swift to Camp Davis in North Carolina?"

"No, you don't say? I heard Minnie Sawyer went to New Jersey."

I hadn't realized they were such good friends.

"Where you want us to store your gear, babe?" The sergeant juggled several bags.

"It's on the third floor. I'll show you," Myrtle led the two service men up the stairway. They followed, struggling with Delores' things.

"It's a nice room," Emmie said as she put her arm around Delores' waist. "Your bed is near the window not far from mine."

They started up the stairs after Myrtle and the men. "I'm sure it'll be great," Delores' voice wafted after her like her floral perfume. "It's all uphill after the bays at Sweetwater."

The factory girls went back to their games. I sat down on the piano bench and played Chopsticks but it wasn't fun anymore. Delores was a bit much for ordinary folks.

CHAPTER 2 — EMMIE

"Ace Adams Pitches 62nd Game, Pilot Mabel Rawlinson killed in crash of A-24,
Wallace Beery Stars in Salute to the Marines."
Headlines
~ American View Magazine ~

I want to tell you about my friend Emmie. It still gives me a chill to say that, my "friend" Emmie. I don't remember knowing anyone quite like her. An orphan and then a widow, Emmie never had the advantages I did. She grew up dreaming of things that I took for granted. Yet, when we first met that day at the inn, I realized she knew how to be happy. Imagine!

The day after our arrival, we got up early and stood in line for the bathroom. Although Emmie didn't make her bed as neatly as I would have wished, she did make it. Delores, on the other hand, left her sheets and blankets twisted into a knot, her blue dress draped over her writing table along with her stockings and her shoes under Emmie's chair. I held my breath and counted to ten.

Emmie didn't seem to notice.

Breakfast was quick — toast and Myrtle's strawberry jam. It was a lovely fall day so I wandered out onto the porch as I ate. Emmie was already out there sitting on the swing. Her hair didn't seem so dowdy in the sunshine.

"Shirley!" Emmie beckoned me over. "I've been chatting with some of the *Wiley* girls. Seems we have a real romance going on here."

"What do you mean?" I sat down beside her on the swing, nibbling on my toast.

"Jerry Kline has a crush on our Miz Myrtle."

"No!"

Myrtle had to be pushing fifty — a little old for hanky panky, if you ask me.

"Yes! He juggles his lessons with the *Wiley* girls so he returns the last student of the day to the factory just in time to pick up Miz Myrtle and bring her back here to the inn. Every day."

"How long has Myrtle been alone?" I asked.

"I don't know. Long enough, I suppose." The bus appeared at the crest of the hill a couple of blocks away. Emmie stood up and slung her bag over her shoulder. "All I can say is good for Myrtle."

The bus pulled up in front of the porch, little American Flags mounted on each of the front fenders. The girls spilled out of the house in twos and threes. The driver pushed open the door.

Emmie came up behind me and put her arm around my waist. "Go get em!" She whispered in my ear. I turned around to protest, but she shook her finger at me and got on the bus, grinning.

I followed her, my cheeks burning, hoping the bus driver didn't notice. "Good morning," he said as I went by. His voice had a flat nasal quality about it. I nodded and hurried to my seat.

Myrtle hurried out of the inn, a yellow scarf wrapped around her head and tied in a bow over her forehead. Her hands were bright red. I wondered if anyone had helped her with the breakfast dishes. She climbed on the bus and sat in the seat right behind Grant Logan. "We got one more," she told him.

"Delores must be running a little late," Emmie guessed. "She was worn out from her long train ride."

I glanced over the bobbing heads of the girls sitting next to us out the window. Where was she? It was rude to keep people waiting especially on our first day.

Old Mr. McKensey came out the door. The girls whistled and gave him catcalls. He scowled and walked around the bus to his car muttering to himself.

"It's part of the routine," Myrtle explained. "They always give Mr. McKensey the business."

14

"I see," I said, but I didn't.

Delores bounded out of the house, still buttoning her uniform blouse. "Sorry," she said to the driver who put the bus in gear and pulled forward as soon as she was seated.

"You're late," Emmie hissed.

"I was busy," Delores took out her compact and powdered her nose. I caught Grant Logan looking at her in the rear view mirror. Men!

Myrtle glanced at Delores and mouthed 'Thank you.' Delores pursed her lips and shook her head. Myrtle smiled. It was then I realized Delores' hands were as red as Myrtle's.

Wiley Aircraft consisted of two main buildings, a hangar, and two runways, side by side. Grant pulled the bus up to the door of the red brick assembly building in the back and unloaded the chattering women. "If you ladies can wait here for a minute, I'll get the girls started. Then I'll take you over to the office building to get checked in. Since this is your first day, you'll probably just do some testing, but we got a lot of planes to be ferried out to Camp Morgan. I imagine you'll be headed west tomorrow morning."

"Whew!" Emmie fanned herself as Grant followed Myrtle into the building.

"He's swell." Delores peered out the bus window at his retreating figure.

"Shirley's set her cap for him," Emmie announced.

I spun around to stare at her in horror. "EMMIE!" How could she say something like that? "I've never even been formally introduced to him."

"I betcha Myrtle will take care of that for you." Delores applied way too much dark red lipstick, rubbing at a smear near the corner of her mouth with her pinkie. Betty Grable would kill for lips like hers.

"I-I'm not interested." I hated the way they looked at each other and smiled, like they knew a secret I didn't.

"This should be a pretty easy gig, don't you think?" Delores changed the subject and I was grateful. "They are only making one kind of plane for the war effort — the little *Wiley Fox*. The military uses them to transport generals around and for battlefield scouting. They don't have to do aerobatics."

"Doggonit." Emmie snapped her fingers. "I thought we'd get to fly some hot planes. That's one of the reasons I joined up."

I couldn't imagine any of us flying 'hot' planes. "What did you do before?" I hoped my skepticism didn't show.

"I dusted crops in Indiana."

My father had once done a story about crop dusters. They did crazy things with a plane. Swooping down to within inches of the plants and then pulling back on the stick and climbing almost straight up to avoid trees or houses or telephone poles, tight stalling turns, and then back along the first swath. It was demanding work. I looked at Emmie with new interest. "How did you get into that line of work?"

"Hoppy, my husband." That was the second time she had mentioned him. My eyes flitted to her left hand. No ring.

"Go ahead, tell us." Delores patted Emmie's shoulder. I didn't like that Delores seemed to know more about Emmie than I did.

"I grew up in an orphanage in southern Indiana," Emmie started. "As I got older, I helped with the little ones and worked around the place to pay my way, but eventually I had to learn to take care of myself. They couldn't keep me forever so, when I was fifteen, they sent me to secretarial school. Turns out, I didn't have the knack for shorthand and I washed out of typing class. As you have already seen, I'm no good in the kitchen and I only lasted one day as a waitress. To keep the head mistress off my back, I went to work as a flagger for a bunch of crop dusters. That's the person who marks the swath so the pilot can judge where to begin his next run."

It sounded boring, but I said, "That's interesting."

16

"There was a lot of standing around waiting for something to happen. It didn't take long to spray a field, but then you'd have to tromp over to the next one. There were bugs and worms everywhere, of course. At the end of the day, I was sunburned, sweaty, and itchy from dozens of mosquito bites.

I squirmed in my seat and scratched my cheek.

"One day they set me up to flag for a pilot I'd never met before. He wasn't handsome but he was oh so good looking." Emmie clasped her hands over her bosom and sighed. "He had these weird boots — all worn down on the heel, black and white cowboy boots. He was such a flirt. He'd wink at me and I'd blush and giggle like girls that age do."

I didn't want to remember being so young and silly. Delores caught my eye and winked. I looked down at my knuckles and then back at Emmie.

She continued. "I worked three days a week flagging and then the other days I did chores at St. Michael's. The first time Hoppy came by, I was in the side yard watching the little ones scamper around when this bright yellow biplane floated over the tree line. The kids danced around waving and calling to him. He banked and tossed something out of the cockpit. It drifted to the ground like a little parachute.

"A boy named Lonnie got to it first and brought it to me. It was a piece of paper, tied to a rock and a handkerchief. The paper said, 'Beautiful Emmie'." She coughed into her fist and I looked away.

"Oh, Emmie." Delores reached out to squeeze Emmie's hand. "You never told me this story before."

"I haven't thought about it in a long time. Oh, he was sweet." She pressed her index fingers into the inside corners of her eyes.

"So what happened next?" Delores nudged her.

"He started flying over St. Mike's any day I didn't flag. He dropped me little notes and circled until I read them. I waved and giggled

17

until he flew off towards the farmland south of us, waggling his wings as he crossed the tree line.

"Then one day — it was a Sunday — he landed his WACO in a field a half-mile from the orphanage and hiked over to see me. We sauntered down the road towards a little grove of apple trees. I yammered on about Lana Turner and Clark Gable. He listened to me as if what I said mattered. It wasn't until we were in the orchard that he held my hand.

"I asked him what it was like to fly and he promised to take me up. We walked back to his plane. It had HOPPY written in large red letters across the side. He leaned down and kissed my cheek before crawling back in the cockpit. He took off, banked, and flew over my head. I blew him a kiss. He was swell in his goggles and leather helmet."

She took a deep breath and smiled at me. I couldn't help but smile back.

"You are such a romantic, Emmie." Delores snorted when she laughed. It was most unattractive. Of course, when you look like Delores, men will ignore even that.

I frowned at Delores and turned back to Emmie. "So then what happened?"

"The next time he flew over, he dropped a box weighted down with rocks. Inside was a locket with my name on it and a note that said, 'Sunday, 2 pm, lunch?' I looked up, mouthed 'YES,' and bobbed my head." Emmie pulled the delicate silver locket out of the neckline of her uniform to show us.

"It's lovely," I said imagining the young man who had given it to her.

"Thank you."

"So you went to lunch?" Delores prompted.

"I had one nice dress. It had puffy sleeves, a low neckline, a high waistline, and a bow in the back. I made it myself. Well, to be honest, Miz Clooney at the orphanage helped with the sleeves. It was baby blue with blue birds embroidered on the bodice. I loved it." She stuffed the locket back down inside her blouse. "As you can see, my hair is straight as a board, but Miz Clooney went to work on me with a curling iron. What do you call those long rolled curls?"

"Banana curls?" Delores twirled her index finger in the air.

"Yeah, that's it," Emmie said. "Miz Clooney got me all duded up with ribbons and banana curls. I didn't have any stockings but I did have some nice little anklets with lace and patent leather shoes. Actually, the shoes were the only dress shoes in the orphanage and they were tight in the toes. I wore them anyway."

"You wore shoes that were too tight?" Delores shook her head with a smirk. "Tsk, tsk, tsk! What we'll do for a man!" She winked at me again, her dark lashes fluttering against her cheek. It was a bad habit.

"I expected Hoppy to pick me up in a car, but he showed up in his WACO. When I came to the door made up like a 5'8" Shirley Temple doll, I could see he was trying not to snicker. He took my hand and we walked out to the field where he'd parked his plane. By the time we got there, my toes were numb. The patent leathers hadn't been worn much and the soles were still smooth. In the damp grass, my feet went out from under me and I sat down hard." She laughed at the memory. "And of course, I got green stains on the back of my beautiful blue dress."

"Oh, Emmie. You are too much."

I resisted the urge to glare at Delores for teasing Emmie, but Emmie didn't seem to mind. They had obviously been friends a long time.

"There's no way to crawl into one of those old biplanes in a dress and retain any sense of modesty. Hoppy boosted me up into the front cockpit pretending he wasn't looking at my bare thighs. You could always tell when Hoppy was about to laugh, his chin quivered and

19

his eyes twinkled. He made me promise to leave the stick and rudder alone. He pulled a thin leather helmet down over my beautiful curls, squashing them flat. Then he added the most glamorous pair of goggles you've ever seen before buckling me in with a thin leather strap.

"'Hang in there, darlin. I'm going to give you the ride of your life,' he told me.

"I nodded and held onto the sides of the fuselage. He slipped into the cockpit behind me and hit the ignition. The power of the engine made the plane quiver. We started rolling, slow at first — then faster and faster. The trees at the end of the field seemed closer than they should and taller than I remembered. The back of the plane came up. It looked like we were going to smash right into the orchard. I screamed. The nose of the plane came up in front of me and I was pushed back against my seat. I closed my eyes for a moment and when I opened them, I saw blue sky beyond the propeller.

"Hoppy banked and I looked down the right lower wing and saw St. Mike's below. Then he straightened and we headed towards Madison Lake. The wind in my face took my breath away so I looked down over the side of the cockpit. You could see miles and miles of farmland stretching in all directions. The ends of my curls hanging out the back of the helmet blew straight and then tangled. Up ahead, there was an open field near the lake. Hoppy took us down, first slipping to one side, then to the other — losing altitude quickly. The front wheels hit the ground and we bounced back up into the air, then down again. As we slowed, the back wheel came down. We taxied towards a clump of trees at the far end of the field and Hoppy cut the engine.

"'Come on, darlin,' he said as he helped me out. I put my arms around his neck and slid down the front of his body as he released me. I wasn't sure if it was Hoppy or the airplane that had me so excited. He held me in his great big arms and I felt loved like an orphan can only dream of. I stood on tiptoe and kissed him."

"Aw. I love the mushy stuff." Delores sighed and patted her chest over her heart.

"Me too." I was hanging on her words, breathless.

"I was lucky to know him." Emmie lowered a dusty window and stuck her nose out the crack. "Where is Grant?" He'd been gone ten minutes.

"It's not that far over to the other building, why don't we walk?" Delores collected her purse.

"Nonsense. He left the keys in the ignition." Emmie crawled over the guardrail into the driver's seat and started the bus.

I gripped the seat in front of me. What would Grant think when he came back? Would we be in trouble? "Maybe we should stay where they can find us," I said as Emmie revved the engine.

She released the clutch and we began rolling. "We're just going over there. He'll see the bus and know where we are," she grunted as she struggled to get it into second. "Oops!" she called as she spun the big wheel and we swerved to the left to avoid hitting the corner of the building.

"Yeeha!" Delores cheered.

I held my breath.

After fifty yards, Emmie jammed on the breaks and we slid to a stop. "There ya go." She turned off the engine and opened the door. Delores and I got out while Emmie searched for the emergency brake.

Emmie jumped out of the bus. "Relax, Shirley. What are they gonna do? Send us to the work farm for driving across the parking lot?"

I struggled to look like I was having fun too.

We went into the building and up a short flight of stairs. A young woman sat at a desk chewing gum and reading a comic book. "We are the WASP assigned to test and ferry aircraft out of here. As I

21

understand it, we are supposed to meet someone this morning." Delores said in a la-di-da tone.

"Do you know who?"

"Either of you know?" Delores looked at Emmie who shrugged and then at me. I shook my head. "Not a clue," she said as she smoothed the hair curling from their pins at the nape of her neck.

"I'll call Mr. Wiley. Have a seat." She nodded to the reception area.

We sat down. "Hurry up and wait," Delores picked up an *American View* magazine and fanned through the pages. "Oh look," she said. "This is the one with Cornelia's article in it."

"So when did you and Hoppy get married?" I asked Emmie.

"Well, that very day, actually." Her eyes sparkled. "Here I was in my grass-stained dress, too tight shoes, leather helmet and goggles — kissing Hoppy like there was no tomorrow. He pulled the goggles off and hung them inside the plane, then the helmet. My hair was waist length then — two feet of rats, knots, and tangles. Now that I was standing up again, my feet were killing me. Hoppy knelt down in front of me, put his arms around my waist, and laid his chin on my breast. I ran my fingers through his curls. 'I know this is a little fast, Emmie,' he said. 'But I knew you were what I wanted the moment I saw you at the end of that row. I can't promise you riches, but we'll always have fun.'

"Well, I loved the idea of having fun. After all, I lived in an orphanage I had already outgrown. What did I have to lose? 'Are you wanting to get married?' I asked him.

"'What did you think? That I wanted to keep you for a pet?' The man always could make me laugh. I practically screamed, 'YESSSSSSSS!'

"We unloaded our picnic lunch and spread out under a huge tree near the lake. I sat cross-legged nibbling on a drumstick. I'd just had my first airplane ride and a strange man proposed to me. It was the best day of my life. I didn't know a thing about Hoppy except he dusted crops for a living and I loved him."

"My God, Emmie. What if he beat you? What if he made you unhappy?" Impulse decisions scared me. Seemed like a good way to get hurt.

"I was sixteen," Emmie laughed. "I didn't know what the hell I was doing. I just went with my heart. I didn't have a head yet. I think now if he had hurt me I would have run away, but who knows? Turns out there wasn't a mean bone in Hoppy's body. He was a big old potbellied teddy bear."

"Still." I shivered. Maybe she was just lucky.

"Anyway, so we sat there eating our lunch and Hoppy said, 'When?'

"I couldn't stand the thought of going back to St. Mike's. I'd already moved on in my head. 'How about now?' I said.

"'I knew it,' he said. 'I told dad I could talk you into it. He bet me you wouldn't.'

"'You bet your dad you would marry me today?' I was shocked.

"'No, I bet him I would bring you home today.' I choked on my chicken and he ended up pounding my back to get me to breathe again. 'Are you sure, Emmie?' he asked me and I was suddenly afraid he might change his mind. Why would he want an ignorant little girl like me?

"'Let's go do it now,' I said."

"You are a wild woman, Emmie." Delores blew smoke out of her nostrils and crossed her legs. "Even I wouldn't marry a man on the first date."

I had to ask, "Did you really get married?"

"Sure. We crawled into the plane and flew to Hoppy's farm. His old man Red is about as sweet as they come. He welcomed me from his wheelchair and pointed me towards the bathroom. I guess he thought I needed to freshen up. When I saw myself in the mirror, I couldn't help giggling. My hair looked like a witch's mop and my lipstick was smeared over the side of my face. I guess it is love if you look like hell and he asks you to marry him anyway."

"I must be doing it all wrong," Delores said as she tapped her cigarette against the edge of a glass ashtray. "Maybe I should start dressing down and I'll meet a better breed of man."

No matter what Delores did, she'd be beautiful. That kind of beauty was frightening. Who knows what it might attract?

"The preacher was a boyhood friend of Red Hopkins. He came out to the farm after Sunday evening services and performed the ceremony. I'd washed my face and worked for an hour on my long ratty hair with Hoppy's tiny tortoise shell comb. There was no way, so I borrowed Red's scissors and cut it all off. It was a little ragged, but I wasn't going to get married with tangled hair. I couldn't stand the shoes anymore, so I got married in my stocking feet. To be nice, Hoppy took off his God-awful black and white cowboy boots and stood before the minister in his socks too. We didn't have a ring. He promised he'd buy me one, but he never got around to it.

"The next day Hoppy went to work and Red and I started to make each other's acquaintance. I tried to help around the house but it was hopeless. I broke his favorite glass mug right off the bat. Then, I burned macaroni onto the bottom of one of his pots. Twice I stood too close behind him and he backed his wheel chair over my toe. Hoppy teased me about being 'underfoot' all the time. Ultimately, I was relegated to feeding the goat and washing silverware. Red had been taking care of the house and the business ever since he had his accident. He didn't want or need me in his kitchen."

"What happened to him?" Delores lit another cigarette from the butt of the first.

"He and Hoppy were barnstorming in two different planes. They said it was a maneuver they'd done a thousand times — but something went wrong and Red went down."

24

I shuddered at the idea of being in a wheelchair for the rest of my life, having to rely on someone else for every little thing. I like things to be just so. You can't count on other folks for that.

"Red is a nice old guy," Emmie said. "He's long gotten used to his situation. He can do anything you can except walk."

Somehow, I doubted that, but I nodded.

"Anyway, after a week, he suggested that Hoppy teach me how to fly. Every day, Hoppy would get up before daylight and go dust his fields. Then he'd come home and we'd go flying together. After all the trying and failing, I finally found something I was good at. The WACO was a sweet little plane. At first, Hoppy took me up and taught me straight and level, stalls, full throttle stalls, and turns. Then he taught me to take off and land. We worked on it every day for weeks. He taught me about the plane, the instruments, the control surfaces – and true to his word, we had fun. Soon we were doing barrel rolls and spins. Flying with Hoppy was heaven. Whenever he took the controls, I held out my arms and put my head back and enjoyed the air rushing over me.

"It seemed only natural after I got my license and I'd been flying a few months to learn to dust crops. Red encouraged it. The idea of two pilots bringing in cash was attractive. More importantly, it kept me out of his hair. Hoppy took me out to a big empty field and showed me what to do.

"'Practice till I get back,' he told me as he took off in the pickup to go talk with a farmer.

"I watched him drive away, his elbow resting on the window frame, a toothpick sticking out the corner of his mouth. I remember thinking he was the best thing that ever happened to me. Because of Hoppy, I was going to be a crop duster!

"I started the engine and took off. Swooping down over the crops, I flew the length of the field, turning and flying another swath parallel with the first. It was great fun at first. Back and forth, back and forth. After about an hour, I had to pee. I was quite a ways from town and I didn't want to go find a farm house, so I set the WACO down in a field of weeds near a thicket."

I looked up at the receptionist in alarm, hoping she wasn't listening to our conversation. She seemed busy with her comic book.

"Relax, Shirley. Even receptionists pee."

I didn't like Delores' mocking tone.

Emmie smiled at me. "I'll lower my voice. How's that?"

Sometimes I feel like such a fool.

"Anyway, so I crawled out of the plane and ran towards the trees. I was zipping up my jeans when I heard growling in the weeds a few feet away. A farm dog had come out to investigate the big yellow bird in his field. He didn't know what to make of the WACO, but he sure didn't like me. He put his ears back and his upper lip quivered over his canines. He was about thirty yards in front of the plane so I decided to make a run for it. Of course, there was no way I could outrun him. I got to the plane and threw a leg up over the fuselage to get into the cockpit when he hit me. He grabbed hold of the leg of my pants and pulled me backwards. I fell so hard it took my breath away. Snarling, the dog went for my throat. All I could think to do was to curl up in a ball. He bit at my arms which I'd thrown over my face, but I rolled just enough for him to do this." She lifted her bangs to show the ragged scar I'd already noticed. "I think he would have killed me but there was a big explosion in the distance. He startled and let go. I took the opportunity to climb up into the WACO. When he realized I was gone, he was furious — barking hysterically, throwing himself against the side of the fuselage. I was hesitant to start the plane for fear I'd hurt him, but after a minute, I got to thinking he might jump into the cockpit with me. Frankly, I'd had enough of this mutt.

"There was black smoke on the horizon. I hit the ignition thinking the noise would scare that dog off. I got to give it to him though, he was brave. As I started rolling down the field, he chased me — biting at the wheels. Blood dripped into my eye as I pulled back on

26

the stick. There was a little 'thump' and a wild howling. I must have hit the doggone thing. I figured him for dead, but there he went squealing through the tall grass as I flew off towards the smoke.

"Fire trucks raced along the roads below me, their sirens muffled by the roar of my engine. I rubbed the blood out of my eye and squinted. A bright red plane had crashed into a barn and the two were burning. A short ways away, I saw Hoppy's truck parked on the side of a dirt road. I circled, looking for him. Finally, I landed in the closest field I could find. I ran forever it seems.

"I headed toward a group of men huddled around a lump on the ground covered with someone's old black raincoat. I remember noticing the pocket was torn. Sticking out from under the raincoat were Hoppy's worn-heeled, hand-tooled black and white cowboy boots. I screamed and tried to get to him. Because I was bleeding, everyone thought I'd been in the crash with Hoppy at first. The sheriff who was a friend of Hoppy's held me back. 'He wouldn't want you to see him this way,' he said.

"'But why was he in this plane? Whose plane is it? I don't understand,' I cried.

"Someone dabbed at my cut with a bandanna and tied it around my forehead. 'He was buying it for you, Emmie. He was testing it to make sure it was safe.'"

We sat there in the lobby of *Wiley Aircraft*, the image of Hoppy's body stamped into my mind.

Emmie sniffed. Both Delores and I reached for her hand this time. Delores' red-nailed fingers curled around Emmie's freckled ones. I withdrew, wishing Delores wasn't around.

An older gentleman came out of the back office. "Welcome, welcome," he said. "I'm Mr. Wiley. Usually I don't get to meet the new ladies, Grant takes care of all of that — but he tells me you took things into your own hands."

Mr. Wiley knew about the bus and he didn't even seem mad. I didn't know what to think.

I still think about Emmie and Hoppy sometimes — and those early days when we were getting to know each other and learning our jobs. It already seems like such a long time ago.

CHAPTER 3 — THE FIRST TRIP

"Italy's Surrender Shocks Stock Prices, Steel Production Sets New Record, Australian Nurse Offers New Treatment for Polio in Minneapolis Hospital."
~ American View Daily ~

Our first day at *Wiley Aircraft* was uneventful. Grant Logan gave us a tour around the factory. We met just about everyone and saw how everything worked. Emmie waved at Mr. McKensey who was pushing pieces of lumber long-ways through a table saw. He frowned behind his goggles and his mouth moved but we couldn't hear his lecture over the scream of the equipment. Myrtle and a few of the girls were busy covering wing frames with heavy linen. Others installed instruments into the dashboards of partially finished fuselages while young boys and old men hoisted shiny new engines into the air with chains. At the far end of the factory floor, teams of masked women painted completed planes dark Army green. As we were leaving, Grant handed us flight manuals for the *Foxes* we were to test. The one thing we didn't do was fly.

The next day, we reported for duty in our baggy jumpsuits and Grant assigned us three *Wiley Foxes*. We sat down together and figured out our flight plan. I figured with good weather, it would take three days. Emmie was the most experienced pilot of the three of us, so we decided she should navigate. The *Foxes* were two-seater monoplanes with 65 hp engines. The yellow arc on the airspeed indicator was set at 90 mph, the red line at 120 mph. They were simple, utilitarian, and easy to fly. We packed a change of underclothes, some money, and several bottles of water. Myrtle provided us with egg sandwiches and oatmeal cookies made with molasses. By 9 am, we were ready.

We crawled into our respective planes, taxied to the end of the *Wiley* runway and took off. Once in the air, Emmie checked on each of us with the radio. "I guess we test these birds before we head west. I'll go first."

"I hear you," Delores keyed her mic.

"Okay by me," I answered.

"Climbing to four thousand feet, no problems." Emmie put the plane through its paces — climbing, diving, stalling. "Not a Stearman but a nice little plane," she said into the microphone when she finished the standard procedures. "You want to go next, Delores?"

"I'm on it." Delores wasn't as precise as Emmie, but she ended each of her maneuvers with a flourish, waggling her wings like a punctuation point.

"Your turn, Shirley." Emmie's squeaky voice sounded like Donald Duck over the radio.

"Okay, here I go." I was slow and exact, careful. It took me longer than either of them. When I finished, Emmie pointed her nose west and we followed. It was a sunny day and we flew in loose formation for a couple of hours.

Around 11 am, we crossed the Indiana state line and Emmie keyed her mike. "You guys ready for a bathroom break?"

"I was ready an hour ago," Delores answered.

"Okay." I was embarrassed to discuss the bathroom over the radio.

"This is my old stomping ground. There's a little strip near here. We can refuel, take a break, and eat our lunches."

Delores and I acknowledged by clicking our microphones and followed Emmie down. It was a short, grassy strip but these were little planes and we had no problems. We taxied up to the hangar and cut the engines, eager to stretch our legs.

"What the hell is this?" An apple-shaped man in a stained tee shirt came out of the hangar, wiping his hands on an oily rag. I guess he never had three women in military planes take a break at his airport before and he was suspicious.

30

"Nub, you old buzzard, it's me, Emmie Hopkins." Emmie took off her sunglasses.

"My God, little girl. Does Red know you are here?" He picked her up and swung her around. I cringed at the thought of the greasy handprints he left on her jumpsuit.

He set Emmie on her feet and slapped her on the back with enough force that she took a couple of steps forward. "Naw, I haven't had time to call him. We're gonna buzz the old place," she said.

That was news to me.

"Nub, I want you to meet my friends — Delores and Shirley."

Fortunately, Nub just nodded and didn't make a move to pick us up or shake our hands. "So what are you young ladies up to?" His voice dripped with disapproval.

"We're delivering aircraft for the government. They are recruiting women pilots to free the guys for combat." Emmie put her arm around his furry shoulders and walked him towards the hangar. He wore his pants so low that Delores and I stole amused glances at each other at the sight of his scrawny, hairy behind. "We're going to need to refuel. I have papers explaining what I'm doing and I have the money."

He scratched his spotted head. "How long you gonna be here?" His voiced faded away as he and Emmie disappeared inside the hangar.

"Why is it bald men are covered with hair everywhere else?" Delores whispered.

I covered my mouth with both hands to smother a giggle. Father was a bald hairy fellow too.

"Well, I don't know about you, but I'm ready to find a bathroom. You think they got one in there?" Delores started towards the hangar.

"We haven't been invited in yet," I protested, but I trailed behind her, looking over my shoulder in case someone might disapprove.

31

The restroom was as filthy as I feared it might be. I looked around, but there wasn't another building in sight. It dawned on me it would be cleaner to go in a field. I took a small bottle of lavender scent out of my bag and spritzed the place. After doing my business and washing my hands, I wrapped several lengths of toilet paper around my wrist and then folded it and slipped it into my purse just in case I was faced with a dirty bathroom again. I had to flush the toilet twice and the water was still running when I opened the door. Delores was waiting for me — her arms folded over her chest, tapping her toe. She was so impatient. I avoided her eyes as she squeezed past me. She didn't take long in the bathroom. I hoped she washed her hands thoroughly. She emerged fresh and pretty as a picture post card.

Together, we went looking for Emmie. She had collected our lunches and was sitting on an ancient picnic table beside the runway. "Nub gave us some cokes from his cooler." She tipped the small bottle to her lips. She had unzipped her jumpsuit and slipped her arms out of the sleeves. I hated how it looked, but she seemed cooler than Delores and I did. "He's refueling the planes as we speak."

"You think we are going to get the evil eye everywhere we stop?" Delores straddled the bench and picked up her lunch.

"We are like the freak show at the circus, that's all." Emmie bit into her egg sandwich. "People aren't used to women pilots."

Delores picked through her lunch bag. "I'm not sure I like being eyed like I'm a prized cow."

Delores turned heads wherever she went. I wasn't sure how this was any different. I walked around the weathered picnic table trying to find the cleanest place to sit. It was covered with dried bird droppings and splinters. I decided to eat standing up.

"Did you hear about the girl who got forced down in Alabama due to a storm? She landed at a strip near this dinky little town and went looking for a place to eat. No place in town would serve her." Delores munched on one of Myrtle's cookies. She always ate her dessert first if she could get away with it. "Just goes to show we should always have food with us."

"I'm sure we'll run into all kinds of folks." Emmie finished her sandwich and wadded up the wax paper. "We'll just grin and bear it when they are snooty."

I couldn't get over how Emmie took things in stride. I worried about the bigger airports with air traffic control or military bases. What if they wouldn't let us land? We'd heard stories of girls sleeping on the ground under the wings of their planes.

"The men pilots come and go as they please and no one thinks anything about it. It's not fair, that's all I'm saying." Delores' voice took on an argumentative tone. "And I'm tired of all the studies trying to decide if we are losing our feminine qualities."

"Aw, Delores. If you have a period every month, you are still a woman. Don't let them get your goat." Emmie finished her coke and stood up. "Just do your job. Ain't no skin off your nose one way or another. You should have seen the look on these farmers' faces when I showed up to dust their fields instead of Hoppy. Like everyone else, they had this idea women couldn't do the job for them. It was their respect for Red that made them give me a chance. Once they saw I could handle it, they didn't care if I was a girl or not."

"What was it like?" I asked to keep the topic away from Delores' monthlies. I was intrigued Emmie had taken over Hoppy's business after he died. The very idea of diving on a field of corn scared me to death.

"Better than flagging." Emmie laughed. "You have to concentrate all the time and keep an eye out for obstructions. When you are flying that close to the ground, there are trees and buildings and telephone poles and electrical wires and windmills ready to jump out and grab you. And of course there are all those other flying objects in the area. I had a bird smack me on the shoulder once. He didn't make it and I just about didn't either. Broke my collarbone and I was

33

down for the count. Fortunately it was at the end of the season and we didn't lose too much."

"How'd you get that plane down?" My shoulder was aching at the idea.

"Well, I crashed, of course."

"Oh my God, were you all right?"

"Naw, I died." I stared at her with my mouth open for a moment. She kept a straight face for two more beats before she thumped me on the arm and laughed. "It's an old joke, Shirley."

"Oh." It wasn't funny but I forced a faint laugh.

Delores stood up. "Emmie, you keep scaring Shirley like that and she's going to punch you."

"No, no. I'd never do that," I said and they both laughed again.

"It's time to get going. We've got a long haul ahead of us." Emmie wiped her hands on the seat of her jumpsuit. "Let's see if Nub's got us all fixed up."

We trooped into the hangar for one more go at the bathroom, before crawling back into our *Foxes*. Emmie headed south which puzzled me as Delores and I followed her. When she dove towards a small farm with three cars sitting out front, I understood. One by one, we swooped down on the house. After a few minutes, an old man in a wheelchair rolled out into the yard, waving his hat.

Emmie stuck her hand out the side window of her *Fox*. Below her, some kind of animal tugged on the back of one of the cars.

"What the heck is that?" Delores said into her mic.

I squinted. "A goat I think."

We circled for another look. The old man was yelling and smacking the goat on the hindquarters with his hat.

"Beulah's eating Uncle Clyde's license plate," Emmie chuckled into the radio. "Uncle Clyde is Red's brother from Illinois. They made

34

their license plates out of soybean and paper pulp this year. The livestock loves them."

Red Hopkins was herding Beulah back into her pen as we flew away.

A couple days later, we landed at Camp Morgan for the first time. We were tired and hungry and in need of a shower. My mouth tasted like a dirty birdcage and I was eager to brush my teeth. As we emerged from our *Foxes*, a tall, slim Colonel marched across the tarmac to greet us. He cut quite a figure in his leather jacket, blouson pants and knee-high boots. He even sported an ivory-handled colt .45 in a holster strapped to his hip. A younger, shorter man with red hair followed a step behind him.

"I'm Conrad Simpson," the colonel said as he grasped Emmie's outstretched hand. "I don't usually meet ferry pilots but I am a personal friend of Jackie Cochran and you are the first girls to land here."

"Nice to meet you, Colonel Simpson." Emmie flinched, opening and closing her reddened fingers once he released them. "This is Delores Lieberman."

Delores shook hands with the big man and whimpered.

"And this is Shirley Maxwell." His grip was absolutely crushing. I rose up onto my toes trying not to squeal. His lips twisted into an unmerry smirk. I refused to cry out in pain and he refused to release my hand.

Something flickered in his eyes. "Hello, Shirley," he said. "Your father called the other day."

I froze, my mouth open. "Do you know my father?" I felt sick.

"I do now." He turned to the lieutenant standing behind him. "I'd like to introduce you to your instructor. This is Lieutenant Thomas A. McDougal. War Hero."

35

The young man stepped forward. He greeted each of us pleasantly, but of course, his eyes clung to Delores. The three of us couldn't help but stare at him in horror. A thick red scar snaked from his hairline above his right eye, across his forehead, the bridge of his nose and down his left cheek. I imagined the wound that made that mark and shuddered.

"Call me Tommy," he said. "We need you to go back to Ohio and bring out three more *Foxes*. You'll be doing this through the New Year, I'm afraid. We are behind in getting those little grasshoppers out to their units." Tommy was about the same height as Emmie and Delores — and, of course, they all towered over me. "You leave on the first train going east in the morning which is at 4:30 am. So I suggest you get to bed early tonight."

Sleep sounded great to me.

"We thought we'd escort you to dinner to welcome you to Camp Morgan. Anything for Jackie." Colonel Simpson looked at me like he was appraising a cantaloupe. "And for George Maxwell."

What had Father said to him? While I was blushing, Delores blurted out, "We'd love dinner, but we didn't bring anything but the clothes on our backs and a change of underwear."

"No need to dress up, we'll go to the Officer's Club. I presume you are wearing uniforms under those jumpsuits." Simpson raised one eyebrow. "However, I'm sure you'd like to freshen up a bit and I want to put in an hour or so at the firing range. Tommy, why don't you show the ladies to their barracks? Come back for me when you are ready." He didn't wait for an answer and strode off across a grassy field headed toward a building just over a rise.

"He likes target shooting." Tommy shrugged.

"Nice boots," Emmie giggled.

"I don't know — I kind of liked the pants," Delores said.

"Wait till you see the rest of his outfits. He's jealous of those Nazi bastards and their fancy uniforms with capes and cloaks. He'd have

36

a monocle if he wasn't afraid we'd all laugh at him. He's never gotten over the Cavalry's move from horses to tanks. It was a personal disappointment even though George Patton is his hero now." When Tommy smiled, the scar lifted his lip higher on one side of his mouth. "But for all his flamboyance, Colonel Simpson is a good guy. Once you get used to him, you'll like him."

Emmy rubbed her hand. "I'd like him a lot better if he didn't break my hand right off the bat."

Tommy led the way to a long Quonset hut the other side of the admin building. "He was showing off. He's not all that keen on you all being here. He thinks there will be trouble."

"That's what they all think." Delores sighed.

"Simpson's not your problem here." He opened the door to our barracks and bowed as we filed in. "I'll wait for you. You should find everything you need in the bathroom."

"What is our problem?" I stopped in front of him.

"The men."

I bit my lower lip and went in.

#

As we walked back across the tarmac, our hair damp, and our underwear clean under our smelly, unpressed uniforms, we saw crews pushing the shiny new *Foxes* we had flown into a hangar.

"What will they do with them?" Delores asked.

"Check them out, register them, and then a pilot will ferry them to wherever they are needed. I think these are slated for one of the aircraft carriers," Tommy said.

The men paused when they saw us coming towards them. A few pilots in flight jackets stepped out of the hangar. A balding mechanic with 'Wilson' on his jumpsuit saluted, but others scowled.

"We don't need your help," a short fellow shouted.

37

"What kind of women are you?" Another taunted.

"If you don't have anything to do, I can find something for you." Tommy pointed towards the hangar.

"I never thought I'd see the day," someone grumbled.

"Get back to work." Tommy waved them off and we walked through the crowd towards the firing range.

The mechanic bowed and pretended to take his hat off with a flourish. "Wayne, you're an asshole," a voice inside the hangar called.

"At least they didn't call us dykes," Delores whispered.

"That's next."

It was warm in California, but I felt a chill.

#

The next morning, Tommy McDougal saw us off at the train station. "You are on your own from here on out," he told us.

"I think we can handle it." Delores waved at him through the train window. We sat facing each other as the train pulled away from the platform. It was still dark and I closed my eyes as we rocked side to side.

"That is so beautiful." Emmie lowered her voice to just above a whisper.

"It was my grandmother Lieberman's and she got it from her mother. She gave it to me on my seventeenth birthday. It's a Kashmir Sapphire mined back in 1885."

"I've always liked sapphires. The color is so intense."

"This is my favorite stone. My grandma's eyes were this color. I remember looking into them when I was a little girl and seeing this pendant hanging around her neck."

38

I watched Delores through my lashes. She held the gem in her palm, looking at it with affection. "I thought she was perfect —," she said, "perfectly beautiful, perfectly kind, perfectly good. All her life she has tried to do good things. She once baked a honey cake and wrapped it up in cheesecloth. Then we took a streetcar downtown where there were people sleeping on the street corners. We gave the cake to a guy with no teeth because she thought he was probably hungrier than some of the others. I asked her why we were giving cakes away and she said, 'It's a mitzvah to give. It's part of being Jewish — being good to other people for no reason.' When we went back home to Squirrel Hill, there wasn't enough flour for us to have a cake that night. I felt wonderful all the same."

I opened my eyes. "What's a mitzvah?"

"A blessing."

"It must be nice to know your mother and father — and your grandparents." Emmie's eyes were wistful. She was naïve, I thought. Knowing your parents isn't all it's cracked up to be.

"It's wonderful, Emmie," Delores said. "You'll have to come home with me sometime. You can meet everyone — my mother and father, and my little brother Arty. My cousin Gretchen who escaped from the Nazis lives with us now too. You will love them all. You must come too, Shirley. Mama makes the best pot roast."

She was probably just being polite but I hoped not. I'd love to have pot roast in Pittsburgh with a happy family. Of course, we never got a chance to do that. I sometimes wonder what it would have been like.

That was our routine for several months. We flew new planes to Camp Morgan — sometimes stopping to have lunch with Red Hopkins, sometimes just buzzing his farm. Then we spent the night at Camp Morgan before catching the early train back to Ohio.

As usual, I've gone on way too long and my hand is stiff. When I was in school, the nuns cracked my knuckles with a ruler when I wrote with the wrong hand. Father was so unhappy to have a lefty in

the family that I had to learn everything backwards. It's exhausting –
– having to think about everything all the time, but it's the rule you
know.

CHAPTER 4 — MAGS

"Some flowers overpower the rest."
~ *George Maxwell, Bon-vivant*
Late-October, 1943

It is time to tell you about Mags Strickland. To say I never met anyone like her would be an understatement. She lives in a world of her own making and has no regard for what anyone else thinks. She laughs at the conventions the rest of us accept without question, challenges our most basic beliefs, and refuses to be bound by even the most minimal of social bonds. Yet, I find her utterly charming. Everyone does.

Emmie, Delores, and I had been flying *Wiley Foxes* to Camp Morgan for six weeks. I sat at my writing table composing a thank you note to Father. He'd sent his driver with his old 1935 Plymouth sedan. It took old Buzzy over a week to drive from New Jersey since the speed limit was 35 miles per hour and it was sometimes hard to find gas. He didn't stay at *The Windshift Inn* very long. Myrtle packed him a lunch and Buzzy took the first train back. That was fine with me. I didn't like Buzzy anyway. He smelled like Limburger cheese and onions. I didn't ask Father for the car, but I have to admit, it was nice having it at the inn.

Delores sat on her bed painting her legs. Stockings were very dear. We hadn't been able to buy silk in a long time and nylon was rationed since the Army used it for parachutes.

"How do you do that? Every time I try to paint in the seam, I get it crooked. I can't bend myself into little knots like you can." Emmie struggled to sew a strap back onto her slip without taking it off, her chin pressed against her chest.

"I'm double jointed." Delores lifted one painted leg straight up by her ear and then lowered the toe behind her head to touch her opposite shoulder. She looked like a pretzel. I hated when she did that. It was so immodest.

"Dammit!" Emmie stabbed herself with the needle and her slip sagged lower on one side.

"Why don't you take it off first," I suggested as I filled my fountain pen from a half-empty bottle of Scripps ink.

"That would be too easy. I like a challenge." Emmie stuck her tongue out the side of her mouth as she concentrated on tacking the strap.

"Oh no, we can't do things the easy way. Where's the fun in that?" Delores extended the painted seam up the back of her thigh. I couldn't watch either of them. I laid my pen down and walked over to the window. It was late fall. The trees were brightly colored. It was taking longer and longer to fly the *Foxes* to California as we had fewer hours of daylight and often flew many miles out of our way to avoid storms. I tucked the blackout cloth up over the curtain rod to get it out of the way.

A young girl pulling a wooden wagon full of cans of leftover cooking fat made her way down Cold Creek Road. The back wheel caught on a rock and she turned to tug at the handle.

I heard Myrtle's voice from the porch below me. "You come for the left over lard, Pammie?" Pam was a chubby little thing in faded overalls, scuffed saddle shoes, and a torn red shirt. She must have tried to cut her own hair because it hung longer on one side than the other.

"Yes, ma'am. You are my last stop."

"I don't have as much for you this week. I try and use the bacon grease several times before I save it."

"What do they use this stuff for?" One of the *Wiley* girls stepped out from under the overhang and loaded two big sealed cans onto Pam's wagon.

"I don't know exactly — explosives, I think," Pam said.

42

"How's your daddy doing today? You heard from Danny?" Myrtle stood in the yard with her arms crossed over her breasts. It was Saturday and she wore a plain housedress under her frilly apron. It was the first time I'd seen Myrtle in anything but overalls. She looked like everyone's idea of a mother.

On the other hand, Pam looked like everyone's idea of a tomboy. "Daddy's fine. It's been a couple of weeks since we got a letter from Danny. Daddy says not to worry, because Danny's probably out to sea right now."

"You listen to your daddy. He knows what's what." I wondered if Myrtle knew her voice softened whenever she talked about Jerry Kline. Emmie was right. They were definitely sweet on one another.

"Yes, ma'am." Pam picked up the handle to her wagon and turned to hike back up Cold Creek Road. That kid was up and down the hill between *The Windshift Inn* and Jerry's airport four or five times a month, collecting for one thing or another — metal, rubber, nylon. She and Grant Logan cornered the market on home front patriotism.

Mr. McKensey pulled his rusty old car into the turnaround. He scowled when he saw Pam.

"Morning, Mr. McKensey." Pam waved at him.

"What do you want this time, you little thief? You already got the bumpers off my car." He braked as she grunted to pull the wagon out of his way. Sure enough, slabs of wood adorned the front of his vehicle instead of chrome.

"Just fat today." She smiled at him and he frowned back.

A bright red biplane roared over *The Windshift Inn* so low the windows shook. Pam dropped the handle to her wagon and ran out into the side yard beyond the oaks, shading her eyes with her hands. Myrtle followed.

"What the heck was that?" Delores fanned her legs to dry the body paint.

43

"Looks like a Stearman to me." I raised the window and stuck my head out. The plane climbed vertically several hundred yards and then looped down to buzz us again.

"What is that idiot doing?" Mr. McKensey shook his fist out the cracked window of his old Ford.

The red plane swooped over the inn upside down. Several of the factory girls were out in the yard now. Emmie ran down the steep back stairs pulling a dress over her head. Delores joined me at the window. The pilot rolled the plane and climbed for another loop-de-loop.

"Show off," Delores grumbled as she lit a cigarette, dropping the spent match out the window. I glared at her and she shrugged, good-natured and unrepentant.

With a flourish, the Stearman made one last pass at the inn and headed towards Jerry Kline's airfield a mile away. The girls in the yard went about their business now that the performance was over.

"Shirley, Shirley!" Emmie danced below me waving her arms to get my attention. Pam stood beside her, looking up at me with huge solemn eyes.

"Look at that nut!" Delores waved back. "She forgot to put on her shoes, running around barefoot in October. She'll catch her death."

"Her slip's showing," I said.

"Fercryingoutloud!" Mr. McKensey inched his way through a group of Myrtle's chickens near the back of the driveway. "It's like Grand Central Station at mid-day without a traffic cop around here."

"What do you want?" I called out the window to Emmie.

"Bring my shoes! Let's go meet this guy with the Stearman." Her voice was shrill.

"I don't want to walk that far." It was at least two miles if you followed the roads, a mile if you crawled down the hill and hiked cross-country.

"Neither do we. Bring the keys to your car." Emmie's smile won me over. I sighed and reached for my sweater, buttoning it up to the throat.

"She is crazy." Delores laughed. "And so are you."

I found Emmie's shoes under her bed and picked up my keys. The idea of a ride down country roads on a lovely autumn day infected me with Emmie's sense of fun. "Are you coming?" I called to Delores as I started down the stairs.

"I have a date coming by in a few minutes." She was still in her brassiere and slip.

"You are going to be late."

"No I won't. I'll beat you downstairs."

"You'll have to hurry, I'm going down now." I headed towards the landing on the second floor.

"You're going too slow!" She called after me.

"HA!" I raced down the last two flights of wooden steps, ran through the kitchen and onto the back porch, the screen door slamming behind me. Hurrying around the corner of the house, I skidded to a stop. Emmie was helping Pam load her cans of lard into the trunk of the old Plymouth and Delores was leaning against the side of the car, grinning.

"How did you do that?" I put my hands on my hips.

"Jumped out the window." It was a good thing she wasn't wearing stockings. She had a long scratch down the calf of her left leg, but she was fully dressed including shoes if you didn't count the fact she was unbuttoned and unzipped.

"It's a wonder you didn't break your neck." Delores and Emmie made me laugh, but someone was going to get hurt one of these days if they kept playing around like this. Jumping out of a window, indeed!

45

"Yes, but the drain pipe was right by the window. I slid down it. Fell on my keester when I landed, of course." She hitched up her dress to show a big bruise forming on her thigh.

"Are you coming with us?" I opened the back door of the sedan and Pam crawled in.

"Naw, you tell that guy I can out-fly him any day of the week and twice on Sundays. Bennie Bermeister is taking me for a ride in his Uncle's convertible."

"You watch out for him!" Pam rolled down the window and stuck out her head. "He's a friend of Danny's and he's a two-legged wolf."

I slid in behind the steering wheel. Emmie got in beside me and busied herself with putting on her shoes.

"Don't you worry about me, Miss Kline. I'm a two-legged wolf tamer." Delores straightened her dress and zipped the side zipper. As we drove away, I saw her checking her painted-on stocking seams in the rear view mirror.

I drove slowly to minimize the dust.

"Doggonit, Hoss. I can walk faster than this." Emmie's thin cotton dress was too light for the weather. Either she didn't mind being cold, or she didn't have anything warmer.

"I always drive just below the speed limit," I said as I turned onto Kline Road and headed towards *Jerry's Flying School*.

"That's a shame. This is a nice car. It's got some horses under the hood." She thumped the outside of the door like she was playing a drum. Father would have a heart attack if he saw anyone beating on his car like that. I pressed down on the accelerator, spinning the tires in the loose gravel.

"Now that's more like it." Emmie stuck her head out the window, the wind blowing her hair back from her face.

I pulled into the airport and parked beside the main hangar. *Jerry's Flying Service* was housed in a small cement block building with an office and pilot's lounge in front and a service area in back. Two silver hangars housed Jerry's fleet of four small *Wiley* trainers. Two runways intersected at right angles, the paved main one going east-west and a smaller grass strip running north-south. Jerry lived with Pam and Danny in a white house behind the airport. An unpainted barn and a corral lay across a pasture to the left.

Jerry Kline stood outside the office talking with a tall, slim man in a leather flight jacket, high boots, and jodhpurs. They were smoking long, skinny cigars and laughing loudly. The red Stearman sat in front of the bigger hangar. Jerry nodded and the two men shook hands.

Pam jumped out of the Plymouth and ran ahead of us.

"Pam, this is Mags Strickland." Jerry put his arm around the little girl's shoulders. "Mags, this is my daughter, Pam."

I was shocked. This slender Conrad Simpson look-alike was a woman.

"That was some flying!" Pam pumped the stranger's hand.

"It's a pretty day." Mags grinned at us as we approached, the cigar clinched in her teeth. Her heart-shaped face was delicate, her auburn hair no more than an inch long. "You must be the other WASP."

"Nice to meet you, Mags. I'm Emmie Hopkins."

"I'm Shirley Maxwell."

"George Maxwell's girl?" Mags blew smoke out of her nose.

Did Father know everyone?

"I flew through New Jersey on my way over here and he had me bring you some things." She rummaged through her leather knapsack and produced some small blue boxes with silver wings — powder, lipstick, and eyebrow pencil from Jackie Cochran's

47

exclusive line of cosmetics. I knew Father was making nice with Jackie Cochran but I liked having new things.

"Thank you." I stared at the toes of Mags' expensive leather boots – – her feet were long and narrow — like the rest of her.

"That's some plane," Emmie said. "Can we look at it?"

"Thanks, she's getting old now, but she's still a dear. My favorite ride." We walked over to the Stearman. "This is the plane I learned to fly back in 1928. I went up with a man who was trying to seduce me. The next day, I cut my hair and bought his plane. I've been flying her ever since."

"Well, did he succeed?" Emmie's dimples deepened and her eyes sparkled mischievously.

"Of course." Mags puffed her cigar. "But the airplane was a much better deal."

Emmie roared with laughter. Pam looked at me with a blank expression, not quite sure she got the joke. I glanced at Jerry. What must he think of this kind of talk?

"Why are you late?" Pam inspected the airplane. A custom leather boot that snapped onto the fuselage to form a tight seal covered the front cockpit.

"Everybody else got here last month."

"I didn't get back from England until the middle of September and I ran down to Key West to see a friend of mine."

"How long were you in England?" Jerry picked up the rear of the airplane. Mags and Emmie took the right wing, Pam and I the left. We pushed the Stearman into the hangar, positioning it so that the wings were well clear of Jerry's two *Foxes* parked nearby.

"Over a year. Went in August of 42. Ferried aircraft for the RAF." Mags stepped up on the wing and unsnapped the leather cover over the front cockpit. She handed a large sealed carton down to me and I staggered under the weight of it. Pam picked up the leather knapsack, Emmie collected Mags' suitcase and we all walked back to the Plymouth.

The trunk was full of Pam's grease collection and her wagon. Jerry helped her unload and carry the cans of used fat over to a large stockpile inside the hangar. We stuffed Mags' things inside and closed the lid.

"The area is beautiful." Mags looked at the surrounding countryside. "Are there any stables nearby? I like to hire a mount ever once in a while. A ride is relaxing after a long flight."

"No need for that, young lady. I have several horses that need to be taken out and exercised. You are welcome to join us anytime," Jerry said.

"I find handling a spirited horse similar to dealing with the male of our own species, don't you?" Mags nudged Emmie with a sharp elbow. Her eyes included me, accepted me. I waited for the punch line. "They need a strong hand, an educated seat, and a lot of praise."

For the second time since meeting this strange person, Emmie threw her head back and laughed. Normally, this kind of talk embarrassed me, but Mags' had a way of incorporating you into her joke. I felt like she liked me right off the bat. I laughed too.

The backdoor of the Plymouth opened outward from the mid post. Emmie crawled in. I stood by the driver's side, holding the keys.

"It was nice to meet you, Jerry. I'll be back over in a couple of days with my fuel ration stamps. Maybe we can ride your horses then." Mags walked up to me, standing by the car. "This is a nice car, Shirley. Do you mind if I drive?"

Normally, I prefer to drive — especially Father's Plymouth, but I dropped the keys into Mags' outstretched palm and went around to climb in the passenger door. Mags got in and started the engine. She steered with her left hand, her right never leaving the gearshift. She released the clutch and accelerated out of the airport, turning away from the inn onto Logan's Run Road.

"We should have turned the other way," I yelled over the road noises.

"How's about we take a little ride," she said out of the corner of her mouth, her eyes on the horizon in front of us.

"Oh, of course," I glanced over my shoulder at Emmie who showed me her broadest grin. "These old country roads always end up in Cold Creek anyway."

We headed off in the wrong direction, the wind roaring in the open windows, clouds of dust churned up by the big wheels billowing behind us.

"Where are you from, Mags?" Emmie grasped the back of the front seat. Her lips were bluish. I wore a jacket and I was cold. I don't know how she kept from shivering.

"I was born in South Hampton, England, but my family lives in St. Louis. My mother's folks are in the brewing business there. Actually, I was nearly born and died on the Titanic," Mags shouted over the sound of the big engine.

"That big ship that hit an iceberg?" Emmie and I stared out the windshield in horror as we approached a crossroads with no sign of braking.

"Yep, Mamà went into labor the day they were to board and they ended up missing the boat due to my imminent arrival." She pronounced Mamà the same way FDR did. Mags hit the brakes and spun the steering wheel. Emmie squealed with laughter. We slid around the corner and headed towards Cold Creek on Sugar. "So you see, I saved my father's life at the very least by being born at the right time." We zoomed past a sign that proclaimed the speed limit to be 20 mph.

I grabbed the window frame and braced my feet, a grimace frozen on my face.

50

"There's Delores!" Emmie pointed to a small convertible coupe up ahead of us. A young man in uniform crouched in the passenger side, his hat blown into the rumble seat. Delores was driving nearly as fast as Mags. The little car leapt over a large rut, Delores and the soldier rising into the air above their seats. We took the rut just as fast. The Plymouth was heavier but the three of us were thrown upwards as well.

A chicken truck came toward us a few hundred yards away as Mags pulled into the opposite lane to pass Delores. Delores accelerated to keep us from getting around her. The soldier's eyes were wide, his mouth open in a soundless scream. The Plymouth was faster. Mags zipped around Delores and back into the proper lane a second before we reached the chicken truck, which had stopped dead in the road, chickens squawking as their cages slid forward, feathers floating in the air. Emmie waved at the white-faced driver as we sped past.

Mags took the next two left turns equally fast, and we headed back towards *The Windshift Inn*. Delores was on our back bumper, beeping the horn and trying to get around us. A mile from the inn, Mags slammed on the brakes and Emmie and I flew forward, grabbing onto anything we could. A row of ducks marched across the dirt road. Delores slid sideways to avoid hitting the back of our car. We could hear her cursing. The last duck in the line turned to us and quacked as if to thank us for not running them down.

Mags hit the gas and we raced towards the inn with Delores close behind. We flew into the turnaround stopping just feet from the front porch. Mags turned off the engine and the three of us sat in silence. Delores squealed to a stop behind us. Bennie Bermeister jumped out of the car and ran into the inn, his face pasty white — his hand over his mouth. I fumbled for the door handle.

"Yeeha!" Delores yelled from the convertible, her fist in the air.

Mags tossed me the keys and got out of the Plymouth. "That's some pretty good driving there." She extended her hand to Delores.

"I'll get you next time," Delores grinned.

51

I got out of the car and leaned my forehead against the roof. Emmie crawled out and put her hand on the small of my back. "Get a grip, it's only fun," she said so the others couldn't hear.

"We could have been killed. We could have wrecked Father's car." My teeth chattered and I thought I might throw up on Myrtle's yellow mums.

"It's over now. We tested death and He passed us by. Breathe deep. Doesn't the air taste wonderful?" Her eyes sparkled with some mysterious emotion I'd never felt. She went to join Mags and Delores and I stood there alone, wondering what in the world she meant.

Myrtle came out onto the porch and Delores introduced Mags.

"We got a bed all ready for you," Myrtle said.

"Thank you, ma'am. I brought you something from Syracuse. I stopped by there for fuel. A friend of mine runs a grocery." Mags opened the trunk of the Plymouth and hefted the big box onto one thin shoulder. "No, that's all right. I'll carry it in," she said to Myrtle who tried to take the box. "It's mostly Spam, but there are several cans of ham, Vienna sausages, and a couple of big salamis as well. I don't eat meat, but there's no reason you can't use my rations."

I caught the look of delight on Myrtle's face. She already loved Mags too. Emmie tossed Mags' knapsack over her shoulder and I picked up the suitcase. Bennie Bermeister staggered out onto the front porch and dropped into one of the gliders.

"Ready for another ride?" Emmie asked as she went past. He suppressed a gag. "So much for the two-legged wolf," she whispered to me as we trudged up the stairs with Mags' things.

That was our first adventure with Mags Strickland. From the moment they met, Delores was obsessed with beating Mags at something. Every night, Delores fought to win at Euchre. Every night Mags cleaned up. Every time we took the *Foxes* up, Mags outflew Delores. Every time we went for a drive in the Plymouth, the two of them wrangled over who would drive. Mags had the confidence of someone who's always had money — a born winner, yet she was as generous as a monk — giving away money, clothes, ration coupons, time.

I wasn't sure Delores was ever going to warm to Mags. Then, several weeks after Mags joined us, Delores heard about the death of a fellow WASP. They had been close during training at Sweetwater and Delores was devastated. The girl crashed when a flirting male pilot got too close and knocked the tip off her wing. Since the government considered us civilians, there was no money to send her body home and no money for a funeral. We might die for our country but our country wasn't going to take care of us in death. Delores was furious, but helpless.

Mags, who knew as many people as Father, arranged for the body to be brought back to Savannah. She and Delores met the train and escorted Delores' friend back home. We never knew what happened, but when they got back to *The Windshift Inn*, they were the best of friends. That's not to say Delores wasn't still determined to beat Mags at something — anything. As for Mags, she played with Delores — letting her think she might win, before lowering the boom. They were spoiled children playing dangerous games, if you ask me.

CHAPTER 5 — THE STEARMAN

"It's easy to be generous when you know there is more to be had."
~ George Maxwell, Philanthropist,
November, 1943

The Saturday after Mags arrived, we drove out to *Jerry's Flying Service* to take Mags' fuel ration coupons to Jerry. He and Pam were locking the airport office when we arrived. Pam's face brightened and she ran up to take Emmie's hand as we got out of the Plymouth.

Jerry tipped his stained cowboy hat. "I was just about to take the horses out for a run, what do you say?"

"I've never ridden a horse but I'd love to try." Emmie clapped her hands together.

"Neither have I." The closest I ever got to a horse was when Father took me to the races when I was eight years old. We went down to the paddock and he let me pick one to bet on. I selected a mottled gray mare. She came in dead last.

Mags herded us towards Jerry's stable behind the airport. "If you can fly a plane you can ride a horse," she said. Emmie, Delores and I stumbled along like sheep. With the exception of Delores who was in her uniform, we were not dressed for this unexpected adventure. Emmie's dotted Swiss dress seemed too frilly for a horseback ride and I wore my usual wool skirt and sweater.

"Don't you worry — a couple of my darlings are used to greenhorns." Jerry clapped Emmie on the back. I guess that was supposed to reassure her. I tensed in expectation, but he never touched me.

Pam tugged on Emmie's hand. "I'll show you, don't worry. It'll be fun."

Emmie ruffled Pam's hair. "I'm up for it."

We leaned against the corral fence chatting while Jerry and Pam saddled the horses. The animals stamped and whinnied inside their stalls. A cool breeze carried the smell of straw and manure to our noses. I fidgeted thinking about how I might get out of going riding with the others.

Mags unzipped her leather jacket. "Emmie, you have to be cold in that dress. Why don't you take my jacket?" I felt bad I hadn't offered my sweater. It was like Father said — I was selfish and thoughtless.

"Oh no, I'm fine. I'm hot-natured." Emmie peered into the dark stable trying to see what Pam and Jerry were doing. She acted like we went horseback riding every day and she was impatient to get started. "Another trip back to Camp Morgan on Monday," she said as she rubbed her upper arms. "There will be four of us this time."

"I'm looking forward to it." Mags re-zipped her jacket.

Delores rummaged through her purse, took out a compact, and reapplied her lipstick. "Do you know Conrad Simpson?"

"Old Connie? Sure, he came to visit my father back in St. Louis all the time when I was a kid. He used to bounce me on his knee and steal my candy." Mags chuckled at the memory. "Does he still have that gigantic sweet tooth? He could put back a whole pecan pie in one sitting. It was enough to gag a goat."

"He's in charge of Camp Morgan." Delores didn't like Colonel Simpson and it was clear he didn't like her. He was the only man I ever knew who seemed untouched by her stunning physical beauty. Whenever they met, they exchanged chilly nods and kept as far apart as possible. "He's our boss out there." She made a face to demonstrate her disdain.

"Well, good for him. He always did want to be in charge. He used to tell me it was his destiny to lead." Mags threw a long leg over the top rail and straddled the fence. "Connie is a big history buff —

56

especially the Civil War. He thinks he is the reincarnation of George Custer. He just missed World War I. It ended before he finished training. I'm sure he thinks this war is his chance to make a big splash."

"I don't think he likes us being there," Delores said. "He treats us like we don't exist."

"I wouldn't be surprised. We are hardly what he expected. He dreamed of charging up San Juan Hill not babysitting a bunch of female ferry pilots. Even so, Connie is a pussycat. Bring him candy and he's yours for the asking."

The barn door swung open and Pam brought out a tall black gelding.

"Oh my," Delores' eyes widened. "What's his name?" She walked around the enormous creature, patting his back as if she knew everything there was to know about horses.

"Horace." Pam giggled as Delores walked around the enormous creature. "You will like him. He's a character."

"Why do you think I'd like him?"

"He snorts when he laughs."

Emmie elbowed Delores. "Just like someone else we know."

We all laughed at that one — even Delores.

"How do you know that a horse is laughing?" I wiped the corners of my eyes with the tips of my middle fingers. Horses were one of the few things that didn't interest George Maxwell and so I'd grown up in sublime ignorance of the species.

"Watch this," Pam handed the reins to Mags. "Can you count to ten, Horace?" She pulled a carrot out of her back pocket and held it so that he could see it.

The beast nodded his head. I swear, he really *did* bounce his head up and down. Emmie clasped her hands over her mouth, her eyes sparkling over her knuckles.

"That's mathematics, not merriment," Mags pointed out.

Pam gave the horse the carrot. "Keep watching. Hey, Dad!"

Jerry tossed her a turnip and she showed it to Horace. "Do you want this?"

"I'd have taken the carrot over that ugly thing," Emmie whispered to me between her fingers.

Apparently, Horace agreed with her because he shook his head from side to side.

"Don't horses like turnips?" Delores asked.

Horace shook his head again.

"He did not do that, did he?" I was astounded.

"What do you really want, Horace?" Pam put her fists on her hips.

The horse took a step forward and nuzzled her pockets, first on one side and then the other.

"Not there, eh?" Pam taunted.

Horace nosed around until he found the last carrot in her back pocket and stole it.

"You are a bad boy, Horace." Pam shook her finger as the animal chewed the carrot.

In response, Horace laughed. He snorted and showed his teeth and bounced is head. I swear it sounded just like Delores.

"Looks like this is the perfect horse for you, Delores." Mags tossed her the reins.

Delores patted Horace on the nose. "Looks like it's you and me, boy," she told him as she slipped a foot into the stirrup and swung herself into the saddle. She seemed totally comfortable with the animal. I sighed. It was just one more thing that I didn't know how to do.

Jerry led a smallish brown mare into the yard. "This here is Pokey. Pam used to ride her when she was little," he said. Emmie grabbed hold of the saddle horn, slipped one foot into Jerry's cupped hands and swung her other leg over the back of the horse. "Whee!" She chortled, her dress hitched up over her bare thighs.

My horse was named Easy. I was trembling when I put my foot in Jerry's hands. Mags and Pam pushed on my behind. After several tries, I straddled the horse. Her back was so broad my legs dangled several inches above the stirrups. Jerry adjusted them and I slipped my oxfords into the foot straps. Easy turned to look at me as I squirmed and tugged at my skirt. "What does she want?" My voice quivered despite my attempts to keep calm.

"She doesn't want anything, she's checking you out." Jerry handed me the reins. "Pokey and Easy are pals and one doesn't go anywhere without the other." He patted Easy's neck. "You just relax and Easy will follow Pokey."

"I *am* relaxed," I said through clinched teeth. I gripped the sides of the horse with my thighs and held onto the saddle horn with both hands. Within a few minutes, we were ready to hit the trail. Mags' horse was a hoof-stomping, wild-eyed stallion. She wheeled him around and galloped off over the hill, with Jerry close behind her. Horace trotted along behind them. Delores sat straight in the saddle with a pained expression on her face.

"I'll wait for you," Pam said as Emmie and I struggled to get our horses to move. She was riding a cute little paint named Speedy who danced sideways on delicate hooves. "Just give them a kick in the sides and say 'giddyap'.

"Giddyap!" Emmie nudged Pokey who had discovered a bit of greenery a few steps beyond the corral gate. The little mare ignored her and munched on the bush. Sensing the person on her back was a rookie, Easy joined her pal for a quick snack. Emmie and I sat in our saddles while the two horses grazed.

"Now what?" I hoped this would be my chance to climb down and go back to the inn, but Pam slid off Speedy and tied my reins to a rope she looped around her own saddle horn.

"What about me?" Emmie called.

"Just hold on. She'll follow Easy." Pam climbed back on her horse and trotted off after the others. Easy had no choice but to follow. After a moment, Pokey followed too.

"Oh God, Pam, slow down!" Bouncing in the saddle, I gripped the horn with both hands. I could hear Emmie giggling behind me as Pokey hurried to keep up. As we crested the hill, we saw Mags and Jerry racing across a meadow. Delores wasn't too far behind them. She was leaning forward in the saddle. I couldn't tell from her posture if she was urging the horse to go faster or if her legs were hurting.

"Lean back as we go down the hill," Pam instructed as we picked our way down a rocky path. The others disappeared into a small forest before we reached the pasture. We found them a half-hour later sitting under a shade tree taking a break. Jerry puffed on a beat-up Meerschaum and fussed with the horses. Mags lounged on a bed of golden leaves, her hands behind her head, her legs crossed at the ankles, staring into the branches over her head. Delores sat on the ground, inspecting a long scratch on her forearm. She spit on her finger and dabbed at a streak of blood on her elbow. She looked as miserable as I felt.

"Was that great?" Mags called to us as we plodded up to them.

"Fabulous." Emmie's face was rosy. She acted like every little thing — a mangy chipmunk, a black squirrel, a scrawny jackrabbit — was special. Had we really just done the same thing?

Pam dismounted and hurried to help us. Emmie jumped down on her own, her skirt billowing around her. "Whoa!" She giggled as she staggered around bowlegged for a moment.

I stood in my stirrups and swung one leg around, feeling for the earth with one toe. It was far below me. Jerry gripped his pipe between his teeth and lifted me down off the horse. My knees buckled as he set me on my feet. Pam took my arm and led me to the trunk of the tree where I reclined, my thigh muscles trembling.

"Where are we?"

"Not too far from the airport as the crow flies." Jerry pointed back through the woods with his pipe. "Maybe a half hour if we use the lane." A deeply rutted logging road was visible about 50 yards away.

Easy found a nice scratchy bush and rubbed her rump against it. I was sure she was frowning at me. I leaned against the tree and took a deep breath.

"You don't look so good," Delores said to me.

I shrugged. She had scratches on her left cheek and brambles caught in her hair. "What happened to you?"

She flipped open her compact and touched the cuts gingerly. "The damned horse decided to take a short cut through a bunch of trees with low hanging branches."

I stretched my legs out in front of me. "I'll never make it back," I groaned as my thigh muscles twitched. I was sure the others were annoyed with me and I felt guilty for spoiling their fun.

"Sure you will, Shirley. You're tired right now. You'll make it." Emmie was refreshed and ready to go again.

"How's about we walk a bit before getting back on the horses," Jerry suggested hooking his pipe into the corner of his mouth.

I closed my eyes trying to keep from crying. "It's so far."

"You are tense," Mags said from her prone position. "Relax! Let Easy do the work."

"Relaxing is hard for me." The small of my back ached and my buttocks were sore. All I wanted was to be in my bed curled up with a hot water bottle between my legs.

Mags got up. She reached her hand out to me. There was a freckle in her right eye — a minute flaw in a perfect face. "Let's start now," she said.

I allowed her to help me to my feet. I had to grab her arm to keep my balance. I hated that — depending on anyone to simply stand.

"We'll head towards that farm about a half mile away," she told the others. "Take your time."

"Don't worry." Delores picked a leaf out of her hair.

Mags took Easy's reins and we strolled towards the road with the horses following us. I glanced back at them from time to time. They seemed tame enough but I felt tiny and vulnerable all the same.

"They aren't going to hurt you." Mags read my mind.

I limped along beside her. "I've never been around animals."

Mags nodded her head as if it was okay.

We reached the road and turned right, the horses' hooves clattering over small rocks. Nervous as they made me, the beasts were well behaved and eventually my mind began to wander. "What was it like in England?" I asked thinking of Mags' experience with the British Air Transport Auxiliary.

"Cold. Foggy. War torn. I spent a few months in London years ago and it was heartbreaking to see the bombed out areas now." Easy stopped to nibble on a bush. Mags made kissing sounds and tugged on the reins, "It was a wonderful experience — some tricky flying though."

"What kind of planes did you fly?"

"The ATA had us flying two- or four-engine bombers mostly, but I liked the fighters best — the Hurricanes and Spitfires. Everything was a challenge." Mags paused to light a cigar. "We didn't have radios or navigation equipment except a compass. Those items were saved for planes going on combat missions. The weather was incredible. We'd wake up to a bright sunny day only to have fog blow in before we could get in the air."

I shook my head. "Bad weather scares me. I once got caught in a cloud. I couldn't tell which way was up and which way was down. I pushed the stick forward in a panic. As I came out of the cloud, I missed a church spire by just a few feet. Father had a fit because I jostled him. I land at the rumor of storms now."

"Weather was only one of our problems. In southern England, the British sent hundreds of huge balloons up to 1000 feet tethered with cables to discourage Germans from strafing factories and aerodromes. You get caught up in one of those and you are going down. Friend or foe, you had to keep your wits about you at all times." Mags held her cigar between her thumb and forefinger, her face serious. She'd been where it was dangerous. Not like the rest of us who would never leave the North American continent.

We crested a small rise.

"Well what is this?" she asked as we came upon a rickety barn beside the road. A broken door hung from a single hinge and we could see a wrecked airplane parked inside.

"Looks like an old Stearman to me," I said.

We led the horses through a shallow ditch and into the grass in front of the rotting building. She wrapped our reins around a fence post.

I looked around, afraid someone would catch us snooping, but Mags stalked into the barn without hesitation. I took a deep breath and followed.

"I'll be damned." She squatted to peer under the torn fuselage. "Looks like a C3 — maybe 1927 or 1928." A scarred wheel leaned against the wall. The engine was dismounted and in pieces, the propeller missing. The wings on the left side were broken. Unidentifiable pieces of wood and torn fabric littered the floor.

Something moved in the loft. Birds? Mice? Standing around in a barn that looked like it might fall on our heads at any moment — looking at the pieces of a smashed Stearman was not my idea of fun. Besides, it was dark and close.

"I need some air!" I stepped out into the sunshine and leaned my forehead against a nearby tree, my heart pounding. I was pulling myself together when the others rode up the road.

Pam urged Speedy forward. "Is something wrong?"

"No, we just found an old airplane."

"What kind of plane?" She slid out of her saddle and tied Speedy up with the other two horses. Emmie trotted up behind her. You would think she'd been riding for years. Delores and Jerry brought up the rear. Delores met my eyes. I could tell by the way that she sat the horse that she was hurting.

Pam and Emmie ran into the barn to examine the relic.

"This is the McKensey barn. I'm surprised it's still standing." Jerry said as he got off his horse.

"That nasty old man living at the inn?" Delores asked.

"He lost the farm back in the early thirties when the Depression hit. His wife was already dead." Jerry took his pipe out of his pocket and knocked it against the heel of his hand. "He's been living over at Myrtle's for years. When the war came, Grant Logan offered him a job at the Wiley Plant. We went from not having enough jobs to not having enough people. It took him by surprise but he was glad to be needed again. He acts like he hates it but he loves having something to do."

"Why is he in such a bad mood all the time?" Delores winced as she moved in the saddle.

"Well, you work all your life. You think you'll have something for your older years and then it slips away from you. Here he is in his eighties and he's still got to work for a living. He doesn't have any family to take care of him."

Mags, Emmie, and Pam emerged from the old barn, wide grins on their faces. "Okay, what now?" Jerry laughed when he saw his daughter's face.

"Mags is going to buy the plane so we can fix it up."

Jerry's face darkened. "*You* are going to fix it up?"

"We'll drag it back to the big hangar and we'll work on it after school." Pam smiled up at him, her eyes wide and innocent. I recognized that look. It was the one I used on Father when I was a kid.

Jerry's jaw moved back and forth. It took me a moment to realize he was gritting his teeth. "It costs money to fix up something like that and even if you had money, airplane parts aren't easy to find these days. Especially parts for something that's been rotting in a barn for the last umpteen years."

"Please, Daddy?" Her broken front tooth made her smile all the more charming.

"I'll pay for it." Mags stuck her hands in her pants pockets and hunched her shoulders, looking away from Jerry.

"And I'll help her work on it when I'm here," Emmie said.

"None of you look like a mechanic. How will you repair that engine?"

"We'll find a way." Pam untied Speedy and caressed his neck. The horse made a soft sneezing sound.

"Supposing you do find a way — what then?"

"I'll fly it." Pam climbed back up onto Speedy and grinned at Jerry.

I folded my arms over my chest. If Mags wanted to help this kid, why didn't she get her tooth fixed?

65

"Whatever happened to playing with baby dolls, Pammie?" Jerry grumbled but everyone knew he was giving in. "What am I going to do with you?"

"Thanks, Daddy."

"Let's get these horses back, it's getting late. Mags, you let me know when you work your deal with McKensey. I'll tote it to the hangar with the pickup."

I remounted Easy with a lot of help. I was terrified the malevolent beast would turn around and bite my thigh or maybe buck me off. Mags, Pam and Emmie went on ahead while Delores and I plodded along with Jerry.

"I don't like this," he said. "This isn't what her mother had in mind for her."

"She's a beautiful little girl," Delores lied.

Jerry grunted. "You are nice girls. I like you, but you aren't normal, no offense. You don't live everyday lives like the rest of us. After the war, you'll go off somewhere and do God knows what. Pam will stay right here. What will happen to her then? She needs a mother — someone ordinary who can teach her how to be ordinary."

"She'll do fine, Jerry," Delores said.

"You are making her want things she can never have."

We rode on in silence. Jerry's mouth was a grim line across his face. I didn't blame him for being worried, but Pam was a tomboy long before we came on the scene. We didn't dress her in overalls and flannel shirts. We didn't hack off her hair. Besides, Emmie and I never had a mother and it didn't seem to do us any harm. Then again, maybe that's why we weren't normal.

The airport appeared up ahead and the stables behind it. Easy raised her ears and whinnied when she saw Pokey. I hung onto the saddle horn and screamed as the little horse broke into a trot. Emmie was already off Pokey, the reins wrapped around one wrist. Pokey raised

66

her head and saw Easy. She snorted and trotted out to meet us. Emmie ran four steps before she fell on her face, Pokey dragging her by one arm through the dusty corral.

"Let go of the reins!" Mags chased after Emmie yelling, "Let go!"

"Whoa! Pokey, whoa!" Pam's voice rose above the noise of the horse's hooves. Pokey and Easy met midway across the grassy field between the runway and the stables nosing each other and stamping their feet. Jerry and Delores galloped up behind us to see about Emmie. I sat on top of Easy, frozen. I wanted to scream but my mouth was dry and nothing came out. I swallowed and tried again.

Mags knelt beside Emmie's body and unwrapped the reins from her wrist. They turned her over. Her skirt was torn loose from the waistband and dirt and grass stains covered the bodice. Her forehead was scraped raw and there were scratches on her arms and legs. Her hand was unnaturally white and there was a deep, bluish bruise around her wrist where the reins cut her.

"EMMIE! EMMIE!" Pam crouched beside her.

"I'm okay. I'm fine." Emmie struggled to get up.

"You lay there a bit, young lady." Jerry pushed her back down with a gentle hand on her shoulder. Mags felt her arms and legs to make sure nothing was broken.

"No, let me up. I'm okay." The sound of Emmie's laughter filled me with joy. Now I could breathe again.

"Do you hurt anywhere?" Jerry asked.

"Well, yeah, Hoss. I hurt everywhere." She winced as she sat up. "It was stupid. I'm sorry." She lifted her skirt. Both knees were skinned.

"We need to get you back to the inn." I found my voice. "Someone help me off of this damned beast and I'll get the car." Delores and Jerry lifted me down. "I'll be right back." I ran towards the airport where the Plymouth was parked, the pain in my legs and back forgotten. By the time I drove across the field, they had helped Emmie to her feet. Jerry led the horses back to the barn, bending over to pick up Emmie's shoes — one in the grassy field, the other in the corral where Pokey jerked her off her feet. Mags, Pam, and Delores gathered around Emmie. I pulled up and reached behind me to open the backdoor.

"Don't look so scared, Shirley." Emmie told me as she limped towards the car on her own power, "I'm fine."

Jerry stepped out of the barn. "I'll be there as soon as I get the horses taken care of," he yelled across the field as everyone crawled into the car. Mags and Pam snuggled next to Emmie in the backseat, Delores ran around to the passenger front seat. I released the clutch and spun the wheels on the slippery grass before she got the door closed. The big tires found purchase and I pulled onto the road in front of Jerry's house.

"Dammit, Shirley. Don't kill us all." Emmie said from the backseat. I glanced at her in the rear view mirror and wanted to cry. She was starting to get a black eye too.

"Damn horses!" I screamed as I made the sharp left onto Logan's Run. I felt their eyes on me. Delores sat sideways, her mouth a round O. Mags and Pam were quiet. What had I done? I spun the steering wheel hard left once again and headed south on Cold Creek Road.

The Windshift Inn was in sight. I braked and pulled into the turnaround beeping the horn. Myrtle ran out onto the porch, her face creased in alarm. She hurried down the steps as I stopped the car. Pam threw open the back door and they helped Emmie out feet first.

"I messed myself up a bit, Miz Myrtle," Emmie said as Myrtle and Pam guided her into the kitchen.

"I've seen worse, you'll be fine." Myrtle told her as the screen door slammed behind them.

I was trembling. Mags opened my door and squatted beside me. "I think maybe you are in worse shape than Emmie."

Tears rolled down my cheeks. "I didn't give her my sweater." I hiccupped. "She was cold and I didn't think to offer her my sweater."

"She wouldn't take it, you know how Emmie is," Delores said.

I glared at her. How would she know how Emmie is? Delores had friends everywhere she went. Emmie was the only friend I had. It wasn't the same thing.

"She's skinned up and she's going to be sore for a few days, but she's not hurt bad. She'll be back in the *Foxes* with you on Monday. Don't you worry, okay?" Mags helped me out of the car.

Jerry pulled into the turnaround in his pickup truck. He slammed the door behind him and tossed Emmie's shoes to Delores. We followed him into the kitchen. Emmie sat on the table, her bare feet on a chair. Her insteps were skinned and bruised. Myrtle was dabbing at her wounds with small squares of cloth dipped in peroxide. Pam sat beside Emmie tearing a sheet into strips to be used as bandages.

"Look at you," Delores handed Emmie her shoes. "You are almost dressed down enough to get married."

"My hair isn't messed up enough," Emmie gritted her teeth as Myrtle doctored her toes. "How's Pokey?"

"Pokey's in her stall having dinner as we speak." Jerry patted her back and examined her wounds.

"Looks like you got a broken toe here, Emmie. You sure you won't let me get the doctor out here?" Myrtle held up Emmie's foot. The little toe was swollen and crooked.

Emmie was pale but she pretended to be okay. "No, you are doctor enough for me." Delores handed her a soapy washcloth and Emmie wiped the dirt off of her arms and face.

69

"This is going to sting like the dickens." Pam put Merthiolate on Emmie's forehead and on her knees.

"Oh yes, it does." Emmie gasped. Pam jerked back, horror on her face.

"You are doing fine, Pammie." Myrtle patted the little girl on the back.

"You sure are." Emmie pointed to her elbow, which was also skinned. "You are gentle. Think how much it would hurt if someone like Delores was doing it." Pam's face glowed. Delores stuck out her tongue. Emmie had a knack for making everyone else feel better.

"What were you guys doing when this happened?" Myrtle asked as she bound up Emmie's toe.

"We found an old airplane in Mr. McKensey's barn," Emmie said.

"Mags is going to buy it and we're going to fix it up." Pam put Merthiolate on the scratches on Emmie's arms. "You'll help us, won't you, Daddy?"

Jerry looked worried, but he said, "You know I will."

#

Emmie slept soundly that night. I know because I was wide-awake fighting muscle cramps. So was Delores. The next day was Sunday. Emmie's knees were so scabbed up she couldn't straighten her legs. Her left eye was black and a stained bandage covered her forehead. Her broken toe must have hurt the way she favored it as she hobbled around the inn, but that evening, she was singing off-key while Delores played the piano. On Monday morning, she crawled onto the bus with the rest of us.

"It's Mags' first trip west as part of our group," Emmie explained as she settled into the seat across from me. "I don't want to miss that."

Mags wore her WASP uniform — a white blouse and khaki slacks. She looked even skinnier without her leather jacket and boots. They

70

kept promising us real uniforms but so far, we were still making do. Myrtle and Delores were last as usual.

Grant put the bus in gear and we headed towards the factory. Everyone squealed when they saw Mr. McKensey — including Emmie and Delores. He ignored us, muttering to himself as he hiked back towards his car. All was right with the world.

Emmie was healing up by the time we returned from Camp Morgan. Mags worked a deal with Mr. McKensey somehow since technically he didn't own the farm or anything on it anymore. Emmie and Pam cleaned out a space in the big hangar at *Jerry's Flying Service*. Jerry, Grant Logan, and Mags brought the last piece to Jerry's airport the week before Christmas. They spent hours sorting through the pieces. Mags, Jerry, Pam, and Emmie went horseback riding almost every weekend. I couldn't get over Emmie doing that after what that monster did to her. Wasn't any way you were going to get me on a horse again.

Delores and I ignored them and each other. She was always busy writing letters and making phone calls to Pittsburgh. I got the impression there were family problems. I curled up with a book, helped Myrtle in the kitchen, and listened to the radio in my off hours.

CHAPTER 6 — CAMP MORGAN

"Allies aren't necessarily friends and enemies aren't necessarily bastards."
George Maxwell, Interview
~ American View Magazine ~
January, 1944

O hio winters can be beautiful. Deep snow coats the countryside around the inn, the air is clear and crisp, and children delight in building snow GIs who stalk snow Nazis with broken broomsticks for rifles. Although winter flying can be great when the weather is nice, it didn't cooperate this year. We spent many afternoons playing cards in the parlor or sliding down the hill in front of the inn on Myrtle's large wooden trays stolen from the kitchen when she was at work. Sometimes, bored and guilty at wasting so much time, we pushed the bounds of safety and headed west in brand new *Foxes* only to be stranded somewhere between *The Windshift Inn* and Camp Morgan waiting for a snow storm to pass and visibility to return.

The inactivity especially frustrated Emmie. She moped around the inn after Myrtle and the other factory workers piled into Grant Logan's bus and disappeared down the icy roads towards *Wiley Aircraft*. At first, she was underdressed for cold weather. Other than her uniform, her wardrobe consisted of thin cotton dresses, anklets, and thin-soled flats. Then one day, I caught Delores rummaging in Emmie's chest of drawers. She spun around and pushed the drawer closed with her behind.

"Ssssh!" She warned me with her finger over her lips. I frowned and made a note to check my own area to make sure nothing had been taken or moved out of place.

"My grandmother knitted it for Emmie," she said turning to reopen the drawer and holding up a thick red wool sweater. "I don't want Emmie to know where it came from."

I was ashamed. Why I hadn't done something when I noticed Emmie shivering by the wood stove in the parlor, her arms prickly with goose bumps and her fingers blue?

Emmie was thrilled with her present from some secret friend and wore the sweater whenever she was out of uniform along with an unfashionable but warm wool dress that appeared one day, laid out on top of her bedspread along with a pair of handmade mittens. I figured that one for Myrtle but I couldn't prove it.

Eager to get into the act, I had Father send me a couple pairs of long john underwear to wear under our uniforms and jumpsuits. On clear winter days, it could get cold in the planes we were flying. I draped one over Emmie's bedstead and pretended to be asleep when she found it.

In the middle of the night, she sat on the side of my bed. I lay there with my eyes closed. "Don't think I don't know where these came from," she whispered as she pulled my covers up higher on my shoulders. "I feel like I have sisters at last." Long after she'd gone back to her own bed and I could hear her snoring, I lay awake. It was the first time I remember being happy with myself.

Mags outdid us all. She laid a big box on each of our beds. We all squealed with delight when we saw them. They turned out to be brown leather flight jackets like Mags' only these had our names emblazoned on the back. Delores and I knew our jackets were to hide the fact Emmie had no coat at all, but we loved them anyway.

Mags and Emmie were growing tired of ferrying *Foxes*. They both wanted assignments that were more interesting. Delores was irritated by the way the men in California treated us. She was also angry about the endless rules that governed our existence. Our trips to Camp Morgan became more contentious as the three of them cornered Conrad Simpson about one thing or another. I was afraid the complaints would worsen our position there so I kept my mouth shut.

74

"How the hell do they know when we have our periods?" Delores grumbled as we flew west the week after the New Year. "Who's going to check? Colonel Simpson? Tommy McDougal?"

"I won't tell if you don't," Emmie keyed her mic.

"It's one of the silliest damned things I ever heard of — grounding us when we're menstruating." Delores continued over the hum of the 65 hp engine. "And what's this about not letting us catch rides back east? They'd rather pay train fare than deal with gossip? What do they think we are going to do?"

"They think we are going to seduce the pilot, of course." Mags chuckled. "And not letting us fly alone with a male pilot is going to prevent that."

"If I was going to seduce someone, there are lots more comfortable locations than the back seat of an A-24." Delores was on a roll.

"There's not much Connie can do about those rules. They come from Jackie Cochran or the Army. He's got to enforce them." Mags had a tendency to take up for the target of Delores' current complaints.

"It's not like he pays much attention to us one way or another," Emmie joined in. "Did you see that box of Hershey bars on his desk? I keep thinking he'll offer us one whenever we go in there, but he never does. One of these days I'm going to raid it — for Pam, of course."

"Of course," Mags said.

We all knew how much Emmie loved sweets. I'd once come downstairs in the middle of the night to find her sticking her finger in Myrtle's sugar bowl. It wasn't the crime of the century since she anteed up all of her sugar coupons just like the rest of us, but it was disgusting. She laughed at me and sucked the glistening little granules off her fingers.

"Only reason he buys us dinner once in a while is because we bring him goodies from Myrtle," Delores interjected. "He doesn't listen to anything we say."

"I hope he likes apples." Emmie had a bag of Rome Beauties tucked away in the backseat of her *Fox*. She and Pam had a great time picking apples for Myrtle in the Logans' orchard outside Cold Creek. I didn't feel it was dignified to crawl around in trees, but Delores and I helped Myrtle make several pies and cobblers.

"Oh, don't worry about Connie. He'll love them," Mags assured us as she dove on Red Hopkins' farm. We all followed, buzzing around the small house like angry bees until the old man rolled out into the yard waving and shouting. Emmie flew low over the animal pen and tossed Beulah an apple, which smashed to the ground a few feet in front of the goat.

"Yeeha!" Delores congratulated Emmie on her aim.

When we landed at Camp Morgan, Mags and Delores marched off across the tarmac to find Colonel Simpson. I don't know why they bothered. He was never in his office anyway.

Emmie and I unloaded our *Foxes* and turned them over to a brawny young mechanic named Wayne Wilson who had eyes for Emmie. She signed the papers on his clipboard and smiled at him.

"I got one for you, Emmie." He popped his chewing gum.

"Okay, I'm listening." She liked big homey guys.

"What do you call a German plane?"

"You got me." She glanced at me. Pam Kline had told us this one last week.

"A SNOTSIE!" He slapped his own knee and let out a bark like a hound dog.

Emmie's laugh sounded sincere. "That's a great one, Wayne." She swung her duffle over her shoulder and took two steps.

76

It wasn't funny the first time but I managed a weak smile. I longed for the Quonset hut and the hot shower that awaited me. I picked up my duffle and followed her.

Wayne hurried along beside us. "I have something for you."

"What?" Emmie stopped again.

It's embarrassing to watch someone else flirt so I pretended not to notice.

He took a piece of paper from his clipboard. "It's *Fifinella*."

"Oh, Shirley, look at this!" Emmie was delighted. Wayne was quite a cartoonist. He'd drawn the WASP emblem of a wide-eyed imp in a red dress with hip boots and gossamer wings and then superimposed Emmie's pixyish face on it.

"Wayne, this is extraordinary." I took the paper and examined it. Father would love to have someone with his talent working for the magazine.

"My compliments to Walt Disney." His eyes were on Emmie who was flustered. Our *Fifinella* patches, designed by Walt Disney, were based on a friendly wartime gremlin who caused all kinds of mischief but brought good luck. We even sang a song during training, *Buckle down, Fifinella, buckle down.* It was a thoughtful thing to do and I looked at Wayne with wiser eyes.

"I … uh … thank you, Wayne," Emmie said. "Can I have it?"

"Of course, I drew it for you." He took it out of her hands, slipped it between two pieces of cardboard, and put it into a manila envelope. The man was prepared — I'll give him that. He must have been waiting for us to land. I don't know how many points Emmie gave him, but I gave him a bunch.

"I can't tell you how much I appreciate this." Emmie studied her own boots.

"Naw, it's nothing. I'm glad you like it." Wayne waved as we trudged off towards the Quonset hut.

"I can hardly wait to show this to the other girls," Emmie said. I felt Wayne's eyes on our backs. Emmie must have too. Halfway there, she turned around and smiled, wiggling her fingers.

"You like him," I said. Emmie loved to tease me. It was only fair I turn the tables on her.

"He's okay."

"Uh huh. Wait till I tell Mags."

"Oh, I can't wait to tell Mags." Once we were inside the Quonset hut, she danced a little jig. "He's nice, don't you think?"

"Yeah, I do think he's nice, Emmie."

"You mean it?"

I did.

As I expected, Mags and Delores came in while I was showering. Delores stripped down to her underwear and wrapped a towel around her middle. She stood in front of the sink, pin curling her hair in the steamy bathroom as I emerged from the shower stall.

"Didn't find Colonel Simpson?" I asked as I toweled off.

"Oh, we found him. At the firing range."

"Doesn't he do anything else?" I slipped on clean underwear and felt much better. I sat inside the curtained dressing area to put on my shoes and socks.

"Eats candy." Delores took off her towel and hung it on the hook outside the shower. I glimpsed her nakedness through a gap in the curtain and looked away. I could never get over her lack of modesty. I'd never think of taking my clothes off before I got into my private area.

"Did he listen?"

"How can anyone hear anything over there? There's ten guys gunning for the bull's eye with twenty different kinds of pistols. Simpson's got four or five himself."

78

"Father has several but all he ever does is clean them. I've never seen him fire one."

"It's part of being a man." Delores turned on the water and I heard her step into the tiny stall. I buttoned the top button of my blouse, smoothing the front placard with my fingers until it lay just so over my bust. "I think they like shooting better than they like whoopee, if you know what I mean." She raised her voice to be heard over the water.

I hated when she talked that way. I was sweating in my wool skirt and sweater when I pulled back the curtain and stood in front of the sink. I used a washcloth to wipe the steam off the mirror so I could put on my makeup. "So are we on our own tonight? Or are we having dinner with the Colonel?"

"We are supposed to meet Simpson in his office in about an hour. He'll be out of bullets by then, I trust. Then you and Mags and Emmie are having dinner with him. I have a date." Delores gurgled as the hot water hit her face.

"Anyone I know?" I sketched in my eyebrows.

"Lieutenant McDougal, War Hero." She turned off the water and her voice seemed overloud.

"What happened to him?" I pursed my lips and applied my lipstick.

"Rode a B-17 down after the Germans shot one of the engines. The second engine on the same side took shrapnel and flamed out too. The co-pilot took a round in the head and Tommy caught a piece of shrapnel in the face. The crew thought they were dead, but Tommy landed that plane anyway. Even the co-pilot survived although they say he's going to be slow from here on out."

"He *is* a hero, then." I dusted my cheeks with face powder to take down the shine.

"Oh yeah, but he doesn't like talking about it. He's trying to find a way to go back but the Army has other ideas." Delores stepped out of the dressing area, her damp hair curling around her face, a towel wrapped around her body.

I swear the woman didn't even need makeup — her complexion was flawless. I put my compact away. "Seems like both you and Emmie have Camp Morgan boyfriends."

"Tommy is helping me get checked out in some of the bigger planes. It's an opportunity." She pulled a cotton slip over her head.

"An opportunity for what?" There wasn't going to be much of a demand for women to fly fighters or dive-bombers after the war.

"I want to get as good as Mags and Emmie. I'm thinking when it's over I'll go to Europe and look for some of my family. She slipped the huge sapphire around her neck. "Maybe they'll let us fly one of these planes over one day."

"Are they lost?" I was puzzled.

"My mother's brother and his family. They lived in Mannheim up until 1940 when they disappeared. We think they were deported to a camp in the French Pyranees, but we aren't sure. Mama meets the mailman at the corner every day, but there's never anything from them."

Suddenly it struck me. "Oh, Delores. I'm sorry. I didn't know."

"My cousin Annaliese has a baby girl named Rosa. Her husband was arrested and marched away on November 9, 1938 — Kristallnacht. The baby was born six months later. We've never seen her. It breaks my heart to think of a baby in one of those camps, but we are hopeful."

I tried not to look into her eyes, but I couldn't help it. She was lying. She had lost hope a long time ago. "Maybe Father can help." It was a silly, impulsive thing to say.

Disbelief flickered across her face. "Maybe." We both knew it was hopeless. Not even George Maxwell could rescue a Jewish family from the Nazis. I resolved to ask him anyway.

She stepped into a dark blue and white tailored dress. She was stunning. I guess that's not enough sometimes.

#

When Mags and Emmie were ready, the four of us walked across the Camp to Colonel Simpson's office.

"Come on in," he called when Mags knocked. We filed in and stood in front of his gray metal desk. We lived an odd half-life. We were trained by the military, flew military planes, obeyed our military commanders, and observed military courtesies. However, we were civilians with few of the advantages extended to the military like insurance or death benefits. Colonel Simpson gave us a quick salute that was almost insulting in its sloppiness. He didn't stand when we came in but continued playing with a big pistol he held in his lap.

"Colonel Simpson, we want to make a request." Delores's dress emphasized her figure. She'd pinned a fresh gardenia over her right ear. With her dark hair arranged on top her head, her perfectly shaped eyebrows, and long curly lashes, she was the epitome of femininity.

Conrad Simpson ignored her.

Mags lounged on the corner of Simpson's desk and handed him a cigar. The two of them lit up. "You're not taking advantage of all your resources, Connie. You got some damned fine pilots here."

"I realize you are something special. Hell, I saw you out-fly that loud-mouthed, wing-walking bastard down in Stuttgart that time. I'll even take your word these young ladies here are pretty good. However, I got a camp full of problems and I don't need any more. I got these men convinced you are here to ferry the little *Foxes*. They don't like it, but we are making do. I give you the men's assignments and there'll be hell to pay." He spun the cylinder of the .45 and peered down the barrel, holding the cigar between his teeth.

"What do they like doing the least?" Delores demanded.

81

"Look girls, Camp Morgan's a busy place. Aside from checking out the planes you bring us, we have to fly them out to whoever needs them. We also fix planes damaged in combat, test them, and try to get them back into service as quick as we can. We don't have the parts half the time and we have to fabricate them ourselves without the proper materials. Then we got to tow targets for the new artillery boys who can't hit the side of a barn twenty foot away with a cannon." He rubbed the pistol barrel with an oily rag.

"Why can't we do that?" Delores leaned forward and put her hands on his desk.

"Now why would a little girl like you want to pull a target back and forth all day while boys who haven't been changing their own pants more than a year or two take pot shots at you?" He blew a series of smoke rings and broke them with the pistol. "The men hate that assignment. They don't want to take a chance getting killed before they get their crack at the Luftwaffe."

"Then why would they have a problem if we did it?" Delores was relentless.

Simpson glared at her.

Mags stood up and paced in front of Simpson's desk. "At least think about it, Connie. The boys might not have as much problem with us if we are taking jobs they don't want anyway."

"Mags, your mother would have a fit if she knew you were doing such a thing." Simpson laid the pistol on the desk and packed the cleaning cloth back into the bottom drawer.

"Mamá has fits all the time, it's good for her health." Mags lifted her cigar in salute, keeping Simpson distracted while Emmie pocketed two chocolate bars from the box on his desk, her face never changing from its serious, attentive expression.

I'm sure my mouth was hanging wide open. The scowl on Delores' face melted and she pursed her lips, her eyes wide in surprised merriment.

"I could set you up to ferry the fat cats from here to there if you want." He looked at each of us. Mags and Delores were less than enthused, but Emmie and I smiled. I'm sure Emmie smiled because she'd stolen Simpson's candy, but I liked the idea of giving Generals and Admirals and Ambassadors rides. It was easy duty, similar to what I'd done for Father so many years — lots of straight and level. "The only other thing we do here is practice dog fighting with the young chaps before we send them off to duel with der Fuhrer," Simpson continued.

"That's perfect!" Mags spun around.

"Oh no you don't." Simpson shook his finger at her. "There are some things you can't change, war or no war."

"You know anyone who could do it better than me?" Mags demanded.

"There's no one like you, Mags," he acknowledged. "Not even Hank would do the things you do."

"Hank would approve even if Mamá wouldn't."

"I'll think about it, that's the most I can promise right now."

"Aw, Connie. You're the best."

"Let's go eat before you convince me to send you back to Europe. Jackie'd have my butt for that one."

Emmie swiped one more Hershey Bar as we started out the door. "Chocolate," she mouthed to Delores as we followed Simpson and Mags out the door.

"Save me one," Delores answered as she slipped away for her date with Tommy before we got to the Officer's Club.

Mags and Simpson spent the evening talking about Hank Strickland while Emmie and I ate our dinners without saying much. I didn't understand why Mags called her mother Mamá but referred to her father as 'Hank.' I'd never think of calling Father 'George.' The very thought made me sweat.

83

Later that night, Emmie, Mags, and I fell onto our cots exhausted. I was drifting off into a dream where a ghostly Hank Strickland and I were having cocktails with Ernest Hemingway in Key West when Delores tiptoed into the room. "Emmie," she whispered. "Emmie, wake up."

"You might as well forget just waking one of us up." Mags stretched and turned on the lamp. Delores held what looked like a rat in her arms. Its eyes glittered in the half-light.

"What is that?" I pulled the covers up to my nose, my eyes glued to the tiny animal.

"A gift from Tommy." Delores sat on her bed and put the creature on the pillow.

"Is that the cutest thing you've ever seen?" Emmie jumped out of bed. She wore her long johns even in California. She knelt down beside the cot and the little bat-eared creature scurried into her arms. "What's his name?" she asked as she cuddled it.

"I thought maybe I'd call him 'Señor.' What do you think?"

"Why Señor?"

"Tommy bought him for me in Mexico. 'Señor' is the only Mexican word I know."

"What is it?" I'd never seen anything like Señor.

"He's a Chihuahua, of course. A puppy." Delores stroked the tiny dog snuggled up in Emmie's lap.

"He's precious." Emmie held Señor on his back like he was a baby.

"But what am I going to do with him?"

"Myrtle doesn't allow pets at the inn," I said. "And the Army would have a fit if they knew he was here." Señor *was* cute. He was cream colored with light brown spots, huge pointy ears, and big brown eyes.

84

"I need someplace to leave him where I know he'll be okay while I'm flying. Kind of like a baby sitter without the baby." Delores' face lit up when she looked at the dog. I didn't understand it. I'd never had a pet — and besides, animals didn't seem to like me. My unfortunate adventure with Easy and Pokey came to mind, but Señor was little. I was overcome with the desire to touch him. I crept from my cot and advanced a step at a time.

"Why don't we leave him with Red?" Emmie suggested. "We can drop him off when we go back. Might have to hide him on the train, but that shouldn't be too difficult — he's small enough to fit in a coffee mug."

"You think that would be okay with Red?" Delores rubbed Señor's belly with her knuckles.

"Are you kidding? Red would love this little guy. He'd have the run of the house."

"That's what I should do." Delores bit her lip and her eyes welled.

"Do you think I could touch him?" I stood over them in my pajamas.

"Well, sure. He's a dear." Delores smiled at him with affection and the little dog basked in her love.

I reached out to touch him. His ears perked and he rolled to his feet, growling. "What's wrong?" I jerked my hand away and backed off.

"He's just tired. Tommy and I played with him most of the evening. He'll get used to you. Let him smell you."

I held my hand close to him. With a sharp bark, Señor snapped at my hand, missing my pinkie by millimeters. He scuttled into Delores' lap, his tail between his legs, yapping at me.

"He doesn't like me." I sat down on my bed — offended. What was wrong with me? Everyone said animals know if you are a good person or not. Señor growled every time I looked at him. What did that say about me? I wanted to cry.

"Maybe he doesn't like your perfume," Mags patted the little monster who accepted her caress without complaint.

"I'm not wearing any." I took deep breaths.

"He's a puppy, Hoss. Give him time." Emmie sat down beside me and took my hand. I stole a quick peek at the dog. He bared his teeth, his upper lip quivering.

CHAPTER 7 — THE WACO

"Ensign Eloise English Launches Destroyer, Robert Walker to Star in 'Taps for Private Tussle,' Tired Women Impair War Plants."
Headlines
*~ **American View Daily** ~*
Late February, 1944

W e stopped in Indiana on the way back to Ohio to leave Señor with Red. Red was delighted to see us. He wheeled around the little house preparing a terrific dinner of chicken and dumplings. We sat at the kitchen table laughing as he told stories about some of Emmie's more unfortunate adventures — like the time she put the old yellow Waco into a spin and then got her shoelaces caught on the rudder pedals. Or the time Hoppy took her up into the tree house he built in the back pasture when he was a boy and she fell through the floor and dangled from a tree limb by one arm until he rescued her. Delores had to tell the story of when Emmie found a scorpion in her bunk at Sweetwater during training after she went to bed. Emmie sat next to Red with her elbows on the table and her chin in her hands watching each person tell stories about her, the corners of her mouth turning up in an almost smile.

After dinner, Emmie volunteered to wash the dishes but Red shooed her outside saying he and Mags and Delores could handle it. I got the impression Red feared for his chinaware. Emmie and I went for a walk.

"What did you think of our little show the other day?" She asked as we headed towards the animal pen with a handful of raw vegetables for Beulah.

"I don't think Colonel Simpson knows much about flying."

"Me, either," she said, her breath fogging in front of her lips. "I think he'll go with whatever Tommy McDougal says." The goat saw us coming and trotted up to the fence.

"You and Mags are great pilots. I'm sure he was impressed with all those rolls and spins. Delores is pretty darned good too, but I doubt he'll want me flying anything bigger than the *Foxes*. I'm not sure I want to. I don't have the nerve for it." I crossed my arms over my chest and hunched my shoulders against the chilly breeze.

"At least he gave us a shot. I'm sure he did that because of Mags." She poked a carrot through the fence and Beulah gobbled it up. "Wanna give her one?"

"Oh no, you do it." I put my hands behind my back.

A half-grown pig hurried up the fence wanting his share. She squatted down to feed him. "So you think we'll get to tow targets?"

"Depends on how much the guys hate doing it, I guess." I winced as the pig's snout rubbed up against her hand trying to get the last trace of potato.

"I think they aren't going to like anything Colonel Simpson gives us to do," she said. "Do you see the way they look at us? The other day I was walking across the Camp and there were some guys patching the tarmac. They whistled and hooted. At first I kept walking but then I thought, 'Why is that insulting? Maybe it's a little crude, but it's just their way of recognizing my femininity. Maybe we've been too stand-offish, too easily offended."

I ignored the catcalls and lewd comments. Delores gave back as good as she got with curses and angry gestures, but that made things worse. The men were especially obnoxious to her.

Beulah stuck her nose through the fence, begging for more food and I backed away.

"So, anyway, I waved and smiled — nothing inappropriate — just a smile like this." She stretched her lips over her teeth in a parody of her natural grin. "You know what they did? They got nasty. They laughed and elbowed each other and called me names like 'Whore' and 'Bitch'." She chuckled, rubbing her hands together to warm them. "Makes you wonder what they are so afraid of, doesn't it? If they are so good at everything, why are they scared of what we might be able to do?"

I knelt beside her and gripped the fence. "Men can be cruel." I didn't succeed in keeping the bitterness out of my voice.

"They aren't all like Hoppy, that's for sure." She gave Beulah the last turnip and stood up, wiping her hands on the seat of her pants. She looked into my eyes. I was afraid of what she might see but somehow I found the courage not to look away. "Come on, I want to show you something," she said.

Beyond the animal pen and down a small slope was a long meadow. A red barn sat at the far end. As we got closer to it, Emmie's pace increased. Her legs were longer than mine and by the time we got there, I was panting. She struggled with the heavy doors, pulling them back against the outer wall of the building. It was dark and musty inside. Emmie disappeared into the gloom as I stood at the entrance, afraid there might be animals in there — barnyard cats or maybe an owl or bat. A burst of light illuminated the interior as she opened the big doors on the opposite side. It was then I realized I was looking at a hangar.

"It's beautiful, Emmie." I ran my fingers over the wooden propeller of Hoppy's WACO. The old biplane made Emmie's loss seem more real.

"It is, isn't it?" She leaned against the right wing. "Help me here, will you?" Together we pushed the old plane out into the bright sunshine. She tossed me a pair of goggles. "Get in." She gestured towards the front cockpit.

I didn't even think about refusing. I grasped a small metal handle on the upper wing, stepped on the roughened surface of the lower wing near the fuselage and climbed in. I straddled the stick and I fidgeted trying to pull my skirt down around it. There was a soft leather helmet connected to the dash, which was barren of the multitude of instruments we relied on nowadays.

"It's one way," she said as she pulled on a pair of thin leather gloves. "You can hear me, but I can't hear you." I nodded, a little surprised that the plane was wired for electricity. I pulled the helmet down over my head and tightened it under my chin before slipping the goggles in place. "You might want to zip up your jacket too."

Other than a heavy coating of dust, the bright yellow WACO was in pristine condition, just as she left it after her last air show in Cleveland. She went to New York the next day to interview with Jackie Cochran. The plane shifted as she took her position in the rear cockpit. She started the engine and the propeller spun — slowly at first, then faster, becoming a blur. I felt the vibrations through the seat, almost like a tickle.

I was strapping myself in with a thin leather belt that looked like the one holding up Father's britches, when her voice came into my head through the earphone set into the left flap of the helmet. "Hang on, Hoss." I held up my left thumb to acknowledge I'd heard her.

The plane accelerated across the pasture. I was startled by how easily it rose into the air. It reminded me of the Otis Elevator in Father's building. The day was cold and clear. I had been a pilot for a long time, but it still took my breath away as we cleared the tree line.

We weren't three hundred feet in the air when Emmie rolled the WACO. "That was for Mags," she said into my ear. She circled the farm before we headed south. "You know, Shirley, we are seldom alone. I've been meaning to talk with you for a long time, but every time I try, you change the subject or walk away. Consider yourself kidnapped."

My mouth went dry and I clung to the edges of the cockpit with chilled fingers.

"I consider you a good friend and I can't help but notice you are unhappy," she continued. "I want to stick my nose in your business and ask what's wrong, but I won't. I'll just tell you a little story about me. Okay?"

I held up my thumb. I was glad I didn't have to say anything. She was being kind, I reminded myself. She was being Emmie.

"When Hoppy died, I thought I might die too. That didn't happen. I went on living. Then I thought maybe I'd never have fun again. That didn't happen either. Fun happens every day. You just gotta be tuned into it. After enough living and enough fun and enough thinking, it didn't hurt quite so much that Hoppy died and I began to appreciate the fact Hoppy lived at all. I decided I could choose happiness or unhappiness. Whatever is bothering you, it's time you make your decision, Shirley." She banked the WACO and we headed back toward the farm.

My goggles fogged up. I didn't bother to take them off and wipe them. She made it sound so easy, but then she was much stronger than me. I was doing the only thing I could think to do. Hold on. Hold on tight. Keeping the lid on things took all my effort. There was no time for happiness. I didn't know what it was, anyway.

She slipped first one way and then the other, bringing the old plane down effortlessly. We bounced along the meadow on the front two tires for several seconds before we slowed enough for the tail to lower. She cut the engine as we approached the red hanger and we coasted the last few feet.

#

Red rolled his wheelchair out onto the front porch with Señor in his lap. "Nub's on his way to pick you all up. You better get your things."

"I got something for you, Red," Emmie skipped past me and into the house to get her duffel. I sat down on an old wooden bench. Señor stood up in Red's lap and growled at me.

"Why does he do that?" I slipped my hands into my jacket pockets.

"Cause it bothers you, young lady." Red scratched the little dog's ears.

"Of course, it bothers me. Wouldn't it bother you?"

91

"He's trying to show you who is boss. They do that, you know. There's a pecking order in most animals. He's asserting his place in that order."

I stuck out my lower lip. "How can a little dog want to boss me around?"

Red's booming laugh revealed his pink gums. His false teeth were in a glass of water by the kitchen sink.

"I need to get my bag," I said and stood up.

Emmie was on her hands and knees, rummaging through her duffel. Clothes were scattered everywhere on the living room floor. Mags and Delores sat on the sofa with tall glasses of something that looked like pale iced tea. I nudged a pair of panties with my toe. "Emmie, that's downright embarrassing to have your underwear lying out in front of God and everybody."

"I'm looking for that little white box. I know it's here." She stuck her head in the duffel, her rear end in the air.

"She's looking for a white box." Mags lifted her half-empty glass in a salute.

"A white box," Delores repeated as she held up her glass.

"You want me to help?" I sighed.

Emmie was like a dog burrowing under a fence, tossing her clothes behind her like soft clods of dirt. "I know it's in here." The canvas bag muffled her voice.

I gathered up her clothes and folded them into a neat stack. There under her pink dress, which was wadded up and thrown into the corner, lay the white box. "Is this it?" I held it up.

She pulled the duffel off her head, her hair crackling with static electricity, "That's it. Thanks, Hoss." She caught the box I tossed to her and stood up. "Are you all ready?" She said to Mags and Delores who were sprawled out on the couch like rag dolls. "That stuff Red makes is pretty potent. I'd quit if I were you."

"Oh, we quit." Mags chortled and set the glass down on the coffee table with a loud thump. Delores pounded the arm of the couch with her fist laughing without sound. I blinked. They were drunk! How the hell would we get them onto the train in this condition?

Emmie swung her repacked duffel over her shoulder. "We better get you two out in the fresh air. Nub'll be here any minute."

Mags and Delores struggled to get up, clinging to each other and giggling. I presumed this was their latest challenge to each other and wondered who had won the drinking contest. Nub drove up in his old pickup truck as we came out onto the porch, the cold ground crackling under his tires.

"What did you give them, Red?" Emmie stood in front of the wheelchair, her hands on her hips, her head cocked. Señor sat up, his ears alert, his tongue dangling out of his mouth.

"Nothing special — just some of that last batch of hooch. You know how Beulah likes it so we gave Señor a thimble full of it too." Red slapped the armrest of his chair and cackled. I didn't know why he thought it was funny. Even though I wouldn't have touched the stuff, I was a little offended he didn't offer me any. After all, even the goat got a share.

"I bring home my friends and you get them crocked." Emmie shook her finger at him.

"I used to get Hoppy's friends crocked, too. What's the big deal?" Red always looked like he knew something you didn't — a secret, funny something.

"You old rascal." Emmie glanced over her shoulder as Mags and Delores started a rousing chorus of Yankee Doodle.

"I got to admit, they did pretty good for girls." Red pointed to Mags and Delores who were cavorting in the front yard, their arms around each other's shoulders like can-can dancers. It was embarrassing and funny at the same time. Nubs stood by the front fender of the pickup, smoking a cigarette and smirking.

93

"Here, I bought this for you in California." Emmie thrust the box into his hands and picked up Señor who snuggled against her breast with a blissful doggy smile.

"Well, what is this?"

"Open it." Emmie rubbed Señor's round little tummy, which was extended like a drum from the tidbits everyone fed him during dinner.

"Well, I'll be damned. Isn't that something?" Red held up a silver pin. It said 'Remember' in script. A good-sized pearl was mounted beneath the first 'm' and then the word 'Harbor'. "I think it is the best one yet."

"Red has a collection of Pearl Harbor paraphernalia," Emmie explained as I peeked over her shoulder at Red's prize.

"Yep, I got everything from cigars to posters to stamps."

"Don't let Mags know about your cigar," I smiled at him.

"There it is. I knew you could do it," he winked.

"What?" I looked around, wondering what he was getting at. Nub was loading our bags into the back of the pickup.

"Smile."

I blushed, but it was a nice moment.

"You all ready?" Nub called.

"We're coming." I shook Red's hand. "Thanks for your hospitality."

"You girls come back anytime." He was a nice old man.

Emmie hugged Señor and leaned down to kiss Red. He patted her back and took the dog.

"I'll see you soon," she said in his ear.

Mags and Delores clambered into the bed of the pickup. "Don't you think you'll be cold back there?" I opened the passenger door of the truck. After the ride in the WACO, the warm cab was attractive.

94

"Oh, I don't think so." Delores yawned and stretched before lifting the collar of her leather jacket and stuffing her hands into the slash pockets.

Mags waved at the old man sitting in his wheelchair. He was hatless and in his shirtsleeves, his nose dark bluish red. "That was some great anti-freeze, Red. Thanks."

"Best way I know of to keep warm!" He blew her a kiss. Señor put his front paws on Red's chest and laid his little head on his shirt.

Emmie and I got into the cab of the truck with Nubs. "Bye, Red! Bye, Señor!" Emmie called out the window. Nubs started the engine.

"Stop, stop!" Delores pounded on the back of the truck. Nubs sighed and turned off the ignition. She crawled out of the truck and ran back to Red and Señor. We waited while she said one last goodbye to the drowsy little dog. When she got back into the truck, Nubs drove us to the train station.

At the platform as we got out of the cab, Emmie and I found Mags and Delores asleep in the bed of the truck with their heads on their duffels, their coats zipped to their chins, their fur collars up around their ears — and Señor snoring loudly from the inside breast pocket of Delores' flight jacket.

CHAPTER 8 — MEN AND WOMEN

"Change confuses everyone."
~ *George Maxwell, Social Scientist*
Early February, 1944

Everyone in Cold Creek fell in love with Señor especially Pam. We drove out to Jerry's airport in Father's Plymouth the day after we returned from Camp Morgan. As usual, Señor snuggled inside Delores' jacket. It was a beautiful winter day, only traces of snow on the ground. Mags was eager to take her plane up. Emmie wanted to see how Pam was doing with the wrecked Stearman. Delores and I went along for the ride. It was better than playing dominoes with old Mr. McKensey who asked you to pull his finger and passed gas every time he won a hand.

Delores set Señor on the ground as we got out of the car and he lifted his leg against the tire of one of Jerry's Wiley Trainers.

"Where did you get him?" Pam leaned against the doorway of the hangar, her hands shoved into the pockets of her overalls watching the little dog release a long stream.

"Someone gave him to me." Delores waited for Señor to finish his business and then tugged on the leash attached to his Sapphire studded silver collar, which used to be her favorite bracelet.

"A boy friend?"

"A friend."

Pam held out her arms, making kissing sounds. Señor went right to her wagging his tail. "I bet he *wants* to be your boyfriend."

Emmie came up behind Delores and said in her ear, "I bet he's got a pretty good chance, too."

Delores pretended she hadn't heard her.

"What's his name?" The dog rolled onto his back so Pam could scratch his belly. What was it about that animal? Everyone wanted to touch him. There are people like that in this world — people who draw other people. Then there are others who are never touched.

"Señor." Delores gazed down at the squirming puppy with unbridled love. I thought she was getting carried away. He was just a dog. Even so, I was still hurt by his inexplicable behavior towards me, especially when he was sweet as pie to everyone else.

"No, I mean the boyfriend."

"You aren't as young as you appear to be, are you?" Delores put her hands on her hips and raised one eyebrow.

"I'm a kid, I'm not stupid."

Delores snorted. I could tell she liked Pam. They were a lot alike. Neither of them ever met a stranger and they both always had something on their minds.

"Pam won that one." Mags picked up a small leather bag that held her maps and headed towards her plane.

"It's cold as hell up there," Delores told her as she walked away.

Mags continued walking, lifting her hand over her shoulder to wiggle her fingers in a small wave. "I never let being cold stop me."

"So we noticed!" Emmie yelled after her.

Señor yapped twice after Mags' retreating figure.

"What kind of dog is he?" Pam dug a ragged Tootsie Roll out of her pocket and unwrapped it.

"Chihuahua. Tommy said he wouldn't grow to be more than four pounds. He's a puppy now."

Señor tugged on his leash as Pam bit off half of the Tootsie Roll and offered him the other half. The little dog chewed violently turning the candy one-way and then another, his eyes bulging with determination. He was still chewing as we headed into the back corner to look at the wrecked airplane after Mags took off. "I don't think we have the whole airplane," Pam complained as she picked through the pile of parts. "I bet Mr. McKensey sold bits and pieces of it over the years. We got the frame even if it is broken up — but most of the engine is gone."

"The problem is, we don't know what it's supposed to look like." Emmie got on her hands and knees and burrowed through the wreckage head first.

"Doesn't Mr. McKensey have the manual that came with it?" I sat down near the unsorted pile. It reminded me of the mess around Delores' bed.

"Mr. McKensey never learned how to read," Pam explained like I was a slow two-year old. "Besides his son found this thing wrecked in one of their fields after a barnstormer hit the ground a little too hard."

"What happened to the barnstormer?"

Pam mimicked cutting her own throat, dropping her head to one side with her tongue stuck out the corner of her mouth.

"What happened to Mr. McKensey's son?"

"He got run over by a John Deere. Mr. McKensey was furious because he never wanted that tractor anyway. He said if Mac had listened to him and stuck with a horse and plow it would never have happened. He's so mad he won't even go visit Mac's grave. He lost the farm not long after that. Daddy says he lost his taste for farming when Mac died anyway." Pam found another wing rib and laid it with the others.

"Maybe you can write to the company and get a manual." Delores turned an unidentifiable piece of metal around in her hands.

"Where would I get the address?" Pam asked. "The library?"

Emmie picked up a piece of rotting wing. "I got a friend might be able to find you one."

99

"A picture would help," Delores said. "I used to patch airplane wings back in Pittsburgh. It's a long boring job, but I know how to do it. We'll need Grade A Cotton and waxed string — maybe some pinking tape. Maybe we can steal people's bed sheets."

"I vote for larceny." Emmie held up her hand. "It's more fun."

"That's the least of our worries. If we can figure out where all the pieces go and if we can fix the broken ribs, how we gonna find dope?"

"Pam and I will scavenge some. She can con the good people of Cold Creek and I'll see what I can scare up at *Wiley Aircraft*." Emmie held up a water-soaked chunk of wood. "I don't know what this was, but we're going to have to get some lumber and fabricate new pieces for parts too damaged to use."

Señor tore a piece of rotted fabric from the wing and gnawed on it. "Even if we get the fuselage and wings repaired, do any of us know how to rebuild the engine?" I felt like a party pooper when I saw Pam's disappointed face.

"Daddy will help some, but he's no mechanic. We had a guy working for us but he got drafted so we are making do." Pam straddled one of the sawhorses and pursed her lips, thinking. "Maybe Grant Logan can help. I mean they put engines in the *Foxes* at the plant."

"Where are you going to get tires? One is ruined and the other one doesn't look like it'll stand up to a hard landing," I said. Señor trotted over to Emmie who was focused on the conversation.

"Maybe we can trade them for some better used ones or for enough money to buy used ones." Delores scratched her head.

"We'd have to rob a bank to buy a set of tires." I nudged them with my toe.

"Shirley's right," Emmie said. "I think theft is our best option there too." When Emmie didn't give Señor the attention he wanted, he looked around the room, his bright eyes inspecting each of us.

100

"Just be sure you steal ones that are better than these." I shook my head at the sorry-looking hoops of rotted rubber.

"Looks like Mr. McKensey took the compass and the air speed indicator and sold them." Señor's leash rattled along behind him as he went back to Pam. She tickled him under the chin.

"I'm not sure those old planes had many instruments to begin with," Emmie said.

"Well, whatever they were, there are two big holes in the console." Pam pointed to where it lay.

Señor trotted across the room to within a few feet from where I sat. He crouched down, his belly almost touching the floor, his snout on his front paws and squirmed closer, one paw at a time. I ignored him for fear he'd snap at me again. "Maybe it was an oil pressure gauge," I guessed.

"On Hoppy's WACO, we used to hang a key on a string from the dash and that would tell us if we were straight and level or banking." Emmie leaned back on one elbow and stretched out her legs to the side. "We're spoiled now what with all the fancy equipment."

"You need to get organized first. Lay things out in some order. Right now you can't tell heads from tails." The mildewy smell of the rotten cloth gave me a headache. "Get rid of stuff you can't use again."

"You know I'm no good at that. Will you help?" Emmie had me and she knew it. I could feel Pam and Delores' eyes on me. The last thing I wanted to do was fool around with a lot of dirty, stinking, bent, rotted and broken stuff.

"It would be easier if we had a schematic showing us how all the parts fit. I doubt that would be in a flight manual." Even though I'd agreed to help, I wasn't optimistic. We were pilots, not designers or engineers.

"If you'll help, we'll find a way."

101

"I'll help." Other than doing an inventory and recording what they had and didn't have, I wasn't sure how much help I'd be. At least, things would be neat.

"Will you look at that?" Delores caught my attention then darted her eyes downwards.

Señor had worked his way to where he was only a few inches from me, his eyes on my face. Enchanted, I smiled. He wiggled once more and laid his chin on my foot. I looked around, surprised. Everyone was smiling.

"Go on, pet him," Emmie whispered.

I reached down and touched his head with my fingertips between his ears. With that little encouragement, he crawled into my lap and lay still. I look down at him, both my hands in the air for a moment, my mouth open. I was afraid to say anything. Afraid the little darling would growl or bite or run away.

"It's okay. You can touch him now." Emmie's eyes sparkled. It dawned on me. She was happy for me. I looked around. They all were.

"Pet him, Shirley." Pam gestured with her head. "Pet him."

I caressed his back with trembling fingers. He snuggled down. I stroked him again. My nose burned and my eyes filled. "He likes me," I said in wonder.

\#

Things changed after Señor made peace with me — or maybe I changed. All I know is that I felt good for the first time in a long time. It was during this same week I was sitting in the parlor listening to Buddy's Big Band on the radio when Myrtle came into the room and sat down on the sofa across from me. "We need your help, Shirley. I need your help."

"What's wrong?" I lowered the volume.

She sat with her knees together and her hands folded in her lap. Three lines creased her broad forehead below her widow's peak. "I just got a phone call from Grant Logan. There's a girl at the factory who needs help."

"For what?"

"She's going to have a baby, Shirley. She isn't much more than a baby herself, but nature does take its course — war or not."

"What's he going to do about it?" I never figured Grant for someone who'd get a girl in trouble. He seemed too serious for that kind of thing.

"There's a home up in Cleveland that'll take her. She was trying to save enough from her salary to get there, but she's already quick. People are going to start noticing soon. A bigger woman might have gotten away with another month, but Lizzie is tiny. We were hoping you'd drive her up there in your father's car. Grant will go with you of course. This little one is having a tough time and it would be good if someone went with her who could talk with her. I'd go, but I gotta take care of the rest of you."

I frowned and leaned forward in my seat, my elbows on my knees. "Why doesn't he marry her?"

"He's off fighting the Japs."

I raised my head, confused.

"This isn't Grant's baby, honey. The daddy is one of our neighborhood boys, a friend of Jerry's son. I'm sure he would have married her if he were here."

"Why did you ask me? Why not Emmie? Or Delores?"

"Grant asked for you." She stood up and patted me on the shoulder. "He wanted that pretty little thing with the Plymouth."

No one ever asked me to help before. Now, within a week, I'd been included twice — and Grant picked me over the others. "When do we go?"

103

"He's bringing her over now."

"I need to get some fuel ration stamps and buy gasoline." I started up the steep steps to freshen my make-up and change my blouse.

"You can do that on the way. Jerry will give you fuel ration stamps and I'm sure Grant will bring some. I'll make lunch to take with you."

I hurried into the dormitory. Delores lay on her bed with Señor, feeding him bologna. I crossed to my dresser pulling my blouse out of my skirt.

"Where ya going?" She tore a tiny bit of meat off the main slice and tossed it to Señor who caught it mid-air. As usual, her area was a total mess. Her laundry lay in a huge pile on the floor at the foot of her bed. It was ten o'clock in the morning and she hadn't gotten around to folding them yet.

"Thought I'd take a little trip up to Cleveland." I selected a round-collared white shirt, which was hanging in the blouse section third from the left on my clothes rack.

"Something wrong?"

"Don't you think that's going to make him sick?" I went behind the small screen near my bed, stripped off my blouse, and replaced it with the fresh one. Tucking it into my skirt band, I slipped on my gray cardigan and buttoned it up to my throat.

"He's crazy about it." I heard the snap of Señor's jaws as he snapped up the next piece of bologna.

"They are rationing meat and you are feeding Myrtle's baloney to a dog." I'd have given Señor my ration if I'd known he liked it.

"I'm going to be alone here with Señor and Mr. McKensey. Maybe I'll sleep the afternoon away." Delores yawned.

"Where's Emmie?"

"She and Mags are out at the airport. It might snow this afternoon so Mags wanted to take her plane up while she can."

104

"Well, then. No one will miss me."

A slow smile spread across Delores' face. "An adventure?"

"Maybe." I darkened my eyebrows and rouged my cheeks.

"Yeeha!"

I put on my coat as I clomped down the stairs with the keys to the Plymouth in my hand.

Grant Logan stood in Myrtle's kitchen with a thin girl. Broken blood vessels webbed the whites of her eyes. Had she been crying? Vomiting?

"Shirley, I'd like you to meet Lizzie Langer." I didn't even realize Grant knew my name.

"Nice to meet you, Shirley. Thank you for helping me." She had changed from her *Wiley Aircraft* overalls and wore a dark dress that was about two sizes too big. Holding a small valise in her left hand and carrying her coat draped over her forearm, she looked like a child dressed up in her mother's clothes.

Myrtle thrust a box of food into my hands. "Y'all be careful now. The roads get a lot slicker as you go north."

Grant turned to face Myrtle as she spoke, his eyes on her lips. "We'll be fine," he said.

We tromped through crusty snow to get to the Plymouth, which was parked out back by Mr. McKensey's old Ford. Gray clouds were rolling in and it was cold. Lizzie crawled into the backseat and wrapped herself in the thick blue blanket Myrtle gave her. Grant got into the front passenger side. I started the car and backed around. As we passed the inn, I saw Delores peeking out the third-floor window. Turning onto Cold Creek Road leading into town, we could look down over the hill and see Mags landing her red biplane at Jerry's airstrip.

"Where are we going?" I asked as we turned north toward Cleveland.

105

"What?" He cupped his ear.

"Where? Where are we going?"

"St. Jerome's Home for Foundlings. It's in Bay Village west of Cleveland not far from Lake Erie. They know we are coming," Grant looked over his shoulder at Lizzie. "She's asleep, thank goodness. She's had a bad couple of days."

"How did you get involved in this?"

"I'm her boss."

"No offense, but my boss would be the last person I'd confide something like this to." Fat, wet snowflakes splattered against the windshield and I turned on the wipers.

"What?" He touched his ear and cocked his head once again.

I turned to face him. "I wouldn't tell my boss about this."

"She was working the assembly line and fainted. I picked her up and took her to the nurse's office. It was pretty obvious what was wrong."

"Does anyone else know?"

"Just the nurse and Myrtle and you and me."

"What about her parents?"

"I told them we needed Lizzie to work in the Cleveland office for a few months."

"*Wiley Aircraft* doesn't have a Cleveland office."

"Right."

"She's a kid. Who did this?"

"A home town boy. Been in trouble all his life."

"Does he know?"

"I doubt it. It doesn't matter. Once Lizzie has the baby and it's adopted, it'll be like it never happened. No one else has to know. She'll be home by summer."

"Problem solved." I gripped the steering wheel and squinted as the icy drops came down faster.

"You have other suggestions?" It was hard to tell his emotions from his atonal voice.

"No," I sighed. "It's the way things are."

"That baby's life would be hell if she kept him. He'd be labeled a bastard all his life. What about Lizzie? Her life would be ruined. She's only a kid as you say."

"She suffers through this alone and he gets off scot-free?"

"She shouldn't have let Bennie near her."

"So it's her fault?"

He glanced over his shoulder again and put his finger to his lips to warn me to lower my voice. "Don't you think it's her fault?"

"What about Bennie?"

"Boys will be boys. They are going to try. It's up to girls to control these impulses."

I bit my lip and drove through the snow in furious silence. When the heat was on them, men talked a whole different line. 'You'd do it if you loved me.' 'I thought I was special.' 'That's why I want you — because you are a virgin.' Then if you give in or if they force you, you are dirtied forever. As Father always said, a man wants a clean woman to bear his children. Little Lizzie in the back seat would have to pray we all kept her secret forever.

"You want me to drive?" He turned sideways to face me, his back against the door, the final word on womanly responsibilities having been said.

"No, I'm fine." The road became treacherous and I slowed to 20 miles per hour. "You like working in the factory?"

"It's not where I'd be if I could choose, but Mr. Wiley's been good to me."

"Where would you be?"

"Marines. Wherever they are these days."

"Maybe you are supposed to be here doing what you are doing." I braked as we came up behind a truck, conscious of Grant pressing his right foot into the firewall.

"It's pretty hard to be the one left behind. I hoped they would have something I could do." He was healthy — I'm sure it was embarrassing for him to be stuck in Cold Creek.

"You do a lot of things for the effort."

"I try, but it doesn't seem enough when my neighbors get telegrams from the War Department about their sons. A friend of mine died at Pearl Harbor. I wanted to go after those bastards myself — to smash their bucktooth, slant-eyed faces in." His face contorted into a snarl. I was taken aback. Then before my eyes, his face relaxed and went back to the soft, good-hearted contours of a man willing to rescue a teenage girl in trouble. "I'm sorry. I need to control that."

"We are all angry at what's happened. This war has hurt a lot of people. None of us wanted it, but they forced us into it."

"My own hatred scares me sometimes." He flinched as I pulled out to pass a slow moving car in front of us.

"How were you raised?"

"Catholic. I was an altar boy."

"My mother was Catholic and I went to Catholic schools, but Father is fallen away. I guess that makes me fallen away too."

"You ought to come to Mass with me someday. My parents were married at St. John's. My brothers and I were baptized there. You'd love it."

He wanted to take me to Mass. I couldn't remember a man wanting to take me to church. "I'd like that," I heard myself say.

Lizzie awoke and stretched in the back seat.

"Are you all right back there?" He turned to look at her.

"No! You better pull over." The girl made gagging sounds. The berm was miniscule but there was a ditch along the side of the road. I turned on my lights and braked. As the car stopped, Lizzie threw open the door and lay on her stomach, her head outside the car, throwing up into the snow.

I stared out the driver's side window, avoiding Grant's eyes and trying not to hear her retching.

"There, that's better." She sat up wiping her mouth with a handkerchief.

"Are you sure?"

"Yeah. We got anything to eat?"

Grant and I looked at each other with horrified amusement. He handed her Myrtle's picnic basket.

#

It took four hours to get to St. Jerome's. A nun met us at the door and collected Lizzie. Since neither Grant nor I were related to her, the nun discouraged us from going in. Lizzie turned to us with frightened eyes. I held out my arms and she ran to me.

"You can call me at *The Windshift Inn* if you need anything." I shoved a ten-dollar bill into her hand.

"You don't even know me."

I squeezed her hand, at a loss as to what to say.

Her bottom lip quivered. "I'll write to you, okay?"

"I'd love to hear from you, Lizzie."

She turned to Grant. "Thank you, Mr. Logan."

"No problem. You focus on having that baby. Your job will be waiting. Don't you worry, no one will ever know."

The nun led her away. We stood in the foyer of St. Jerome's, looking around. It was a great big lonely house. The orphanage was in the back like an afterthought.

"She'll be okay," he said.

"I know." I teared up.

"Do you like spaghetti?"

I wiped my eyes with the back of my hand. "Sure."

"I know a good place for spaghetti on the road back to Cold Creek. Can I buy you dinner?"

He put his hand on my back as we made our way down the icy steps of St. Jerome's. He opened the car door for me and I got into the passenger side.

"This feels better," he said as he started the car.

"What do you mean?"

"Men should drive."

"You don't think much of us, do you?"

"I think you are trying to be men."

"Funny, I thought we were serving our country."

"We need you right now, but that doesn't change the fact that you have your place."

"Let's not talk about it."

"The war will be over some day. The guys will come home. No one is going to want a woman coarsened by working in a factory or flying an airplane. Those boys are heroes. They deserve better."

"What do you suggest?"

"I'm not suggesting anything. I'm telling you nothing has changed. Don't expect any man to accept this. They are going to want you to put away those slacks and dress like a lady. They are going to want women who'll take care of them and have their children, not someone flying around all over the country."

"Why are you telling me this?"

"I'm getting it out of the way."

He pulled into *Mama Leone's*. He got out and hurried around to my side of the car, opening the door for me. He took my arm as I got out. "When you are with me, we are doing things the old fashioned way." His sudden smile was dazzling.

I let him lead me into the restaurant. We sat at a table with a checkered tablecloth in the front window. He ordered antipasto, pasta with marinara and red wine from a cheerful woman who turned out to be Mama Leone in the flesh.

"You are a bad example for Pam Kline." He continued as he buttered the crusty Italian bread. "She doesn't have a mother to show her how to be a woman. She wants to be a pilot now."

"Jerry mentioned it."

"You could fix that."

I was beginning to feel like a true freak — the half man / half woman character in the sideshow. Grant Logan was beginning to remind me of George Maxwell, the bully. "How can I fix anything?"

"A man likes to think he's in charge. It's a little upsetting to think his wife could challenge him to an arm-wrestling match and win."

"Grant, I promise I won't hurt you." I was getting good at making jokes.

He was quiet for a minute and I thought I had offended him — then that bright smile again. Grant Logan had a sense of humor too, it seems.

"Thank God. I was worried." He bit into his bread.

"Good. Don't worry about Pam. She's a smart little girl. She adores you, I hope you've noticed."

"She misses her brother. She's a loud-mouthed, little tag-along, but she and Danny are close. I remind her of Danny."

"There are worse things in the world."

"There are indeed. You could help her if you would."

"Teach her to sew? Cut her hair? Dress her up like a doll?"

"All of those things."

I shook my head. "What if she wants to learn something else?"

"Teach her about that too."

I sat for a minute digesting what he was saying. "Oh?" I flushed. "Oh!"

I went home that night with a lot to think about. If the WASP were in an odd position with respect to the Army, we were also in a new world where men and women no longer knew what to expect of one another.

CHAPTER 9 — TARGET TOWING

*"First Lady Fights for Equal Rights for Women, Enemy Fighters Smash US
Bombers in Battle over Frankfurt, Cats Help Train War Dogs"*
Headlines
~ American View Daily~
March, 1944

The next time we returned to Camp Morgan, Tommy McDougal informed us we were to check out in the 1000 hp A-24 dive-bomber. Mags, Emmie and Delores jumped around with excitement. I was less than thrilled. This was quite a change since the *Foxes* were nothing like the A-24. We'd trained on AT-6's, which were more powerful than the *Foxes*, but it had been six months since we'd even seen one.

"Conrad says these planes are no longer necessary for combat so he doesn't see any reason why you can't fly them," Tommy said as we followed him to take a look at an A-24 parked on the apron.

"The planes are dispensable and so are we." Delores' grumbling had grown louder as the situation at Camp Morgan became more frustrating.

Tommy put his hand on the wing and turned to us, ignoring Delores' sour expression. "He wants you checked out in them right away. You'll be towing targets when you come back next time so we'll be working hard the next few days."

"Okay, let's get on with it." Mags walked around the plane, touching it here and there, noting this or that characteristic. Emmie squatted to look at perforated extensions along the trailing edge of the wing. Dive brakes. This was a much more complicated plane. I had grown comfortable with the *Foxes*. I followed Mags around the aircraft eyeing it with apprehension. The wingspan looked to be about 40 feet or more and it was maybe 33 or 34-feet long. It would be the biggest plane I'd ever flown.

"Who's going first?" Tommy asked all of us, but he was looking at Delores.

"I'll go!" She held up two fingers.

"Fine. Climb in. By the way, you can't take that dog."

"What dog?" Delores batted her eyes at him.

That's all it took.

He shrugged and they got into the plane with Tommy in front and Delores behind him. Tommy taxied out to the runway. As they took off, we could see Delores in the gunner's seat through the canopy, her face serious as she concentrated on the instruments in front of her. We knew Señor was riding along with her. He wasn't quite as tiny as he used to be, but he still fit comfortably inside her baggy jumpsuit.

The rest of us stood there in the sudden silence after they left. "What are we supposed to do now?" I folded my arms over my chest, unhappy with the idea of standing around waiting for Tommy and Delores to come back.

Mags strode into the hangar where other A-24s were parked. A group of mechanics and male pilots were standing around a plane near the back of the hangar discussing something. Their voices were raised, their faces angry. When they saw us, they lapsed into sullen silence — eyeing us with hostility.

"Can I help you?" Wayne Wilson approached, glancing behind him and scratching the bald spot on the back of his head.

"We just wanted to look one of these over," Mags said. "Are there any manuals?"

He chewed his gum a bit faster. "I think I can find you a manual. Someone checking you out?"

"McDougal."

"You could do worse. He knows his stuff."

114

"You mind if we take a look?" Mags nodded towards the A-24 parked near the men who were glaring at us.

"Be my guest." He winked at Emmie and she smiled back. "I got a good one for you."

"Okay, I'm listening," Emmie said as we headed towards the A-24. The men scattered as we approached, glancing back at us with frowns.

"Okay. There's this waitress, see. And she's pouring this soldier a cup of coffee. And she says, "Looks like rain." And he says, "Tastes like it too. Bring me some tea." He opened his hands and grinned, waiting for our response.

"Oh!" Emmie slapped her own forehead and rolled her eyes.

"It was that awful fake coffee, get it?"

"I got it." She laughed. Wayne stuck his hands into his pockets, grinning and looking around at the rest of us. He reminded me of a big puppy.

We crawled up to sit in the cockpit one by one. Wayne answered our questions patiently. "This baby has a range of 950 miles fully loaded. She'll max out around 250 mph, but cruising speed is 175," he said as I sat in the front cockpit reviewing the instruments. Unlike Mags, Delores and Emmie, I was going to need to sit on my parachute to be able to see over the dashboard. I stretched out my legs. My feet didn't quite reach the rudder pedals. I hated using blocks, but the aircraft was designed for someone several inches taller than me. I checked the Form One as we'd been taught to do at Sweetwater. It was a record of each plane's airworthiness and repair history. This particular A-24 was a mess. There were a series of problems noted by the various pilots who had flown it in the last two weeks and one of the mechanics had red-lined it. That meant a lot of repairs were required, but the plane could still fly. I glanced at Wayne who lowered his eyes. Something was wrong here. I could feel it. I made a note of the aircraft number — 49.

115

Rummaging around in the side pocket, I found a funny-looking plastic packet. "What's this?" I asked.

Wayne flushed. "You don't need it."

I was puzzled at his reaction. "But what is it?"

"It's a … uh…a pressure relief valve."

I held it up to the hangar light above me. I couldn't make heads or tails of it. "But for what?"

"Let's get you out of there before McDougal gets back and starts looking for you." He hustled me down out of the plane so fast that my heels slid on the cement floor and I almost lost my balance. He crawled down after me and went around to the other side of the plane as if to get away from us.

Mags and Emmie stepped back with exclamations of surprise. "What was that all about?" Emmie asked.

"I don't know. Did you see that thing in the side pocket?"

"No, what was it?"

"I don't know, but Wayne got all bent out of shape when I asked about it."

"You mean the relief tube?" Mags' mouth twitched.

"I guess." I looked from her to Emmie.

"It's a portable urinal. So they don't have to land to go to the bathroom."

I covered my face with both hands, my face burning — but I giggled in spite of myself. "Well, I guess Wayne's right. I don't need it."

Emmie leaned against the fuselage, her head thrown back, holding her sides. Mags wiped first one eye and then the other one. Our laughter echoed in the hangar and the men standing a few feet away scowled at us.

116

After we collected ourselves, we realized Wayne was no longer hovering around us and we went looking for him. He was looking through a shelf of books in one of the meeting rooms.

"Give me a second, I know there's a manual for the A-24 in here," he said. He had a greasy rag stuffed in his back pocket. I made a note to check the seat of my pants in case he'd been sitting in the cockpit of the A-24 before me.

"Take your time. We appreciate you doing this for us." Mags wandered around the room, looking at the calendars and pin-ups and bulletin boards. The wall behind the bookshelf was full of Wayne's cartoons — some of them poking fun at Hitler or Hirohito, others were caricatures of Simpson, McDougal, and some of the male pilots. There were even cartoons of FDR and Patton and Eisenhower. On the far side, there was a picture of Mags in her barnstorming get-up and a sketch of a sour-faced woman climbing into a Fox with a bathing beauty sash across her uniform that said 'Virgin Queen.'

"What *is* that?" My voice was shriller than I intended.

Everyone turned to look at me, even the men on the other side of the hangar.

"What's what?" Emmie whispered, taking hold of my arm.

"*That*!" I snatched the cartoon off the wall. "How *dare* you put me up on the wall like some … some ..." I couldn't think of anything bad enough to say. I dug my nails into the palms of my hands.

Wayne wouldn't look me in the eye. "It's a joke. I didn't mean anything by it."

"Oh sure, a joke!" I threw the wadded up paper at him, turned on my heel and marched away.

Emmie hurried after me. "It's nothing, Shirley. He didn't mean anything by it."

"Didn't he?"

117

"It was in fun. He did one of me, don't you remember?"

"He didn't hang it up for the entire world to see. He didn't make fun of you."

"Shirley, he didn't mean it that way."

"It's not the first time I've run into that kind of thing. My father owns a magazine with all kinds of funny guys — cartoons all over the place."

"But this isn't the magazine." She had me there. I looked around. Everyone was staring. What had I done? I'd been so careful up till now. Would Mags and Emmie still like me?

Tommy and Delores landed and taxied back towards the apron.

"Come on, Shirley. We gotta learn to fly this bird." Emmie mock-punched my arm like the guys did to each other.

"I'm sorry, I don't know what got into me."

"It's okay. Let's go." Emmie herded me towards the area where Mags awaited. Mags patted me on the back and everything seemed okay. I glared over my shoulder at Wayne who turned on his heel and went back to join the cluster of pilots and mechanics on the other side of the hangar.

Tommy braked not far from us. They slid back their canopies and got out. Since they didn't make flight suits for women, we were issued men's sizes. We all rolled up the sleeves and legs, but the bagginess couldn't hide Delores' extraordinary figure. I could only imagine what Wayne Wilson would do with her caricature.

"Damned thing about brained me," she said as she approached us, rubbing her forehead.

"Any of you ever been in a dive bomber before?" Tommy asked. We all shook our heads. "Guess I better warn the rest of you, then. These things are built for landings on aircraft carriers. They are equipped with hydraulically operated dive brakes."

"We noticed." Emmie and Mags nodded.

118

"On landing, you fly these things nose down until the last minute, and then you pull up just before the wheels hit the ground."

"I didn't expect that and banged my head against the gun sights." Delores had a small bluish bump on her forehead.

"Great." Emmie pushed back Delores' dark curls to examine the bruise, her eyes filled with concern.

I made a note to hang on during landing.

"It's hard to know much about what he's doing, too. The back seat doesn't have all the same instruments. You gotta guess what's happening." Delores stroked a wiggling lump over her left breast. Señor stuck out his nose and yapped.

"Only dog to ever fly in a dive bomber." Tommy reached over to scratch Señor's ears like a proud papa.

Mags zipped up her flight suit. "Well, I guess if a dog can do it, we should be able to. I'm ready to go next."

We spent the day flying with Tommy McDougal — the first time up with him flying the plane, the second time with each of us in the pilot's seat and him in the gunner's seat behind us. As Mags was making her second landing in the A-24, the left front wheel blew and she fought to keep the plane from skidding off the runway. That was it for us until they could repair the tire. It was almost 2:30 pm by then anyway. I was more than willing to call it a day.

"Wayne says keeping these planes in tires is becoming harder and harder. Spare tires with any life in them are sent overseas," Emmie said as we trudged back towards the Quonset hut.

"These planes are stuck together with chewing gum." Delores put Señor on the tarmac and he trotted along beside us. "Someone's going to get killed in one of these crappy birds."

"Did you see the Form One in the plane sitting in the hangar?" I interjected. "It was red-lined."

"That's probably why it was sitting in the hangar, waiting to be fixed," Mags said. "Makes you wonder about the maintenance program here. How do you fix anything if you don't have spare parts?"

The whole thing left a sour taste in my mouth. The next morning, it was my turn to take the A-24 up. Tommy got in the back seat and I settled myself in the front. I took a look at the Form One and shuddered. The engine started up easily but ran rough as I was taxiing out to the runway. During the run-up, it died. Tommy keyed the mic. "Let's take it back."

Together with Wayne Wilson, Tommy and I drained almost a cup of water out of the carburetor. I should have done something about it right then and there. I should have called Father or Jackie Cochran. There must have been something we could have done.

Camp Morgan began to keep us busier. It was still cold in Ohio and even though there were planes waiting to be ferried, there was work to be done in California. We often stayed several days before taking a train back to *The Windshift Inn*. Before long, the problems at Camp Morgan began to wear on us. Even Mags and Emmie were worried.

CHAPTER 10 — B-17

"Allies Blow Up Nazi Robot Tanks, 2,000,000 Women Sought for Jobs, Wiley Plant turns out 2,500[th] Fox."
Headlines
~ American View Daily ~
April, 1944

I dreaded going back to Camp Morgan. The mechanics were tense, unhappy men who had more work than they could do. The male pilots were either eager to get back to the real war or eager to find ways to stay out of combat. All we wanted to do was fly. The problems of Camp Morgan impacted anyone who sat in the cockpit of a poorly-maintained plane. You'd think we'd work together on it — but, they kept their distance, sullen and hostile. Mags and Emmie made friends with a few of the mechanics and of course, Delores was seeing Tommy McDougal. None of the others accepted us.

It turns out Mags and Emmie didn't have to tow targets after all. Conrad Simpson sent them to B-17 school. The taller girls caught that assignment — and the best pilots. Delores and I started towing targets near the end of March. I wasn't looking forward to it and wariness turned out to be warranted. It was terrifying. The A-24s were falling apart. There wasn't a single pilot, male or female, who hadn't experienced a blowout on landing. Decent tires were few and far between. Even the ones being sent overseas were in bad shape. It made me appreciate Pam Kline's zeal for collecting rubber. One of the planes had a sticky throttle that scared me to death every time I had to deal with it and Number 49 had a broken latch on the canopy. You could get it to close, but it was impossible to open from the inside. Every time we went up, we reported problems on the Form One, but these A-24s were low priority and parts were scarce. Basic things like sparkplugs were coveted.

The job involved flying up and down a beach towing a long piece of muslin while novice artillerymen opened up on you. A frightened young private sat in the gunner's seat behind the pilot playing out the target cable. Of course, I understood their fear. Being shot at was scary enough, let alone riding with a woman pilot. Twice I landed to find new bullet holes in the fuselage. Everyone had a story to tell about nervous trainees aiming at the plane rather than the target. In fact, Delores became famous her first day over the beach.

She wasn't happy with the plane she drew that day. It had so many problems she wasn't sure she was going to get it into the air. The engine cut out twice while she was on the ground, but finally, it caught and she and her target handler took off. It was his first day as well and he looked terrified. She made a long slow turn coming out of the airport and headed towards the beach.

"Good to see you." I radioed her. I'd already made several passes and the underarms of my flight suit were damp.

"I was beginning to wonder if I'd ever get the damned thing off the ground," she answered.

"Come in like you are gonna strafe the beach," the instructor on the ground told her.

"On my way." She aimed the nose of the A-24 at a grove of bushes on the edge of the beach. The wind howled over her wings as she went into a steep dive. Through the canopy, I could see the boy in the back seat — his eyes bulging, his lips stretched over his buckteeth. Delores pulled back on the stick, skimming the water and sand before climbing steeply at the end of her run. Machine gun fire riddled the muslin target streaming behind her.

"Damn, no one ever did that before," someone drawled over the radio.

"You asked, you got." Delores keyed her mic as she circled at altitude.

"How about a nice slow pass this time around 800 feet?"

"Roger."

I was less than a mile away at 3000 feet when it happened. As Delores flew down the beach, the anti-aircraft fire came too close to her engine cowling.

"That's flak!" The kid in the gunner seat yelled as puffs of black smoke surrounded the plane.

The whole thing infuriated Delores. "What idiot did that?"

The next shot blew her tail clean off and she started down with very little altitude to work with. "DAMMIT, WHAT THE HELL DID YOU CRAZY ASSHOLES DO TO ME?"

"Watch your language," the instructor radioed her.

"WATCH MY LANGUAGE? ARE YOU KIDDING? YOU ASSHOLES SHOOT ME DOWN AND YOU ARE WORRIED ABOUT MY DAMNED ..." The plane disappeared into the treetops beyond the beach. I abandoned my route and flew towards her, circling above the swath cut into the brush by the crashing A-24. My heart pounded as I waited for the explosion, but fortunately, it never came. The plane was crumpled. I couldn't see anyone, but I radioed the coordinates and waited as a rescue crew rushed to the area.

The instructor keyed his mic. "Get back to your assignment, Maxwell."

I circled once more and returned to my sector. As I swooped low over the beach, my target handler released the cable and the muslin target drifted to the ground. Several soldiers rushed to evaluate the results of their practice. By the time I got back to the airstrip, Delores and her private, a freckled-face boy from Alabama, had found their own way home. They hiked through the woods until they found a road and hitched a ride with a tank headed back towards the base.

As I taxied up to the apron, Delores stood at attention in front of an angry lieutenant six inches shorter than her. He was pacing back and forth and shaking his finger under her nose. Her large breasts were about eye level for him and he was trying not to notice them. It would have been funny if it hadn't been so tragic. She'd nearly been killed! The young private stood behind her, his chest stuck out, his chin tucked in. Red-faced and flustered, the officer finished his tirade, got in a jeep and sped off. Delores relaxed and said something to the boy. He slumped for a moment, then turned and loped off as if glad to be away from her.

I shut my engine and crawled down. "Are you okay?" My own target handler raced off to catch up with the young Alabaman who was already half way across the field.

"Just peachy." She unzipped her flight suit and a big-eyed Señor peeked out at me from her bosom. No wonder the lieutenant had been so distracted. Not only were her breasts big, but they were wiggling. "He chewed me out for cussing on the radio and chewed me out for leaving the damned plane. Seems they are still out there looking for us in the woods."

Her cheeks were flushed and one strand of hair had slipped from its pins and curled down over her forehead. I didn't know what to think. Seemed to me losing an expensive plane would be more of a problem then cussing on the airwaves, but the rules at Camp Morgan were foggy at best. "Conrad Simpson wants to see me. Can you take Señor?"

"Sure, we'll get cleaned up and go for a walk."

"That bastard is probably going to chew me out too."

"Watch your temper, Delores!" I didn't blame her for being angry, but throwing a tantrum in front of Simpson wouldn't make things better.

I cuddled the little dog and he laid his chin on my shoulder like a baby. Taking a deep breath, Delores headed off across the tarmac to Conrad Simpson's office. I wished Mags or Emmie were here, but they weren't due back for a couple more hours. Mags would handle Simpson and Emmie would handle Delores. I felt helpless.

124

I was sitting on my bunk feeding Señor when Delores came in. Señor perked up his ears and wagged his tail. "They are grounding me for a couple of weeks for cussing on the radio." She slumped down on her own bed.

"I can't believe it," I said. Señor wiggled his whole body when he wagged his tail. I sat him on the floor and he trotted over to her. He stood on his hind legs, patting her shin with his front paws.

"Lets you know where we stand, doesn't it?" She picked up Señor and he licked her face. "You know, I thought I was doing something good — something patriotic, but they make me feel like I'm a criminal, like I'm intruding on some private male domain."

"I know what you mean," I said. "When all those people were killed in Hawaii, I felt like there was nothing I could do about it. Lots of people put flags up outside their houses, but that seemed like a gesture with no power behind it. Then this came up and I thought I'd be useful. It was tangible." I stared at my hands, a little embarrassed by this admission.

"Did you ever play stick ball with a bunch of boys?" Delores hugged the squirming puppy.

I shook my head. "I never played any kind of sports."

"Everyone forms a line and they choose up sides. They never pick you to play until there's no one else left. They assume you can't play. When it's your turn at bat, they all inch forward. I loved knocking the ball over the back fence of the field where we played. They never expected it. The damned fools."

"Did that change their minds? Did they ask you to play after that?"

"Hell no, they figured it was a fluke. As we got older, the other girls started accepting it — gathering on the sidelines and cheering. They prepared their hope chests and worked on catching a husband. They turned into a bunch of silly fools, if you ask me, even letting boys win in the few games it was still permissible to play like chess or bridge. If I were a guy that would piss me off. What fun is it to win

125

if someone lets you?" She peeled her flight suit down over her boots and threw it on the floor inside out. Señor grabbed hold of the sleeve shaking his head and growling.

I felt like I had to explain. "Some of us just want to get along, Delores. Dodge as many bullets as we can."

She looked up at me and shrugged. "Maybe the best strategy is to outrun them."

"Like today?" I said and we both laughed.

"It's a losing battle sometimes, that's for sure," she said. "When I was in the tenth grade, I had the highest average in the geometry class, but I didn't win the geometry prize. I asked the teacher why and she said it was given out for potential. It seems my lack of a penis limited my potential for geometry."

"Perhaps you needed something to measure with," Mags said from the door.

Señor let go of Delores' flight suit, his ears alert. "I could get something like that at the dime store." Delores answered without blinking an eye. I was beginning to enjoy their repartee as long as they didn't do it in front of anyone else.

"I hear you had an interesting day." Emmie came in behind Mags.

"I wanted to start out with a bang."

"And you were exceedingly successful," Mags tossed a cartoon onto the bed. It was one of Wayne Wilson's best. It showed an even more voluptuous Delores, without a plane, flying with her arms stretched out like wings and a row of pimply-faced, grinning privates taking shots at her round rear end. The caption said, "Taking a crack at a little WASP tail."

"It's a good likeness, don't you think?" Emmie took off her blouse and tossed it into her bed.

"I'm going to get that little bastard." Delores held the cartoon up and pointed. "My boobs are much better than these."

126

I would have been offended, but she took it pretty well. She was much more upset about being grounded. I would have considered it a nice vacation. One day of flying those rickety planes was more than sufficient for me.

"Are you going back to *The Windshift Inn*?" I asked.

"Nope. Tommy is taking me to the movies tonight. We have a date tomorrow night, too — and the night after that. I'll just hang out here and go back with you on Thursday."

I was relieved. Mags and Emmie weren't going back for a couple of weeks. I didn't like the idea of a four-day train trip by myself.

"What are you going to see?" Emmie raided the bag of jellybeans I'd been feeding Señor.

"*The Uninvited*. It's a ghost story."

"Oh good, let's go too." She picked out all of the black ones and lined them up on her pillow. Kicking her boots off, she removed her uniform pants and hung them over her locker door. Then she stuck her head inside her duffel rummaging for clean clothes tossing them out behind her. Emmie was the only woman I ever knew who stumbled around in her panties and those pointy cotton brassieres with a duffel on her head. I couldn't help laughing at her. None of us could.

"If you come dressed like that, I'll pretend I won't know you." Delores tossed Señor a red jellybean and he snapped it up. "Tommy and I will be in the back row eating popcorn and watching the movie."

"I know how that goes." Emmie found her chenille robe and put it on. Then she pulled the bag off her head. Her hair stood up on the crown of her head, crackling with static electricity.

"Don't you worry about it, Lieutenant McDougal doesn't want any part of us tonight," Mags stretched out on her bunk, her hands behind her head, her legs crossed at the ankles. "He's in a snit right now."

127

"A snit?" Delores taped the cartoon on the wall over her bed. "You didn't get him in a bad mood, did you?"

"Mags was bad at B-17 school today and the teacher would have sent her to the principal if he could." Emmie popped the first black jelly bean into her mouth and stuffed all the clothes she'd just pulled out of her duffel back into it.

"Okay, what did you do, Mags Strickland?" Delores unpinned her hair and brushed the leaves and twigs out of it. For a woman who had crash-landed a plane and hiked through the woods, she was in a remarkably good mood.

Mags yawned and stretched. "I rolled it."

"Rolled it?"

"Yep."

"What did you roll, Mags?" I was confused.

"She rolled the B-17." Emmie's tongue was jellybean black. Señor trotted over to her and whimpered. She gave him a red one.

I was shocked. "I can't believe you. You've only been flying them a week. Weren't you scared?"

"Well, yeah! But it was fun anyway."

"Tommy must be furious," Delores said as she collected her shower things.

Emmie talked with her mouth full of candy. "Yeah, he was going to throw us out of the program, but he had second thoughts about trying to explain it to Conrad Simpson. He thought our attitude was — what did he call it, Mags?"

"Irresponsible."

"Yeah, light hearted and irresponsible."

"But we did do it. I think he was impressed after he got over being mad. Course he's still pretending to be mad, but he's only in a snit

128

now." Mags lit a cigar and blew smoke rings into the air above her bunk.

"I'd never dare try something like that. What was it like?" I hugged my knees and imagined the B-17. The Flying Fortress was huge with a wingspan of over 100 feet and it was almost 75 feet long. Four engines. An expensive long-range bomber, it was armed with 13 machine guns — under the chin, on top, the ball and tail turrets, waist and cheek guns. I'd never even ridden in anything so big, let alone fly it. Only Mags would think of rolling it.

"It's a great plane," Emmie said. "There are windows everywhere around the cockpit — six surrounding the pilot and co-pilot, two over your head. You can see forever."

"Whatever made you want to roll it, Mags?" Delores was intrigued too.

"I've rolled every plane I ever piloted. Why should this one be any different?" Mags acted nonchalant, but I knew she got a big kick out of flying that monstrous plane. It was right up her alley.

"Is it hard to fly?" I asked.

"She's just big. You have to worry about four engines, of course. To be honest, I nearly blew it. If it hadn't been for Emmie, we might not have recovered."

"And Tommy would have been even more pissed." Delores stripped off her uniform, wadded it up and threw it on the floor with her jumpsuit. "Hope he cheers up before the movie tonight."

"It was a bit of surprise to him. We were flying along, straight and level. Mags was in control, I'm in the right hand seat. Tommy was sitting in the jump seat behind Mags." Emmie held up a jellybean for Señor. He ignored her and lay down under Delores' bed. He'd had enough.

Mags lay on her bunk, her hands behind her head, holding her cigar with her teeth as she spoke. "We're up about 8,000 feet just cruising along and down below us I see this huge cotton field. It went on and on in all directions and it reminded me of the place where I used to practice aerobatics. Anyway, I get an urge to roll this big bird. I turned the ailerons hard left and hit the left rudder — and over we go. Tommy screams and holds onto the side of the plane. Emmie just sits there. Real quiet at first, then she chortles like a hyena. Took about thirty seconds to get all the way over and as I approach the start position and begin trying to recover, the damned thing wants to roll again and nose down. I pull back with all my might on the controls and try to give her some right rudder and aileron. I glance at Emmie wondering if she's going to help. Takes her a second to realize rolling over and auguring in nose first wasn't what I had in mind and she hollers over the dive whine, "What the hell's going on here?" before she grabs the controls on her side and we recover together. By then, Tommy was in a snit."

"That spoilsport." Emmie stuffed a bar of soap, a washcloth, and a bottle of shampoo into the pockets of her robe and tossed a towel over her shoulder.

"Why did it want to go over again?" I asked.

"Controls jammed I think," Mags said. "Tommy's going to have the mechanics take a look. There's gonna be some flex in the structure of any plane when you do maneuvers like that, but that wasn't what we expected."

I shook my head. "I doubt the B-17 was built for that."

"Straight and level, high altitude, long distance," Mags agreed.

"Let me get this straight. You roll a B-17 bomber and the worst that happens is that Tommy's in a snit?" Delores shook her head. "I get my tail shot off, literally, and I get grounded for cussing into the radio. Where's the fairness here? You should at least have to go to bed without dinner."

CHAPTER 11 — ROMANCE

"The heart is simple, the mind complex."
~ George Maxwell, Romantic
May, 1944

Delores and I climbed on the train back to *The Windshift Inn* the Thursday after she was grounded. Even though it was early morning, the train was crowded with service men — many trying to capture Delores' attention with little success. We dozed in our seats as the train pulled away from the platform. As usual, Señor curled up in Delores' large canvas bag on the floor under the window.

Delores was in a somber mood. Our few days in California had not been happy ones. Aside from her crash, there was a small faction among the men whose hostility boiled over now that our assignments included more than ferrying the *Wiley Foxes*. One especially unhappy fellow bristled whenever he saw us. Mags and Emmie refused to acknowledge his existence. I ducked my head and scurried past him enduring his barbs and sullen glares, but Delores answered back with growing rage. In the course of the last week, she ended up in a cussing match twice. The second time, Emmie and Tommy McDougal rescued her when the conversation escalated to yelling and pushing. The angry young man, taught never to hit a girl, withdrew at Tommy's command, his fists clenched and his face red with outrage.

Delores was cursed with ambition. Unless you are a nurse or a schoolteacher, the world can be a frustrating place for an ambitious woman. If she had been dull or plain, she might have been forgiven her assertiveness. As it was, men felt compelled to conquer her and women viewed her with a mixture of disapproval and jealousy.

Tommy McDougal was in love with her. I do think Delores liked Tommy more than she liked most men, but they were as different as two people could be. He was Episcopalian, she was Jewish. Having

131

already risked his life once over Germany, he was cautious. Delores pushed herself, her airplanes, and everyone around her. She wanted things he couldn't imagine. I wasn't hopeful for them. Yet, they spent every moment they could find together and she at least seemed happy with the status quo.

The train chugged through miles of orange groves. When the sun burst through the window a couple hours later, her eyes glittered with tears. I handed her my handkerchief. The chain around her neck no longer held her Grandmother's sapphire. She saw my gaze and touched the empty necklace at the base of her throat, her upper lip quivering.

"What happened to it?" I asked.

She blew her nose. "I hocked it."

I leaned forward in my seat. "But why, Delores? If you needed money, you could have come to me or Mags."

A sob caught in her throat — an odd, choking sound. "There's nothing you can do, Shirley. The world has gone crazy or maybe it was always crazy and I never noticed."

"What's happened?"

"The Nazis are killing people. Whole communities. Thousands at a time."

My heart dropped to my toes. "Your cousins?"

"Everyone."

"Oh, Delores, that can't be true." The Nazis stomped around in high boots and funny mustaches. They were fools, not monsters.

"One of the boys got out. He got into some kind of trouble early on. I never did find out what he did. Anyway, he left Mannheim in early 1940 and headed east. The war followed him. He got as far as Lithuania and for a while, it looked like the jig was up, as the German advance seemed unstoppable. Then he found out that there was a chance he could get out through Russia before the Soviets closed the border. The Japanese counsel in Kaunas was leaving himself, but he spent three weeks giving out transit visas. People were standing in line day and night to get one. "

"A Japanese?" I was astounded. It wasn't the image I had of Japan.

"Hans was one of the last ones to get a visa. He went to Moscow while the going was good. Somehow from there he got to Japan. He wrote a letter to his parents back in Mannheim. My cousin Gretchen told us about it when she came to Pittsburgh back in 1941."

"My God, Delores."

"I know. I can't figure it out either. How could they rescue so many people from the Nazis and then turn around and bomb us?" The train rocked back and forth. She reached out to steady herself as we made a long slow turn.

"What happened to the others?"

"You know I told you they were sent to some kind of camp in France?"

I nodded, remembering the night she'd told me about her cousin Annaliese and Annaliese's little girl, Rosa.

"The Red Cross told us that the Nazis liquidated the camp they were in and nobody knows where they took them."

"I'm sure they are fine." I tried to reassure her.

"Now we are hearing that the Germans have set up extermination camps."

"What's that?"

"Where they take people to be gassed and cremated." She bit her lower lip.

"You can't mean that!" I gripped my purse. "All of them?"

"Grammas and Grampas and babies. Jews mostly — but others too. Communists. Gypsies. Retarded people."

I sat back in my seat, biting my lower lip. "It's rumor, Delores. We gathered up all our Japanese citizens when the war first started. You have to do that during times of war when you don't know who is or isn't an enemy. They are in a camp somewhere. When the war is over, they will send them home."

She blew her nose. "I hope you are right. My great aunt is in her seventies. She's my grandmother's twin sister. All this moving around can't be good for her. It scares me that no one knows where they are."

"That's why your grandmother's sapphire?"

She nodded, twirling the empty chain with her long lovely fingers. "It's chaos over there. We are trying to find them and bring them here to the States. It takes money, Shirley. The sapphire will do more good sitting in that pawnshop than hanging around my neck. Maybe I'll get it back someday."

I decided to talk to Father again. Perhaps the magazine had information to ease Delores' mind. Maybe Father could find Annaliese and little Rosa.

Señor whimpered in his sleep and she covered him with a baby blanket. "Tommy took me dancing at the Hollywood Canteen last night after I wired the money to my father. I couldn't think. I couldn't talk. We just held each other and shuffled around the dance floor."

"Tommy's swell," I said.

"Yeah, he's swell." She turned to watch the landscape flash past our window.

#

Grant Logan met us at the train station around noon three days later. "GRANT! GRANT!" Several cars away, he couldn't hear me over the wheezing train. Holding a small bouquet of daisies wrapped in newspaper, he scanned each car. I leaned out the window and waved until our eyes linked.

"Hello! There you are!" He hurried to meet us as we stepped onto the platform. He seemed flustered by Delores' presence. He shook my hand and then he gave me the flowers. Blushing, he shook my hand again. I was touched and pleased.

"You are in time for the Blood Drive," he informed us, shifting from foot to foot.

"Oh good, a Blood Drive." Delores set Señor on the platform and attached a leash to his silver collar. The little dog sniffed Grant's shoe and raised his leg.

Grant jumped backwards in alarm. "Don't you think that collar is a little la-di-dah for a male pooch?"

Señor strained at his leash looking for another object to mark. "He is offended that you question his masculinity," Delores said. "It's been a long way since our last stop. I wouldn't get in his way if I were you."

Grant fiddled with his hearing aids. "I think he's embarrassed to be seen in public in that thing." His voice was over loud.

"I think you are jealous because you don't have anything quite so grand, Grant Logan." Delores paused to allow Señor to snuffle around a garbage can and then a few steps later, he lifted his leg at a fire hydrant.

"How are things going at the factory?" I asked.

Grant took my elbow and led me towards Father's Plymouth, which was parked at the far end of the platform. A soft spring breeze caressed our faces. Delores trailed along behind us, letting Señor get some exercise and giving me a little privacy with Grant. "You got a letter from Lizzie." His voice almost too low now.

"How is she?"

"I didn't open it. It was addressed to you in care of me at the factory. I gave it to Myrtle and she put it with your other mail at the inn."

"That was thoughtful."

135

"I'm a thoughtful guy." He tossed my duffel and Delores' into the trunk of the Plymouth. He glanced back. Delores and Señor were still several yards back. "I missed you."

No one had ever missed me before. "I wasn't gone that long."

"That's not what you are supposed to say." He took my right hand and held it in both of his.

It was the first time he'd ever touched me that way. "What did you want me to say?"

"That you missed me too. That it seemed like forever."

I opened my mouth to say just those words but others came out. "You are nice, Grant." I stumbled. "It was a complicated week, but I did think about you."

"NICE?" He put his lower lip out like a naughty boy.

I laughed. There was something about Grant I couldn't put my finger on. Something familiar. I liked him but I couldn't understand his interest in me. "Well, you *are* nice," I said, blushing.

He lifted my hand to his lips. His kiss was proper, yet my body tingled. "I want to take you home to meet my folks, Shirley. You'll like them and they'll like you." He opened the passenger door.

"Sure," I said, my mind focused on my physical reaction. It was troubling and intriguing at the same time. "When?"

"Tonight."

"Oh, Grant. I just got home. I need to unpack, take a bath, wash my hair."

"You have all afternoon. I'll come for you around six. Mom is fixing something special, an old family recipe, Sauerbraten. She saved all our ration stamps for a week to get the roast."

"You were pretty sure of yourself. What if I was busy tonight? What if the train had been delayed?" I was torn between being annoyed and being flattered. Grant was as pushy as he was sweet.

136

"Not me. Mom. She was sure you'd come. She's making a peach kuchen for you."

I wasn't sure what a kuchen was, but the idea of someone preparing something just for me was enchanting. Of course, there's no way I could have refused after his mother went to such trouble.

Delores and Señor approached the car. Grant closed my door and hurried around to help Delores and Señor into the backseat. I glanced over my shoulder. No longer joking, Delores shuttered her eyes against the spring sun, sitting quietly with Señor in her lap stroking his head with her knuckles.

At *The Windshift Inn*, Grant helped us unload our bags before parking Father's car out back. "I'll be back at six," he waved as he crawled into the *Wiley Aircraft* bus. Everyone was at work and the house was quiet. Delores and Señor climbed the backstairs slowly as if very tired. I set my duffel by the kitchen door and fixed myself a small lunch. I found it hard to eat on the train. Sitting at Myrtle's butcher-block table sipping a glass of milk and snacking on toast spread with apple butter, I opened Lizzie Langer's letter. It was only a few words in smeared ink. *"I'm afraid. The baby is a monster eating me alive. I don't even recognize myself anymore. I'd rather die."*

Choking on my lunch, I checked the date on the envelope. It was postmarked a week ago. I hurried to the phone hanging on the wall in the hallway.

"Hello, Virginia? Can you get me Myrtle Jones? She's at work. At *Wiley.*"

The operator assured me *Wiley Aircraft* would not allow women on the assembly line to come to the phone. I sat down, wringing my hands. Lizzie was so far away, so young. It would be several hours before Myrtle came home. Maybe I should call Father. Thoughts bounced around in my mind like careening billiard balls.

"What's wrong?" Delores stood on the stairs with Señor under her arm. She'd changed out of her slacks into a long sleeved wool dress

137

and scrubbed her face clean of any makeup. It was one of the few times I saw her wear her hair down.

My eyes met hers. No one was supposed to know about Lizzie — only Grant and Myrtle. "Someone's in trouble," I whispered, echoing Myrtle's words to me the day I first met Lizzie.

"The girl you took to Cleveland?" She must have been guessing. Then of course, she was there that day, watching me pull out of the driveway with Grant and Lizzie in the car. Numb, I handed the letter to Delores who scanned it. "Let's send her a telegram," she folded it in quarters and handed it back to me.

"Yes. Let's do that." I went back to the telephone. "Virginia? This is Shirley Maxwell. Can you connect me to Western Union? Thanks."

Delores opened the icebox and poured Señor a small saucer of milk. He lapped loudly as I dictated the wire.

"Dear Lizzie. Stop. Please call me at *The Windshift Inn*. Stop. Shirley Maxwell. Stop."

I hung up the phone. "Do you think she will?"

"What else can you do, Shirley? You let her know you care. Now, you go about getting ready for your date."

"What if she calls back?"

"I'll be here — and Myrtle. If she calls, we'll have Virginia transfer the call to Grant's house." She sat at the table, rolling a small blue marble from hand to hand.

"You aren't going out?" I was surprised. She had at least four boyfriends in Cold Creek.

"I don't feel like it. Think I'll just sit in the parlor, play a little piano, listen to the radio."

"Are you sick?" She was pale, but I knew what was bothering her. At a stopover in Indianapolis, I'd wired Father with questions about what was happening in Europe. I hoped he'd get back to me with news soon. I couldn't stand seeing her this way.

138

"Just a little blue. You go get ready for Grant. I'll stand guard duty for Lizzie."

I stood at the foot of the stairs trying to decide what to say. "It can't be true, Delores. It just can't be. The Germans are civilized. Civilized nations don't kill innocent people."

The marble rolled off the table and rattled across the kitchen floor. Señor chased the small glass ball until it bounced off the wall and went under the stove. "I hope you are right," she said.

I went upstairs to get ready.

#

Myrtle stood at the foot of the stairs, a frilly white apron over her coveralls, her hands covered with flour. "Goodness, you look beautiful."

I smiled at her. I did look nice, I thought. I'd smoothed my pageboy back from my face and covered it with Emmie's crocheted hairnet. The other girls wore hairnets all the time, but I'd never tried it until now. It was a bit trendy for me. I spent a long time choosing my clothes. I wore a borrowed dark green dress with a wide black belt, padded shoulders, and short sleeves. The bodice was too low for my taste, so I covered my upper chest with a deep red scarf and secured it with a round gold pin near the throat. Instead of my usual oxfords and anklets, I wore low-heeled black pumps and my one pair of nice stockings. I finished the costume with dark red wrist-length gloves.

"You look great in green." Delores stuck her head around the doorframe behind Myrtle. Señor poked his head between their legs and yapped. I started down the backstairs hanging onto the banister. I wasn't used to dress shoes and I was afraid of sliding down the wooden steps on my behind.

"Look at Shirley, Mr. McKensey," Myrtle turned as the old man came in the kitchen door. "She's going to have dinner at the Logans' tonight."

139

Mr. McKensey growled as he clumped up the stairs towards me. I shrank against the banister to give him plenty of room to pass. "Not bad, kid," he whispered as he turned at the landing and headed towards his room. I negotiated the last few steps smiling in spite of myself.

"What did he say to you?" Delores asked. "You are thirteen shades of red."

"He didn't say anything."

"Nasty old curmudgeon." Delores went back to her potato mashing.

"That's a mighty big word, Delores." Myrtle teased. "You know what it means?"

"Yep, I looked it up in the dictionary after I met Mr. McKensey."

Someone knocked on the front door.

"I'll get it," One of the *Wiley* girls called from the parlor.

"No, I'll get it." I ran to get there first. As soon as I hit the hardwood flooring in the hall, my slippery heels skidded and I swung my arms to keep my balance just as the young girl opened the door. My eyes met Grant's. I smoothed my skirt and patted my hair, pretending to be calm. I heard Myrtle and Delores laughing in the kitchen.

"Hi, Mr. Logan." The girl stepped back in surprise. "What can I do for you?"

"I came to pick up Shirley." He nodded towards me. I was frozen like a dressmaker's dummy.

She turned to look at me in my finery. "Oh," she said. "OH!"

"Cut that out," he laughed as he stepped inside the door.

"Yes sir!" She went back into the parlor. "Hey, guys. Mr. Logan's here to pick up Shirley." We heard giggling and a half-dozen heads peeped around the doorframe at us.

"I think we better get out of here, don't you?" Helping me into my sweater, he leaned down and whispered into my ear, "You are lovely, Shirley."

I beamed with delight knowing Myrtle and Delores were watching. Grant guided me down the stoop, his hand at the small of my back. He was driving his father's delivery van, a woodie with *Logan's Groceries* painted in bright red block letters. He lifted me up into the high seat. The delivery van was better than the *Wiley Aircraft* bus but not much.

Mr. and Mrs. Logan were shorter, rounder, and blonder than Grant. They lived in a large apartment above the store on Sugar Street in downtown Cold Creek. Everything was scrubbed and in perfect order. Stepping into the living room, I was assailed with bright colors and a thick, cinnamon scent. Grant's mom buzzed around with a plate of goose liver hors d'oeuvres and pressed a cup of warm apple cider into my hands. Mr. Logan examined me over small gold-rimmed glasses and offered me his favorite chair. As I sat down, I saw a large crocheted American flag mounted flush to the wall over the mantle.

Family pictures filled their home. There were two boys younger than Grant. One was in the Navy. He joined the same day as Myrtle's son Ricky and Jerry's oldest Danny back in 1942. The youngest Logan boy, only seventeen, was in basic training in North Carolina. Mr. Logan picked up each framed photograph and gave me a detailed assessment of each boy's military career. Mrs. Logan talked about the joys and tribulations of raising three sons in a small town. She described their growing horror when they realized Grant couldn't hear. They saved for years to provide him with hearing aids. She regaled me with stories about his fascination with noise when he got them at aged fourteen. From crumpling paper to a whistling teakettle, he was delighted with each new sound. I laughed at the image of Grant at seventeen sticking his head inside the horn of the Victrola and tapping his toe to the music of Rudy Vallee.

141

Dinner was hearty and delicious. Kuchen became my favorite dessert. I didn't talk much. I didn't have to. Arial and John Logan filled the air with chatter about the life of merchants, the ration system, and the hell of the Depression a decade in the past. I was surprised to learn they went to school with Jerry and Suzie Kline and Myrtle and Richard Jones back in the early years of the century. Everyone got jobs and married and began their families in the mid 1910's. They grieved when their friend Suzie Kline died of measles in 1937 leaving Jerry to cope with two children. When Dickie Jones was run over by a Cleveland streetcar, Myrtle had been inconsolable. She struggled for years barely making do with the income produced by *The Windshift Inn*, which had been Dickie's old family home. Then the war came along and business at the inn picked up. She also got work at the factory as a welder, of all things. Finally, their worries for Myrtle had waned. It was an odd fact that their eldest son was now their school chum's supervisor.

"You must come see us again," Arial held both my hands.

"I'd love to come back. Thanks so much for having me. The kuchen was divine."

"Let her go, Mom. We have places to go and people to see." Grant held up my sweater and I slipped my arms into the sleeves.

"You are a good girl, Shirley. We like you for our Grant."

I flushed. "Thank you, ma'am."

"Good-bye, Shirley. We look forward to seeing you again." John Logan stood inside the screen door, his arm around his wife, as Grant helped me down off the loading dock.

"Shall we go for a walk before going back?" Grant took my gloved hand.

We walked around the corner of Sugar Street and headed down Main. "Your family is wonderful, Grant. I've never been around a home where there is a father and a mother."

He cupped his ear.

"YOUR MOTHER AND FATHER."

He nodded. "I wish my brothers were here so you could meet them too."

"I look forward to that. I can't wait until the war ends."

"I'm afraid it won't end anytime soon. The Germans will fight every step of the way back to Berlin."

"I'm frightened. What if they win? What if they do take over the world? Delores says they are killing civilians."

"People get killed in war. Bombs can't tell the difference between soldiers and grocers," he said.

"No, not like that. She says they are gathering up everyone in small towns and neighborhoods and taking them to camps where they are gassed." I shuddered at the thought.

"Where did she hear that?" He frowned as we stopped in front of the Rialto. *Going My Way* was showing.

"Rumors."

He wrung his hands and paced back and forth. "I don't believe it," he said finally. "I can't believe it."

"I sent Father a telegram to see if he heard anything about it. If they were killing that many people, don't you think we'd know?"

He grabbed my upper arms and turned me to face him. "Please don't say anything about this to my parents."

"What do you mean?"

"Their parents came from Germany. It was a horrible position to be in during the first war and it's no easier now. People look at us and wonder — are we spies? Are we the enemy?"

"Grant, you are as American as anyone I know. You are involved in home defense, blood drives, and worker productivity. Both of your brothers are in the service." I touched his cheek with the back of my

143

fingers — and then jerked them back slightly. It was the first time I'd reached out to him.

He put his hand over mine and pressed it against the side of his face. "I love this country. I was born here. My parents were born here. My family has been here since 1886. My grandfather changed his name to Logan in 1914. Cold Creek is my home and these are my neighbors." He gestured with his head to the darkened town around us. "I've never even met a German who lives in Germany. All the same, I am German to a lot of people. If this is true, it won't make things any easier."

"It doesn't make sense," I said. "Why would they invade a country, then gather up people, and kill them? I thought they wanted to be Masters of the World. I thought they wanted natural resources. Aren't people natural resources?"

He stared at me for a moment. "They most certainly are. That's why we have women and old people working at the factory. We need those resources for the war effort. When the war is over, we'll have plenty of men, and the women can go back to their homes and families and the old folks can return to retirement." He took my hand and we headed back towards Logan's Groceries.

"You wouldn't think of killing your workers," I said. His stride was twice as long as mine and I puffed to keep up with him.

He stopped and turned to me. "They do hate Jews. They feel about the Jews like we feel about the Japanese and Negroes."

"We haven't killed those people though, Grant."

He seemed relieved at the thought. "No, we haven't."

#

Back at the loading dock, he lifted me into the passenger seat of the old truck. Crawling in on the driver's side, he started the engine. "Are you too warm?" He scooted towards my side of the bench seat and reached around me to roll down my window. A cool breeze

144

filled the compartment with the scent of flowers. I stiffened, terrified and thrilled.

"Shirley." He turned my face towards his and kissed my lips. It had been thirteen years since I'd been kissed. The kiss went on for several moments. He smelled of good things — comforting things like starch and soap and tooth powder and cinnamon. The kiss deepened. Something inside me burst and I kissed him back sliding my arms around his neck. He grunted in surprise and his tenderness turned to passion. He nuzzled my neck below my left ear and I pressed myself against his body. Every nerve ending was alive for the first time in my adult life.

"Wow," he said before I covered his mouth with soft kisses. He pulled away panting.

I took a deep breath, smoothing my clothes. Trembling. I only half-remembered these feelings. I had kept them at bay for a long time. I was embarrassed. "I … I'm sorry," I said, afraid he was put off by my forwardness.

"Don't be." He leaned over to kiss me again, this time only grazing my skin. "But I think I better take you home. I can't stand much more of that."

"Me either." I pulled the hairnet off and shook my head. I felt better — more like me.

He put the truck in gear and we headed out towards *The Windshift Inn*. We spent several more minutes in the turnaround wrapped in each other's arms. Even though he was close shaven, my cheeks burned from rubbing against his face. "I think we better stop now," I said. "I need to think about this."

"So do I." Grant straightened himself and got out of the truck. Instead of setting me down on my feet, he carried me to the door of the inn and gave me one last kiss before putting me on the steps. "Tomorrow night?"

145

"Tomorrow." I waved as he disappeared into the night. Inside the door, I hurried to the darkened parlor to watch him leave through the front windows.

"That was some pretty good kissing." Delores switched on the lamp. She was sitting on the couch beneath the windows. Señor sat up in her lap, his bat ears perked.

I knelt on the couch beside her and lifted the shade to peer out. Grant's taillights were disappearing. "I can't believe myself," I said.

"You are human, Shirley. When are you going to allow yourself that pleasure?"

"Tonight, I guess."

Delores stood up and put her hand on my shoulder. "Good for you."

"You got a telegram tonight." She said over her shoulder as she and Señor went up to bed.

I sat for a moment, my mind full of Grant and how he felt in my arms. Going into the kitchen, I collected my telegram and poured myself a small glass of milk. The thought of sleeping in a real bed after the long, long train trip was inviting. I started up the steep steps. At the landing, I peered down the hallway. A beam of light glowed beneath the closed bathroom door. Delores must be taking a bath, I thought. In the dormitory, I opened the telegram. It was from Father. I took a sip of milk.

"RUMOR OF EXTERMINATION CAMPS MIGHT BE TRUE. STOP. EVIDENCE. STOP. NO PROOF. STOP. FATHER."

CHAPTER 12 — SEÑOR

"Dionne Quintuplets Celebrate 10th Birthday, French Patriots Hit Enemy Supply Lines, Ice Cream Quota Up 30,000 Gallons
Headlines
*~ **American View Daily** ~*
Early June, 1944

Lightning lit up the windows and rain pounded on the roof. There was a noise downstairs. I snuggled under my blankets, not wanting to wake up. Mags and Emmie clambered up the steps of *The Windshift Inn*. Señor, sleeping under the covers at the foot of Delores' bed, squeaked with alarm. I got up to let them in, flipping on the overhead lights. When I opened the door, the rank smell of damp, unwashed bodies wafted over me. They came in, dropping their duffels at their feet.

"Wake up, sleeping beauties." Mags stripped off her khaki slacks and her yellowing white blouse and tossed them into her laundry basket. "I'm so glad to get out of these nasty things."

"What are you guys doing here?" Delores sat up in bed, yawning. "I thought you had assignments at Camp Morgan." Her eyes were puffy and red. I wondered how much sleep she got any more.

"Connie sent us to deliver a couple of generals to Texas." She put on a long red flannel robe.

I scurried back to bed, pulling the blankets up around my chin and covering my face with my pillow. "You've been to Texas since we left Camp Morgan?"

Emmie pulled off her boots. The sour odor of her wet socks filled the room. "We've been to jail since we last saw you."

"Jail?" I pulled my pillow down to my chest. "Why were you in jail?"

"Our main offense was being in Texas as I understand it." Mags gathered up her towel, washcloth, and expensive soap. "It was icky

147

in there too." She shuddered and stuck out her tongue in disgust. "I'm off to the showers, before the hordes take over." Her bare feet thudded against the cold floor as she hurried down the hall.

Emmie, dark circles under her eyes, stripped off her damp uniform. Then, she lay back on her bed, in her underwear.

"Well, I, for one, can't stand this. You must tell us what happened." Delores sat with her legs crossed Indian style, wrapping her quilt around her shoulders. Señor stood beside her, his tail wagging.

"The same day you left, Colonel Simpson called us to his office and asked if we'd take these two generals to Austin using a B-17 which would be picked up by two other pilots and flown to Florida. That was easy. Then, in Austin, they had a trainer they wanted us to deliver to Sweetwater. That was kind of fun — to go back, you know. We had dinner in that little diner where we used to go, remember?" She nudged Delores' bed with her foot.

"Did you get some lemon pie?" Delores picked up Señor and rubbed his belly.

"Oh yeah, it was marvelous." Emmie smiled at the memory of that particular sweet. "Anyway, they had a couple of AT-6s they wanted us to deliver to a small field in Oklahoma where they installed new radios. Then they wanted us to take them back to Sweetwater and at Sweetwater, they had a couple of *Wileys* that needed to go to Houston. By then we'd been flying for three days with nothing but catnaps here and there and we were looking pretty bedraggled."

"Bedraggled doesn't begin to cover how you look." Delores yawned and stretched.

"I've run into dead polecats smelled better than we do." Emmie sniffed her own armpit and made a face. "We thought we would be back to Camp Morgan the same day so we didn't even bring a change of clothes. We rinsed our underwear in bathroom sinks, and brushed our teeth with our fingers."

"So what about jail?" I sat with arms wrapped around my lower legs.

"Hold on, Hoss. I'm getting there," Emmie chuckled. "We got out of Sweetwater late in the afternoon. It started getting dark soon after we passed Austin, so we found a small town with an airstrip and landed. Right off the bat, we ran into this fellow who was hesitant about letting us leave the planes at the airport overnight. He said he'd never seen anything like us and how did he know we weren't spies."

"Spies? That's a new one." Delores laughed.

"I guess he was pretty scared because he called the sheriff after we left. We were walking down Main Street looking for a place to eat when this old cop stopped us. We told him who we were. We were even wearing our wings. He explained that this was a decent town and they didn't take to strange women in pants." Emmie unwrapped a candy bar. She must have raided Simpson's office again.

Mags stood at the door rubbing a towel through her short hair. "The word got out. There were people peeking out windows and standing on the street corners. This little town didn't have any war industries. No Rosie the Riveters and they didn't want any either, just a farming community with not much contact with 'big city' folks." She sat down on her bed and stretched.

"Old Sheriff Trembly was a nervous guy. His hands shook and the left side of his face sagged. He should have been in the hospital rather than out arresting smelly women in slacks." Emmie collected clean underwear and her robe out of her chest of drawers. "Speaking of, I better get my shower too," she said with her cheeks full of chocolate.

"Please do." Delores held her nose between her forefinger and thumb.

"No, finish telling us what happened," I insisted.

149

"Not much more to tell. Needless to say, Sheriff Trembly was unimpressed with our explanations. He never heard of WASP and he was mighty suspicious of our presence in his fair town. FDR would never allow such an outrageous thing as women pilots so clearly we were lying. He even asked if we were a couple of perverts." Mags laughed.

Emmie paused at the door. "I figured him for an uninformed Democrat, but Mags thought he was a fallen away Republican. Anyway, rather than let us sully up Main Street, he threw us in the clink."

"They didn't even clean out the cells from the last residents who had very poor aim when it came to the toilet, by the way. We did see an old friend while we relaxed in our odiferous accommodations." Mags held up her khaki pants. The knees and rear end were stretched out. "Another day and they could stand up by themselves." She crawled into bed and snuggled under a fluffy blanket.

"Okay, I give. What old friend?" I asked.

"Kilroy." Mags rolled over to face us. "Written on the wall in chalk or something."

I didn't understand why everyone thought it was so funny to draw big-nosed, round-eyed gremlins on every fence or wall or rock in the country and then scrawl below them, 'Kilroy was here!' I mean who the devil was Kilroy and who cares if he's been there? "So how did you get out?"

"We called Connie." Mags voice was muffled, the blanket pulled up to just under her nose.

"And he got you out?"

"Actually, no. He told Sheriff Trembly that nothing better happen to that B-17 and when he realized we had already delivered it, he hung up." Emmie leaned against the doorframe and sighed. "The old fool didn't know what to do so he left us to deal with it ourselves."

150

"We called Jackie but she wasn't there and didn't call back until yesterday morning. She chewed Sheriff Trembly out left and right. We could hear her voice over the phone. The poor old fellow was insulted to have a woman talk to him that way but he finally understood that we worked for the government." Mags yawned. "His fear of G-men over-rode his disapproval, so he let us go."

"We were starving by that time so we went to a coffee shop on Main Street and ordered breakfast," Emmie said. "The waitress, the cook, the other customers all glared at us like we'd come in to rob the place. These folks were worse than the guys at Camp Morgan. They acted like they hated us. I was glad to get out of there." She sighed and wandered down the hall to the bathroom.

"It gets to you after a bit, doesn't it?" Delores' eyes gazed inward. "If they can hate you for no reason, they can kill you for no reason too."

Mags lifted her head up over her covers to look at Delores and then me. I shrugged. "It's not personal. We are changing things. The war is changing things. That scares folks. Scared people are angry. Let's face it, a lot of the fellows at Camp Morgan went to Connie before we got there and wanted to be transferred. They didn't even know us. They were just trying to protect their way of life, where the rules make sense to them."

"Where the rules *favor* them," Delores murmured.

"Well, sure. That's why they are scared." Mags winked at me and pulled the covers over her head.

#

We slept until noon. After raiding the refrigerator, we decided to go down to Jerry's and work on the Stearman. A big stack of sheets lay in the far corner. Other than that, not much had been accomplished. Delores set Señor on the floor and he trotted over to chew on the wing tip. Mags went off to check on her plane while Emmie and I wandered through the wreckage picking up first one piece and then another.

"It seems hopeless," I tossed a wing rib back into the pile. "I don't have a clue where to start."

Emmie laid an altimeter on the floor. "Wayne found this for us. The faceplate was smashed. He replaced the glass but he doesn't think anything else is broken — maybe the rim is bent a little bit." Señor sniffed it.

"You think it works?"

She shrugged. "He hasn't found much information yet, but he did suggest it might be easier to build a whole new plane from the parts we have. He drew up this plan."

The drawing was detailed yet simple — a beautiful piece of artwork. I didn't trust Wayne since the cartoon incident and I wondered if he was giving Emmie parts stolen from the government. However, the man was an artist. I had to give him that. I unfolded the plan and spread it out on the floor.

"Maybe we should tape it up on the wall?" Emmie squatted beside me.

I smoothed the wrinkles, careful to avoid smudging the crisp pencil lines. "Thumb tacks on a piece of plywood, I think." We smiled at each other. I was enthused about the project for the first time.

"He's good, isn't he?" She beamed with pride.

"He has a great future after the war. I'll talk with Father about him."

"That would be nice, Shirley. Wayne needs something to go right for him."

"You've been spending time with him?" Delores asked as she sorted through the sheets Pam had collected over the last few weeks.

"On and off. Right now we are off." She wore her faded blue jeans and red sweater under her leather jacket, her face dark and sad.

"What's wrong?" I asked.

"Wayne and I were getting along pretty well. He took me home to meet his family last week. They have a farm near Camp Morgan not far from the Pacific — thousands of acres of cotton, some soybeans. They told me how afraid they were right after Pearl Harbor. People were sure the Japs were going to hit us again so they were carrying guns and shooting anything that moved. Wayne wanted to get into the fight. Coming from a farm family, he wanted to be a crop duster. After everyone got so frightened, he thought about patrolling the coastline from the air."

"Tommy will teach him to fly," Delores said. "You know how sweet he is about that kind of thing. He says he can teach anyone who's willing to work."

"He tried already and washed out in the first week."

Señor whimpered and Delores knelt to put his leash on his collar. "I'm sorry, Emmie. You know how the military is. They try to rush a bunch of people through and they don't have a lot of time if you have problems. Wayne needs someone to take him up and work with him." She propped open the backdoor. Hooking the leash over the doorknob, she set Señor outside to do his business. I zipped my jacket higher under my chin and stuffed my hands in my pockets.

"I tried that too. I told him he needed time on the stick and he wanted to believe me. So last weekend, we rented a PT-17 and I took him up. We hadn't gotten 100 feet in the air when I hear him gagging. I looked around and he was clinging to the fuselage trying not to puke."

"Vertigo," I whispered.

"Yeah."

"Poor fellow," Delores said as she collected Señor and closed the door. "No wonder he's so hard to figure. He's got to resent us. We are living his dream — and we are girls."

"There's some of that. He's not like the others but it does gall him," Emmie said. "I landed right away but he was embarrassed. I told

153

him it didn't matter. He said, 'Doesn't matter to you,'— and stalked off. He's nice enough when he sees me around Camp Morgan, but something's changed. Somehow seeing me deepens his humiliation."

"Not everyone is meant to fly," Delores said as she examined Wayne's design for the new plane. "Look at this! The man is a great mechanic, a great artist. Hell, he can even design planes. Those talents are beyond most people."

"We want what we can't have," I said. "In fact, how many people appreciate what they have?"

"Me!" Emmie held up her hand and we all laughed.

#

Jerry and Pam Kline were coming to dinner at the inn. Myrtle seemed flustered by the visit and fussed over every detail. Mags donated a ham to the occasion and the rest of us pitched in to make this a special meal.

"Where are those tomatoes I put up last fall," Myrtle muttered as she sorted through a cabinet full of jars.

Delores pushed open the door from the cellar with her behind. She held an armful of potatoes, carrots, and onions she'd fetched. "I couldn't find lima beans, but you have some dried pintos."

"I don't know if Jerry likes pintos," Myrtle said over her shoulder. "Maybe we should just give up the idea of beans?"

"We already have three vegetables," I said as I mixed up batch of cornbread.

"I just want everything to be perfect." Myrtle set two big jars of tomatoes on the counter. "What do you think about applesauce?"

Delores glanced at me, before dumping her armful of vegetables in the sink. "Everything you cook is swell, Myrtle. Not to worry, this will be too."

154

"Delores is right," I said. "When is the last time anyone complained about your food?"

Myrtle wiped her forehead with the back of her hand. "I wish I knew what Jerry likes."

"So what do you want me to do now?" Delores put on an apron and washed her hands.

"Maybe cut up the potatoes and get them boiling. Then grate carrots and onions real fine?"

"Potato pancakes?"

"Do you think he likes potato pancakes?"

Both Delores and I burst out laughing.

"What?" Myrtle glanced from one of us to the other, eyes wide.

"You are as nervous as a long-tailed cat in a room full of rocking chairs." Delores filled a pan with water and set it on the stove.

"I am?" Myrtle covered her mouth with both hands, her round cheeks glowing. "I've known Jerry since we were kids."

"Apparently not well enough to know what he likes to eat."

"Well, I don't know him that way."

"Oh sure," Delores snorted.

"It's just that this war has interrupted everyone's family life." Myrtle turned her back on us and rummaged in a drawer. "And we need to … uh … try to …uh …"

"What are you looking for, Miz Myrtle?" Emmie came into the kitchen with a bag of pecans.

"A knife," Myrtle bent to her task. "To pry open these jar lids."

"You mean this one?" Emmie picked up a flat bladed knife lying on the counter above the drawer.

"Oh!" Myrtle took the knife from Emmie and marched into the dining room which was a dead-end. "Oh!" She turned back around, laid the knife on the counter and went upstairs.

We all giggled.

"What's with Miz Myrtle?" Emmie grabbed a spoon and scooped a mound of sugar into her mouth.

I shuddered and tried not to watch her. "Will you cut that out?"

"Myrtle's nervous because Jerry Kline is coming to dinner."

"And you two have been teasing her?" Emmie spilled the bag of pecans into a bowl and sat down with a nutcracker.

"Of course." Delores grinned.

I felt guilty, but of course, I'd enjoyed the whole thing too.

"Naughty!" Emmie licked the spoon and put it in the sink.

By the time Myrtle composed herself and came back downstairs, I had cornbread in the oven and Emmie had shelled the pecans. Delores had cut-up the potatoes and put them in cold water on the stove. I was grating the carrots and Emmie worked on the onions.

"You girls are wonderful," Myrtle said as she took over for Emmie.

"You know we love you, Miz Myrtle." Emmie pressed her cheek against Myrtle's, trying not to touch her with her oniony hands.

"I'm glad you are back," I said. "None of us has a clue how to make pancakes."

"I'll show you," Myrtle said.

Emmie washed her hands and turned to the jars sitting on the counter. "What did you want to do with the tomatoes?"

"Stew them with some of these onions." Myrtle kept her eyes on the vegetables she was chopping.

156

"Oh, I love stewed tomatoes. So does Father." I had no idea if Father had ever had stewed tomatoes but I wanted to make Myrtle feel good about her choice.

"I like them too," Emmie said as she dumped the contents of the jars into a big sauce pan.

"Well, look at you all." Mags leaned against the doorframe, her arms folded over her chest. "Since when did the three of you get so domestic?"

"We're helping with dinner." I imagined her amusement at seeing George Maxwell's neurotic daughter cooking. I laid down the grater, checked the potatoes and turned up the fire under them.

Mags took off her leather jacket and hung it on the back of one of the kitchen chairs. "Okay," she said, "What do you need me to do?"

#

"Howdy," Jerry Kline took off his hat and held it in front of his chest. He had shaved so close that there was a shiny red abrasion on his chin.

I stepped back to let him in the door. "You're timing is perfect. Dinner will be ready in about fifteen minutes."

"Hi, Shirley!" Pam bounded in the door after him. "I saw your daddy's picture in a magazine down at Logan's store today. He wrote an article about the steel mills in Cleveland."

"That sounds like Father," I said as I hung Jerry's jacket in the hall closet.

"Is he someone important?" She asked as she unwound the scarf around her neck.

"Well, he's important to me."

"Shirley's dad owns that magazine, Pammie," Jerry told her. "He owns a lot of magazines and newspapers around the country."

She blinked. "Wow!"

157

I leaned over and whispered in her ear, "He's just like anyone else's dad. You'd like him."

"Can I meet him someday?" She whispered back.

"I imagine you will. He's always popping up unexpectedly."

"Yeah, my dad does that too," she said as she handed me her coat.

"Hi everyone." Myrtle came down the stairs. She'd changed out of her housedress into the shirtwaist that she usually wore to church.

"Don't you look nice," Jerry told her.

Pam counted the place settings I'd carefully arranged on the dining room table. "Aren't the other girls gonna eat with us?"

"They all have dates, it seems," I told her. "It's just the seven of us and Mr. McKensey."

"Well, where is he?"

"He's still up in his room," Myrtle said. "Why don't you go tell him that dinner will be ready in a few minutes?"

"Do I have to?"

"Pam!" Jerry seemed shocked by Pam's rudeness.

"It's okay," I said. "I have to run upstairs anyway." I thought I understood her little rebellion. Mr. McKensey wasn't the friendliest soul. Even so, I felt bad for him. He seemed so upset all the time.

"Thank you, Shirley. Remind him that Jerry and I are going to the movies tonight, so we are going to eat a half-hour early."

"I will." I climbed the backstairs, pausing on the second floor. A board squeaked underfoot when I approached Mr. McKensey's door

"I can hear you out there. Don't think you can sneak up on a fellow and get away with it." Mr. McKensey's voice was hoarse and I knew I'd caught him smoking.

The door was ajar. I rapped lightly on the frame. "It's me, Mr. McKensey. Shirley Maxwell."

158

"Don't just stand there. Come on in."

He stood in front of his slightly open window, blowing smoke out and breathing in the cold night air. He half-turned to face me. "Ever think about the past, young lady?"

I opened my mouth, but nothing came out.

"I thought not. Young people look forward."

"Maybe the past is too ugly," I said.

Mr. McKensey cocked his head. "Maybe. At my age, you realize there's not much future left."

I looked around. His bed was made. A stack of books sat on his nightstand with a pair of reading glasses and a lamp. He'd carefully arranged old photographs on top of his bureau. I wished Emmie and Delores kept their things as neat. "I realized that a long time ago, Mr. McKensey."

He put out his cigar and closed the window. "So what do you want?"

"Want?" I racked my brain. I wasn't sure there was anything that I wanted. To avoid trouble, maybe? No, trouble was what I didn't want. That wasn't the same thing as wanting something.

"You didn't come up here for a visit." Mr. McKensey sat down in an overstuffed easy chair.

"Oh." I avoided his eyes. "Yes. Myrtle wants to go to the movies with Jerry Kline tonight. So dinner will be a half hour early. She wanted me to remind you."

"Ha!"

His sarcastic laugh embarrassed me more. "I'll see you at dinner, Mr. McKensey." I closed his door behind me a little harder than I intended. The old coot!

#

159

"That little stinker sure loves ham," Myrtle chuckled as she slipped Señor a piece under the table.

"You spoil him." I crinkled my nose. "All of you do."

Everyone burst out laughing.

"Like you don't?" Delores nudged me with her elbow.

"What does that mean, I wonder," said Emmie.

"What does what mean?" Delores leaned down to feed the sweet little creature something from her plate.

"What does it mean to spoil someone?"

I bit my tongue. Everyone knows what it means to be spoiled, for goodness sake.

"It means that someone gets everything that they want," Pammie spoke up.

"What's wrong with that?" Emmie looked at me and raised one eyebrow.

"Spoiled people are ungrateful for what they have. They misbehave," I said. "They don't appreciate what others do for them."

"I don't think Señor is ungrateful." Delores smiled down at the little dog licking her fingers.

"Maybe it means that someone gets something that he doesn't deserve?" Pam tried again.

Mags poured herself another glass of wine. "Why wouldn't someone deserve a piece of ham? Or anything really?"

I could understand Mags. She and I were the children of wealthy families. We had nice clothes and good food and plenty of toys and books. We'd gone to good schools. I don't think I'd call either of us spoiled, exactly.

160

"I've always wondered how having something nice could be a bad thing," Emmie said. "Seems to me that generosity teaches someone how to be generous."

"Seems to me, that being spoiled means that you have received gifts but don't feel any responsibility for returning kindness back to the giver." Mr. McKensey caught Myrtle's eye and winked. "I don't see anyone like that sitting around this table."

#

Myrtle and Jerry left for the movies. Mr. McKensey went back to his room. The rest of us cleared the table and washed the dishes before retiring to the parlor. Delores knelt in front of the big Zenith radio, twisting the knobs until the soft strains of Tommy Dorsey's band floated through the room. She closed her eyes and hummed — her arms outstretched, swaying to the beat. Señor stood at her feet, wagging his tail.

I sat in the caned-back rocking chair, my knees together — not rocking. Myrtle's tiffany lampshade softened the light. It was more peaceful here than in California. Normally, we weren't allowed to stay on military bases. It was another case of Colonel Simpson stretching the rules for Jackie Cochran. I didn't fool myself. If anyone ever complained, we'd be stowed in a cheap tourist court in the blink of an eye. Besides, the Quonset hut was military drab inside and outside — not very homey.

"What happened to your arm?" Delores pointed to a bandage on Pam's wrist, peeking out from her cuff.

"I burned it. Caught my sleeve on fire putting wood into the heating stove at the hanger."

"My God! Is it a bad burn?"

"No, not bad, but I'm afraid of fire. Danny and I saw a big fire at the circus the summer he left. All the animals burned up. My wool shirt smelled like those poor lions and camels and zebras and elephants. I acted like a baby and got Daddy all upset." Pam ducked her head

161

and fidgeted. I could understand why Pam was embarrassed. I hated when my father got upset too, especially when it was my fault.

"Hey, I would have cried too. Fire is pretty scary stuff." Emmie comforted her with a quick hug. "Don't be so hard on yourself."

"I couldn't sleep for a while after the circus. After I caught my sleeve on fire, I sat up all night thinking about dying." She shuddered.

Delores shuddered too.

Emmie peeled back the tape and examined Pam's burned forearm. She could look right at things I couldn't bear to see. I didn't remember my mother, but I sometimes imagined she was like Emmie — someone who could look at the ugly parts and still like you. "It's not too bad," she said as she replaced the bandage. "It's already healing."

"Yeah, I'm fine now."

Emmie stroked her ragged hair. "What happened here?"

Pam touched the shorter side of her bangs. "It was singed around the edges so I cut it off."

"Mm. I bet you'd look cute with your hair fixed up like Delores'." I could never figure Emmie. Here we were talking about bad dreams, then out of the blue, she starts in on Pam's hair.

"Sure, I think it would look great on her," Delores agreed. "We'd need to wet it down and then pin curl it, but I think it would take. If not, I have a curling iron." With all this fuss over Pam's hair, I hoped someone would trim it evenly.

"Why don't you stay with us tonight, Pammie? We'll have a pajama party." Emmie wrapped a strand of Pam's dark hair around her finger and cocked her head to evaluate its curlability. "Let's make popcorn and hot chocolate."

"Yeeha!" Delores perked up. It was like the effort to be cheery cheered her. I wasn't sure what was going on. Delores and Emmie

162

did that a lot, like they knew something, the rest of us didn't. "We can do your hair, sit up all night, and talk about men."

"I don't know anything about men." Pam's eyes were huge.

Delores mimicked Mae West, one hand on her hip, one patting the back of her hair. "Sure you do, you just don't know you know it yet."

"I do?" Pam stood up and mimicked Delores, rocking her hips from side to side and grinning. It was pretty funny. Delores turned the radio up and pivoted around, shaking one finger in the air to the upbeat rhythm. Pam giggled and copied her movements as best she could. Emmie clapped her hands with delight and I smothered a smile. Emmie jumped to her feet and pulled me out of my chair, whipping me around in an awkward jitterbug. Emmie wasn't a good dancer but she was enthusiastic. She held one of my hands and we leaned back and spun in a circle. I stumbled along trying to follow her lead, gasping for breath. It was the most fun I'd ever had. On the final chords, Emmie and I flopped down on the sofa, her full skirt settling over her like a parachute.

After a moment, Frank Sinatra's mellow voice filled the room.

"Oh, I love that song," Emmie squealed. "I'll be seeing you ...," she sang, hugging herself, her eyes closed. Pam made a face like she tasted something sour and I shrugged. Delores frowned at both of us and began singing loudly too, her arms around Pam, rocking back and forth. I guess how well you sing doesn't matter if you are having fun. After a moment, Pam and I sang too.

As the last note faded away, I noticed tears in Emmie's eyes. "It makes me think of Hoppy," she smiled.

I hadn't realized. "I'm so sorry," I said.

"Don't be. It's a happy memory."

"But it made you cry!" Pam's face melted.

"Not all tears are bad." Emmie rubbed her eyes and sighed. "Sometimes they are a sign of how much something touches you."

Pam and I stared at her blankly. I had no idea what she meant. You cry when you are hurt, when you are mad, and when you are sad. I didn't understand tears like hers.

"I've been so lucky in my life. Each day has been special." Emmie seemed overcome with the thought. Her chin quivered and I wondered how she could say such a thing. Abandoned in the back of a hay wagon as an infant, she watched other children — prettier children — being adopted while she lingered through her teenage years at St. Mike's. She found the love of her life early and lost him early. She stumbled through her days bumping into things, but she nursed her wounds cheerfully as if they didn't matter at all. Nothing ever quite worked out for Emmie and yet everyone loved her. I was in awe of Mags and I was jealous of Delores, but Emmie was different. Even though I didn't understand her at all, being around her was a comfort.

"Why lucky?" Pam asked.

"Because I know you." She patted Pam's head. "And you and you and Mags." Delores and I smiled as Emmie looked at each of us in turn. "Because someone figured out how to build airplanes and Hoppy taught me how to fly them. Because I got a chance to love Hoppy. Because I know Red."

Pam frowned. "Who's Red?"

"He's my father-in-law, Pammie. He's the sweetest old man in the world."

"Sweeter than Mr. McKensey?" Pam giggled.

I looked around, hoping Mr. McKensey wasn't lurking in the stairwell.

"No one is that sweet," Delores said.

We all laughed.

164

The music came to an end. We stopped talking as a squeaky-voiced announcer came on.

This is Elvin "Scooter" McClelland with Scooter's Fast News on Thursday, February 24. The WASPs are stirring things up again. Imagine them wanting the same benefits as our brave boys in uniform, stealing jobs away from REAL pilots! They can't fool you. Congress is getting letters and answering calls telling them the truth — women are less trainable than men and more in the way than helpful. It's time to reconsider this program and get these 35-hour wonders out of the sky! Until next time, keep the fire burning till our boys come marching home.

Silence filled the room.

"Why don't they like you?" Pam pushed her lower lip out.

"They do like us, honey. They just don't want us flying." Emmie said. "They think there aren't enough flying jobs for everyone and they think men should have the jobs that are available."

"Cause men learn better than women?"

Delores knelt down beside Pam. "Don't you believe it, Pammie. They tell you that all your life, but you know it's not true, don't you?"

"Why do they say it then?"

"I don't know why they say it, but look at Emmie — she had over 2000 hours of flying before she joined WASP," Delores said. "Mags won speed races, performed in air shows, and even flew all over Africa on her own. How many men have done that? We have to meet the same qualifications as combat pilots, Pammie."

"But that man said WASPs had only thirty-five hours."

"Just because he said it, doesn't make it so."

The whole conversation was getting on my nerves. The civilian pilots didn't want us. The military pilots didn't want us. Squeaky-voiced reporters said bad things about us every day. Even Congress

165

had it in for us. Why were we even doing this? The good mood was over.

"Whatever you hear, Pam, you can always come to me," Emmie said. "If you have questions, just come ask me."

"Okay."

Delores turned off the radio. "I'm ready for some of that popcorn."

#

"Señor's not going to fit inside your jumpsuit much longer," Mags said as we loaded our new *Wiley Foxes*.

"I know," Delores said. "I hate leaving him behind though. He's been crawling up on my shoulder after we are aloft and cuddling near my cheek. I don't feel so alone when he's with me."

I had to laugh. Delores was never alone unless she chose to be. She opened the door to the cockpit of her *Fox* and set Señor on the seat. We gathered around.

Mags stroked the little dog. "He's a growing puppy but it's not just that — he's fat. Look at that belly. We're all to blame. We feed him anything we are eating. He can eat more jellybeans than Emmie." Señor wiggled happily, his tongue dangling.

"That's cause we loves hims, isn't that right!" Delores held up a piece of cookie and Señor sat up on his haunches, pawing the air with his front legs.

There were only three planes to deliver to Camp Morgan this time. I was scheduled to tow targets all the next week so I was hitching a ride in the backseat of Emmie's *Fox*. Since she'd been in B-17 school, we'd not been able to spend much time together and I'd missed her. She was the first person I'd let myself get close to in years. Grant was the second. Her advice had been golden. I was letting go of the bad stuff and embracing the good.

"Do you want to stop at Nub's on the way back? We can have him take Señor to Red." Emmie leaned forward to let Señor lick her face, slipping him a piece of cookie.

"Maybe on the way back. I'm not ready to hand him over," Delores said. "Besides, I think Tommy would like to see him again."

"You are as bad as that guy who used to fly with a lion cub until it got so darned big it could fly the plane without him." Mags petted Señor one last time.

"You mean like an African lion?" I thought about the cubs I'd seen in the zoo. A lion cub was a lot bigger than Señor ever would be.

"It was part of his act along with his fancy mustache. He loved that little thing until it started tearing him up — sharp teeth and claws, you know."

"Señor isn't a lion. He's a lamb. He's no trouble at all," Delores insisted.

"Uh oh." Emmie nudged me. "Look who's here?"

I glanced over my shoulder. Grant was walking across the tarmac. Joy flashed through my body. He'd come to say good-bye.

"Go, Shirley," Emmie whispered. I smiled at her and went out to meet Grant. We'd seen each other every day — going to movies, to church, to dinner, snuggling together inside the truck, kissing for hours.

"I wish you didn't have to go." He paused a few feet from me.

"Me too." I tucked my chin, embarrassed to have this conversation in the middle of the *Wiley Aircraft Airport* but also proud that the other women could see that my fellow cared.

He handed me a small blue envelope. "This came for you."

I glanced down. It was from St. Jerome's. I sighed with relief. Lizzie Langer must be okay. I tucked the letter inside the zippered pocket over my left breast. "Thanks for bringing it to me," I said.

167

"You know I hate this."

"What do you hate?"

"You doing this. I hate for you to be so far away. I want you with me."

"It's my job."

"It's not your job forever."

"As long as we are at war."

"What?" He cupped his ear.

"It's my job as long as we are at war."

"The war won't last forever, Shirley."

"For the foreseeable future." That was what Father always said. 'The foreseeable future.'

"I'd like you to think about it."

"About what?" Was he saying what I thought he might be?

"Quitting. Resigning. Giving it all up." His eyes drew me in, charmed me. I wanted to run away very fast.

"I'll think about it," I said, but I wasn't going to quit. Not now. No way!

#

We had good weather all the way to Camp Morgan. Emmie and I lagged behind Delores and Mags. We were in a great mood, singing our lungs out over the hum of the engine. We stopped in all our favorite places to eat or sleep or go to the bathroom or to get fuel. We buzzed Red's house, laughing and waving. Beulah kicked the pig. Red sat on his sidewalk, a huge gummy grin on his face.

"Wish we were stopping now, I could use some of that hooch," Mags said into the radio.

"What I don't understand is why it puts Mags and me down hard, but it never effects Red," Delores said.

"He's been drinking it since he was ten years old." Emmie wagged her wings at Red and headed west. The others followed and eventually passed us.

"Tamales in Arizona?" Mags radioed as we lost sight of her.

"Tell Shorty I want two tamales and a tall glass of beer," Emmie answered. I leaned back to enjoy the ride. I thought about Grant. I liked him, but he wanted things from me. Why do people want things from other people? I thought of the letter in my breast pocket. I took it out and ripped it open.

Miss Maxwell,

In response to your telegram, Miss Langer left St. Jerome's the afternoon of May 27. She left no forwarding address.

Sister Gabriella Griffith.

I folded the letter and put it back in my pocket.

#

We landed at Camp Morgan three days later. Emmie and I taxied up to the hangar just as Delores met Tommy McDougal. They walked off together, eager for privacy, I guessed.

As we crawled out of the plane, stretching and stamping our feet to get the tingles out, Wayne Wilson came to the door of the hangar. He caught Emmie's eye for a moment, then went back inside. A moment later, another mechanic came running out to handle the paperwork. Emmie sighed and I squeezed her shoulder.

Mags was showering when we got to the Quonset hut.

"Will you look at that?" Emmie stood at the foot of her bunk. Hanging on the wall above the headboard was a cartoon depicting the four of us in our leather jackets with bird's wings sprouting from our backs — sitting in a round bird's nest. Under the picture, in

169

large print, Wayne had written, "WASP's NEST." A rose and a note lay on her pillow.

"Well, open it." I nudged her.

She ripped the envelope with her thumbnail. "Oh!" She held it out to me. It said, "I'm sorry! If you forgive me, come to the door. WW"

"Are you going to do something about it?" Mags had slipped up behind us and read the note over my shoulder.

"What should I do?" Emmie picked up the rose and held it beneath her nose.

"Go to the door, silly!" Mags gave her a little push.

Emmie stumbled towards the door. I'd never seen Emmie like this. Wayne must have meant more to her than she let on. She put her hand on the doorknob, turning to look at us.

"Do it!" I whispered.

"Go on!" Mags gestured with her head.

She opened the door. Wayne stood there with a bouquet of what I guessed were eleven more roses and a mock pitiful look on his face. Emmie covered her mouth with one hand. The fellow did sorry right — I'll give him that. I couldn't decide about him. One thing for sure, he better not hurt Emmie again. I realized that my fists were clenched.

That night, Mags and I had dinner with Conrad Simpson.

"I got a bone to pick with you, Connie." Mags stabbed at the air over her salad with her fork. "Next time you leave me incarcerated without a by-your-leave, I'll have your butt on a platter."

I picked at my food, watching them through my eyelashes.

"Aw, Mags. What the hell did you expect me to do? I didn't know this character calling me up in the middle of the night."

"You knew me, Connie."

"I didn't know you were on your way to Houston. You were going to Austin with the generals the last I knew."

"I don't care. When you get a call from anyone using my name, I expect you to do something. Even if it wasn't your job, you owe me."

"I know, I know." He squirmed in his seat. He was decked out in his jodhpurs and knee-high boots — medals dangling from his chest, his hair slicked back. I wondered why he owed her anything. "How is your father, Shirley?" He turned his attention to me.

I dropped the lettuce off my fork. "He's fine, sir."

"George is a mighty fine man."

"Yes sir." I stared at my plate.

"Count your blessings."

"Oh, Connie," Mags groaned and smacked him on the arm with her napkin.

#

The next morning, Delores and I got up early and went out to the hangar where we were assigned our A-24s. Mags and Emmie were once again assigned the task of ferrying a few passengers — this time to San Francisco. It didn't seem fair. I'd have loved that duty. So far, I had found nothing to like about target towing.

It was Delores' first day back after her grounding. "No matter what happens, watch your language," I told her as we waited for our target handlers.

"I will, I will." Delores' evening with Tommy seemed to have cheered her up. She held Señor in her arms. He was squirming around trying to lick her face.

"Boy, Señor is feisty today."

"We had a good time last night, didn't we boy?"

171

"Here come the troops," I said. Two lanky young privates were headed our way. They stopped when they realized we would be their pilots. We watched them argue a few yards away. One turned around and went back to the hangar. The second one shrugged and came towards us.

"A brave man," Delores whispered.

"I'm Private Segretti." He shook our hands.

"Good morning, Private." I smiled.

"Mr. Segretti," Delores said. Señor growled and Segretti jerked his hand away in surprise. "I'm Delores Lieberman and this is Shirley Maxwell. Is there a problem?"

"Yes, ma'am. Private Johnson isn't feeling well this morning. He's got himself a little old stomach ache." The young man glanced over his shoulder as the other soldier disappeared into the hangar. "There's a lot of that going around."

"What now?" I asked.

"Oh, they'll assign someone else. They got a whole bunch of guys with loaded guns waiting for us this morning."

"That's good to know." Delores chuckled. "Should one of us go on up?"

"You go. I can wait." I wanted to put target towing off as long as possible.

"Okay, Señor and I'll take them on. Which plane do you want?"

"I had my eye on this one. I checked the Form One and it looked like it might be in fairly decent shape." To be honest, all of these planes made me anxious. It was like choosing between a bottomless pit and an empty well.

"I'll take the other one, then." She unzipped her jumpsuit and tucked Señor inside. He'd gotten so big that he didn't quite fit anymore. He snuggled down, pinned to her chest — his chin on her shoulder.

172

"No, no. Don't do that. You take this one. I might not even get up today by the time they find a replacement."

"Whatever you say. I'm more worried about one of those clowns shooting me down again than something being wrong with the plane."

"YOU were the one they shot down?" Private Segretti's eyes grew larger. He looked from me to Delores.

"What's wrong? Afraid to go up with me?" Delores teased.

He frowned and straightened his shoulders. "I ain't afraid of anything."

"Fine. Crawl in the plane." She winked at me as the young man scrambled aboard and took his position. "I'll give him the ride of his life," she said. "Maybe a roll or two. A spin?"

I laughed. "You devil. You be good even if he isn't."

I could see Señor wiggling inside her jumpsuit as she started the engine. I backed away and she taxied towards the end of the runway, sliding the canopy in place. I squatted in the shade of the other A-24 as she took off. She climbed and started her turn around headed towards the range.

I knelt there, relaxing — thinking about Grant Logan. The sound of the engine changed. Delores was slowing. Then she sped up. What was going on? I stood, shading my eyes with my forearm. Something was definitely wrong. She was trying to bring the plane back in, but I couldn't tell why.

I jumped into the parked A-24 beside me and turned on the radio, searching for her frequency.

"Looks like elevator cable snapped." Her voice was calm.

"We are clearing the area." Someone told her.

"Using the trim tab instead. It's a little crazy, but it's working."

"Bring it on in, Delores," I whispered.

The plane went up slowly and down slowly. Revving the engine, she lined up with the numbers.

I gripped the yoke of the A-24 as if by doing so I could ease her way. "Please God, bring her in safe. Please."

She aimed the plane at the runway. She was going too fast.

"Oh God! She'll never get it stopped," I muttered under my breath.

Her wheels hit the tarmac with a loud screech and she rolled forward. I climbed out of the parked plane and ran toward her. She zipped past me still going too fast. I hoped her tires would hold. A blowout would be catastrophic. She was coming to the end of the runway and her rear wheel was still off the ground. I could imagine what was going on in her head. If she hit her brakes too hard, she'd nose over. She eased down on them. The plane slowed. There was a small clearing before a row of trees after the pavement ended. Her tail was down. She stood on her brakes and hit her left rudder, sliding sideways. The plane stopped abruptly and Delores cut the engine.

I kept running. The back canopy slid open. Private Segretti climbed out and ran to the side of the tarmac to lose his breakfast. I could see her inside the plane but there was something red everywhere. As I got closer, I heard her screaming.

I climbed onto the wing, the propeller still wind-milling. Tommy McDougal wasn't far behind me. I heard his feet on the tarmac. I tapped on the canopy. "OPEN IT! DELORES! Open the canopy." She looked at me wild-eyed. Her screams intensified. Señor lay in her lap — his brains dashed out on the windshield.

Tommy McDougal pushed me aside and reached into the plane to retrieve Señor. Delores' screams melted into sobs as Tommy laid the little dog's bloody body on the grass beside the runway. She was still strapped into the cockpit, her jumpsuit ripped where Señor had been thrown forward against the gunsights when the plane stopped abruptly. I fiddled with her harness, trying to get her out but she fought me in her hysteria.

174

"Delores! DELORES!" I backed away, sliding down the slope of the wing, stumbling as my boots hit the ground. "DELORES!"

Tommy lifted a finger to his lips. His scar burned dark red across his face, his eyes stern. "Stand over there by Wayne and I'll get her out, okay?"

A small crowd of mechanics and target handlers gathered a few feet away. Wayne stepped forward and took my upper arm, pulling me back up the runway towards the Quonset Hut.

"Let's get you back to the nest." His words galled me and after a few yards, I jerked my arm away from him.

"Come on, Shirley. This is no place for a woman." His voice was soft, wheedling. I couldn't tell if his eyes were kind or accusing. I looked back to see Tommy helping Delores out of the plane.

"No."

"Shirley." Wayne reached for me again.

I slapped at him with both hands, "NO!" He ducked, grabbing my wrists. I locked my knees and pulled back.

Delores tore loose from Tommy and rushed forward to beat Wayne on the back and chest with her fists. "Stay away from her!" she screamed. "It's your fault. It's your job. All you have to do is keep them flying and you can't even do that!" She went after him with her nails. He let go of me and I fell backwards onto my behind.

Steel arms encased me and lifted me to my feet. I kicked and twisted, recognizing Private Segretti. Tommy pulled Delores back and Wayne retreated. His eyes reminded me of a wounded deer I once saw dying on the side of the road. His nose was running and there was a deep scratch on the side of his face. Did I do that? Or was it Delores?

"It would be different if your butt was on the line." She lunged at him. "You don't care if we die."

175

Tommy struggled to restrain her. She was an inch taller than him and filled with rage. "Get the hell out of here, Wayne," he yelled.

Wayne ran off across a grassy field with his hand to his cheek. A couple of the other mechanics followed him, heads ducked, shoulders slumped. Tommy nodded and Segretti released me. I glared at them both as I smoothed the wrinkles out of my clothes.

Tommy loosened his grasp and Delores turned in his arms, her head on his shoulder, her arms around his neck. I couldn't stand watching them.

#

Delores sat on her bunk playing with Señor's silver and sapphire collar. "He was so trusting and innocent," she said.

I lay on my bed with my arms folded over my chest, hating her. My mouth was dry, my eyes gritty. I wanted her to shut up so I could float away and dream of nothing.

"Tommy gave him to me the first time we slept together. Did you know that? We went to that tourist court out on Palm Avenue and when I unbuttoned his jacket, there was Señor in the chest pocket of his shirt. Remember how little he was that night? Mostly eyes and ears." She touched the sapphires with her fingernail.

I rolled over to face the wall. I didn't want to hear about her slutty behavior with Tommy McDougal. I didn't want to think about how she murdered Señor — she and Wayne and Tommy McDougal. The swirls in the wood looked like tiny tornadoes.

"I fell in love with him that night." I wasn't sure if she meant Tommy or Señor. Her breathing quickened and I realized she was sobbing again. Good. Her selfishness put Señor in danger. My stomach soured. I couldn't put all my anger on Delores. I was the one who chose the plane. I was the one who let them go first. I dug at my right forearm with my fingernails like I used to do before Father made me a pilot.

176

"How are you two doing?" Emmie's fragrance filled the room like opening a bar of soap. "Tommy told me what happened." I heard the bed squeak as she sat down beside Delores.

"I don't think I can bear this." Delores' voice quivered.

"You can bear it," Emmie whispered. "You must. What other choice is there?"

"I should never have given my heart to that silly little animal. It hurts too much."

"Of course you should," Emmie said. "Loving is part of living."

"I should have left him with Red like Mags said."

I grunted and closed my eyes. If she had left him with Red, he'd be fine right now — eating Red's beef stew and lapping up a saucer of hooch.

"You didn't leave him with Red. There's nothing you can do to change that, so why think about it?"

Delores hiccupped. "I was nasty to Wayne. Did they tell you? I was upset about the plane and about Señor. I wanted to hurt someone so I hurt Wayne. I'm ashamed."

"He's worried about you, Delores. He knows what that dog meant to you. He's as upset about those damned planes as you are."

I sat up, my eyes crackling with anger. Emmie's arms were around Delores, her back to me. "Then why doesn't he fix them?" My voice quivered. "Why does he let us take them up when they have all these problems?"

"My God, Shirley. What have you done to yourself?" Delores stared at my arm, dabbing her eyes with the edge of her sheet. Emmie turned, concern coloring her face.

I looked down. Blood trickled from four long scratches on my right forearm. The pain started as soon I saw the wounds. I whimpered, my mouth open. Emmie hurried into the bathroom and came back

177

with a wet cloth. It wasn't fair. Delores was beautiful even in sorrow. My crusty ugliness went on forever.

"Stop this. Stop it now." Emmie shook me until I looked at her and then she hugged me. I held out my arm and she wiped the blood away. "You are in worse shape than Delores over this."

"I don't know what you mean."

"You've got to let things go. If you are mad, be mad. If you need to cry, cry. Then you gotta let it go and just relax. You hear me?" She looked into my eyes. Her kindness made me feel even guiltier. "No more scratching yourself?"

I shook my head unsure I could keep that promise.

"I guess I owe Wayne an apology," Delores said.

I hated him! I hated everyone but Emmie. "Me too," I mumbled.

"Apologies will be appreciated, I'm sure." Emmie took each of our hands. "But there's a bigger issue here. The male pilots are scared too — and the kids that ride with us. The mechanics are frustrated – – not enough parts, not enough time. We need to stick together on this and see if we can figure something out."

"They don't give a damn about us." Delores echoed my thoughts.

"They do want the airplanes we all have to fly to be airworthy."

"What do you propose?" Delores asked.

"Mags is talking with Conrad Simpson now. Tommy is talking to the men. We want to meet — first thing in the morning." Emmie took a candy bar out of her duffel and broke it into three pieces.

"It's useless," I said. "If there aren't any parts, what can we do?" My anger turned to despair.

"We can refuse to fly planes that shouldn't be flown." Delores lay back on her bunk.

"We can work with the guys to make sure everyone knows which planes are suspect," Emmie said.

"They are all suspect." Delores put her forearm over her eyes.

Emmie nudged Delores' bed with her toe. "You know, they tell me it took some pretty good piloting to bring that plane in today."

Delores rubbed her eyes. "Not good enough or Señor would be alive."

Emmie patted Delores' foot. "You can't control everything." She looked at me and raised her eyebrow, "Right, Shirley?"

She was wrong. Control was everything.

#

The next morning we gathered in the back hangar. Conrad Simpson stood before us like a foppish martinet — slapping a horsewhip against his thigh and caressing his holstered .45 from time to time. Mags sat in a folding chair near the front of the room talking with some of the men pilots. They were all smoking cigars and a haze of blue smoke floated upwards over their heads. The mechanics clustered together, shuffling from foot to foot. Emmie and Delores sat near the rear of the room. I stood by myself in the far corner near a wall covered with diagrams of the various airplanes we flew at Camp Morgan. Every so often, Emmie looked back at me. She was worried that I'd do something stupid.

Wayne Wilson caught my eye and I nodded. Sometimes he seemed so nice. He had accepted our apologies with more grace than I would have been able to muster. We stood in a small awkward circle — Wayne, Emmie, Delores, and I. Delores had done all the talking. I was grateful for that.

"All right, let's get this meeting underway." Simpson tapped a metal table with the butt of his gun to get our attention. The mutterings of a dozen conversations muted and we turned our faces towards him. "We all know there have been problems here at Camp Morgan and I've called this meeting to enlist your help in solving them."

"He never called this meeting." Delores's stage whisper was loud enough for everyone to hear it. Tommy frowned at her and so did I.

179

Emmie leaned over and said something. Delores slumped in her chair and folded her arms over her chest.

"I want you to know that nothing you say here will be held against you. We want to find ways to make sure you all are safe. Does anyone have anything to say about that?"

Delores held up her hand. A good portion of the crowd snickered and applauded. "The WASP who got shot in the tail," someone muttered. She ignored them. "These planes are falling apart. We take our lives in our hands every time we go up. Are you guys trying to kill us?"

A short fellow with dark shadows across his cheeks shook his finger at her. "You think you are the only one whose ass puckers on take-off?" My head snapped towards him, my mouth open. "Oh, excuse me, ma'am." He took off his hat and bowed. "But every one of us has ridden one of these birds down. Engines cut out, control cables bust, missing instruments — you name it. We've taken it up with the mechanics more than once." I remembered the angry faces of the pilots the day Wayne showed us the A-24.

"We only got two hands." Wayne leaned against a workbench, chewing his gum vigorously. "If we had more mechanics — more parts."

"Tires. If we had some decent tires." Another of the mechanics moaned. Everyone began talking at once.

Simpson banged on the table again. "D-day alone used up more stuff than I ever dreamed we could put together. All that got us was a toe hold in Europe. We still have a lot of fighting to do to get rid of Hitler and then, we have to deal with Hirohito. The country is doing without just about everything to get us what we need to do that, but we all know how much this war is consuming. Let's face it — parts are scarce. Tires are scarce. People are scarce. The steel mills in Cleveland and Pittsburgh are doing the best that they can. The folks at Boeing are putting out the planes, the navel yards are working at capacity. Bill Wiley is working his people to death too. It's taking

180

all of them to get us where we are now. It's taking everything we can do. I know it's not enough. I know you are scared. Hell, I'm scared, but sometimes you just have to make do. This is one of those times."

"Is that why they are here?" The lieutenant who harassed Delores on a regular basis jerked a thumb her way. "You are making do?"

"All right, Ewell. I've had about enough of this." Delores tried to stand up, but Emmie hung on to her waistband and pulled her back into her seat.

"Can it, Lieutenant. The presence or absence of these ladies has nothing to do with you." Simpson scowled and slammed his whip against the wall.

"Look, she's been up twice and came down hard twice. She's a hazard, a danger to all of us."

"She got that plane down without a scratch. Could you?" Tommy McDougal yelled. "I seem to remember pulling you out of a ditch when your PT-17 blew a tire."

Ewell clenched his fists. "Sure, you're getting a piece of that hellcat. Why wouldn't you take up for her, McDougal?"

"HEY, HEY, HEY!" Mags threw a chair and it clattered across the room. Shocked silence descended on the room. She took her cigar out of her mouth. "Look, we're here. It's a fact. Who knows how long we'll be here. That's a fight for another day. Right now, we need to pull together. If one of those birds isn't fit to fly, it could be any one of us that draws it. On this one thing, we need to agree."

The tension in the room simmered. Men preparing for combat had to be trained. Planes going to Europe or the Pacific had to be repaired. The available parts had to go to them. Conrad Simpson was right. We had to make do. The only thing Mags accomplished was that we all agreed to work together and avoid blaming each other. I suppose that was a victory.

#

Our newfound collaboration with the men didn't last a month. Delores and I continued to tow targets. I spent longer and longer on my pre-flight inspections, pouring over the Form One. Twice I refused to go up until Wayne fixed small things. He accommodated me without comment. In fact, we persuaded him to ground number 49 — a troublesome plane which, among other problems, had a broken latch on the canopy. It was the plane I'd vowed to avoid when I first saw its Form One.

Mags and Emmie checked out in a number of different planes and were given a variety of assignments. Although we weren't allowed to leave the continental United States, they tested and flew repaired aircraft to any number of in-country locations.

When Simpson assigned Mags and Emmie to fly the B-26, a plane the men considered unsafe, the pledge of cooperation between the sexes was over. As Lieutenant Ewell shouted to Mags, "He's using you to force us into flying this dog."

"What do you expect me to do?" she'd answered. "Refuse to fly a perfectly good plane?"

It was back to everyone for themselves after that.

#

I spent many of my evenings alone. Mags was often on overnight trips. Emmie spent time with Wayne. Delores and Tommy were inseparable. I thought of Grant, but I wouldn't let myself miss him. He sent me a small heart-shaped pin with two red-metal hearts pierced by a golden arrow and white enameled lacework around the edges. I hid it inside the zippered pocket of my jumpsuit.

The last night before our return to *The Windshift Inn*, I settled in for a long evening in the Quonset hut with a sandwich and a glass of milk.

"Oh no, you don't," Emmie said as she ironed her uniform blouse. "We are going to *Wings & Swings* tonight and you are coming with us."

"I don't feel like it."

"Doesn't matter. Wayne bought you a ticket. You have to go."

"He didn't!" I was horrified.

"Put down that sandwich. Dinner is included."

"Oh, Emmie. I don't want to go on your date with you."

"It's a party. We want you. Wayne wants you. Delores and Tommy are going to be there."

I was quite sure this wasn't Wayne's idea at all. "I didn't bring anything to wear."

"Wear your uniform, that's what we are doing," she said as I put my dinner aside. "And get that glum look off your face. We are going to have fun tonight. We've been down in the dumps long enough."

We had to stand in line to get into *Wings & Swings* even though we had tickets. Tommy Dorsey was playing and the place was packed. Our table was toward the middle of a hundred others surrounding a little hardwood dance floor. Delores and Tommy were dancing — pressed against each other, eyes closed dreamily. We took our seats and ordered drinks.

"I'm glad you came tonight, Shirley." It was the first time I'd seen Wayne without his chewing gum. "I've wanted to tell you how sorry I am about Señor."

"He was Delores' dog."

"I'm sorry about everything."

I didn't doubt his sincerity. "I'm sorry too." I choked on the words.

"I'd like to start from scratch. Okay?" He stretched out his hand.

I felt Emmie's eyes on me. The moments stretched on and the silence made me nervous. I couldn't help but notice the dark hair on his knuckles. "Okay." I closed my eyes and shook hands with him.

183

"You two are my best friends," Emmie said. "I want you to like each other." Liking was a bit much to ask, but I resolved to try and get along.

The waitress brought our drinks and we sat back listening to the music. A blonde-haired woman in a peacock blue evening gown sang plaintive love-songs in a low alto. My eyes drifted from Emmie and Wayne to Delores and Tommy on the dance floor. I thought of kissing Grant in the delivery van.

"Emmie tells me you all are building an airplane back in Ohio." Wayne took a sip of beer and set the mug back onto the table.

"I'm not doing much. Emmie and Delores are working on it."

"You should meet Pam, Wayne. She's the cutest little girl. She's got this thing about 'Der Fuhrer's Face.' Every time we turn around she's singing it," Emmie said. "She marches around holding a broom like a rifle and spitting like Donald Duck."

"A little kid like that is learning to fly?" Wayne popped a peanut into his mouth.

The incredulous tone in his voice raised my hackles. "She's almost fourteen and she's smart as a whip!" I knew Pam didn't need me to defend her. Why was I?

"I took her up in one of her dad's *Fox* trainers the last time we were there," Emmie said. "She's comfortable with the basics. We did some climbing turns, some straight and level, some descents. She was doing well so I decided to show her stalls."

"I remember my first stalls," Delores said as she and Tommy joined us at the table. "Scared me to death. I busted my instructor's eardrums."

"Delores can put out the sound, that's for sure." Tommy kissed her cheek as he helped her scoot her chair up to the table. Unlike the rest of us, Delores was wearing her blue-flowered dress and a white gardenia above her ear. "I didn't have any idea what a stall was." He

184

laughed and sat down beside her. "I thought it was when the engine died. I was only sixteen when I learned to fly."

"I don't know what Pam thought, but I didn't want to scare her. I explained things and then showed her so she'd know what to expect. It was a clear day. I took her up around six thousand feet and let her rip." Emmie took a sip of her beer. Her eyes sparkled as she warmed to the story. "We're flying along straight and level. She slows the plane while pulling back on the controls. The stall horn made her jump. You should have seen the look on her face when she started losing control effectiveness. She squealed when the plane dropped and I expected her to give up control to me and let me recover. I mean, she's only thirteen. But no, she had the presence of mind to put the nose down and push in the throttle."

"Good girl!" Tommy snapped his fingers for a waitress. "Beer and a rum and coke." He pointed to Delores and the woman nodded.

"She loved it. Right away, she wanted to do it again. So we did." Emmie laughed. "We must have done ten, fifteen stalls. She'd put that nose down and squeal with delight as the wings regained lift. You'd think she was on a roller coaster."

Delores accepted her drink from the waitress. "Go, Pam!"

"It is a thrill," Tommy said. "I used to practice over a big cornfield because I had it in my head that if I went down, the corn would soften the crash."

"Oh no, what disabused you of that notion?" Delores lifted her rum and coke.

Tommy clinked his beer mug against her drink glass. "I crashed."

"Were you hurt?" I asked.

"No, I died." They all said together. I blushed. I never got that joke. In fact, I didn't get this whole conversation. I hated stalls. Wayne squirmed in his seat. I wondered what he was thinking. He must have felt me watching him because he glanced my way. I drained my wine glass to avoid him.

185

"Well, anyway. She kept on doing stalls until she got cocky. I don't know exactly what she did. I'm guessing she tried turning right when we were too close to stall, but we went into a spin. Now that did scare her and she let go and screamed. I got the ailerons neutral and kicked the left rudder. Then I put the nose down and eased us out. Believe it or not, that kid watched every move I made. I was ready to land, but now she wanted to do a spin herself."

"You're kidding," Tommy laughed. "I've never seen anyone do that."

"Me either. It took me weeks to work up to a spin," Delores said. "Pam's a gutsy little girl."

"Here's what I'm getting at. She did it perfectly! She stalled the plane, put it into a spin and recovered just as I had done. Not only wasn't she afraid, it made sense to her. She understood what she was doing." Emmie beamed like a proud parent.

"Sounds like she's a natural — fearless and smart." Tommy snapped his fingers at the cigarette girl who was wandering past in a skimpy costume.

"She's smart and she wants to build this plane Wayne designed. She goes to the library several times a month and has been reading up on aerodynamics and physics," Emmie said. "Her father owns the airport so they have plenty of space to work."

"She went around the neighborhood and collected people's old sheets," Delores added. "Grant Logan got her a couple gallons of dope from the *Wiley Aircraft Plant*. The problem is going to be the engine. It's going to have to be rebuilt or replaced I'm afraid."

"One thing at a time. I think she's got a few months of work before worrying about the engine," Wayne said. "If she can get the plane itself built, I'm sure we can work something out."

Wayne was a strange man. He was excited someone was going to build his plane, even if that someone was a thirteen-year-old girl. This was the same guy who made fun of us with his cartoons.

186

We left the next day, riding together on the train, stopping so Emmie could see Red and so Mags and Delores could get drunk with him. The closer we got to *The Windshift Inn* the lighter my mood. Once I was safely in Grant's arms, I never wanted to go back to California again.

CHAPTER 13 — PROPOSAL

"Sharon Rogers Band Swings at Coney Island, Bay Village Doctor Held on Abortion Charges, Waldo Peirce wins first place in Pepsi Cola Portrait of America painting contest."
Headlines
~ American View Daily ~
July,1944

None of us were looking forward to telling the folks in Cold Creek what had happened to Señor. The factory girls loved him. Myrtle baked him doggie biscuits. Mr. McKensey's gruff complaints were so insincere that no one was surprised when he tossed an old child's squeeze toy across the kitchen floor for Señor to chew on. Everyone was heartbroken and concerned about Delores — no one more than Pam.

"I know it hurts." Emmie put her arm around her as they sat on the couch in the parlor. The little girl laid her head on Emmie's shoulder. Her nose was running, but Emmie didn't seem to care. "Everyone dies, Pam. We can't control that, but we can make sure life is good while we have it. Señor had a short life, but it was a happy one too."

"I know." Pam sniffed and wiped at her nose with her sleeve.

I gripped the arms of my chair and leaned forward.

Emmie pulled a red bandanna out of the back pocket of Pam's overalls and held it while Pam blew her nose.

I relaxed.

"Where are Myrtle and Jerry?" Delores looked around. Even the factory girls who usually spent their evenings playing cards and listening to the radio were gone.

"They go out together sometimes. I don't know where they go." Pam wiped one last tear from her cheek. "I'm awful sorry about Señor, Delores."

"Thanks. It's been a hard couple of weeks."

"It's hard to lose someone you love. Dog or not," Emmie said.

Delores looked tired. Every night, I heard her thrashing about in her sleep or sobbing into her pillow. It wasn't just Señor or the mess at Camp Morgan. She was worried about her relatives lost in Europe. Her mournful mood made my eyes sting. I looked away. I had problems of my own. I didn't want to feel bad for her. Besides, what could I do except tell Father?

I checked the grandfather clock in the hallway. "I'll be out for a while but I'll be back."

"Shirley has a date," Emmie teased.

"Not really a date." I hurried to explain. "We are just going to go for a little ride. In fact, I better get ready." I hurried up to the dormitory to avoid any more conversation. I was emerging from a quick bath when I heard Mags coming up the backstairs. I wiped my face with a towel, already sweating under my sweater and wool skirt.

"Grant's waiting for you downstairs," she said as she pulled off her boots. Her hair was damp and droplets of water dotted her leather jacket. She rode that damned horse in all kinds of weather. We no sooner stepped off the train than she was off to the woods, content with her own company and that of the stallion. "He's showing them how to make popcorn his way."

"I didn't know there were multiple ways to pop corn." I combed my hair and applied new makeup.

"Grant was meant to be the boss."

"It's not that. He likes things to be in order, that's all." My words seemed idiotic once I heard them. "I'm sorry, I know you weren't criticizing him."

"No problem."

"It's nothing really. I barely know him."

"Okay."

190

"We don't have a thing in common."

"I understand."

"He's too bossy. Just like Daddy." I couldn't stop blabbing.

Mags took off her jacket and hung it on her clothes rack. "Well then, it must be his body. You go out there and enjoy him while he's young and perky."

I blushed before I giggled. "How do I look?"

"Like you are contemplating sin."

"Oh, Mags!" I threw Delores' petticoat at her.

#

We headed towards the woods north of Jerry's Airport. Warm rain splattered against the windshield of the *Logan Groceries* Van. Roselawn Cemetery was a few yards past the turnoff. Grant drove down a dark muddy lane and parked, turning out the lights. It was a perfect spot, secluded and yet we could see Cold Creek City lights in the distance.

"I've waited a month for this, Shirley." Grant took me in his arms and kissed me. "Did you think of me?"

"You always ask me that."

"And I'll keep asking it until you learn to lie or you learn to miss me." He bit my bottom lip playfully.

"It was a bad few weeks."

"You always say that."

"It's always bad."

"Then quit, Shirley. Throw in the towel. Tell them where to stow all the garbage and come back to Cold Creek and marry me."

My mouth went dry. It had been a long time since any one had asked me that.

191

"What *is* it? Why do you go catatonic on me whenever we start getting close?" His grip was too tight. I couldn't squirm free.

"I'm not ready to get married."

"I love you. Let's make the leap and have a bunch of kids." He kissed me. I couldn't breathe and struggled to get away. "Come on, baby. Don't be like that," he said as I pressed my back against the passenger door.

"How do I know you mean it?"

"You think I propose every night of the week?" He seemed incredulous, angry.

"No."

"Do you love me, Shirley?"

I pondered the question. I loved being in his arms. I loved the way my body responded to him, but I wasn't sure that feeling was enough to wager my life. I liked Grant. When he wasn't griping about me being in the WASP, he was fun to be around. After a long while, I nodded. My palms were wet.

"Then what's the problem?"

"I didn't plan on getting married."

"Why?"

"I don't know."

"Children?"

I shook my head.

"What kind of girl are you? All the unmarried gals in Cold Creek have been filling their Hope Chests since they were ten years old."

"Then why not ask one of them?"

"Dammit, Shirley, because I want you." He lifted my chin. "Come on, now. You aren't happy flying airplanes cross country every couple of weeks and from what you say, flying up and down a beach

192

with every Tom, Dick and Harry shooting at you is a good way to get killed. I have prospects. We have similar beliefs. My folks are crazy about you. You are what I want. Quit, Shirley. Just like that. Quit." He took me in his arms and kissed me, his tongue forcing open my mouth. I accepted it gingerly at first — and then that explosion of feelings hit me again and I writhed in his arms. He savored my response for a few minutes before pulling away. I smoothed my hair and buttoned the top of my cardigan.

"Here, I have something for you." He dug into his pocket and produced a small ruby ring.

I turned on the dome light over our heads and examined it. It slid onto my finger with ease. "How did you do this?"

"I got Pam to steal one of your rings and we used it for size. Then she slipped it back into your jewelry box while you were in California."

I cringed at the thought of Pam pawing through my things with a runny nose. What if she'd touched my jewelry with dirty hands? On the other hand, I loved perfect fits.

"So what do you say?" He asked.

"Can I think about it?"

"Tell you what. Why don't you put this on your right hand while you think about it? Then when you decide you want to marry me, we can put it on your left, okay?" He slid the ring on my finger, lifted it to his lips and kissed it, his eyes probing mine.

"Okay." I mumbled but he read my lips.

"In the meantime, quit."

"I'll think about that too." I needed to talk to Father about it before I knew what I wanted. The news from Europe was getting better. Some of the pilots who'd completed their tours started coming home for a well-deserved rest and a domestic assignment. Maybe now *was* the time to leave the WASP.

193

A week later, we flew back to Camp Morgan.

"You want to buzz Red?" Mags keyed her mic as we crossed into Indiana.

"He's not been feeling up to snuff and it's pretty hot out today. We can catch him on the way back." Emmie answered as we took off from Nubs' airstrip after refueling. It was windy and we were eager to get out of the area before it got too late.

"How are things going with the Stearman?" Delores asked a few miles beyond Indianapolis. Emmie and I had gone out to *Jerry's Flying Service* the day before with a part that Wayne Wilson had found for us.

"We have the frame pretty much put together following Wayne's plan. We'll start work on the wings and fuselage when we get back from this trip," Emmie answered. "It's taking a while to collect all the hardware we need. It's not clear if we will need a new engine or not."

Mags keyed her mic. "You are going to need help, I think."

"I have a two-week layover coming up in August. I'll work with her then. Wayne's been giving me pointers."

"I'll help, Emmie," Delores said. "I have some time too."

"I'll be there too," I said.

"Thanks everyone."

We arrived at Camp Morgan near sunset two days later. Wayne Wilson was waiting for Emmie as we taxied up to the hangar with the new *Foxes*.

"Hey Emmie, how many speeds on a German tank?" He trotted along beside Emmie as we headed towards the Quonset hut.

"How many, Wayne?"

"Four." He held up four fingers. "Slow Forward, Fast Reverse, Very Fast Reverse and Extremely Fast Reverse." He popped his gum and bowed. Emmie giggled, shaking her head.

"You make this stuff up." Delores laughed.

"Well of course I make this stuff up, what do you think? I'm a plagiarist?"

That got all of us and we were still laughing as we hurried into the WASP's Nest for our showers.

#

The next morning, Mags left to ferry a fighter up the coast. Delores and I were to tow targets as usual, but the general Emmie was to fly to San Diego canceled at the last minute.

"Take the morning off, Emmie." Tommy McDougal told her. "Or wait until I get everyone in the air and I'll take you up in the B-29. They are looking for a couple of girls to learn it."

"I'd love it, but why don't I tow some targets while you finish up and we can take the big lady up this afternoon?"

"I'm not sure we have a ride for you. You talk to Wayne and see if there's an A-24 available. You'll need a target handler too."

"You can take mine." Delores joked. "Every time I go up in one of these things something bad happens."

"Sure, I'll take it." Both Delores and I were surprised since we hated the A-24s. "After all these weeks and all that training, I've never gotten a chance to do any target towing." Emmie zipped up her jump suit and brushed her longish bangs back from her face. "You can take over this afternoon."

"Don't look so happy, Delores." Tommy shook his head. "Go talk to Wayne and he'll set something up for you."

I could understand Delores' reluctance to go back up after losing Señor.

195

Our target handlers stood waiting for us as we approached the planes. "Damn," Segretti whispered to a scrawny boy named Petersen who was to fly with me." I just get used to Lady Blue Eyes and they swap out powder puff pilots on me."

Emmie shook hands with him and started her inspection of the plane. She might have been a giggly, sweet-faced girl off base, but she was a professional when it came to flying. We climbed into our planes. I could see Emmie scanning the Form One as I started my engine and taxied towards the end of the runway. As I did my run-up, I caught her out of the corner of my eye as she pulled in behind me. I stuck my hand out of the canopy and waved before closing it. I pulled onto the runway and centered it. I glanced over my shoulder. Petersen was strapped in and ready. He gave me a 'thumbs up.' I accelerated down the runway and took off.

"See you at lunch," I keyed the mic.

"I'm right behind you," Emmie answered.

I continued my climb-out and banked hard to the right headed towards the beach.

"Something's wrong with your friend." Petersen pointed out the side of the canopy.

I banked so I could see the airport. Emmie's plane was struggling to gain altitude. "What's wrong?" I asked her.

"Engine cutting out. Plus Segretti can't close his canopy. We're circling to set it down."

"Be careful."

"You got it."

I wasn't worried. Emmie was a lot better pilot than any of us except Mags. She climbed a few hundred feet more as she circled the field. Inexplicably, the nose dropped. She already had it lined up with the runway, but she was going down too fast. The wheels hit the top of the trees at the edge of the airstrip and she crashed in the grass. I

196

flew over her immediately. The plane had broken in half. Segretti was thrown through his open canopy and was rolling on the ground holding his head. I could see Emmie struggling with something inside the cockpit. I decided to land and started around. Delores was running down the tarmac headed for Emmie's plane. A stream of pilots and mechanics followed her — then Tommy McDougal in a jeep.

I made a tight turn and started back towards Emmie. A finger of flame sprang from the engine. Emmie still wasn't out. Delores was a quarter mile away. By the time I flew over again, the cockpit was burning. Emmie's screams pierced my heart. I landed a few feet away. Petersen jumped out ahead of me and ran towards Segretti. I jumped from the wing as Delores ran past. Emmie's shrieks stopped.

"NO!" Delores tugged at the canopy. The metal glowed. I watched her hands blister. Inside the cockpit, I saw the little scar on Emmie's forehead before the flames ignited her hair. The silver locket she always wore around her neck melted before I looked away. I knew it was useless. It took all my strength to pull Delores away. She collapsed on my shoulder holding her burnt hands in the air. Black smoke billowed out of the plane and covered us. The flames roared. We staggered backwards and knelt in the grass a few yards from the plane. It was then that I noticed it was plane number 49.

CHAPTER 14 — FUNERAL

"To her, life was delicious."
~ George Maxwell,
Obit for Emmie Hopkins,
American View Magazine

Two days later, we took Emmie home to Red. Tommy McDougal drove us to the train station in Conrad Simpson's car. The corners of his mouth turned downward as he helped Delores climb the steep wooden steps onto the platform. She should have been in the hospital. Her arms were bandaged to the elbow and she smelled of ointment and gauze. Crusty red patches dotted her forehead and left cheek. She was so pale I was afraid she might faint and I didn't know what I'd do if she did. I focused on the concrete beneath my feet as Tommy led us towards the refrigerated car near the back of the train.

The hearse was parked in the parking lot and a black-suited, red-cheeked gentleman stood beside it holding his hat over his heart. A simple wooden coffin rested on an iron-wheeled baggage wagon. Mags and Conrad Simpson waited beside it. I looked around — still no Wayne Wilson. He'd been missing since the day Emmie was killed. I wanted to be as angry with him as I had been when Señor died, but I couldn't summon any emotion at all. I just wondered where he was.

"Thank you for coming, sir." Tommy shook Simpson's hand. The medals on the Colonel's chest glittered in the sunshine. My eyes clung to the Ivory handled pistol on his hip. Being shot would be better than burning, I thought. I closed my eyes until the images drifted away.

"I wanted to be here." His face was a masculine version of Mags'— almost too delicate for the carefully put-together military outfits he wore. "This has diminished us all. I wanted to tell all of you how sorry I am."

Delores was drugged but she drew back when Simpson tried to touch her. I let him shake my hand and didn't even flinch when he crushed my ruby ring against my other fingers. What did it matter?

Railroad workers pushed back the wooden doors of the baggage car. I tried not to be surprised that they were women. There were other coffins inside — and blocks of ice. The cold air raised gooseflesh on our arms. The laborers rolled Emmie's casket into the car and we heard scuffling sounds as they unloaded it from the wagon. Mags patted Simpson on the shoulder and said something to him. He nodded, tipped his hat and went back to his car.

"Let's find our seats," she said.

I followed her down the long string of railway cars. Tommy and Delores lagged behind. I heard them murmuring to each other. Delores would not be coming back to Camp Morgan until she was fit to fly again. After we buried Emmie, she was going home to Pittsburgh. It might be a long time until she and Tommy saw each other again.

"Here, Shirley." Mags took my arm and led me to our seats in the train. She stowed my bag on the shelf over our heads. Then she sat down beside me — a million miles away.

The whistle blew.

A minute later, Delores made her way down the aisle, staggering sideways as the train moved forward, unable to grab anything to balance herself with her burned hands. Mags rescued her and helped her get settled in her seat. The train was packed with servicemen who turned to look at her as usual, only this time they were wondering what happened. She pressed her face against the window. Tommy McDougal trotted along on the platform beside us for a few yards.

I closed my eyes as the train picked up speed. The wheels rattling against the rails sounded like a voice saying, "Let her go, let her go, let her go, let her go." I can't, I thought. If I hold on tight, I'll wake up from this nightmare and Emmie will be fine.

200

"Shirley?" Mags nudged me.

"What?"

"I have to deliver a *Fox* to Key West next month. Why don't you come with me?"

"I don't think I have the energy."

"Think about it, okay?"

A sailor in the seat in front of us coughed into his fist. I hated being cooped up in this closed box with a bunch of sick people. I thought about Emmie closed up in a box in back of the train and closed my eyes again.

#

It was raining as we pulled into the Cold Creek Station. Grant waited for us with an umbrella. Delores curled in her seat, her arms crossed over her chest. The pain must have been intense because she twitched and whimpered in her sleep and cried out when Mags woke her. I gathered my things and stood in the aisle while Mags guided Delores out of the train.

"Stand right there under the awning, Shirley, while I get Delores on the bus," Grant called out to me as I stepped onto the platform. The *Wiley Aircraft* Bus was parked a few yards away. Grant held his umbrella over Mags and Delores as they climbed aboard. Then he came back for me. "You look terrible," he said as he took my hand. "Let's get you out of here."

I sat on the bench seat behind him. The gears screeched as we pulled out onto Elm Street and headed south towards Logan's Run Road.

"I missed you." I knew he couldn't hear me over the noise of the engine and he couldn't read my lips. That made it easier to say.

#

Myrtle fussed over Delores and put her to bed. Pam hustled around underfoot, trying to help. Her thick dark hair curled in a distant

201

approximation of the upsweep Emmie had created for her a mere two weeks ago. Her eyes were swollen from crying.

Jerry sat in Myrtle's kitchen drinking fake coffee and smoking with Mags. He'd brought Myrtle home from *Wiley Aircraft* so she could get things ready for us.

"How are you doing, Shirley?" His eyes probed mine. He was trying to be kind.

Pam offered me a cup of tea. I realized she no longer wore a bandage on her forearm and the burn had scabbed over. My stomach rolled and I demurred. She stared at me for a moment — and then, as if understanding, sat down at the table and spooned honey into the mug. She glanced at me from time to time as she stirred, her young face serious.

"Shirley and I are going to take the bus back to the factory and pick up the girls," Grant informed everyone. I accepted this information without comment.

"You get her back here for supper, Grant Logan. That little girl needs some fattening up." Myrtle shook a long wooden spoon at him.

"No problem, but remember Mama wants a crack at her tomorrow night." He ushered me out into the yard and we crawled back into the rickety bus. He closed the door and took me into his arms. I let him hold me for a while, accepting his kisses. Then, he guided me to the seat behind him. I could see his troubled eyes in the rearview mirror. "You know, we are the perfect couple. I can't hear and you don't talk." He winked. "Let's go get the girls, okay?"

I smoothed the wrinkles out of my wool skirt, my legs crossed at the ankle. He started the engine and pulled out of the turnaround onto Cold Creek Road. The rain had stopped, leaving large puddles alongside the road. Within ten minutes, we pulled into the parking lot at *Wiley Aircraft*. Assembly line workers stood out front waiting for us. They rushed toward the bus giggling and talking among themselves. When they saw me, they lowered their voices, their faces curious and somber. The girls living at *The Windshift Inn* nodded to me, as they filed past headed towards their favorite seats.

A tiny girl brought up the rear and found a seat across from me. She sat with her knees together, her lunch bucket sitting in her lap. Her coveralls were too big, the sleeves and pants rolled up several times. She lit a cigarette and released smoke from the corner of her mouth. She couldn't be more than sixteen, a strange mixture of delicacy and coarseness. She looked familiar, but I couldn't place her.

As we pulled out of the parking lot, Grant slammed on the brakes and we were all thrown forward when Mr. McKensey cut in front of us. The girls whistled and flashed toothy grins at him — the daily ritual. He stuck his hand out of the window with his middle finger extended. The women tittered. McKensey spun his wheels in the muddy road as he headed towards *The Windshift Inn*. The war had done strange things — putting the very young and the very old to work in the same factory. Neither seemed to appreciate the other's situation.

Grant circled through Cold Creek letting women off from time to time. As we approached a dilapidated house on the corner of Sugar and Wiley Road, the girl leaned forward and touched my arm. "Thanks, anyway." Images of a heavier young woman vomiting out the back door of Father's Plymouth filled my head. Lizzie jumped down out of the bus like a carefree teenager, unlatched the gate of the unpainted picket fence, and ran up the steps, her ponytail bouncing.

A familiar-looking young man in uniform stood on the porch holding the door open as she scurried under his arm and into the house. He pitched a cigarette butt into the bushes beside the porch.

"Yo, Bennie!" Grant lifted a hand.

The scrawny young man waved and followed Lizzie into the house. I recognized him as Delores' date back on the day we all met Mags. I caught Grant looking at me in the rear view mirror. I raised my eyebrows and he shrugged. It had been only four months since we'd

203

left Lizzie in Bay Village — she was still a long way from her due date. I turned around to inspect the old house as we drove away. I didn't understand. Why had she left St. Jerome's? What happened to her baby? I turned back to Grant's eyes in the mirror. He nodded almost imperceptibly. It was the way of the world. Nothing I did changed anything.

#

Dinner at the inn was solemn. Jerry and Pam joined us as did Grant. The workers sat around the table chattering about boyfriends and movie stars. I thought about that dinner we'd had a few months back — we'd been a family that night.

Delores sat next to Mags. Myrtle had helped her wash her hair and it was still damp. She couldn't hold a fork so Mags spooned food into her mouth until Delores shook her head and refused any more. She hadn't eaten much since it happened — not even dessert.

"Shirley, your daddy called while you were out," Myrtle said as she dipped cabbage, onions, and carrots onto a plate. "He said for you to call him tonight after eight o'clock."

"Yes, ma'am."

"He seems like a nice man."

"Yes, ma'am."

"I told him I thought you oughta stay right here at the inn. You have lots of friends here to watch after you. Pam wants your help building that crazy plane and Jerry says you can help him teach people to fly." She passed the plate to Jerry.

"Thank you, ma'am. I'll think about it."

Grant put his arm along the back of my chair. I knew this was his doing and it annoyed me.

Jerry passed the plate onto the next person. "Don't think, little girl. You do what Myrtle says. She knows what's best."

I stared at my vegetables.

"Stay, Shirley. We'll have a wonderful time." Pam's earnest smile was shiny white but my eyes were drawn to that broken front tooth. I glanced around the table. Serious faces studied me, waiting for my answer.

"They are expecting me at Camp Morgan next week. I have my new uniform." I hadn't taken a bite yet and my mouth was dry.

"Let them get their act together out there. Take a rest. You all need to rest," Myrtle said as she sliced a loaf of rye bread.

My schedule was set. I was supposed to go back to target towing. Get back up on the horse that threw you, as Conrad Simpson said. He and Jerry were always saying crazy things like that. They meant well, but I had no desire to crawl back into any saddle. I didn't want to get in trouble with Jackie Cochran, but I didn't want to upset Myrtle and Jerry, either. I took a deep breath. "Okay."

"I couldn't hear you." Grant cupped his ear.

"OKAY."

"That's our girl." Myrtle took a bite of cabbage. They thought it was all settled.

#

After calling Father that evening, I wandered out on the front porch. The stars were like ice cubes in the night sky. I sat on the steps and watched them glitter.

"What did he say?" Grant sat down beside me.

"He said I should go home."

"Don't."

I dug my nails into my forearm.

"Here, let me hold your hand." He kissed my left palm. "How's that?"

"Fine."

205

"Talk to me, Shirley. Tell me what's going on in your head."

"Nothing."

"Quit. Please, please quit. You don't belong in the air. Things are changing all the time. They don't need you as much. Don't go back."

Actually, going back was the last thing I wanted to do, but the mere fact that everyone thought I should quit, made me think twice. "I said I would."

"People will understand. Stay here. Marry me."

Father wanted me home, Colonel Simpson and Jackie Cochran wanted me in California, Myrtle and Jerry wanted me at the inn, Grant wanted to marry me. They were all trying to fill up my time so I wouldn't think of Emmie. It was nice of them, but I didn't need them. I didn't need anyone. It was clear to me now — as clear as those icy stars.

I turned to Grant. "Will you get me a glass of iced tea?"

"Come inside. We'll sit in the parlor and listen to the *Hit Parade*."

"Okay. Give me a minute."

He stood up. "I'll get the tea ready."

"Thanks."

As soon as I heard the door close, I stuffed my hands into the pockets on my jacket and dashed across the front yard and the turnaround. Chunks of white gravel on Cold Creek Road glistened in the moonlight. I stepped over a low barbed-wire fence and slid down the steep hill on my behind. It was easier to see once I was away from the lights of the inn. Grass and dried weeds crunched under my saddle oxfords. The cool air felt good on my cheeks. I walked faster.

Behind me, I heard doors slamming, car engines revving, and voices. I hadn't been gone five minutes and they were already looking for me. I gritted my teeth and ran. A rock rolled under my foot and I fell hard. My skirt hitched up over my raw knees. I lay there for a moment, panting. I rolled over onto my back, staring at the sky.

"DAMN, DAMN, DAMN!" I drummed my heels on the ground. I was tired of being treated like a child. I was tired of never being alone. I was tired of nothing ever being perfect. I was tired of trying to keep it together when so many bad things were happening around me. I screamed louder. My voice echoed in the field. I screamed until I was breathless. Then I cried for Emmie.

#

I lay there as long as it felt right. Then I got up and climbed the hill below the inn. I was breathless by the time I crawled over the fence and crossed Cold Creek Road. I tiptoed into the foyer. No one was around, so I hurried up the backstairs.

Mags lay on her bed reading. Delores was drugged and snoring.

"Where is everyone?" I picked leaves and grass out of my hair.

"Looking for you."

"And you stayed to take care of Delores?"

"You are a big girl. I figured you'd come back when you were ready." She turned a page of her book.

That was the most thoughtful thing anyone ever did for me. "Thank you, Mags."

"No problem."

I gathered up my things and went down the hall to the bathroom. I soaked in the tub for a long time, the hot water warming and relaxing me. I felt lighter. I still missed Emmie. Heck, I still missed Señor. I always would, but the grinding pain was in control. Wrapping a towel around my head, I paused. I'd forgotten to bring my clean clothes to the bathroom with me. I'd never forgotten something like that before. I pulled my robe tight around me and opened the door a crack. Not seeing anyone, I scurried down the hall to the dormitory in my bare feet.

207

Mags was still reading.

I stood at the foot of her bed. "I think I'll go to Key West with you."

"Good." She kept her eyes on her book.

I went behind my screen and put on my pajamas. I was in bed when we heard them all come back into the inn. I pulled the covers around me and rolled over to face the wall.

#

It was a beautiful Saturday morning. Delores looked better — at least not so pale. She sat at the dresser, holding her bandaged hands across her breast.

"I'm going to miss you," she said as I helped her slip into her long johns. "We've been through a lot together."

"Yes, we have." I couldn't bear to look into her eyes. I was embarrassed by her partial nudity, discomfited by her helplessness. I glanced at my own hands and wiggled my fingers, appreciating their length and strength.

"You'll have to come see me sometime. Drive the Plymouth over or fly Mags' plane," she said as I buttoned her blouse.

"I promise I will."

"It should have been me, you know. I was supposed to fly that plane." Delores's voice quivered with anguish.

"I could say the same thing. I'm not as good a pilot as you. If I'd taken that plane up, I would have been killed instead of Señor." I straightened the collar of her blouse. "I was heartbroken that Señor was killed, but the thing that got me — and I hate to say this even now — the thing that got me was that I was relieved it wasn't me." My shame was overwhelming.

"Look at me. No, look at me." She touched my chin with her bandaged hand. I lifted my eyes reluctantly. "Lord knows I loved that little dog. So did you, but if I have to choose, I choose you. You understand?"

208

I blinked to clear my eyes. I'd never liked Delores. She was too wild, too pretty. I wanted the things she had — her beauty, her sapphires, her family. Here she was being nice to me. I struggled to zip the side seam of her slacks.

"Did you ever think," she said. "That maybe the fates are against me? First taking Señor, then Emmie? Maybe I'm the one that's supposed to be dead now."

I shook my head. I could imagine myself dead, but not Delores. She was too vivid. "All I know is strange things happened around that place — and they didn't want us." I was sure Ewell and his gang had sugared that engine. It was the plane Delores was scheduled to fly and he hated her. I figured she had the same suspicions, but neither of us could say it.

"Wayne would never let anyone hurt Emmie," she said.

"Then where is he? Where did he go?" I was willing to condemn all of them, including Wayne and Tommy.

"I think he's hiding, licking his wounds."

"In that case, I hope he's hurting bad."

"I don't doubt that he is." She sat down on her bed, holding her arms in front of her. She gestured with her head towards Emmie's chest of drawers. "We've put it off for too long, I think."

I sighed. "Maybe we should wait for Mags."

"Mags is getting the plane ready. We'll be out of here by late morning."

I pulled open the top drawer — Emmie's panties. "You take them. They are too big for me." I took them out and folded them. Emmie wasn't as big a slob as Delores, but her underwear was in a tangle.

"Put them in my duffle. I'll donate them to a charity. It'll be a mitzvah."

"Keep these." I handed Delores Emmie's long johns. "I'd like to know you are wearing them when it gets cold."

"Thanks, Shirley."

I pulled out the hand-made red sweater. Delores' eyes welled. "I can't take it back to Grandma. I'll wear the long johns if you'll keep the sweater."

I laid it on my bed and continued going through Emmie's things, folding them before placing them in the appropriate stack. "Oh, Delores. Look at this." I held out a small package, covered with paper and tied with a string.

"Open it."

I pulled on the string and the paper opened. Inside was a small rock. The note said, *"Beautiful Emmie."*

"Hoppy!" she whispered, her voice filled with awe. "I wonder if anyone will ever love me that way."

"Tommy does," I said staring at the note. The paper was yellowed around the edges, the ink fading.

"I don't think so, Shirley."

"They all love you. They fight over you."

"It's not what you think. It's not what I want." She reached out to touch the rock with her fingertips. "I would exchange a box full of jewelry for this little piece of sandstone."

"Me too," I said, twisting the ruby ring Grant had given me.

#

I drove her to the airport where Mags was preparing the plane. Jerry opened the car door and helped Delores out. Pam ran to hug her. We helped her into the padded winter jumpsuit similar to the one Mags was wearing. I pulled the goggles down over her eyes and slipped the leather helmet over her head. "Write to me when you can," I said not believing she ever would.

"You write first." She kissed me. I put my hand over my cheek to wipe away the red smudge she usually left before I realized she wasn't wearing makeup.

"I'll be back tomorrow," Mags said as she crawled into the rear cockpit after we got Delores settled. "We'll leave for Key West on Tuesday, okay?"

I nodded.

#

Mags flew off toward Pittsburgh with Delores strapped into the front cockpit. I leaned against the Plymouth's front fender waving until she rolled the red Stearman and disappeared over the horizon. Pam stood beside me, her arm thrown over her eyes to shade them from the sun.

"Are you still flying?" I asked as I opened the Plymouth's front door. I was going to Mass with Grant that evening and wanted to get back to the inn to change.

She stuck her hands into her coat pockets and hunched her shoulders against the breeze. "Not since Emmie took me up."

"Jerry doesn't teach you?"

"Daddy wants me to learn other things." She offered me a jelly bean.

I shook my head. "He's probably right."

"I want to fly! I want to be like you and Emmie. Look at the things you do, the places you go." I wondered if she was special enough, tough enough. Maybe Jerry was right. We were making her want things she could never have.

"Do you know about salmon?" I asked as I started the car.

She popped the jelly bean into her mouth. "Pink fish in a can?"

"Father took me to Alaska when I was about your age. We stayed in a cabin with a bunch of his friends. They all went off hunting in the wilderness leaving me with the cook. Mid-morning she and I went

211

for a walk through the woods. She was an enormous woman with glasses and a shotgun that she carried under her arm. We followed the sound of rushing water until we found a river. Standing on the banks, we watched these crazy fish — thousands of them — trying to swim upstream. The current was strong and they had to work hard to make any progress at all. On the far bank, a huge bear scooped them out with his paw, one after another. The grass was littered with bones and pale flesh. Smaller animals picked at what was left of the carcasses. Eagles swooped down over our heads and plucked salmon from the water with their talons. They even jumped up a small waterfall, searching for that one pool where they could mate and lay their eggs. The odds of any one fish making it to where ever they were going and actually spawning were poor." I squeezed the steering wheel. "We are like that — Mags and Emmie and Delores and I. We are fighting a losing battle. Everything works against us. There are only a few of us, and we have to be exceptional — there's no room for mediocrity. We have to be three times better than men to be accepted into the program. It is not likely things are going to change in the foreseeable future. Do you understand what I mean?"

She bobbed her head. "You have to be lucky. I still want to try."

"We can't afford to lose people like Emmie and Delores. There's no one else like them in the world. When they go, there are no replacements. To get anywhere, there have to be so many of us trying that it doesn't matter when individuals get picked off. It's more than luck. It's determination and talent and a really thick skin."

"I want to try."

"Good." I started the car, put it in gear, and pulled away. She was a brave kid. It's easy to be brave when you are young. It gets harder every year you live — every time you try and fail. I braked at the corner of Kline and Logan Run Road and thought for a minute. I thought of how Emmie never let things going wrong stop her. Impulsively, I did a U-turn and headed back towards Jerry's airport.

Pam was tugging on the door to the hangar to close it. I turned off the engine. "Pam?" I called.

212

"Yeah?"

"Will you take me to see the horses?"

She looked puzzled. "Sure. I gotta feed them anyway. Come on." She trotted on ahead, gesturing for me to follow.

My heart pounded as I crossed the airstrip and picked my way through the pasture to the stables. By the time I got there, she had led Easy out to meet me. The little horse twitched her tail and sneezed.

"Here," Pam said as she handed me a turnip. "Hold it in your palm like this. Yeah, that's right."

I shuddered as Easy took the turnip from me, her soft lips nuzzling my palm. I fought the urge to jerk my hand back and wipe it clean with my handkerchief.

"She's a pretty girl, isn't she?" Pam stroked the horse's nose.

"She's okay." I touched her mane with the tips of my fingers.

"You wanna go for a ride?"

"No!" Images of Pokey dragging Emmie across the corral came into my head. "This is enough."

"Maybe next time." Pam led Easy back into her stall.

Seems I could love a tiny dog, but I was still afraid of a little horse. "Yeah, maybe next time."

#

Grant and I had cocoa and eggs at a café in downtown Cold Creek the morning Mags and I left for Key West.

"Can you give me any hope, Shirley?" His light masculine smell filled my nose and I imagined his big hands on my body. My passion for him was intense. I lay in bed at night thinking about what it would be like to be with him, fighting intense urges.

"I'll think about it while I'm gone," I said.

213

"Why do you have to go at all? I want you here." He reached across the table and put his finger on the ruby. "You can do it, Shirley. Just change this ring from your right hand to your left."

"I can't. Not yet." I cleared my throat several times, glancing around at the other patrons in the cafe.

"Let me announce our engagement. Let me at least tell Mom and Dad. I can't wait forever." He laced his fingers through mine.

I felt myself wavering and panicked. I pulled the ring off and handed it to him. "Then take it. Find a girl who can do this on your timeframe." I sounded angry but I was just flustered.

"No, I didn't mean it that way." He slipped it back on my right ring finger. "Please, be patient with my impatience. I want you to be my wife. I want to have a home of my own and children. I want to come home at night and find you there. I want to wake up in the mornings with you in my bed."

I felt boxed in, trapped in a warm cozy corner. "I'll tell you one way or the other when I come back."

"Fair enough." He paid the waitress and we drove back to the inn. We got back in time for him to drive the *Wiley* girls to work. He kissed my cheek as I got out. "Come back to me, my love."

#

It was a beautiful morning in early August. Mags and I loaded the brand new *Wiley Fox* and carefully balanced it. Unlike the normal Army green, this *Fox* was painted bright yellow. It reminded me of Hoppy's plane and I thought about flying with Emmie over the frozen Indiana fields.

It would be hot in Florida. I left my heavy woolen clothes at the inn and packed light cotton skirts and blouses. Myrtle provided us with a loaf of her wonderful pumpkin bread, a small chunk of cream cheese and a thermos of milk. After so many weeks of stress and sadness, I felt excited, like we were going on an adventure.

214

I didn't bother to tell Father what I was doing or where I was going. It felt wonderful even though I had no illusions I could hide from him. It was my first small rebellion in a long time. I knew I would pay for it, but I didn't care. I felt giddy and reckless.

I'd never ridden with Mags before. She didn't fly the plane — she wore it. I had over 1300 hours flying time, but I never experienced the air the way Mags did. She was an artist and the plane was her paintbrush. We circled the inn and buzzed Jerry's airstrip before heading south.

"I have friends in Georgia we can spend the night with," she said as we found the highway and followed a big cattle truck. "Once we get to Florida, I know people in Islamorada. We can stop there for fuel. After that, it's a short hop to Key West."

"You sound like you are familiar with the area," I said as I relaxed into my seat, enjoying the landscape drifting by below us. "Do you go down there often?"

"I have a special friend in Key West — Randolph Royce Reasoner. Everyone calls him RRR." She trilled the r's as if she were speaking Spanish or Italian. "He was a friend of Hank's. They used to go fishing and drinking with Hemingway before he moved to Cuba. RRR does some writing himself."

"Is your father still down there?"

"Oh, no. Hank was killed in an accident back in 1934. I had flown down to see him a couple of weeks before and we went fishing in the gulf. He had been out of work for years. The Depression hit him hard. He didn't have a penny to his name and yet, he seemed as happy as I'd ever seen him. Half his beard had gone white but he was tanned and muscular. We sat on the beach watching the sun go down, drinking rum and saluting the end of the day. We felt a special closeness. I look like him right down to the freckles in our right eyes. He was excited to have found a job in Matecumbe, building a highway alongside the railroad to Key West. It was a part of FDR's New Deal — hiring out-of-work veterans for the project.

Hank told me about this kind of shanty town where they lived. When I left for Toronto the next morning, I slipped money into his wallet. He didn't want anything from Mamá or her hoity-toity family as he put it — but he accepted a few bucks from me from time to time as if that money somehow came from a different source. Isn't that funny?" Mags' laugh made you want to laugh too.

"I was still in Canada when RRR sent me a telegram about the accident," she continued. "I flew back as quickly as I could. RRR met me at the airstrip and we took a boat up to Islamorada Key where Hank worked.

"I'm so sorry, Mags." I couldn't imagine losing Father — he was like God — stern, unforgiving, and always on my back.

"Thanks, Shirley. I rather liked old Hank. I don't know how he and Mamá ever found each other or stayed together long enough to have me. He left home when I was two and he only came back once in a while to teach me some new outrage if you listen to Mamá. He taught me to ride when I was four, to smoke when I was eleven, to drink when I was thirteen. I saw him more often after I left home myself. He traveled around the world and I went to see him. That's why I went to Africa. He was hunting with Hemingway."

"You've done so much in your life. I envy you." She'd been on her own since she was sixteen. At sixteen, I was in a convent school conjugating Latin verbs with no thought of anything beyond the next day's exam.

"Why? You are making your own choices." Mags lifted her right wing and we headed east.

"Am I?" It seemed my life narrowed further every day. I controlled almost nothing. I could barely meet Father's expectations when I was a teenager, now it was impossible.

"Who else?" She put back her head and laughed, rolling the plane first one way and then the other, a further expression of her mirth. She flew for the pure joy of it. I went along for the ride.

216

"Tell me about RRR?" I steadied myself by pressing my hands against the sides of the fuselage.

"Well, he's probably in his fifties or sixties, I've never asked. We've been lovers since I was 19 years old — a few years before Hank died." Her voice was casual like 19-year-old girls fell in love with men in the forties or fifties all the time. Her comfort with the situation emboldened me.

"What attracted you to him?"

"He knows how to have fun."

"That's it?"

"What else is there for a lover?" Mags glanced over her shoulder at me, her eyes twinkling.

"Stability. Ability to support a wife and family. Fidelity." I ticked off the standard requirements on my fingers.

"Well, I'm not interested in marrying him. I'm only interested in fun."

I was shocked. It was fundamental. If you went to bed with a man, there was the expectation of marriage. You were giving yourself to someone for life when you gave yourself for the night. I'd never known anyone who only wanted fun. Men sometimes reneged on the deal, but never women. I presumed that was the situation with Delores and Tommy McDougal and it was most definitely what Bennie Bermeister did to Lizzie Langer. I opened and closed my mouth several times, trying to think of something to say.

"Are you okay back there?" Mags swooped down over a train chugging through the countryside. Young men stuck their heads out the windows and waved. They weren't in uniform yet so I guessed they were headed towards basic training.

Using my thumb and forefinger, I sharpened the crease down the legs of my pants. "I'm fine. I just never heard anyone say anything like that before."

217

"Like what?"

"That you were looking for fun."

"I like men. I don't make any apologies for that. RRR has a small beach house on one of the smaller keys. We motor out in his little launch and spend days there by ourselves. He reads me his latest story while I sunbathe on the beach. We eat conch and lobster and key lime pie. We go skinny-dipping and make love in the moonlight on his back porch. He's a vacation all by himself. When he's not sponge fishing or writing, he's down at Sloppy Joe's drinking beer and smoking Cuban cigars with his buddies. I go see him a couple times a year and we have a great time."

"Doesn't he want you to stay? Keep his house? Cook? Have children?"

"Well, he might want me to stay longer sometimes, but he has children and he's a big boy, he can keep his own house."

"What if he — well, you know, finds someone else?"

"What if he does? What's that got to do with me?"

She didn't live in the real world with the rest of us.

"Besides," she continued. "I have other friends myself."

"How does he feel about that?"

"I don't know, I never asked him. It's not any of his business."

"Haven't you ever been in love, Mags? Wanted a husband? A home?"

"I've been in love lots of times. As a matter of fact, I love RRR, but I'm not interested in living with him. I'm fortunate in that I don't need a man for money. Mamá's Grandfather left me plenty. I don't want to live in one place all my life. I want to travel and do interesting things and I want to get to know lots of men, not just one."

"What will people think?"

"I don't care what they think."

Once again, I was speechless. It was all about what people thought. That's how the world worked. What people thought determined your position in life, your opportunities, your future. What people thought could impact whether or not we could continue to be pilots. I wondered if she'd thought of that? Then I realized, she would continue to be a pilot no matter what — being a WASP was just one of her experiences. The concept was intriguing, but I couldn't imagine what it would be like not to care.

"How did you get there, Mags?" I asked softly.

"I don't really know — born that way maybe. Courtesy of Hank Strickland."

"It would be so nice not to care."

"Perhaps you care too much."

"I learned my lessons all too well, I guess." My stomach muscles cramped. I peered out the window of the *Fox* as we crossed a huge lake. Our shadow darkened the water below us.

"What do you mean?"

"I had a bad experience in college." We were alone in the air. Could I trust her? I'd never confided in anyone about it before. I'd thought about telling Emmie but I lost her before I could work up my courage. "I was engaged to a nice young man. We planned on getting married after I graduated. He worked for Father at the magazine. In fact, he still does."

"What happened?" I was grateful for Mags casual tone.

"Even though I was a passionate girl, I was a virgin. I thought that was what I was supposed to be. My fiancé didn't want to wait until our wedding night. He kept at me for months. To be honest, I wanted it too. So even though I was still over a year from graduating, I agreed to meet him at a seedy little hotel on the far side of town from campus. I bought a special dress. It wasn't immodest

219

or anything, but it wasn't like what I usually wore, you know." Mags nodded and I continued. "I went to the beauty parlor. I even bought new underwear." I had almost forgotten the excitement I felt that afternoon. I enjoyed the elaborate process of ducking Father. The sense of naughty fun made my palms sweat and my heart pound. "Anyway, I took a taxi to the hotel and waited in the lobby like I was supposed to. I guess I was a bit out of place. Couples were coming and going all afternoon. The desk clerk, a skinny guy with a sinus condition, stood behind the desk leaning on his elbows and watching me. Twice an older gentleman with a monocle asked me for the time. I got there at four in the afternoon. I tried calling my fiancé at six-thirty. By nine o'clock, I knew he wasn't coming. I asked the fellow behind the desk to call me a taxi and I stood outside the door."

"Sounds like he panicked." Mags' voice was sympathetic.

"No. He picked that day to run off and marry someone else. Apparently, she was pregnant." It still hurt to say it out loud.

"Oh, Shirley," she sighed.

"He wasn't meant for me. I was furious with him, of course — not for getting married but for leaving me at that hotel all alone." The memories began flooding back. Anger was only one of the emotions that accompanied them. "Of course, it turned out that he was the least of my worries."

"What happened?"

We'd reached the other side of the lake. We were now far enough south that the trees were leafing and large expanses of green stretched out before us.

"Two men in a car pulled up in front of me as I waited for a taxi. The desk clerk came up behind me with a gun. They tossed me into the car and it screeched off into the night. Needless to say, I was terrified. I screamed and fought them, but they wrestled me to the floor and tied me up. What scared me the most was they put this black hood over my face and held me so I couldn't move." I hadn't

220

told this story since the trial. I was surprised how much it still affected me. I wanted to cry but I sniffed it back. "Anyway, they took me to some old building somewhere and locked me in a musty closet in the basement for two weeks."

Her face was grim. "Did they hurt you?"

"Yeah," I sighed. "They hurt me."

"What did they want?"

"Father's money, of course. Once they had it, they took off without telling anyone where they left me. It wasn't until the police caught one of them — the bastard from the hotel, that they finally found me. I was nearly dead by then."

"Thank God, they found you." I don't know what I expected her to say, but her reaction surprised me.

"In a way, it was harder on Father than it was me." He'd been furious with me for going to the hotel. If I hadn't been there, it wouldn't have happened. If I hadn't called my fiancé or the taxi, the desk clerk wouldn't have known who I was. If I had been more alert, I could have gotten away.

"You are a survivor, Shirley. You've done well."

"Have I?"

"I didn't say you are over it. I just meant you are facing what you have to face with courage. I admire that."

As usual, Mags stumped me. I wasn't sure I was doing that well, but I was trying, and I appreciated her recognizing that.

221

CHAPTER 15 — JACK REYNOLDS

"RAF reports Warsaw Ablaze, 37 New Cases of Poliomyelitis, War Department States 96% of Wounded Recover to Fight Again, Allies Liberate Paris!"
Headlines
~ American View Daily ~
August, 1944

We arrived in Key West the next day. After checking into our hotel, we walked down Duval Street to *Sloppy Joe's*. Everyone in the bar greeted Mags with hugs and pats on the back. Raucous, ruddy-faced drinkers socializing after a long day of fishing filled the place. A huge Negro bartender fixed us Mags' favorite concoction — something with limes and tequila and cointreau. "It's a little something I picked up in Mexico about ten years ago," she told me as we sipped from big goblets.

I made a face. It wasn't what I expected.

"There's my dahlin one!" A great round redheaded man came up behind Mags and kissed her on the neck.

"First time I ever beat you here." She slipped off her stool and turned to kiss his lips. "Out chasing the big one?"

"I already caught the big one. Now I'm going after his brother." He wore shorts, sandals, and a khaki shirt which was open in the front. Graying reddish hair covered his broad chest, his muscular arms, and his thick legs.

She put her arm around my shoulders. "RRR, I'd like you to meet a friend of mine. This is Shirley Maxwell, a fellow WASP."

"I've heard good things about you, little lady." His huge paw enveloped my hand. I don't usually care for big men, but his expression was as cheery and as gentle as Santa Claus. I liked him.

"I've heard you are the master fisherman around here."

Randolph Royce Reasoner beamed. I wished it were that easy to please Father.

"I'm sorry to hear about the death of your friend. I met Emmie at an air show once and found her charming. She was one of the few women who could compete with our little Mags." RRR sat on the stool next to Mags and nodded to the bartender who opened him a bottle of beer.

"She was very special." I took a deep swallow of the strange drink before me. It was so strong that I stepped back, gasping and coughing.

"Good, isn't it?" Mags thumped me on the back and emptied her glass. "Big Skinner, how about another?" She seemed so different down here. Flushed and sparkling, her boyish style emphasizing her femininity.

"Will you come to dinner with us, Shirley?" RRR asked after an hour. He was being gallant. They were eager to be alone. It was written all over their faces.

I smiled and shook my head. My drink had been refreshed once and I was getting sleepy. "I'm going to finish this off and go back to the hotel."

"Sleeping in Key West? I don't know about this one." RRR drained his glass and tossed several bills on the bar to pay for our drinks.

"Are you sure, Shirley?" Mags put her hand on my shoulder.

"I'm positive. You scoot now. I'll be fine."

Mags patted me. "I'll see you tomorrow." RRR took her hand and they went out the jalousie doors onto Duval Street.

"It's about time." A young Naval Lieutenant at the end of the bar winked at me, collected his drink, and moved to the stool next to me.

"I beg your pardon?" I raised one eyebrow.

"Jack Reynolds." He stuck out his hand.

I was used to being tense. It was my most natural response, but something about Jack Reynolds made me relax and smile — or

224

maybe it was the two drinks I'd consumed. He reminded me of Señor, a tiny little guy with bright eyes and a friendly manner. If he had a tail, he would be wagging it in his eagerness. "I'm Shirley." I shook his hand.

"So Shirley, what are you doing here?" He rubbed his nose.

"I needed to get away." I found myself flirting with him. It was easier than I would have thought.

"Away from what? Shirley." He said my name sensuously.

I smiled so wide that my teeth felt dry. I was drunk. "I'm a pilot, Jack — and it's been a hard run lately."

"No kidding? A pilot?" He perked up, his dark eyes glued to my face as he pointed to a set of wings on his own chest. "What a coincidence! I'm a pilot, too. We patrol the gulf, looking for subs, you know."

I was surprised he didn't question my right to be a pilot. He accepted it as something we had in common. "I've been ferrying *Wiley Foxes* to Camp Morgan and towing targets," I told him.

"Whew! That's some job. I had a buddy get shot down towing targets. Scared the hell out of him."

"I had a friend go down that way too. She cussed into the radio all the way down and they grounded her."

"Hell, I'd cuss too if I were her."

I took another drink. Jack Reynolds passed my first test with flying colors. He treated me like a colleague. Not even Tommy McDougal did that. Certainly, Grant didn't. We fell into a long discussion about the US Army A-24 Dive Bombers we flew to tow targets in California. Jack had flown them for the Navy although he called them the 'SBD Dauntless.' Time passed. I was having fun.

We ordered one more drink. I'd grown to like Mags' Mexican drink. Big Skinner set the glass down in front of me with a flourish. I leaned forward and licked the salt off the rim of the goblet.

225

Jack was drinking rum. "I fly a PBY now. A hell of a plane, I tell you. We patrol the coastline although we fly out over the Dry Tortugas once a week."

I saluted a huge silver fish hanging on one wall and hiccupped.

"It's beautiful out there, Shirley. Beautiful," Jack continued, slurring his words. "The water is so shallow you can see the ocean floor if the light is right and you can see turtles and sharks and rays going about their business below the surface." Jack cracked peanuts in his fist and popped the nuts into his mouth. I pretended not to notice when he dropped the shells on the floor of the bar since other people were doing the same thing.

"It sounds nice. I'd love to see it." I held the cocktail in my mouth, enjoying the flavor and the coolness on my tongue.

"Why don't you come with us in the morning? There's a fort out there in the middle of no-where. It's a national monument. A man and his wife live out there by themselves, taking care of it. We fly over once a week to make sure they are okay. Drop them some newspapers. Maybe an *American Dream Magazine*."

"*American View Magazine*?"

He threw back the last of his drink. "Yeah, that one."

"Great rag!" I felt like I was floating two inches off the floor. I opened my arms wide like wings and closed my eyes.

"I never read it myself." He slammed his empty glass on the bar.

Startled, I fell off my shoes and staggered sideways, giggling.

Jack grabbed my arm to steady me and continued talking as if nothing happened. "You aren't leaving are you?"

"I've been traveling for three days. I'm exhausted."

"I'll escort you to the hotel." He swayed a little.

"That's all!" I shook my finger and batted my eyelashes. I might have been swaying a bit too. He took my arm and we found our way

226

out the jalousie doors. Tropical stars sparkled above us as we staggered down the sidewalk singing about the white cliffs of Dover.

"Have you ever been to Dover?" He stepped off the curb into the street backwards. A horse drawn cart nearly ran over his foot.

I grabbed his hand and pulled him towards me in a feeble rescue effort. "I'll tell you a secret," I whispered. He leaned forward with his hand cupped over his ear. "I don't even know where Dover is." We laughed, our voices blending with the other street noises — two more drunks among many. "Why do you really do that?"

"Do what?"

"Fly over that fort and drop *American View Magazine* to those people?"

"I dunno." He rubbed his nose. "Being out in the middle of nowhere like that would drive me crazy. I thought they might like to know what was happening out here in the real world."

"You are a nice man, Jack Reynolds." I was sure Father would think so too. I kissed Jack on the cheek. It surprised both of us.

He touched my hair. "I'll take you up to your room."

"No, I can find it."

"You can trust me."

"I know."

He wasn't much taller than me. He leaned forward and kissed me on the lips. I stepped back. He grabbed my shoulders and kissed me again, right in the middle of Duval Street. "Come with me tomorrow?"

"No."

He kissed me again. "Six o'clock?"

"Okay."

#

As tired and drunk as I was, I found myself wide-awake most of the night. Around five am, I got up, bathed, and dressed in my WASP uniform. I was in the lobby when Jack Reynolds roared up on a motor scooter at six-ten. I looked around hoping there would be a taxi nearby. Early morning sponge fishermen were making their way down to the docks, but everyone else was still asleep.

"Come on, Shirley." Jack slid forward on the seat. I took a chance and climbed on behind him. "Hold on tight," he said.

I slipped my arms around his waist and we roared off. Huge bushes of deep red flowers lined the road — Bougainvillea.

The PBY was a huge, high-winged aircraft. The co-pilot gave up his seat and I climbed in beside Jack as we flew west from Key West. It was an extraordinary plane. I was not used to the engines being over my head but I loved the feel of the controls and the fact that I could see the ocean below me.

"You were right. It's beautiful," I said as I scanned the water.

"You might even see a sunken ship if you get lucky."

"What are we looking for?"

"It's too shallow for subs here, but you could keep an eye out for anything unusual like people in rubber boats with guns in their hands who speak German or Japanese." He tipped his hat forward low over his eyes.

I squinted. "I'll keep an eye out."

We'd been flying just under an hour when he said, "There it is."

The six-sided fort took up almost the entire area of a small key. It was odd to see this man made something so far from the rest of the world. Jack lowered one wing and we circled, taking in the beauty of the area.

"Are you ready back there?" Jack shouted over his shoulder.

"Ready." One of the men hollered back.

He put the nose down and we headed towards the inner courtyard of the fort. We could see a small house, trees, bushes, and other small buildings inside the perimeter.

"Drop it!" Jack yelled over his shoulder.

His copilot tossed a bundle out the window. I watched as it bumped across the sandy courtyard.

A woman ran out of one of the buildings, waving. I gasped, holding both hands over my mouth. The figure dancing below me was Emmie — beautiful Emmie. I closed my eyes for a moment and then looked again. No, not Emmie. She was gone forever. Jack pulled back on the controls and bright blue sky filled the windscreen. I wet my lips with my tongue. I was hung over, dehydrated.

We banked and headed back to Key West.

#

Emmie's life was short, but it was hers. She enjoyed it — every minute. I wanted that too. I was running away — away from Father and grief and trying to be normal. The headache nagged, but I didn't let that stop me. Key West was the perfect playground even in the midst of war. Jack was an eager playmate. Like naughty children, we danced in the streets at sunset for no reason except it felt good — and the Lord knows I wanted to feel good. Big Skinner fixed me cocktails filled with rum and fruit juices and cracked ice. We ate conch fritters under a banyan tree and shrank in horror from the wild chickens that pecked around our feet and snatched up any morsels we might drop from our picnic. We went sightseeing on Jack's motor scooter, circling the island several times. At dawn, Jack hired a small launch and we went fishing.

I lingered longer than our original plan, when Mags ran an errand for Hap Arnold. She returned a week later with no explanations and my extended vacation ended. It was the night before we were to leave. I hadn't thought of Emmie or Father or Grant in all that time. Jack and I wandered down the beach after dark. I took off my new rope sandals and carried them. We'd spent the afternoon drinking at

Sloppy Joe's and I was beginning to sober up. I sat down on the damp sand and let the water wash over my ankles.

"Wouldn't it be nice to live here?" Jack sat down beside me. "Buy a plane and start a business flying tourists up and down the keys. We're both pilots. We could keep the damned thing in the air all the time if we had the business. After a while, we could buy one of those big Victorian houses and fix it up. Have a bunch of kids."

My face burned. "What are you saying?"

"I'm asking you to marry me." He wanted to hold my hand but I pulled away and scrambled to my feet. He was like Grant Logan after all — and the others.

I turned and went back up the beach headed towards my hotel many blocks away.

"Wait, Shirley. Wait for me. I'll give you a ride." He followed on foot for a while. I walked faster. Soon the scooter puttered to life behind me. Sprinting through the deep sand was tiring but I reached the sidewalk about the time he did. He had my shoes.

"NO!" I was hot and sweaty, my face flushed.

"At least tell me what I did wrong."

I sat down on the curb, my hair damp from the saltwater and matted with sand. "I'm not looking for a husband."

He looked like a disheartened puppy. "Well, you are the first woman I ever met who wasn't. Are you already married?"

I shook my head. I felt guilty — so much for freedom and fun.

"Then what's the problem? Why did you let me fall in love with you and then run off?"

"Is that what I did?"

"That's exactly what you did." He handed me my sandals.

I stuffed them in my bag. "It's time to go home. That's all."

"Don't give me that. You are scared!"

"No, I'm not."

"Yes, you are. I know scared when I see it."

"It was great. It's what I've wanted, but then you spoiled it." My feet were sore and the sidewalk was uneven. I stepped off the curb and limped off into the night.

"Okay," he said when I was almost a block away.

"What?

"OKAY!" He yelled. "If you don't want to get married, that's fine by me."

"Sssssh! Be quiet." I shuffled back towards him. "You mean it?"

"I thought all women wanted to get married."

I wasn't quite as sure of my stance now but I faked it. "Well, I don't."

"Fine."

I was disappointed he didn't fight harder. Grant always did. "My feet hurt. Will you take me back to the hotel?"

"Crawl on." He kick started the engine.

CHAPTER 16 — INTERLUDE

"Six Men Arrested for Stealing Nylon Thread for Black Market, Meat Association Fears more Shortages, Cary Grant Charms in Arsenic and Old Lace."
Headlines
~ American View Daily ~
September, 1944

I met Mags at the train station at six in the morning. Fresh from the shower, my hair was damp and my cheeks flushed.

"I'm ready to go home and marry Grant." I told her.

"I'm sure he'll be happy about that," she said as we settled into our seats and relaxed for the long ride back to Ohio. Funny thing though, her eyes weren't smiling.

As always, Grant met us at the Cold Creek Train Station. I threw my arms around him with new passion. He held me tight for a moment and then stepped back, "My God, Shirley. What's with you? Sunburn?"

Embarrassed, I put my hands on my cheeks. "It's sunny in Florida."

He pressed his lips on my forehead and looked worried. "You're in Ohio now."

We drove Mags straight to Jerry's Airport. She climbed out and waved before hurrying into the hangar. She was eager to get back into the air. I should have checked on the plane we were building with Pam, but I wanted to talk with Grant. He drove the *Wiley* bus out to our special spot near the Cold Creek Cemetery even though it was broad daylight.

"We have twenty-five minutes before I have to go pick up the *Wiley* girls. I've been frantic with worry about you, Shirley. I was afraid you were going to leave me — or that you'd put me on hold forever." He kissed the tip of my nose.

I took a deep breath. The time had come. "I know I've not been an easy girl to love. I know it's hard for you to believe, but getting

233

married hasn't been a priority for a long time. I convinced myself I don't need anyone — and I don't. I'm not as wealthy as Mags, of course, but Father has been and will continue to be generous with me. That is if he's still speaking to me."

The sun shining in the bus window caressed Grant's face. Even with his forehead wrinkled in some fearful expectation, he was swell. All he wanted was an ordinary life. Was that so much to ask?

"This sounds like the big kiss-off. Please don't do that to me, Shirley."

I took his hands in mine. "I don't need you, Grant. I do want you. I love you, too. You are a sweet, gentle soul. I can't imagine what you see in me, but if you still want me — I'm yours."

He stared at my lips a moment after I finished speaking. "When?"

"Whenever you want." I took the ruby ring off of my right hand and let him put it on my left.

He started making plans right away — when to tell his parents, when and how to tell Father, where to have the wedding. I sat in the back of the bus listening to him talk. He decided I needed to stay at *The Windshift Inn* until all the arrangements could be made. He wanted me to call Jackie Cochran and resign right away. I'd been traveling almost non-stop for months. He insisted I take a couple of weeks to rest up then we'd drive up to New Jersey to discuss the wedding with Father. I'd been through all of those things before. I was afraid to hope it would go smoothly. Whenever I got close to being happy, something happened, but it was time to put those fears aside.

We picked up the girls at the factory right on time and Grant delivered us all to our doors. As I climbed down out of the bus at *The Windshift Inn*, Myrtle came out on the porch to greet me, and wave at Grant. He grinned and gave her the thumbs up. She gave me one of her big bear hugs.

After dinner, I called Father and convinced him that I was fine. He agreed to send me a new pair of saddle oxfords. I decided not to tell him about marrying Grant — not just yet, anyway. I didn't have the energy to discuss it. I climbed the stairs, laid down on my bed, and fell asleep.

#

"Shirley?"

I struggled to open my eyes. "What?"

"Are you going to get up for breakfast?"

"I think I'll just sleep another hour, Myrtle."

"Sure thing, Sugar. You've been running around for months. You rest until you are all rested up."

"Okay." I rolled over and went back to sleep.

#

I should have been planning my wedding. I should have been going to church with Grant and his family. I should even have been working on the plane with Pam, but I couldn't seem to get myself together. I either dozed in the rocker on the front porch or sat in my room thinking. Sometimes I'd try to help Myrtle clean up after dinner, but she shooed me away and I let her.

I didn't think about Jack Reynolds. I didn't worry about Delores either — or that Mags was off flying for the WASP again. I did think about Emmie — and those bastards at Camp Morgan. Jackie Cochran met with Conrad Simpson and insisted on an investigation. I thought that was a crock. Jackie was more worried about the publicity and what it would do to the WASP program than the fact that Emmie was killed. I didn't expect much to come of it.

I thought about Wayne Wilson a lot, too. He'd promised me he'd keep Number 49 grounded until he figured out a way to fix its many problems. He let me down — he let all of us down, especially Emmie. I couldn't understand where he might have gone but I was

235

sure it was because he felt guilty. Conrad Simpson was searching for him — to put him under arrest for going AWOL, I suppose. Mags was looking for him too. She wanted to ask him the same questions I wanted to ask him.

A couple days after I returned from Key West, Delores came back to *The Windshift Inn*. She was pale and skinny. The carefree way she took over a room was muted now. The dark circles under her eyes told me she still wasn't sleeping. The pain had to be excruciating. Her arms were wrapped in light cotton gauze and she brought a small bag full of medicines to help her deal with her wounds. She couldn't lift a spoon or carry a suitcase. In fact, she was in no condition to go visiting.

"Why did you come back?"

A bearded man in a dark suit helped her out of a big, black car. "Aren't you glad to see me?" She wobbled as she climbed the front stoop.

I hurried to help her up the steps. "Of course I am, but you aren't well. You should be in a hospital." I gave her a self-conscious hug. As I slid my arm around her waist, I could feel the bones in her back.

She leaned down and whispered in my ear. "I'm driving my parents crazy. They need a break from me and I need one from them." Her smile was still dazzling when she put her soul into it. "Anyhoo, it seems I'm too healthy for a hospital and too sick to be left to my own devices. My mother is ill herself — depressed. My father is struggling to keep his business afloat while putting out money to try and find anyone we can. They are both worried sick about my brother who has decided to join the Marines of all things. A bored, cranky invalid is the last thing they need right now so Myrtle has agreed to watch after me for a while."

"I'm on recovery duty as well, I told her. Even though I feel fine, they think I need a rest so here we are — roommates again."

236

Delores and I were as different as night and day. We clashed on every subject, and of course, she was an absolute slob. I have to admit that I felt better with her around though. We were like feuding sisters having to endure each other at the supper table — or at least we used to be. Now, her frailty made her seem less formidable.

We spent the next few days gossiping about the other WASPs, Jackie Cochran, and Conrad Simpson. It didn't look good for the program. Responding to complaints about the resources coming our way, Congress would soon vote as to whether to expand or disband us.

Delores was outraged. I thought maybe fate would make it easier to follow through on my decision to marry Grant. I knew I should do something about it, but I procrastinated. I had run out of energy, it seemed. Grant was frustrated with me but Delores had a pretty good idea of what I was feeling. She was going through something similar.

We must have been quite a handful, or maybe it was because we were now staying at the inn for an extended period of time and we were paying full fare as private customers. Whatever the reason, Myrtle quit her job at the factory and devoted herself to *The Windshift Inn* — and to us. Jerry Kline came over to the inn once a week and mowed the lawn. Each evening, Grant sat on the top step yammering on about the War, the factory — even the future of the WASP program. Delores and I sat out there in the dusk, slapping at mosquitoes and giggling at Grant's long discourses on one subject or another. With Myrtle's good food and the fresh air, Delores was soon well enough to go on long walks with me. Jerry even convinced us to go riding again.

One afternoon, he picked us up in his truck and drove us over to the stables. Pam had the horses saddled. I was brave enough to feed Easy a couple of carrots, but when it came right down to it, I couldn't bring myself to ride her again. It was just as well. It took all of us to get Delores up on Pokey. Riding Horace was out of the question for her. She couldn't hold onto the horn. They wrapped the reins loosely around her wrists. I shuddered but Jerry assured me there would be no runaways. He rode close on one side of Delores and Pam on the other. I waved good-bye as they plodded across the pasture.

It was hot at the stables and huge iridescent flies buzzed around my face. I slapped at them but they were relentless. *The Windshift Inn* was on the hill over the airport. I'd climbed up that hill several times so I started out cross-country. The brush was thick. I'd never gone this deep into the field. Brambles scratched my legs and tree branches smacked my face. After a few yards, I felt queasy. I bent over and closed my eyes waiting for the sickness to pass. When I resumed my trek, I had a headache and the small of my back hurt.

Jerry, Delores, and Pam were back at the inn by the time I climbed that steep hill, crawled over the low fence, and crossed the road. I was flushed and sweaty as I came into the foyer. Dinner was ready but the smell of food nauseated me. Myrtle came out of the kitchen and watched me struggle up the back stairs. At the first landing, I paused and leaned my face against the wall. Sure that I would throw up before I reached the second landing, I staggered down the hall to the bathroom.

Dinner was over and the girls were filing up the stairs to their rooms when I opened the door and hurried to my bed. My period was a little late and I'd thought perhaps I was about to bleed, but there was nothing.

I lay in bed crying. Even though I didn't believe in him anymore, surely God's punishment couldn't be so swift and overwhelming. My throat was raw and the back of my head hurt. It was a few days of fun. Grant would never understand. I thought of Lizzie Langer and shivered at the thought of what might lie ahead. I was thirsty. I'd never been so thirsty in my life. I prayed to my angry God, "Haven't I suffered enough?"

CHAPTER 17 — THE FIGHT

"Did she ask for me?"
~ *George Maxwell, Father*
October, 1944

I thought I knew what was coming. How simple that would have been, but life threw me a curve ball that I never expected. I lay in bed — panicked — waiting for Delores. I didn't want to be alone but I didn't have the energy to get up and go look for her. The pain in my head was intense and my throat was so sore it was hard to swallow. An hour passed, and she still hadn't come back to our room.

I was stiff all over and it was impossible to find a comfortable position. I tried to sit up but my calf muscles contracted. Father used to call leg cramps "Charlie Horses." This was the worst Charlie Horse of my life. It went on and on. When it was over, I was exhausted. All I wanted to do was sleep, but I felt dampness between my legs and realized my period had started at last. I sat up and the nausea returned. I found my way down the hall to the bathroom. Someone was in there. I beat on the door with my fist.

"Please hurry. I'm sick. Please."

One of the factory girls came out. Her irritated scowl changed to alarm when she saw me.

"I need help," I told her.

She ran down the back stairs while I threw up into the toilet. My legs were so weak from the cramping that I couldn't get up. There I was with my chin resting on the commode with a growing red stain on the crotch of my pajamas.

Before I knew it, Delores was kneeling beside me. "Let's get you cleaned up and back to bed. Myrtle will be here in a minute, she's calling the doctor."

She slid her bandaged arms under my armpits and helped me to my feet. My legs were like noodles. They wouldn't support me. Using her foot, she closed the lid on the toilet and lowered me down on it.

I whimpered with humiliation.

"Hush, now. Hush," she whispered. "I won't look at you. You hang on and I'll be right back." She closed the door behind her to give me privacy and I heard her run down the hallway toward our room.

The cramps returned. I wanted to rub my legs, but it hurt to lean forward. If I wasn't pregnant, what could be wrong with me? My head ached so much that I couldn't think. Delores tapped on the door before she opened it.

"Take these." She handed me a sanitary napkin and belt. She also had fresh underwear and clean pajamas for me. "I'll wait for you outside."

I nodded and waited until she closed the door again. I stretched to reach the sink from the toilet. I wet a washcloth with warm water but couldn't seem to wring it out. My damp pajama bottoms clung to my thighs as I struggled to get them off. Every move hurt. I cleaned myself as best I could and slipped the napkin between my legs. Fumbling with the garter clasp, my fingers wouldn't work right. I sobbed in frustration. After several minutes, I had to face the fact I couldn't do this most intimate of tasks for myself.

"Delores! Delores?"

She stuck her head in the door.

"I can't do it." I didn't sound like myself.

"I can't help you either." She held up her burned hands wrapped in layers and layers of gauze. "I'll get Myrtle."

A few moments later, Myrtle knocked on the door. She looked the other way when she saw my embarrassing condition. "I've called the doctor. He'll be here in an hour."

"I'm sorry to be such a bother," I murmured as she clasped the sanitary napkin to the belt. She rinsed the bloody washcloth and wiped my thighs. I bit my lip and closed my eyes. She glanced at me with worried eyes when she touched my foot before slipping my panties over it. She worked them up over my knees. Then she put her arm around me and lifted me upwards.

I couldn't stand.

"Delores!"

"I'm here." Delores hurried to support me while Myrtle pulled up my panties.

"Let's forget about the pajama bottoms." Myrtle puffed from her exertions.

I shuddered at the thought of the long trip down the hallway with my thighs bare, "No, please," was all I could get out.

Myrtle sighed and worked the fresh pajama bottoms up my legs. I was grateful to be clean and covered again. "Okay, let's get you back to bed," she said.

We started out of the bathroom leaving my bloody clothes in a heap. "Oh no, no!" I gestured with my head.

"I'll come back for it. We'll get them laundered, don't worry." Delores whispered in my ear.

We made our way down the hall. I was afraid there might be a stain on my sheets, but Myrtle had remade my bed. I was relieved. They laid me down and Myrtle tucked the covers up under my arms.

"She's so hot!" I heard Delores say to Myrtle. She pulled her chair up beside my bed and sat there, a line creasing her forehead. "Don't you leave me too," she whispered.

I didn't care anymore. All I wanted was to sleep and soon I did.

Sometime later the doctor awakened me by flipping on the overhead light. I didn't know him and I didn't like him. His jacket smelled like mothballs and his breath was rotten. He shook a thermometer

241

and stuck it in my mouth without saying a word. Then he threw back the covers and felt my legs, his fingers digging into my sore muscles. Delores stood beside my bed watching the doctor work. Myrtle hovered in the doorway. I mumbled curses at him but he ignored me. Jerking the thermometer out of my mouth, he held it up to the light.

"Hm," he said.

We waited for him to say more, but he took my hands and crossed them over my chest. Then with a hand on my head, he pulled my head forward sharply — trying to bring my chin to my chest. A burning pain from heels to neck shot through my body and I howled.

"Hm," he repeated. "We need to do a spinal tap. Roll over on your side."

Rolling over wasn't easy but I managed without help. "What's a spinal tap?" I asked.

He pulled up my pajama tops and pushed down the bottoms baring my lower back. Feeling manhandled and cranky, my dislike for him turned to hatred.

"Don't you worry your little head about that. It'll be over in a minute." He rubbed something cold on my lower back. "Miz Jones, why don't you come over here and help me with this."

"What do you want me to do?" Myrtle squatted down beside my bed, facing me.

"Just hold her by the shoulders real tight. She mustn't move while I'm doing this."

Myrtle took hold of my shoulders with one hand, my knees with the other. "Like this?

"Don't let her move. You hear me, little lady? Don't move." He raised his voice like I was deaf.

I never saw the needle, but it must have been thick and very long. It seemed to go in forever. My screams awakened everyone in *The*

Windshift Inn. I bucked, but Myrtle held me tight, staring into my eyes with the utmost kindness and concern. Her eyes scared me more than anything else that night. The doctor left me sobbing into my pillow. Myrtle caressed my hair before leaving. I heard the three of them whispering outside my door.

After a bit, Delores came back to me while the other two went downstairs. She sat where I could see her.

"What is it? What's wrong with me?"

"He doesn't know for sure" I knew she was scared too. I could feel it. She and I had been terrified together before.

"What does he think? Tell me, Delores. Be my friend. Tell me."

"He thinks it is polio."

Polio? Only kids got polio — except for FDR, of course. I'd once seen a bunch of men helping him off his train. We were at the station in DC with a photographer from the magazine. He started to take a picture but Father stopped him. Out of respect, I remember him saying. I asked Father what was wrong and he said the president had polio when he was a young man. OH GOD! Polio. How in the world did I get polio? That meant paralysis or death. "When will he know for sure?"

"When he gets back the results of the spinal tap."

"When will that be?"

"He said tomorrow."

"So what do we do until then?"

"We keep everyone away from you. It seems you are contagious right now. We are moving you down to the second floor. There's a room with a private bathroom so it will be easier for us to take care of you. We work at bringing down that fever. He's telling Myrtle what to do now."

I thought of Red forever condemned to his wheelchair, no longer able to fly. It was the first time I realized flying was important to

243

me. I thought of Jack and the pleasures he taught me. I thought of Grant and his desire for children. "I don't want to be crippled." I was growing drowsy again.

"We don't know that's what will happen. Let's just wait and see."

I closed my eyes. The inside of my eyelids glowed dark red. Everything hurt. Myrtle hurried into the room with a bowl of cold water and small squares of terrycloth. "We have to bring her fever down. I have aspirin."

It was hard to swallow the pills. I pushed them far back into my throat but they wouldn't go down. Finally they dissolved on my tongue and the water Myrtle held to my lips spilled over my lips.

"One of the girls is cleaning up a room for you. Jerry will be here in a minute to help us get you down there, she said as she dried my chin and neck."

When Jerry appeared, the problem of carrying me down the narrow staircase seemed insurmountable. He tried putting me over his shoulder but the pain was too much. I cried and begged him to put me down. Finally, he picked me up under the arms and Myrtle took my feet. After much scuffling and shifting my weight one way or another, they got me down the flight of steps and laid me in the new room.

Myrtle and Delores sat there all night, bathing me with cool water, laying cold cloths on my aching head. I'm not sure what they were doing helped me physically, but I was terrified of being alone and grateful to them for being there. Around three, Myrtle fell asleep on a cot Jerry had brought in. Delores stayed awake all night.

The next morning, I tried to get up to go to the bathroom but I couldn't move. The cramping pain in my muscles was still there, but nothing worked. Alone with me, Delores pulled the gauze from her hands. I couldn't tear my eyes away from her burns. She shrugged and smiled. "So much for beauty."

244

She emptied the water bowl and slipped it under my hips. My humiliation was complete when she wiped me and replaced my sanitary napkin. Her hands were stiff and it must have hurt her terribly, but she managed somehow.

Later, when she returned to my room and realized what Delores had done, Myrtle scolded her while cleaning and rewrapping her hands. Exhausted, Delores catnapped throughout the day. I was afraid she was getting sick too.

The doctor called to confirm his diagnosis around three in the afternoon. I was still feverish and I couldn't lift my head from the pillow.

"Delores?"

"I'm right here, Shirley." She roused herself from a chair beside my bed and leaned over me.

"Will you call Father?" I could see myself in her eyes and the image terrified me.

"We've already talked to him. He's trying to find someone to help you."

"Will you tell him that I love him?"

"He already knows that."

"No, promise me. Okay?"

A little V formed on her forehead.

"Okay?"

"I'm not going to let you die, Shirley."

"Tell him anyway?"

A tear trickled down her cheek. "I promise," she whispered.

By midnight, it was hard to breathe. I'd inhale but couldn't find the energy to empty my lungs. Finally, the air would rush out of my mouth in a long wheeze. Faced with the impossible task of drawing

245

in more air, the time between breaths grew longer and longer. I was sure I was dying.

Delores stood by my bed, the rigid knuckles of her hand pressed against my chest. "Okay, that's good. Breathe in, Shirley. That's it." Her voice dropped to a mumble. At first, it didn't make sense, then I made out her words. "Don't let her hurt, please don't let her hurt."

The pain swallowed me and then I understood. She was right. Why didn't God just take me? It was time. Then as the urge to inhale became more intense, nothing mattered but the need for oxygen. I panicked — eyes wide, mouth moving in a fruitless gasp. Delores couldn't hold out either. She gripped my hand and demanded that I breathe and somehow I did. By morning, my fingernails were turning blue.

"She needs an iron lung. She's losing the ability to breathe on her own," the doctor said as he stood over me. "There's not that many available around here. None that I know of. I'll make some calls, but I don't know how we'd get one here in time."

"Mags is on her way here. She'll find one." Delores stared into my eyes. I trusted Mags. I knew she would do her best, but I wasn't sure this was something even she could do.

Myrtle fussed with my blanket. "Shirley, your father is searching for a hospital to take you. Maybe Warm Springs. There's also a place in Minneapolis that specializes in polio."

"No, no, no! I don't want to leave here. I want to stay here." At least that's what I tried to say.

"You need to be where they can take care of you properly — where they know what to do." Myrtle put a cool washcloth across my burning brow.

I gasped for air. "NO!" It was no longer possible to cry. "I want to be with you!"

The doctor pulled Myrtle away from my bedside. "She's not going to make it anyway. What difference does it make if she dies there or here?"

I was shocked by his bluntness. Did he think I couldn't hear him? I could choose to talk or breathe. I couldn't do both at the same time. "Here!" I croaked.

"Here." Delores stuck out her lower lip. Her beauty always threatened me before and her stubbornness annoyed me, but now those qualities were reassuring. I knew she'd be with me to the very end. Why had I never appreciated her before?

I inhaled but this time, nothing happened. I couldn't push the air back out of my lungs no matter how much I tried. My eyes were wide and my mouth gaped. I thought maybe this was it — my last breath. Life seemed so precious just as I was losing it.

"No, no!" Delores put both scarred hands over her mouth.

The doctor rolled me off the bed onto the floor on my stomach putting my hands under my forehead and turning my head sideways. The pain in my neck and back was excruciating, but not breathing was worse. I felt myself going away, drifting upwards out of my body. He straddled my buttocks, placed his hands on my back just below my ribcage and pushed. The air in my lungs spewed out of my nose and mouth. Leaning forward, he pulled back on my elbows and air rushed in. He repeated the process for the next cycle — and the next.

"Here," he said to Myrtle as he got up. "Let me show you how." Myrtle straddled my buttocks and pushed on my back. "Yes, that's it. Slower. Give her time before you pull back on her arms. Yes."

I was terrified, but I was alive.

"It's useless. I doubt she'll take another breath by herself. The only hope is to keep her alive until you find an iron lung for her — if you ever find one." The doctor put his hand on my forehead while

Myrtle continued helping me breathe. "It's too bad really. She's a lovely young woman."

I was glad when he left.

"What are we going to do?" Delores sat down on my bed watching Myrtle labor over me. I could no longer talk at all.

"We keep her alive until Mags finds the lung." Myrtle was becoming breathless herself.

"How long can we keep it up?"

"As long as we have to. Let's see what Mr. Maxwell wants to do. We'll get others in here to help. Volunteers, of course. Grant is beside himself because I won't let him up here. Well, now's his chance — and Jerry of course."

"What about Pam?"

"She's a child. I don't want to take a chance with her getting this." Myrtle pushed on my back.

"We'll work in teams, maybe. I can pull on her arms, but I don't think I can press her back that way," Delores said.

"I'm good for a while. Go downstairs and see if you can get hold of George Maxwell and Mags. Impress upon them how urgent this is." Myrtle pulled my arms back and I took a breath.

I couldn't see their faces. I lay on my stomach like a piece of meat. Every few hours, Myrtle changed my sanitary napkin and cleaned me in between respirations. Modesty was no longer an option for me.

"What in God's name are you doing to that girl?" It was Mr. McKensey's voice. I'd not even heard him come up the stairs.

"She can't breathe for herself anymore," Myrtle said.

"Poor child."

"Mags is searching for an iron lung. There are only so many of them and what with the war, they haven't been making new ones."

"You mean you have to do this until they find a machine and bring it here?" Mr. McKensey's voice grew louder as his footsteps approached me.

"MR. MCKENSEY! You get out of here right now. You could catch polio."

"Nonsense. I'm too old to get some damned kid's disease, and even if I wasn't, I've lived my life. He smelled like old clothes and shoe polish. "Now you get up from there. I'll take over for a while."

"I can't ask you to take that chance."

"So don't ask. Get your butt downstairs and get some rest."

"Do you know what to do?" Myrtle got up and I heard her dusting off her clothes.

"Get out of here, woman. I watched you just now, didn't I? I'll do fine."

She paused at the door. I felt him straddle my legs. He was rougher with me than Myrtle, but my lungs completely filled with air. I heard her go down the stairs. I could tell from her heavy step that she was tired.

"This is a pretty messed up world when little girls like you get exposed to something like this," Mr. McKensey muttered as he pushed on my back. "In my day, we took care of our women. In my day, we focused on our homes not on flying contraptions. In my day, you worked the land and the land took care of you. Didn't have no damned banks taking over for you. No tractors falling on top of you. No Japs blowing up ships in the harbor."

He developed a rhythm that I could anticipate. It was like dancing, punctuated with his wheezing complaints.

"My daddy was a Confederate soldier," he said. "He fought to keep things from changing. He died while I was still inside my Mama back in 1864. Here we are 80 years later and ain't nothing any better than it used to be and a lot of things are worse."

249

He was muttering about everything that annoyed him when Delores and Grant came to spell him twenty minutes later. "I'll be back, little girl," he said as they helped him to his feet.

Delores knelt beside me. "Your father is arranging to bring a different doctor here to treat you. A better one. Grant's going to take over for a while now, but I'll be nearby if you need me." She stood up and then I couldn't see her anymore.

"Baby," Grant murmured as he took his position. "I'm not letting you go. You hear me? I'm not letting you go." His compressions were almost like caresses.

"Thank you, Mr. McKensey. I'm sure Shirley would thank you if she could." Delores' light footsteps merged with Mr. McKensey's shuffling ones as they went out into the hallway. "That was very brave of you, Mr. McKensey," Delores told him.

"Buzz off," he growled.

After he left, Delores came back into the room. "Let's see if I can do this." She knelt at my head and hooked her forearms under my elbows. "If we do it this way, we might be able to last longer before we have to change."

Grant pushed on my back and Delores pulled on my elbows. It went smoothly and together they worked on me for over two hours. They didn't speak to each other, but bent to their task. My muscles were tight and my hipbones were sore where they pressed against the floor.

Then the footsteps of several people came down the hall together. They paused outside my door, whispering together. Then one of them came into the room.

Delores and Grant paused.

"No," a voice with a strange accent said. "Keep doing what you are doing for a moment." The woman knelt down on the floor beside me.

More footsteps and Myrtle said, "Shirley."

A squeak was all I could manage.

"Shhh, now don't talk. Let them work. This is Sister Elizabeth Kenny. She's a nurse who is famous for her work with polio patients. Your daddy sent her here to help us figure out what to do. Don't you worry. Things will be okay soon."

How many times had I put Father through hell? How many times had he come through for me? I wondered if I'd finally found the one thing that he couldn't fix. I closed my eyes.

Grant pushed on my back and air came out of my nose and mouth. "It's nice to meet you, ma'am," he muttered.

"Just take care of this girl right now, son. We'll handle the amenities when I've examined her."

"Yes, ma'am." I could tell from his voice that Grant couldn't quite hear what the lady was saying.

"Young woman, if you could just pull one more time to fill her lungs," Sister Kenny said.

Delores pulled on my arms, then released me, and sat back on her heels.

"I'm going to roll you over for a little while, Shirley."

It was like holding my breath while someone poked and prodded me, but this woman was gentle and fast. "You can start again," she told Grant as he stood up.

#

Myrtle came to the door. "I just heard from Mags. She's found an iron lung but it's broken. It's in a barn about two hours from here. She's found someone who thinks he can fix it. Jerry is on his way with the pickup truck. They'll be here in four or five hours."

Four or five hours, I thought. I have to endure, four or five hours of this hell. It seemed like forever.

251

"Do you hear that, Shirley?" Delores whispered to me as she worked. "You'll be so much more comfortable in the lung. You'll be able to lie on your back and sleep."

They worked through the afternoon and into the evening, switching off from person to person. Myrtle brought up food and drink for whoever was working with me. She'd spell them until they could refresh themselves. Then they'd start again. Mr. McKensey came back twice more but mostly it was Delores and Grant and Myrtle.

After an eternity, I heard Mags' voice. She'd flown into Jerry's airport and hiked her way back up the hill to the inn. She knelt down beside me, her cheek on the floor so I could see her eyes. "They are coming, Shirley. Jerry and Wayne Wilson. They are coming. Hold on. It'll be better soon."

I couldn't answer her but my mind spun with confusion. Why was Wayne Wilson coming here?

Grant stood up. I could hear him popping his knuckles and stretching. "I'll be back soon. Don't you worry, Shirley. I'll be back."

I grunted even though I knew he couldn't hear me.

"I love you," he said in front of everyone.

I grunted again. He squatted to kiss my head before he left. I hoped my hair didn't smell sour. I heard him talking to someone on the stairs. The nurse? Myrtle?

I heard squeaking and then I realized Delores had curled up on the bed. Before long, she was snoring. It was a sound I recognized from better times when she and Señor snoozed on the cot next to me at the WASP's Nest.

Someone new straddled me. Mags pulled my elbows back and I breathed in. She worked for a long time. It was almost dark when Myrtle came in to clean me up.

"Mags! She's sweating!"

I felt their hands on my arms, my forehead.

"The fever's broken, Shirley. The fever broke." Mags shook my shoulder. "You are getting better."

They rolled me onto my back while Myrtle cleaned me and replaced my underwear. Instead of pajamas, they put a long flannel nightgown on me. "This will be easier for us, Shirley. I hope you understand."

After three days of polio, I didn't care anymore. Here I was in a room someone else set up for me. My things were scattered over two floors. I was sure my brush and toilet articles weren't arranged properly. All I could do was focus on my next breath.

CHAPTER 18 — RESCUE

*"Buddy's Big Band Plays Madison Square Garden, O'Conner Declares Polio
Epidemic Ebbing, Marines Take Pelelieu Airdrome."*
Headlines
~ ***American View Daily*** ~
September 1944

They promised me that Jerry and Wayne were coming. They told me it would be four or five hours. I only had to hang on that long, but they were still not there after nine long hours. Delores and Myrtle hadn't slept in two days except for catnaps. They chased the others out of the room when it was their turn to help me breathe — cleaning me, murmuring words of encouragement. Grant remained the strongest, working over me for an hour at a time, resting twenty minutes before starting again.

Mr. McKensey was an old man. He had done more than his share. They sent him to bed and he slept for several hours. When he awoke, we heard him hacking up phlegm and passing gas in his bathroom. After a few minutes, he shuffled down the hall and saw Mags pushing on my back while Grant dozed in a corner.

"What the hell is this? I thought Jerry was supposed to be here by now."

His voice grated on my nerves. I was close to the edge. Everything irritated me — the small grunt Grant made when he pressed on my back, the smell of Mags' hand cream, the way Myrtle's left shoe squeaked when she came up the stairs, the dust bunny in the corner.

"Why didn't anyone call me?" He sounded furious.

"You needed your rest," Myrtle told him.

"Fercryingoutloud! You get downstairs and make up a pan of scrambled eggs. These youngins have been working all night. They are hungry and tired." I heard scuffling as he pushed Grant aside.

255

"Are you sure you can manage?" Grant yawned and I heard his joints creak as if he was stretching.

McKensey's fingers dug into the flesh of my forearms. "I'll be working when you are in your grave, little boy."

"You'll call if you get tired or if anything goes wrong?" Myrtle asked.

"Get out of here. All of you!" His sour breath seared the nape of my neck and his palms warmed my back through my nightgown. "I won't let anything happen to this little girl."

They all trooped downstairs leaving me alone with the vile, wonderful old man. With every cycle, he cursed bitterly, a continuous stream of profanity and compassion. After his rest, his energy was at a high level and he was almost too rough. I was bruised and miserable. After a half hour, he began to tire and his own breathing became ragged. He was coming to the end of his endurance and we were alone. I was frightened. The time between inhalation and exhalation increased. I wasn't getting enough air. My vision blurred. My fingers and toes were cold. I was going to die alone with Mr. McKensey.

Delores ran up the stairs screaming, "They're here! They're here!"

"Good God, girl! You're busting my eardrums," McKensey snarled as he pulled back on my elbows.

I was far away from them and their voices echoed in my head.

She knelt down beside me and put her face against the floor. I opened my eyes. "They just pulled into the turn around, Shirley. It won't be long now." She touched my cheek with the back of her claw. I remember the faint odor of ointment and the sight of those ugly burns on her hand. It was the last thing I do remember before I drifted into warm darkness.

#

When I awoke, the morning sun streamed in through the window above my head. I lay on my back looking up at the ceiling. A transparent spider dangled from a single thread above my nose. I shuddered. An odd mechanical hiss and pop filled my ears. I smelled lacquer and I wondered if I was in hell. Heaven didn't need a paint job.

"Hey, Shirley," a familiar male voice said. "What's the difference between God and pilots? Can't guess? Ha! Ha! God doesn't think he's a pilot."

I tried to lift my head but couldn't. I sensed something round and metal below my chin. I panicked. Was I in my coffin? I opened my mouth to scream before realizing that I was comfortable. Air was going in and out of my lungs. I must be alive.

A balding man stood up and smiled at me. "Feeling okay?"

My back and legs hurt but that sick dizzy feeling was gone. "Yeah." It came out more of a sigh.

"You've been asleep for hours," Wayne said.

"What are you doing?" At least that's what I tried to say. It was hard to speak above a whisper.

"I'm painting this old tin can. We found it stored in a barn, all scratched up, and chipped. I'm also giving you a little nose art down near your feet."

"Oh?"

"Don't you worry. No Virgin Queen caricature. I put your pretty face on *Fifinella*. You could use a little luck, don't you think?" He winked at me and popped his chewing gum before disappearing. I guessed he'd gone back to his work.

I swallowed. My mouth was dry. "What color?"

"Yellow, of course." His voice seemed muffled, like he might be under the machine. Drunk on oxygen, I felt giddy. I wasn't sure why

Wayne was painting the iron lung yellow, but I felt an odd affection for this strange machine — almost like I did for a new *Wiley Fox.*

"There that's better," he said. "Took me the better part of the night to get this thing running. We were missing some small pieces, bolts and the like — and some big ones. The electric motor was dirty, a few frayed wires, some worn out washers. Don't get too upset with me, but I'm afraid I raided the stash you and Pam were hoarding for the Stearman — even the paint. You didn't have enough for a whole airplane anyway. The pad you are laying on was made from the seat cushions. The leather covering was cracked and they were kind of ratty. We stole some of your sheets and tacked them around the cushions to make you more comfortable. You had been squished on that floor for days and I thought you'd like something a bit softer."

"Why are you here?" I didn't mean to sound ungrateful, but I didn't have enough air to talk much.

"I was working as an orderly in Pittsburgh. Mags came looking for me a few weeks ago. I was AWOL so I tried to disappear. Did you ever notice you can't hide from her? I wasn't ready to talk about Emmie yet, but she cornered me in the employee lounge of the hospital and we had a long conversation. I have to admit, I'd held it in too long. Of course, talking about it doesn't make it go away."

"No, it doesn't." I smacked my lips.

"She told me that Conrad Simpson sent my parents my medical discharge. I don't know how she pulled that off or why Colonel Simpson agreed to it. It was great to get that load off my shoulders. Don't get me wrong, I was grateful, but I was never going back anyway. After what happened to Emmie, I couldn't take it anymore. My nerves were shot,

"I'm not a total shit, though. I still wanted to contribute to the war effort. I made up a name and went to work in a hospital in Phoenix. Then I got to thinking maybe Simpson's MPs were closing in on me, so I took a train east and ended up in Pittsburgh.

258

"So a couple days ago, I was pushing this old codger up one of those steep hills near the hospital and I look up and there's Mags. She told me she needs me. That you do. She found this old beat-up lung in a barn outside of Akron, but she needed someone to fix it. I told her I had a job. I couldn't leave. Mags said, of course, I could and before I knew it, she had me in that red Stearman headed towards Akron. It was the furthest I'd ever flown. I don't know how I made it. I kept my eyes closed and prayed she wouldn't do one of those rolls she's so famous for.

"Jerry was already there. Fine fellow, that Jerry Kline. We dug the lung out of a pile of junk while the farmer watched and gave advice. He was glad to get rid of it. We loaded this metal beauty into the bed of Jerry's truck and started back here. Mags flew on ahead of us. We got into trouble right off the bat. The front right tire blew and we had to wrestle it off and get it patched. That's why we were so long getting back."

Their adventures with the iron lung went on and on, like Huck and Jim floating down the river. Jerry and Wayne became fast friends during the hours they struggled to get that marvelous machine back to *The Windshift Inn*. I lay there listening to him rattle on and my eyes began to droop. I fell asleep to the cadence of his storytelling and didn't awaken until noon.

Myrtle and Mags were fiddling with the lung and muttering to themselves.

"No, no!" I was afraid that if they took me out, I wouldn't be able to breathe again.

"It's okay." Sister Kenny says we need to work on your muscles before they start shrinking."

Mags had a big stick in her hands and she held it so I could see it. "We are going to put hot, wet blankets over you," she said. "It's supposed to help with the healing and keep your muscles soft."

It didn't sound like something I wanted to do, but there wasn't much I could do to stop them. They slid me out of the lung and rolled me

259

onto my stomach. My period was subsiding, but Myrtle had to clean me anyway. A steaming tub full of wool blankets soaking in hot water sat nearby. Using the stick, Mags lifted the top one, put it through a wringer attached to a second tub, and then laid it over my feet. I whimpered as they covered me from heels to neck. As the blankets cooled to body temperature, Myrtle began the prescribed massage and stretching techniques. I was exhausted when they got me back into the lung and soon drifted off to sleep again. A few hours later, they visited me again with more hot, wet blankets. I hated them but there was no squirming away or scratching where the wool made me itch.

I just endured.

CHAPTER 19 — FIFINELLA

"B-29s Strike Formosa, Congress votes to disband Jackie Cochran's Women's Air Force Service Pilots, Physician Declares FDR Healthy"
Headlines
~ American View Daily ~
October, 1944

Lavender! I watched my mother tuck little sachet pillows into my sock drawer, but I couldn't make out her face. Fact was, I couldn't remember her face or her voice. She'd been dead since I was three. All I had was two pictures. One was of my parents on their wedding day. They were looking at each other and not the camera, so it was hard to tell much about either of them. The other was of a solemn-faced little girl holding a ball. As far as I could tell, I didn't look a thing like her. It didn't make sense why she would be in my room, but I knew it was her anyway. "Mama?"

"No, it's me," a gentle voice whispered in my ear.

"Mother?"

Something else filled my nose. Not lavender — something acrid. Tobacco.

"Wake up, Shirley. It's Mags."

"What?" My eyes flew open in alarm.

She smiled at me and stepped back.

The machine wheezed and I struggled to follow her with my eyes.

"I'm leaving in a few minutes, but I have some news for you."

"Not going to like it, am I?"

"It's not the end of the world."

"So it's over?"

261

"We are officially canned as of three weeks ago." Mags sat down on a stool a couple feet to my right. "We heard from Jackie the same night I found *Fifinella* here." She tapped the iron lung with her nails.

I waited until the machine drew air into my lungs and then the words gushed out. "You knew and didn't tell me."

"Didn't seem important at the time."

"I'm not ready. My decision. Not theirs."

Mags shrugged. "You will fly again."

I tried to scowl but wasn't sure if it had the same effect lying flat of my back in a metal tube.

"Everything changes. In this case, I think you changed first." Mags' perspective maddened me.

"Sick. Changing." I couldn't get my thoughts to unjumble.

"All the gals are disappointed, but it's pretty hard to argue with Congress. The war in Europe is winding down. The big show is Japan now. People are starting to think about when the soldiers come home. You know what that means."

I grunted. Grant had told me what it meant many times. It still made me mad. "Girls will go home, too."

"Most will, I think," Mags said.

"Not you."

"No, not me."

I bit my lower lip because I couldn't scratch my arms anymore. "Me either. I'll be here."

"For a while but you are getting stronger every day."

"Myrtle and the women at *Wiley's* …" I imagined them all back in their kitchens.

"It's up to each family to decide what they will do."

I suddenly realized that Mags wouldn't be staying at *The Windshift Inn* now that the WASP wouldn't be flying the *Wileys*. "What will you do?"

"I've been talking with Jackie. Hap might have a little assignment for me in Europe. I'm going to meet with him now."

I knew better than to ask questions. Whatever Mags did for Hap Arnold was better kept between them, but I appreciated her trust in telling me that much. "When …?"

"I'll pop up just like I do now. You can't get rid of me. We are friends."

"Friends." My laugh never came out. "I'd be dead except for you."

"Naw, it was a group effort."

"No. Key West, too."

"Ah, Key West! Yes." She zipped up her leather jacket and pulled her gloves out of the pockets. "RRR told me that Jack sends you his love. He knows that you've been sick and has been worried."

"Ah." It was a soft gush of breath. "Lovely man." There was no longer anything but beauty in my memories of Jack Reynolds — fun, passion, adventure, freedom, the stuff of unrealistic fantasy. He was nothing like Grant who wanted to build something solid, an ordinary life with me. I sighed. The demise of the WASP program made that decision easier. Oh! I was forgetting. Perhaps polio had made that same decision impossible.

"I talked to your father the other day," Mags said.

"I let him down — again."

"Hush now." Mags slapped the machine with her gloves. "He loves you and wants to be sure that you have everything that you need."

"I know."

"He wanted me to tell you that he still needs a pilot for the firm."

I squeezed my eyes close but a tear escaped and trickled down my cheek anyway. Daddy was dreaming. I'd be lucky to walk.

Mags dropped her gloves on the chair and found a cloth on the table beside my machine. Gently she dabbed at my eyes. "He also said that he may have found the girl."

"What girl?"

"Delores' relative."

"Annaliese?"

"No, there's no record of where the Nazis sent them after Gurs. He's found the little girl — Rosa."

"My God." Father's reach amazed me.

"The Quakers have her. They just need money and sponsors to get her here."

"No problem." My spirits rose. Rosa was alive somewhere in Europe. Maybe the others were too.

"He told me to tell you that he'd work on it." She patted my cheek and I realized how deftly she'd changed the subject. Now instead of pondering my own questionable future, my mind was filled with the fate of a little girl who I didn't even know.

It didn't matter though. I embraced the thoughts racing through my head. Maybe we could save her. I'd failed Emmie and Delores. I'd failed Lizzie Langer and her baby. I'd endangered Pam, exposing her to polio and making her think that we could build an airplane and that she'd be able to fly it. In fact, there wasn't much that I'd done right my whole life — but Rosa was alive. Maybe her redemption would be mine.

"Delores know?"

Mags picked up her gloves and headed for the door. "I thought maybe you'd like to tell her."

"I do. Thank you."

264

"Bye, bye." She waved and left.

I lay there in my iron cocoon listening to Mags' light footsteps retreat down the hall. It was October again and it was cold outside. I wanted to tell to her to bundle up before she crawled into her Red Stearman and flew off to Hap Arnold. I wanted her to know that I'd miss her, but it was too late. In the past, I would have shrugged and let her go, but I'd let too many people go already.

"Mags!" It wasn't much more than a whisper. "MAGS!"

I heard her stop. "What?"

When *Fifinella* gave me air, I said, "I love you."

She stuck her head around the doorframe and winked. "I know."

CHAPTER 20 — SURFACING

"Son of Sinclair Lewis killed in action, You Always Hurt the One You Love by the Mills Brother Hits Number 1, FDR wins 4th term in office, defeating Thomas E Dewey."
~ American View Magazine ~
November, 1944

"Is it Thanksgiving?"

"Tomorrow," Myrtle told me as she busied herself with the hot, wet blankets.

"Six weeks," I sighed.

"You are doing better every day."

Better? I wanted to strike back at her — at my situation, at this crazy disease, but I didn't want to hurt her feelings. It wasn't Myrtle's fault that I'd picked up this nasty germ somewhere. Maybe it was one of the many public restrooms I'd used in the last few months. I'd spent time drinking in strange bars in Key West. I'd gotten way too close to Jack Reynolds. He didn't seem sick of course, but who knows about anyone really? I wondered if he was okay. What if I'd given this thing to him? My heart pounded harder. No, that just couldn't be. I thought of all the people packed into the train coming back from Florida. There'd been a lot of coughing and sniffling in our car. I tried to tell myself that it was more likely I'd gotten it there. Then I brought it back to *The Windshift Inn*, endangering the people living here — the workers at *Wiley*, the Klines, and Delores — and my darling Grant. I'd been so absorbed in my own suffering that I'd never even thought of the others. I should have done something differently — but what?

Myrtle worked quickly, but I felt dizzy, eager to get back into *Fifinella*. The machine was now like a welcoming womb — safe and protective. I was exhausted and fell asleep before Myrtle finished her housekeeping chores and left the room.

#

I could see a little white dresser out of the corner of my eye. On it, Myrtle had placed one of her hand-crocheted doilies and set up my collection of Jackie Cochran Cosmetics. Jackie called her little line *Wings*. I smiled to myself. How appropriate! I squinted at the arrangement. It wasn't perfect, but I appreciated Myrtle's thoughtfulness.

The window was further to the right. I couldn't turn my head to see it, but I could hear the wind rattling the shutters and I knew it must be snowing outside. The rattle became a regular beat like music. I hummed. What was that tune? "A pretty girl is like a melody," I said out loud. Where did I hear that? Emmie. She was always singing that song. We heard it together — but where? Oh yes, last spring, she and I ferried an Admiral back to Chicago to meet his wife for their anniversary. While we were there, we saw an all-girl swing band play.

What was the name of that band? I mulled it around in my head. What was it? One dark-haired young beauty stood up front and to the side. She played the bull fiddle. Her name was Sharon. The Sharon Rogers Band! Yes, that was it. Emmie had dragged me over to meet them after the show.

Emmie.

I thought I might go mad lying here with nothing to do but think — and remember.

"How's it going, sweetheart?" Wayne bustled around the room, fiddling with something under my machine, whistling.

I never thought I'd be so glad to see Wayne. "Breathing."

"That's a real good sign, if you ask me."

He seemed focused on what he was doing and given my situation, I decided not to distract him — even though I wanted to ask him to move my little bottle of cologne to the other side of the hand cream. He made popping sounds with his lips as he chewed that horrible wartime gum — or was he fooling around with the wiring? What if

268

he unplugged the damned thing by accident and didn't notice before he left the room? I'd suffocate. I imagined myself locked inside a malfunctioning tube with no one around to notice it had stopped working. Myrtle would come in to check on me and I'd be dead. I imaged her having to call Father with that news. Surely Wayne could hear my heart beating. It was deafening. Sweat broke out on my upper lip and I couldn't wipe it off. I wanted to cry out to him — to beg him to be careful down there, to warn him about unplugging *Fifinella*. I opened my mouth to scream but thought better of it. What if I made him mad? The man had literally saved my life with his mechanical expertise. Would my fears seem irrational to him? Insulting? What if there was an electrical short and *Fifinella* burst into flames?

The image of Emmie's face the moment before it melted popped into my head.

I wanted Wayne out of my sight! Now! I waited for the machine to help me with my next breath —eyes popping, lips stretched wide, ready to belch-out my hysteria.

"Well, look who's awake?" Mr. McKensey stood in the doorway.

I cocked my eyes his way. "I'm smiling, Mr. McKensey." I was ashamed of the nasty tone in my voice.

He slapped his thigh and cackled. "I can see that, little girl. So what's the problem?"

I sucked back my panicky thoughts and almost choked on them. "Bored. Miserable. Scared."

"Who ain't?" He sat down on the stool near *Fifinella*. I strained to see him. "Life ain't easy for anybody."

I didn't care about anyone else's suffering at that moment and grunted.

He chuckled again. "No sense in being a pain in the butt though."

"Not much I can do about it right now."

269

Wayne bumped the machine and I gritted my teeth.

"Sorry about that, Shirley girl." Wayne sounded like he was having the time of his life. After all, he had a project now — something to keep his mind off of Number 49 and Emmie.

"What are you doing down there?"

"Your dad found a manual for this here contraption. I was checking out the schematic. After all, I jury-rigged this sucker up pretty fast considering that I'd never seen one before."

"That's reassuring."

Mr. McKensey howled with laughter.

I rolled my eyes.

"Little gal, you sure are cantankerous. I didn't think anyone could out-do Delores, but you are in the running right now."

"This thing's got to keep me alive," I said with the last of my breath.

Wayne patted the side of the tube. "You can trust me — and *Fifinella* here."

"Trust?" He didn't know what he was asking of me.

"Maybe you need to be alone for a while." The cheeriness had drained from his voice.

The realization that I'd hurt his feelings irritated me even more. I would have apologized anyway, but before I found enough breath to do it, he was gone.

"I take that back, Shirley. You are way more pissed-off than Delores. You are about to pass me up for sheer nastiness." Mr. McKensey struggled to get up off the stool. "You get some sleep, now. We'll all come back when you are feeling kinder toward the human race."

He lumbered out the door and I was alone again.

#

270

I opened my eyes.

"I hear you've been beating up on the innocents." I could feel Delores' breath when she spoke so she must have pulled the stool up close to my prison.

"And doing a damned good job of it, too."

"Getting good at cussing too."

"I'm sorry."

"Oh don't be. I'm impressed."

"You would be."

"Mr. McKensey said you were bored."

"Among other things."

"I'd read to you but there's nothing here but *Wuthering Heights* and a couple of Myrtle's *Ladies' Home Journals* from last summer."

"I'll pass." I wasn't sure which thought annoyed me more — star-crossed lovers on the moors or endless ads for Lux Soap. What did any of it have to do with me right now?

"Grant said he'd bring over a Bible this evening."

"NO!"

"I'm sorry, Shirley. I don't know how to help." She sounded as dejected as I felt.

"It's not that I don't like the bible or anything."

"It's okay. I understand that part."

"It's that things are a mess."

I felt a vibration in the air. She must have moved — maybe looked around the room. "I don't know," she said. "Myrtle keeps a pretty clean house."

How could I explain how I felt to someone who was just as happy with her silk drawers draped over a chair? "My hand cream — it should be on the other side of the cologne."

Delores moved around outside my range of vision. "How's that?"

I strained to see. "Move it back a smidge."

"Okay, now?"

"A little more — and turn it a little bit."

"Now?"

I was pretty sure it still wasn't perfect, but it was better than the way Myrtle had left it. I relaxed. "Thank you."

"Anything else?"

"Where are my clothes?"

"Most of them are upstairs on the rack near your bed."

"And Emmie's stuff?"

"It's where you left it. I promise you that. No one touched it."

I sighed in relief.

"What do you want me to do with this book?" She looked downward.

"What is it?"

"The manual for this thingamajig."

"What is its real name?"

She leaned over and struggled to pick up the book. "It says that it's an Emerson Respirator."

"I like *Fifinella* better."

"Me too."

"How does it work?"

"Why do you care as long as it keeps your comfortable?"

272

"Delores, I need to know."

"Why?"

"I just do."

"Are you sure?"

"Not knowing scares me more than knowing. Okay?"

She sat on the stool with the book in her arms. "We'll learn everything there is to know about this crazy-looking thing. I promise." She caught the edge of the cover with her scar-frozen fingers and opened the manual to the first page.

#

The Windshift Inn was dark and quiet. Everyone else was probably asleep. I stared at the ceiling while *Fifinella* labored through the night — keeping me alive and comfortable. I imagined the moonlight on the snowy field sloping down to *Jerry's Flying Service*. Was it only last fall that we'd gone riding down there? Was it only last winter that Emmie and Delores had slid down that little hill on Myrtle's dinner trays? At the time, I'd thought they were undignified and unladylike. Now, the thought of them romping in the snow like children made me smile.

"A penny for your thoughts?"

"How long have you been sitting there?"

"A couple of hours." Grant stood up and stretched. "You were sawing logs when I got here."

"Don't you have to work in the morning?"

"You are talking a lot better now. Long sentences."

"Finally got *Fifinella's* rhythm, I guess. Why are you here so late?"

"I needed to see you."

He leaned forward and something in his posture seemed ominous. "Is something wrong?"

"I don't know, Shirley. Is there?"

"Other than the obvious?"

He recoiled like I'd hit him and backed into the darkness. "You are so good at that, you know — being evasive."

Anger stole my tongue. I waited until my silence forced him to speak again. I was good at that too.

"Who is this?" He held something shimmery white over my head.

I squinted in the gloom. "What is it?"

He lowered it so that I could see it better. It was a thin piece of paper folded into an envelope adorned with unfamiliar, almost indecipherable handwriting.

"Is it for me?"

"You know it's for you. Who is this Captain Reynolds?"

"Jack?" I was confused. Why was Jack sending me a letter? Had my worst fears come true and he'd gotten polio too? The thought of that muscular young man struck down like this was almost too much to bear.

"Obviously he's someone important." Grant's voice broke.

"Yes." I was too sick to lie.

"Should I be worried?"

"No."

He leaned forward again, cupping his left ear. "What?"

"I love you."

"Are you sure?"

"Yes."

He dropped the envelope on the table and walked out of the room. He was already downstairs before I realized he hadn't touched me the whole time he'd been there.

The inn was waking up. Toilets flushed, footsteps pattered above and in the hallway outside my room. I knew my solitude would soon be over and that it would be Delores who would come to console me. The noise in the kitchen below me rose. There were voices and I could hear cabinets slamming. Eventually, a wonderful smell wafted up the stairs. Something sweet and spicy.

Ah. Thanksgiving!

A wave of sadness filled my eyes with tears that I couldn't wipe away. Last year, the four of us — Mags, Delores, Emmie, and I had spent the holiday at Camp Morgan. We'd had to pay for our dinner of course, but the Army's food was pretty good and we'd had fun. We were just getting to know each other then. I'd been jealous of Delores and scandalized by her behavior. I was a different person then.

I was still sad, when Delores appeared at my door.

"Did you hear already?" I said before she could build up to it.

"Grant brought in the mail yesterday afternoon. I guess he fumed for hours before coming back to confront you about it."

"So everyone knows?"

"Hard to keep a secret at *The Windshift Inn*."

"Why do you think Jack wrote me?"

"Want me to read it to you?"

I thought about it, torn between my need for privacy and my curiosity.

She seemed offended. "I won't tell anyone."

"I know — but once we open it, once we know what's in it, it's real."

She stood with her arms folded across her chest, waiting for me to decide.

"What would you do?"

"Read it."

"You read Tommy McDougal's letters?"

"Every single one."

"Do you answer them all too?"

She sighed and held up her hands. "I used to answer him — before."

"Will you read it to me?"

"Oh yeah," she said with a lot more excitement than I expected. I giggled for the first time since I'd gotten sick. It just came out — as unpredictable as a hiccup.

Delores scooped the delicate piece of paper up into her stiff hands but it floated away from her. "Don't worry, I've got it." I lost sight of her but then realized that she was on the floor, chasing Jack's letter. I imagined her on her knees and elbows trying to scoop it up. She snorted and I giggled again. It was the first time I'd seen the playful, outrageous, charming Delores in months.

"Okay, I've got it." Her eyes rose up beside my head. They sparkled with some of their old fire.

"Let's hear what Captain Jack has to say." I closed my eyes, excited about the letter in spite of myself.

The stool creaked as Delores sat down on it and I heard the paper crackle as she opened it.

Dear Shirley,

RRR tells me that you are out of the woods. I'm so glad to hear that. You had all of us worried. I wanted to fly up there, but Mags told me that you didn't need me and that it might be a problem if I just showed up. That's probably true, but I wanted you to know that I care.

"He sounds swell, Shirls."

I turned my eyes toward her and tried to scowl. "Don't call me …"

Delores grinned and I realized that she was teasing me — and I realized that I didn't mind it anymore.

"Keep reading," I said. "A girl in my condition has to get her thrills somewhere."

Delores laughed. "Good for you."

"Polio makes it hard to be dignified."

"It has some advantages. It got you out of those wool skirts and Peter Pan collars," she shot back.

"Will you read the damned letter?"

She snorted and squinted down at the letter, finding her place.

You are an amazing person, Shirley. I've never spent time with a gal who shared so many of my interests. Few women want to know anything about flying. They listen for a while, but before long they get that bored 'let's talk about me now look.' Not you. One of my best memories of our time together was …

"The day we flew over Fort Jefferson," I sighed.

The day we flew to Fort Jeff.

Delores looked up and smiled. "Must have been wonderful."

"It was swell. The sky was forever and the water was green, only a few feet below our pontoons. It was so clear and shallow that you could see the fish. On the way back, we flew over an old shipwreck."

"Maybe I should have Tommy meet me in Key West sometime."

"It was like the rest of the world was far away and there was only the sun and the sea and Jack and me."

"No wonder Mags keeps going back there."

I lay there, thinking about my little escape from being me. The problem with vacations was that you always had to go back to real

277

life. Delores was quiet too. I wondered if she was thinking about a time when everything was all right.

After a moment, she sighed and lifted the paper again.

I'm writing this because it seems that my time at Key West is coming to an end. Now that things seem to be going well in Europe, we will have a new focus. I decided that sitting out the war in paradise isn't right for me, so I've put in a request for transfer. I can't tell you where they are sending me, but I'm sure you have an idea.

"The Pacific Theater." I thought of the Philippines and Midway Island and Tarawa. Daddy had reported on them in his newspapers, but he didn't print everything that he heard. What he'd heard was ugly.

"Probably," Delores said softly. "I think that's where Arty is."

"Your baby brother?"

"You know he joined the Marines because my mother thought it would be better. If he'd gone with the Army, he'd already be in Europe. She couldn't bear the thought of him being captured by the Nazis. They don't treat Jewish boys well over there."

"Oh Delores." Her family had been through so much. Now her beloved brother was involved. "I'm sure he will be okay."

We drifted into another thoughtful silence. I thought about Jack. I wasn't sure if he accepted me as I was, or if I was just a different person around him. One thing for sure, he liked that I was a pilot and he envisioned a life where we both could fly. Grant wanted such different things from me.

Delores rattled the paper, "There's only a little more. Want to hear it?"

"Yes."

Mags told me that you have another guy there in Ohio. I guess that explains your reaction to my little suggestion. I want you to know that I'm not a guy who gives up. I know what I want and I go after it.

I'll be gone for a while. God only knows how long it will be, but I will write when I can. In the meantime, get well and don't get married before I can get back to make my case.

Love, Jack

"Oh my," I said.

"Old Jack seems like quite a guy. Do you like him?"

"I do."

"What about Grant?"

"I like him too."

"You know what you are going to do?"

"Get well, I guess."

"You know what I mean."

"I can't even think about this until I can breathe and move."

"I love intrigue. Since Myrtle and Jerry aren't keeping their romance a secret anymore, there's been no one for the girls to gossip about." Delores refolded Jack's letter. Usually, her clumsy execution annoyed me, but this time, I felt affection. I knew that it was time to tell her. I didn't really know why I'd waited so long. I told myself it was because Father was still working on it. It wasn't a sure thing. Of course, that wasn't exactly true. It was because I was sick and selfish and I dreaded the conversation.

"What are you doing?" Delores leaned forward and I realized that I could see more of her than I had a few minutes before. "You turned your head."

"No I didn't."

"You did. I swear you did."

I could see her face — all of it. She was right. I must have turned my head somehow. I'm sure that I looked worse than she did, but it was

279

close. Her frizzy curls were out of control. Myrtle kept her clothes pressed, but they were two sizes too big now.

"I have something to tell you," I blurted out.

"Well?"

"Do you remember on the train that time, we were coming back from Camp Morgan."

"We made lots of trips like that."

"Will you be quiet and let me do this?"

She cocked her head and raised one eyebrow.

"You told me about your Grandmother and her twin sister and your cousins Hans and Annaliese and about Annaliese's daughter Rosa."

"And Gretchen who lives with my folks now. They all lived in Mannheim before they were deported."

"When we got back here, I called Father and he sent out queries about them through his contacts in Europe."

Delores covered her mouth with her claws. "He's found them?"

This was what I had dreaded. The good news was so mixed with bad. Father's information was vague. "The Jews from Mannheim were shipped east sometime last year. He doesn't know where they took them, but he's pretty sure that your great Aunt and Annaliese were on that train."

Her face fell.

"He's still looking, Delores. Don't give up hope yet."

"I'll call Mama and let her know" She stood up and turned to leave. "Thank you for trying, Shirley."

"No! Wait," I struggled to turn my head even more. "There's more."

"What?"

"The Quakers have the little girl."

280

"What?" She seemed stunned.

"The Quakers have Rosa."

"Oh, Shirley, I can't believe it. Where is she?"

"Father doesn't have details yet, but he will get her home to your mother. You know how George Maxwell is. He'll get her home."

"I … well, honestly, I don't know George Maxwell at all, Shirls." Her smile was back. "But I'm eager to get to know him."

"You should call him. As you can see, I'm indisposed. Call him and tell him who you are. He will tell you what's going on."

"I'll call him and tell him that you love him." She planted a kiss on my forehead and danced out the door.

Lots of people touch you when you can't do anything about it.

I squinted. There was something on the floor near the door. I turned my head a little more. It was Jack's letter. "Oh, Delores," I sighed.

#

"Mr. Maxwell sent you some presents," Myrtle said as she gave me the hot blanket treatment.

"What does one buy someone who lives in a tube?"

"How about a nice big mirror?" Wayne said from the doorway.

"A what?" This was the worst bad joke in Wayne's long history of bad jokes.

"For *Fifinella*. You know, so you can see around the room a little better."

Terrific. Watching cobwebs form would at least give me a project.

Myrtle closed me in and within a few seconds *Fifinella* started up again. "There you go," Myrtle laid a rough hand on my forehead.

"I imagine it had a mirror to begin with, but it must have gotten broken off and lost or something. Your dad said for me to tell you to

281

give it two days. If you still don't want it, I'll take it off." Wayne held it up for me to see.

I looked like something out of *Flash Gordon*. Myrtle kept my hair combed, but I was pale and my lips were so white they seemed translucent. I closed my eyes. "How did he know I wouldn't like it?"

Wayne shrugged, but I could feel the silent amusement that passed between the two of them.

"We parents know our kids even if the child in question thinks we don't." She gave me a sip of water. "Now you just relax and let Wayne install your daddy's present, Missy."

I hated being called Missy, but I refrained from commenting about it while Wayne fussed with the mirror. There was some kind of a ruckus going on behind me, but I figured it was Myrtle cleaning.

"Have you heard from your boys?" I figured I should be polite.

"One's in France." Myrtle sounded winded, like she was lifting something. "The war news is good and I haven't heard otherwise, so he must be okay. The other one is somewhere in the Pacific, I think. He and Jerry's boy Danny are sailors."

"I'm glad. Delores said that her brother Arty joined the Marines." I didn't know what else to say. I'd never met her sons — or Jerry's boy either — or Arty.

There were other footsteps and scratching sounds and a wonderful smell.

"What are you doing?"

"Okay, I just about got it fixed here," Wayne smiled down at me. "Are you ready to see the world?"

"Ha." I grunted at the idea.

He positioned the mirror he'd been attaching to *Fifinella* and suddenly I saw several people standing behind a little table stacked with plates and glasses.

282

"SURPRISE!" It was Pam Kline. "They won't let me come over there and hug you, but I brought you a present all the same. Maybe you can pretend that I'm giving you a hug."

Someone, probably Myrtle, had trimmed her hair and brushed it back behind her ears. "You look great," I said. "You got taller."

"Everyone looks taller when you are laying down, silly."

"Oh." I was taken aback. "I guess they do."

"*Fifinella* almost looks like a plane."

"Does it?"

"One without wings, of course."

"Oh Pammie, I'm sorry."

"About what?"

"About your plane."

"Miz Pam here helped me find the right parts, Shirley." Wayne tapped the foot of the iron lung. "I couldn't have got *Fifinella* working in time without that old plane and all the stuff Emmie had been collecting for it over the last year."

"Daddy says it was a miracle what with all the war shortages. I thought that Emmie would want me to share them with you. I wanted to…" She ducked her chin, suddenly shy.

I was breathing because of Emmie and Mags and Delores — and that old Stearman lying in pieces in Jerry Kline's hangar. I wasn't sure I was happy to be alive yet, but it was stunning to think about.

"Remember the day we found it, Shirley? It was the first time we went riding."

It was the last time that I went riding.

"I told Daddy that once you were up and around and didn't need *Fifinella* anymore, we'd get all those parts back — and that you'd help me build my plane then — and that I wanted you to teach me

283

how to fly it." Pam prattled on like a little girl, but her voice had deepened. She was becoming a woman in spite of the war and her dad and Mags and Emmie and Delores and me.

Jerry Kline put one hand on Pam's shoulder.

"What?" She looked up at him. "Oh, yeah. Sorry, Daddy." She grinned.

"It's good to see you, young lady." Jerry turned to me.

I found a little smile. "Hi, Jerry."

He reached over and took Myrtle's hand. "We have some news."

"When are you getting married?"

They both beamed.

"How did you know?" Myrtle giggled and blushed.

"Everyone knows."

"And after all our tip-toeing around, Sugar." Jerry winked at Myrtle.

"Cold Creek's deepest, darkest secret." Delores sat in a rocking chair positioned so that I could see her clearly in the mirror. "Look at her." She pointed at me. "I told you she moved her head this afternoon."

I showed off my new skill, turning my head slightly. Depending on my position, the mirror allowed me to see most of the room. Mr. McKensey sat on the stool beside *Fifinella*. I think he smiled. He didn't have his teeth in so I wasn't sure. I turned my head the other way. No Grant. I swallowed my disappointment. "What is this? A party?"

"I didn't think it was fair that you couldn't come downstairs and have Thanksgiving with us," Pam said. "So we decided to bring Thanksgiving up to you."

"We didn't bring up the whole turkey, but we brought you a piece," Myrtle said as she cut it up into small pieces. "I know you like crunchy green beans.

284

Everyone laughed at the memory of Emmie's abject failure as a bean snapper.

"Myrtle made carrot cake," Pam said. "From carrots we grew in the garden out back. And I made an apple pie."

Wayne moved the mirror again to show me the treats sitting on the dresser. Someone had moved my cosmetics again. The muscles in my stomach ached.

"So what's it like to have polio," Pam asked with her mouth full of carrot cake.

"PAMELA JANE!" Jerry nearly choked on his tea. "How can you be so rude?"

"No, it's okay, Jerry," I said. "I don't mind."

"So, tell us then." Delores learned forward in her rocking chair as if she was listening to FDR on the radio.

I glanced around the room. Everyone had their eyes on me, waiting. "It's miserable."

"Aw, I'm sorry. I didn't mean to make you cry," Pam said. "I was just curious. If you can't move your legs does that mean that you can't feel them?"

Fiffinella ground on for a few moments. "I can feel them, Pammie. They hurt. Not as much now as when it first started, but they hurt. I can't move them and they hurt."

#

After about an hour, everyone but Delores said their good-byes and left. The noise of them clumping down the stairs made us both giggle.

"Horses?"

Delores' eyes sparkled with mischief. "Buffaloes."

"Big ones." I couldn't believe my utter naughtiness, but for some reason it felt good.

She held up a thin book. "Are you in the mood for the riveting adventures of the Emerson Respirator?"

"Sure." It was better than being alone with *Fifinella* and my thoughts.

"Eh-hum."

I recognized Mr. McKensey's voice.

"Come on in, Mr. McKensey." Delores turned toward the door. "Can I do something for you?"

"Now don't go being polite, young woman. I came to see that one." He gestured toward me.

"Do you want me to leave?"

"I don't care what you do." His step was distinctive, the left foot hit a bit harder than the other one. It was the first time I'd noticed that.

Delores shrugged and backed away so that I couldn't see her anymore.

"It's good to see you, Mr. McKensey."

"Woo, girl, look at you." His voice was almost tender.

"I think I'm getting better," I lied.

He winked at me and jerked his eyes toward Delores. "Are you going to stand there or what?"

"Well, what do you want me to do?" She barked back.

"Cranky!"

"What did you say?" Delores sounded surprised.

"You two are cranky."

"I think there are three cranks in this room," I closed my eyes in exasperation with both of them.

"I got something here for you." Mr. McKensey got right to the point. "You might as well come look too, Delores."

I opened my eyes again, curious now.

"Oh?" She came closer and I could see her again in the mirror.

"When Mags came to see me about that old carcass moldering in my barn, I was glad enough to get rid of it. Thought maybe I could make a buck or two. Figured Jerry's kid would get bored and that would be that. Thought you all were just a bunch of crazy gals playing at being pilots."

"That's what they …"

"Hush, Delores." I could feel her shock. "I'm sorry," I said. "I didn't mean to snap."

"Will you two let me talk?" Mr. McKensey's voice was as harsh as ever, but his eyes, looming large in my mirror, were kind.

I could tell that Delores was offended and I felt bad. "We're listening," I told him.

"Anyway, I didn't tell Mags everything. I just didn't think it mattered until now."

"What is it?"

"I don't exactly know. My son Jake found that wreck in one of the fields that we hadn't planted in several years. We never did know when it went down, but when he came on it, the pilot wasn't more than a few bones and a leather helmet."

Delores glanced at me and raised her eyebrows. "When was this, Mr. McKensey?"

"Been a long time now. Jake's been dead hisself nigh onto seventeen years this June."

"Jake must have been scared to death, coming upon something like that," Delores said.

"He was. Wasn't much older than Jerry's kid at the time. Voice had just started cracking. I was a couple hundred yards away, walking the old rows — deciding whether or not to replant the area. At first I

287

thought it was a girl screaming, then I realized it was Jake, yelling for me to come quick.

"I hustled on over there of course, but there wasn't anything anyone could do about the pilot. He was all in one piece and it didn't look like there had been any fire. I thought maybe he'd set it down hard and broken an axle or something. I figured that boy probably froze to death. It was a damn shame too. He wasn't all that far from *The Windshift Inn*, if he'd known to look for it."

"So what is that you have there, Mr. McKensey?" Delores pointed to something in the old man's hands.

"Ah, yes." He held up a thin leather book. "Aside from the derelict and the body, Jake found this."

I strained to see. "What is it?"

Mr. McKensey ducked his chin. "I think it's about the plane."

Dolores leaned forward. "Can I see it?"

He handed it to her. "I don't know what it says, of course. Jake saved it but never got around to reading it either. Farming doesn't leave much time for that kind of thing."

"It's a log book, Shirley!"

"Who did it belong to?"

"Looks like it got wet laying out in the weather all that time. It's hard to read most of the writing." She used a fingernail to separate the pages. "Wait, here it is." She squinted. "Tom Harrow, I think — or Herrow, maybe. He was an airmail pilot."

I strained to see more in my mirror. "What happened to Tom, Mr. McKensey?"

"Jake and I buried him where we found him. Said a few words over the grave. His spirit was long gone. I felt bad about his folks not knowing what happened to him, but we didn't have any way of knowing who they were."

288

"That's why we couldn't figure out how the plane was supposed to look." Delores turned another page. "It was a special configuration — C3MB. It had some kind of cargo compartment for the mail instead of a forward cockpit."

"We have to tell Wayne. Now that we know that, maybe he can find drawings." I was excited.

"Mr. McKensey, you are swell." Delores winked at him. "What made you think of this old thing?"

"I guess all that talk about the plane saving Shirley's life." Mr. McKensey seemed embarrassed. "Like it wasn't just Emmie and Mags finding that old thing but how I ended up having it in the barn in the first place — and you know — Jake."

I was possessed of an Emmie-like urge to give the old man a hug — if I had been able to move. Then, I realized that I *had* moved my arm. I didn't remember doing it exactly, but I could feel *Fifinella's* inside wall with the knuckles of my right hand.

Suddenly, the room and Delores and Mr. McKensey were far away. I focused on my hand. Sweat formed on my upper lip. I bit my bottom lip and strained. There was a faint metallic thump.

"What was that?" Mr. McKensey stepped back from *Fifinella.*

Delores frowned and laid a hand on the respirator as if she expected it to be hot.

I tried again and this time the knock was firmer, more controlled.

"Shirley?"

I looked up at them. "Call Father!"

289

CHAPTER 21 — DECISIONS

"FDR – Negro Women can be WAVES, Glenn Miller's Plane Goes Missing, Patton's Christmas Prayer, WASP Flew 75M Miles for Military before Deactivation"
~ American View Magazine ~
December 1944

T he next day, I breathed on my own for twenty minutes before I tired and needed the lung. The next day after that, I could move my left arm and turn my head. That afternoon, I wiggled the toes on my left foot. After that, I was eager for the hot blanket treatments, and my progress was quick. Myrtle and Wayne continued stretching my legs and massaging my muscles. I was embarrassed when Wayne first began rubbing my thighs, but he was careful and respectful. I didn't have much dignity left anyway.

It took several days for Grant to get over the idea that there might be someone else in my life. Myrtle had just helped me back into *Fifinella* and was about to leave, her arms full of warm, damp blankets.

"Well, hello," she said.

"Myrtle," he nodded to her as she squeezed past him and went down stairs.

I could see him in the mirror. "Hi."

"I missed you," he said.

"I'm not going anywhere for a while."

"I brought a book." He held it up for me to see.

"*A Farewell to Arms?*"

He shrugged.

"Okay," I said.

Grant came to see me every day after that. He sat beside the lung and read to me. At first, there wasn't a lot to say. We both knew something had changed in our relationship but neither of us wanted to talk about it. As always, his physical beauty affected me, but our passion was at low tide. I couldn't expect a man to get excited over a cripple. I felt something new. It was more than gratitude although I was certainly grateful. It was respect and friendship. He was supposed to be there for me, and he was. What more could you ask of someone?

"This Wilson is a nice guy," he said one day after I had been weaned from the lung. I lay in bed appreciating the softness of the mattress, the crispness of the starched sheets. "Looks like Jerry is going to hire him as a mechanic."

"I know."

"I hear he's working with Pam on that crazy plane of yours."

"It's not mine. Emmie and Mags started all this. I just played along." I opened and closed my left hand. "Look at this! Movement is such a blessing. I never appreciated it before."

He closed the book and laid it on his lap. "I want you to let it all go, Shirley."

"They can't really do much until we are sure I don't need the lung anymore. He's just got a better idea of what it looked like before it crashed — so that gives us a better idea of how to refurbish it when the war is over."

"That's not what I mean."

I closed my eyes. "I know."

"It's time to just let go and concentrate on getting better for the wedding. Look at you. You think you'd be in this position if you'd listened to me before? Gallivanting all over the country — mixing with crowds, wearing yourself out. It's not right, Shirley. It's just not right. You did this to yourself — to us." He threw the book across the floor and I jumped, dismayed by his sudden show of anger. "Myrtle and Jerry are getting married next Sunday. It should be us. We SHOULD already be married."

"I'm sorry. It's hard to explain."

He turned away.

"I wanted you. I still do, even under these circumstances."

He stared out the window at the snowy slope down to the air field in the valley below *The Windshift Inn*. "But that's not the same thing, is it?"

"Turn up your hearing aid, Grant. It's important that you hear me."

He turned back to look at me.

"I don't want to be bossed around anymore."

His frustration and anger melted away. At first, he was surprised. Then hurt. "It's the husband's place to take care of his family, to be in charge," he said.

He was sweet. My heart filled with affection for him. "We had this conversation once before. You just couldn't hear me and I let it pass. I should have stuck with my guns. I thought I wanted to be like everyone else then. I let you convince me I should want to be married. I came back from Key West ready to make that commitment, but then this happened and things are different now."

"I love you." He stroked my forehead.

"I love you too. Maybe not the way you want me to, but I know now that I do love you. You think we can be friends?" I knew the answer before I asked the question. I was just hoping.

"I want to be your husband, not your friend."

"I can't."

He stared at his shoes. "And what will you do?"

"First, I'm going to get well. I think I'll finish my degree. I still want to fly if my health will allow. Who knows? Father has always wanted me to work at *American View Magazine*. Maybe I'll write a book. Mostly, I want to take care of myself."

He shook his head. "You aren't like Mags and her libertine friends. You will be sorry." He slid the ring off my finger and put it in his pocket. "It will be too late." He got up and went to the door. "For both of us."

I didn't want to be Mags — nor even Emmie anymore, but I understood why he thought that. "I'd love to see you when things cool off."

He ran down the steps and slammed the front door behind him.

I was like a child who has to choose between two birthday parties. I cried, but I'd made my decision.

#

I was sitting up when it was time for Delores to go home a few weeks later. She sat down next to me.

"I spoke with Father last night," I told her.

"I heard that he called you." The dark circles under her eyes were fading. Perhaps the physical pain was easing up a bit.

"He's got the little girl, Delores."

She looked up at me.

"Little Rosa. He found a way to get her to Pittsburgh."

Her gasp was subtle – a soft intake of breath. "How? When?"

"I don't know the details. He said that you should call him once you get home — you and your mother and father."

"Oh Shirley." She took my hand. "What about the others? My aunt and uncle? Annaliese and Jan? Hans?"

I didn't want to talk about the others. "I think he would have said if he knew where they are."

Delores sat back in her chair like I'd hit her in the stomach.

294

I had hoped Father could find all of them. He'd tried. When he heard how Delores braved polio to save me, even though she was suffering herself, he tried harder. When he understood what Delores had come to mean to me, he tried even harder.

Delores seemed torn between joy and sorrow. "Annaliese and I were close when we were girls. I feel bad about missing so much of her life. Now maybe I'll never see her again. And I've never seen her baby — not even a picture."

"I'm sure she's beautiful." I didn't know what else to say.

"You did this."

"I just went to Father like I always do."

"Thank you, Shirley."

"You need to eat more," I told her.

"Look who's talking?" Her snort was a comforting sound now.

"When are you coming back?"

"I don't know. They want to try and do something about these scars. Maybe get back a little movement. Mother is not doing well. Her arthritis is getting her down plus she's worried about Uncle Max and Aunt Sophie and Jan and Annaliese. We haven't heard anything more from Hans since he sent us that letter when he arrived in Japan back in 1941."

She covered her face with her hands as if reality had finally hit her.

"Rosa! Mother will be so excited. Gretchen will have her little niece back. We'll take care of her until we find Annaliese."

"Father will help. I would too but as you see I'm indisposed."

"You'll be well enough to visit soon."

That was too much for me to accept so I changed the subject. "What about Tommy?"

"I don't know about Tommy. I can't think about him now."

"Why not?"

"I'm Jewish. I have a responsibility to my family — to those who have been killed."

"You love him?"

"Yeah. I do." She wiped her eyes and sniffed. "I gotta cut that out."

"You saved my life, Delores. I'm not sure I'm not mad at you about that." I had developed a sense of humor too.

"Tough. You are stuck with it."

She was still striking, but the robustness of her personality had faded. At least I didn't have to put up with her messes anymore — or trip over all those mooning soldiers and sailors. "I never thought it would be you."

"How do you mean?"

"I never thought we'd be friends. That you'd be the one, I mean." I was messing it up. "It's not that I didn't like you."

"Don't give me that. You didn't like me at all." She got up to leave. "Some friends. We don't go partying. You never share your fingernail polish with me — and you never tell me shit about you." Delores blew her nose and I cringed at the thought of all the germs she was putting into the air.

"We aren't that kind of friends."

"I thought you were a prig," she said.

"HA! Fat lot you know."

"Goodbye, Shirley. When I can write, I will." She held up her claw.

"Same here." I held up my quivering left hand.

We were in no condition to hug one another so we didn't."

296

CHAPTER 22 — WALDO

"FDR Inaugurated to Fourth Term, Nazi Counter Offensive Collapses, Auschwitz Death Camp Liberated."
~ *American View Magazine* ~
January, 1945

I sat by the window watching someone do 'touch and go's' in one of Jerry's *Wiley* trainers. It was a beautiful day — clear and cold — perfect for flying. I closed the book in my lap and rubbed my eyes. Grant had already picked up the factory girls and Mr. McKensey had already cut in front of the *Wiley* bus, while shaking his fist out the window of his car. It was at least two hours until Myrtle brought me my lunch — and even though I would have relished her company, I wasn't hungry enough to justify having her bring me a mid-morning snack. I yawned, wondering who else might be around.

"Knock, knock?" Wayne Wilson stuck his head through my door.

"You used to just come on in."

"That's when you were too sick to make a fuss."

"That's when I was too sick to chase you away."

"I can still out run you." He winked and we both laughed.

"I want to stand up. Will you help me?"

He came in and set something down on my nightstand. "Where do you want to go? I'll carry you if you want."

"I don't want to go anywhere. I just want to see what will happen."

He frowned. "You won't tell Myrtle, will you? She'll tell your dad and he'll call that Australian lady in Minnesota and I'll be in trouble with everyone."

I smiled. "Mum's the word."

"Okay." He squatted down by my chair. "Put your arm around my neck."

My muscles quivered a little, but my hand went where I willed it.

"Hey, that's great. Good for you!" He slipped his arm around my waist. "Ready?"

"Let's do it."

He straightened his legs and brought me up out of my chair with him. My feet were on the floor, but he was supporting all of my weight. "Okay?"

"It feels odd to be upright. I've been either flat on my back or reclining for months now."

"Want to sit back down?"

"Am I too heavy?"

"Little girl, you are as light as a feather."

I giggled. I was doing a lot of that these days.

He held me erect for a few moments. "What next?"

"More."

He relaxed his grip and I felt my soles flatten on the floor.

"I've got you. If it's too much, just say so."

"No, let's see if my legs will hold me."

"Maybe a little bit at a time."

I was glad he was there to keep me balanced. I focused on my feet as he let me down onto them.

"So far so good," I said through clenched teeth.

"You are almost there."

"Do it."

My knees buckled but Wayne caught me.

"Ready to stop?"

"No, no. Let's try it again."

My knees buckled this time too, but I didn't fall. Gripping Wayne's arm, I slowly straightened up. "One thousand one, one thousand two …"

"Well, la-di-dah — look at you!"

"One thousand five, one thousand six…"

"Hang on, I won't let you fall."

"One thousand eight, one thousand nine, one thousand …" My quivering muscles finally gave out and I collapsed into Wayne's arms, giggling. "I did it, I did it!"

"You sure did, Shirls."

He picked me up and placed me in my chair, wrapping my legs in a warm blanket — while I decided whether it would be okay for Wayne to call me Shirls since Delores did it regularly now.

"I want to do it again."

Wayne poured hot water over my tea ball and handed me my cup. "Okay, we'll do it again after lunch if you are still feeling up to it."

I sipped my tea. "I feel good, Wayne — really good. Do you think you could carry me downstairs for lunch?"

His eyes twinkled and he pretended to pound on his chest like King Kong. "Are you questioning my manliness? Of course, I can carry you downstairs. Myrtle will be thrilled."

I took another sip of tea. "What's that?" I pointed to the small package on my nightstand.

"Oh," he said as he handed it to me. "That's something Mags sent you. Myrtle asked me to bring it up to you. Of course, that's before anyone knew you were so sassy that you'd want to come down to lunch."

I tugged at the string holding the brown paper on the box.

"Look at you — all excited like a kid." Wayne squatted beside my chair.

299

"Doesn't everyone love presents?" Mystified but amused at my own good mood, I opened the box and unfolded a small piece of paper stuck in the lid. "Remember Waldo's Turtles? Love, Mags." I held the note to my chest and laughed before picking up the tiny glass figurine.

"I don't get it," Wayne squinted at my sparkling treasure. "A turtle?"

I set it on the window ledge. "Remember when I went to Key West with Mags last summer?"

"No. You weren't speaking to me back then."

I looked at him — really looked at him for the first time. He was a simple guy — plain, hardworking, and talented. "I was wrong, Wayne. I'm so sorry that I behaved the way I did. I didn't know how to be a friend so it took me a long time to recognize friends. I'm smarter now."

He blinked and looked away. "So tell me about Key West."

"I was such a mess after Emmie that folks around here thought I was crazy."

"It's not crazy to be upset over someone like her."

"You were good to her, Wayne. I'm sorry I ever thought otherwise. She loved you."

He stared at the floor. "Tell me about Key West."

I was touched. After all, I was good at changing painful subjects myself. "Mags took me down to Key West to meet her friend RRR — Randolph Royce Reasoner."

"RRR? Sounds like a buzz saw — or a pirate, maybe."

"He looked like Santa Clause in shorts and sandals."

Wayne laughed. "I'm getting an idea for a cartoon."

"Oh Wayne, Mags would love it. I'll pay you for it."

"No way are you paying me for a cartoon, Shirls. It'll be my pleasure. We'll do it together and send it off to old Mags. You ever notice that gal has a freckle in her eye?"

I covered my grin with my fingers. "When I first met her, I couldn't stop looking at it."

"Let's do one with Mags and RRR." He exaggerated the rolling Rs.

"Let's do." I could hardly wait to get started. I imagined Mags' face when she opened the envelope and tingled with excitement.

"Tell me about this Waldo guy first."

"Oh yeah. Well, RRR and Mags and Jack and I were drinking at Sloppy Joe's. They make this great drink down there – with lime and salt and tequila. Anyway, RRR was telling us about his friend Waldo Peirce who is an artist."

"Waldo Peirce? Are you kidding?"

"You know who he is?"

"He's pretty well known, Shirley."

There was my giggle again. I wasn't able to control it. "Seems that Waldo is a practical joker. RRR told us about a time in Paris when he bought a tiny turtle and gave it to his landlady. She was thrilled and took it to her apartment and lavished it with love and goodies. She made such a fuss about the little creature that after a week Waldo snuck into her apartment when she wasn't there and replaced the tiny turtle with a bigger one."

"Aha!" Wayne grinned.

"She was surprised by how much it had grown but proud as a mama with a baby. She continued to spoil it and feed it and after a week or so, Waldo broke in again and replaced the small turtle with a bigger one still. The landlady was so excited that she went around showing off how big her turtle was getting."

"She never caught on?"

301

"Wait, it gets better. So each week, he continued replacing the turtles with bigger and bigger ones — and Madame was giddy with joy. Then, never being satisfied with one joke, Waldo broke in and replaced the biggest turtle with a smaller one. Now, instead of being happy, the woman was worried."

"Oh he was a stinker, wasn't he?"

"We were all drunk on margaritas so after getting a good laugh at this woman's expense, we got philosophical. I think it was RRR who said, 'When things are getting better we celebrate tiny steps, but when things are getting worse we fear the smallest setback.' And at the time, I got morose and said that I understood how Madame felt because my life had been a series of smaller and smaller turtles." I sighed. "Of course, that was before polio. That was rock bottom."

"So everything is up from here?"

I smiled at Wayne and touched the tiny figurine with a shaky finger. "And this is my first turtle."

#

"Oh my, look at this!" Myrtle scurried around the kitchen to find me a chair. She wiped down the seat with a dishtowel and then threw it over her shoulder. "Be careful, Wayne. Don't drop the little thing. Ease her down."

"Myrtle!" I said, "You sound like Wayne is parking a truck."

Wayne set me down on the kitchen chair and backed away.

"Are you cold? Do you need a blanket?" Myrtle hovered, her hands folded in front of her and her eyes gleaming.

Wayne shrugged. "She wouldn't let me bring a blanket down."

"I'm fine, Myrtle. I just decided to come down for lunch with everyone."

"You picked the perfect day. I'm fixing something special because we have a guest."

"Someone I know?"

"I think you might know me," a deep voice behind me said.

"Tommy McDougal, War Hero?"

Wayne's face lit up. "Lieutenant?"

I struggled to turn my head to look over my shoulder.

"No, don't turn around, I'm coming to you."

His scars were beginning to fade and I could see how handsome he had been before his wound. "It's so good to see you," I said and I meant it.

"Is it okay if I hug you?" He held out his arms.

It was the kind of gesture that would have confused me a year ago. Now, I reached for him. "Tommy, I'm so sorry I was like I was."

"Never be sorry for being smart and competent and beautiful, Shirley." He held me for a long time. "You never did anything but impress me."

"I don't know what's wrong with me today," I said into his broad shoulder, tears streamed down my face. "I'm having a great time one minute and bawling like a baby the next."

"Me too," was all he said.

We held each other for another long moment. I thought about the last time I'd seen him — that day we left California to take Emmie home to Red. The pain was still there, but muted now. I remembered how tenderly he handled Delores and how kind he was to me — things I was too devastated to appreciate at the time.

"Have you seen Delores yet?"

"I'll be catching the train for Pittsburgh this afternoon."

"Does she know you are coming?"

"Of course, although she gave me a hard time about it."

303

"Don't you believe it, Tommy," I said before I thought it out. "She's dying to see you."

The way the scar lifted his lip when he smiled didn't repel me anymore. All I saw was the happiness of a man who would see his beloved soon.

"That's good," he said. "I can't stay away from that gorgeous broad another day."

"Then take Father's car," I said. "You'll get there faster."

Tommy grinned. "Are you serious?"

"It's been sitting out there for ages. Why not use it?"

"That would be wonderful. Thank you, Shirley."

"You drive it though. Delores isn't allowed."

Tommy cocked his head. "Am I missing something?"

I shook my head. "No, it's just a nice memory of some good times when Mags and Emmie and Delores and I were first getting to know each other."

"I'll pry it out of Delores on the drive back here."

"I just need to get keys and gas stamps out of my room."

"We'll take care of that after lunch." Myrtle glanced at the clock over the refrigerator. "Jerry and Pam will be home in less than an hour. How about I shoo you all into the parlor while I finish lunch?"

"That would be fine," Tommy said. "I need to talk to these two anyway."

Wayne picked me up and followed Tommy into the front room. Together, they propped me up on the sofa with pillows and tucked me in with Myrtle's crocheted throw.

We sat in silence for a moment before Tommy clapped his hands together and took a deep breath. "Shirley, Wayne, I know you are surprised to see me — and maybe I should have let you know that I

304

was coming. You see, the truth is, Colonel Simpson sent me to talk to you two — and Delores as well."

"What is it, Tommy? You are scaring me."

"As you know, Jackie Cochran and Colonel Simpson sponsored an inquiry into the conditions at Camp Morgan. While everyone knows that a few of the men objected to your presence at Camp Morgan, most of them expressed their displeasure by griping — a soldier's prerogative, I guess. But one fellow carried his beef a bit further — and directed his rage at Delores. I have had my concerns about him and I relayed them to the investigator during my interview."

"Ewell?" Wayne gripped the arms of his chair and leaned forward.

Tommy confirmed with a nod.

Wayne slammed his fist into the palm of the other one. "That bastard!"

"When they confronted him with my suspicions, he confessed to sabotaging planes that he thought Delores would fly — the A-24 with water in its carburetor that you and I drew that day, Shirley — and the one that Emmie took the day that she died."

"But the latch was broken. I reported it. Everyone knew it was broken. It was supposed to be grounded. No one fixed …"

"He swapped out the Form One on that plane, Shirley."

"Oh my God!" I covered my mouth with both hands. "That's why Emmie didn't suspect anything was wrong."

"He was trying to scare Delores into quitting — I don't think he intended to kill anyone, but maybe he didn't care if that happened either."

I raked my nails down my right forearm. It wasn't carelessness. It wasn't scarcity brought on by war. It was murder. "So what are they going to do about it?" Blood oozed from the long tracks I'd created in my own flesh and I felt the urge to scratch again.

305

Tommy put his hand on mine. "That's what I'm here to tell you. Roger Ewell shot himself in the head before the MPs could arrest him last week. He's dead."

I squirmed, trying to free my left hand from his grasp.

"Shh, no more scratching." His voice was low and firm. "You must not punish yourself anymore."

Wayne stood up, his fists clenched. "I'll go get the Merthiolate."

"Does Father know?"

"Colonel Simpson called him before I left Camp Morgan — and told him that I was coming here and what had happened. I spoke to him myself about an hour ago."

"Why didn't you tell us sooner?"

"You and Wayne and Delores deserved to hear it from me in person. Didn't seem like a telegram or phone call was appropriate after all you have been through."

I relaxed my hand and nodded.

"You didn't do anything to bring this on, Shirley — and Delores isn't to blame either. Ewell did this for his own sick reasons."

I knew he was right. The fury drained out of me, leaving only sorrow.

"Will you promise me that you won't scratch yourself again if I let go of your hand?"

"Yes," I whispered.

"I'm going to need you to help me with Delores."

"How?"

"I'm going to bring her back here after I tell her about this. The two of you and Wayne will need to help each other."

"Like she took care of me …" I looked into his eyes and saw only kindness.

"Yes."

Wayne hustled back into the room with Myrtle's cigar box of bandages and medicines. "Emmie was always worried about you doing this to yourself — afraid you'd get an infection or something. Here, stretch out that arm, let me see what we've got here."

I looked up at him. His jaw twitched and his eyes burned as he washed my arm with a damp cloth and inspected my wounds. Myrtle stood in the doorway behind him, ready to pounce if he didn't fix me up well enough. These people had been so good to me — had kept me alive and stayed with me while I healed. Now once again, I'd scared and upset them with my behavior. I didn't deserve such friendship.

"Wayne, Myrtle, Tommy ..." I glanced at the long red marks on my arms. "I'll never do that again, I promise."

"Good." Tommy glanced over his shoulder at Myrtle. "I'm going to hold you to that."

"Me too," Wayne said as he dabbed Merthiolate on my arm.

"Ouch!" I jerked away. "It stings."

"Tough." Wayne was joking again — sort of.

"Everything under control in here?" Myrtle must have known that Tommy was coming to visit *The Windshift Inn* — and why, but she never mentioned a word of it to either Wayne or me. "I need to get back to the kitchen."

"I'm fine, thanks."

She went to finish lunch.

Tommy turned back to me. "As I said, I talked with your father, Shirley — and with Mags before I came here. Both of them are concerned about how this information will impact your recovery."

I took a deep breath. Something had changed inside me. I wasn't sure when it happened, but I was definitely different. "Emmie and Delores and Mags brought me together within myself, if that makes

307

any sense. Because of them, I began to consider the world in new ways. I thought when I lost Emmie that I'd lost that too."

Wayne put his hand on my shoulder. I'd learned to accept and appreciate his touches over the months that he'd been tending to me. And I'd learned to touch back — that was part of what was different — a touch meant something, but it didn't have to mean everything.

"But now, after being sick — and everything else — I think of how lucky I was to know Emmie." It wasn't something I ever thought I'd say when the pain of losing her had overwhelmed me. "And I'm not going to let this keep me down." I felt silly saying it, but it was how I really felt — at least at that moment.

"I'm glad," Tommy said. "But you have a long haul ahead of you."

"I can do it."

"I'm sure you can."

"I'll help her — and so will Myrtle and everyone else here," Wayne blurted out, his fingers growing firmer on my shoulder.

"Will you calm down? Both of you?" Tommy chuckled. "I've already delivered the bad news."

"Father's not going to make me go back to New Jersey?"

Tommy put back his head and laughed. "George Maxwell can't make you do anything, Shirley. You've been making your own calls for a long time now."

I blinked. "What was this all about then?"

"A gift. One that I'm pretty sure you will love."

I blinked again. "From whom?"

"Mags. Although she said to tell you that it came from RRR too."

I looked around. "So where is it?"

Tommy held up one finger. "Wait one minute, I'll go get it."

I turned to Wayne as Tommy climbed the back steps to the second floor. "Did you have any idea Ewell was capable of this?"

"I knew he was crazy. Everyone thought he was a jerk. That he would actually try to hurt Delores? Naw. I figured he was just a blowhard."

"I should be angrier."

"Killing himself took away any chance of confrontation?"

"Maybe. Then again, maybe it'll come later."

"You've been through a lot since it happened. Comes a time there's not enough emotion left to spend on someone like Ewell. Emmie's gone and knowing how and why she left us doesn't make it any harder — or easier."

"How do you feel?"

He looked into my eyes. "I want to kill him all over again — and since I can't, I hope that he hurt when he went — and that makes me ashamed of myself."

I nodded without breaking his gaze, my eyes welling up with tears. Without a word, he put his arms around me and I laid my head on his chest and cried for all of us.

We heard thumping and the rumble of Tommy's voice over our heads.

"What in the world is he doing up there?" I watched Myrtle's glass light fixture on the ceiling tremble and imagined it dropping down on top of us. Then I heard him coming back down the stairs.

"Here we are." Tommy appeared at the door holding a squirming ball of white fluff. "This is Waldo."

"Oh, Tommy!" I put out my shaky arms and he handed the gorgeous little dog to me. Waldo snuggled against my shoulder, smelling my chin and hair while I stroked his soft curly coat. "Why did Mags send me a dog?"

"That's what I asked her. She said you would know."

I put my hands on either side of the little dog's delicate face and gazed into his soulful dark eyes, falling in love instantly. "He's adorable."

Wayne knelt beside the sofa and petted Waldo who licked his hand but made no effort to leave my lap. Wayne beamed anyway. So did I.

"But I'm crippled here."

Tommy laughed again. "I asked her that too."

"So what did she say?"

"She said not for long."

"She has a lot of faith in me."

"She said that you are past the part of your sickness where you couldn't control things. The rest of it is about determination — and you are the most determined person she knows."

I laughed at that one. "But Waldo needs play and to go out for walks."

"So play with him — and take him for walks."

Waldo looked up at me, his mouth open in what looked like a big smile. "Sister Kenny measured me for braces and Kenny Sticks the other day. She said I might not need them long."

"We could start getting you out with a wheel chair." Wayne got into the act. "I can make you one."

The idea of daily activities beyond the confines of my room — of going outside when the weather permitted — sounded wonderful all of a sudden. "Oh Wayne, I can't wait. Maybe we could go into town and buy Waldo a leash at Logan's?"

I realized that both men were looking at me with amused expressions on their faces. "What?"

310

"You went from sad recluse yesterday to gad-about town with a dog today," Wayne said.

"Mags said you would rise to the occasion." Tommy's lopsided grin was definitely growing on me.

"This has been a big day for me — and it's not quite lunchtime yet." I joked back.

"Let's make it bigger. I have a favor to ask of you," Tommy said. "Of both of you."

"Sure, Lieutenant," Wayne said. "What can I do for you?"

"You know Delores is healing from this last surgery to her hands so she's going to be pretty helpless. I think this stuff with Ewell is going to take the wind out of her sails for a while. Her folks and I agree that she needs to focus on something else — something that will help her get over all the horrible losses she's been through. So I bought her something — a present that I don't want to give her until she's settled down and has moved in here at *The Windshift Inn*. I'd like you two to take care of it until then."

"I'll do the best I can." Like that long ago day when Grant asked me to help Lizzie Langer, I was thrilled that Tommy was asking for my help.

"Okay, hold on. I'll go get it."

While Tommy went back upstairs, I cradled Waldo like a baby and rubbed his belly. I knew how because of all the hours I'd played with Señor. I smiled to myself. It was the first time I'd thought of him in a long time. Then I smiled at Waldo.

Tommy was right to worry about Delores. She was already distressed because of what was happening in Europe, because of Emmie, because flying hadn't changed things enough for her, because of her terrible burns. Realizing that she was Ewell's target when he modified the Form One and put it in Number 49 might destroy what was left of that vibrant spirit that I loved about her. I wouldn't let that happen. I'd be the friend this time — me. I'd not

311

just go to Father for help, I'd watch over Delores like she'd watched over me those long weeks of polio.

Tommy reappeared with a second ball of fluff. "This is Millie. She's Waldo's sister."

"Oh Tommy!" I squealed.

"What's wrong?" Myrtle rushed into the parlor with a spoon in her fist. "My God, Shirley, I thought you'd fallen or something."

"Look at Waldo," I cried. "And Millie. Delores' Millie."

Her face melted just as mine had a few minutes before. "For a place that discourages pets, we sure do have a lot of dogs at *The Windshift Inn*. Now you have to take care of them." She shook the spoon at me and returned to her cooking. I knew she'd been in on this big conspiracy from the beginning, and I loved her for it.

The two little beasts greeted each other with yaps and rolled around in my lap.

"We need to get them blankets to sleep on," Wayne picked up Millie.

"They can sleep with me until Delores is ready for Millie to sleep with her."

Tommy frowned at that.

I laughed. "Just teasing." I had changed, I thought.

"Actually, your Father bought just about anything a little dog could need for Waldo and I did the same for Millie. All of that stuff is up in my room."

"Millie can stay with me in my room." Wayne sounded hopeful.

"Don't you think they would want to sleep together?"

"They will be separated when Delores gets here anyway." Wayne stuck to his guns.

"One thing I need though." Tommy turned serious.

"Yes?"

"Waldo and Millie aren't puppies like Señor was when we got him in Mexico. They are two years old and they grew up eating a special diet that doesn't include bologna or tootsie rolls or jelly beans. That stuff might make them sick."

"I'll buy them anything that they need," I said.

"I have a list of what they can have." He pulled a piece of paper out of his pocket and handed it to Wayne.

"I'm sure the Logans will order it for us. And if they can't, Father will find it for me."

The gravel in the turnaround in front of *The Windshift Inn* crunched under the tires of Jerry Kline's truck. Seconds later, Pam burst into the parlor and shrieked when she saw the two little dogs on the couch with me.

Mr. McKensey came behind her. "Oh Fercryingoutloud." He rolled his eyes.

"US War Planes Firebomb Tokyo, Tennessee Williams' "Glass Menagerie"
premieres in NYC, Private Arthur "Arty" Lieberman, USMC, killed on Iwo Jima,
~ American View Daily ~
March 1945

"Arson Suspected in House Fire That Takes Life of Cold Creek Native Elizabeth
Langer, Aviator Mags Strickland rescues Mother and Two Sons from Displaced
Person's Camp in German, Daniel Kline, son of Jerry Kline, receives Navy Cross
for his action on Iwo Jima
~ American View Daily ~
September 1945

"Benjamin Bermeister Convicted of Deadly House Fire in Cold Creek Ohio,
Americans Enjoy First New Automobiles since Beginning of War, Waldo owned by
Journalist Shirley Maxwell wows Westminster Kennel Club Show at Madison
Square Garden,
~ American View Daily ~
End of Year Retrospective, 1947

"Conrad Simpson Takes Silver Medal in Pistol Shooting at London Olympics,
Shirley Maxwell Weds John 'Jack' Reynolds in Key West, Westinghouse Welcomes
War Hero and Electrical Engineer Thomas McDougal to Pittsburgh"
~ American View Daily ~
April 1948

"Grant Logan of Logan Foods Opens New Store in Cleveland, Former WASP
Delores Lieberman weds War Hero Thomas McDougal in Pittsburgh, Aviation
World Grieves Loss of Lt. General Hap Arnold"
~ American View Daily ~
End of Year Retrospective, 1950

"Dr. Daniel Kline Testifies Murder Suspect Sam Sheppard's Injuries Were
Serious, Pittsburgh Beauty Delores McDougal Becomes Mother of Twins, Olympic
Medalist Conrad Simpson Named Editor of American View Firearms Monthly
~ American View Daily ~
End of Year Retrospective, 1954

"Salk vaccine will change the lives of parents and children around the world."
Interview of Shirley Maxwell Reynolds, President, American View
Communications,
~ American View Television (AVT) ~
1955

"Wiley Aircraft Introduces First New Post War Plane Designed by Famed
Aeronautical Engineer Wayne Wilson, Cold Creek Ohio Resident Lester
McKensey, 92, Dies in Car Crash, Leaves $10M to Myrtle and Jerry Kline, Owners
of 'The Windshift Inn'"
~ American View Daily ~
End of Year Retrospective, 1956

"Unemployed Baker Pamela Kline Inherits 'Jerry's Flying Service' after Death of
Jerald Kline, Delores and Tom McDougal Have Son, American View Magazine
Owner George Maxwell Marries Hollywood Starlet Sheila Monahan
~ American View Daily ~
End of Year Retrospective, 1959

"Physicist Dr. Delores McDougal Appointed to Atomic Energy Commission, Mags
Strickland Attends Funeral of Randolph Royce Reasoner in Key West, Jackie
Cochran Becomes First Woman to Fly Twice the Speed of Sound,
~ American View Daily ~
End of Year Retrospective, 1962

"Grant Logan of Logan's Groceries Buys Fifth Store in Rapidly Growing Ohio
Chain, Myrtle Kline Passes Away from Cancer, Shirley Maxwell Reynolds
Promoted to CEO, American View Communications
~ American View Daily ~
End of Year Retrospective, 1966

"Wayne Wilson Becomes President of Wiley Aircraft, Mags Strickland disappears
in Cambodian Jungle during special mission for Henry Kissinger, Pamela Kline
Declares Bankruptcy - Sells Jerry's Flying Service."
~ American View Daily ~
End of Year Retrospective, 1969

CPSIA information can be obtained at www.ICGtesting.com
Printed in the USA
LVOW040549180412

278104LV00003B/14/P